SCALES of ICE & SHADOW

◆ EMILY SCHNEIDER ◆

PRAISE FOR *SCALES OF ASH & SMOKE*

*"…a masterful work of YA fantasy fiction which contains
all the must-have ingredients for a thrilling read, from
a compelling central pair of characters to a lavish and
atmospheric setting filled with danger and intrigue."*
—Readers' Favorite

*"I. Am. Obsessed… The romantic tension between Kaida and Tarrin is
just so well written (*internal squealing*), so if a (non-toxic) enemies-
to-lovers trope compels you to pick it up, this book will deliver."*
—Marissa Lete, author of *Echoes*

*"I loved this book from start to finish…I was thoroughly
intrigued and found myself desperate to get to the next page…
and the next…just to see what was happening next!"*
—Goodreads Review

*"Tarrin, the main male character, is a cinnamon roll wrapped up
inside of a flaming ball of sass and feels. I would die for him, honestly."*
—Goodreads Review

"My new favorite literary couple!"
—Lucia Ferrara, editor

*"I LOVE this book! Finally found a book
with dragons that is so so good!"*
—Goodreads Review

"Every detail was described to perfection."
—Goodreads Review

*"The writing was absolutely wonderful, and the plot was interesting.
We got a unique spin on some well know creatures, and the
authors spin is fascinating. This book is great for anyone who
loves fantasy, mixed with some enemies to lovers romance."*
—Goodreads Review

DON'T MISS THE AWARD-WINNING FIRST
BOOK IN THE ASH & SMOKE SERIES:

SCALES OF ASH & SMOKE

FANTASY WINNER OF THE 2021
BEST INDIE BOOK AWARD

For all the dreamers who refuse to give up.

PRONUNCIATION GUIDE

Characters:
Kaida: KYE-duh
Tarrin: TARE-in
Eklos: ECK-los
Lita: LEE-ta
Eldrin: EL-drin
Martik: MAR-tick
Roldan: ROLL-den
Barden: BAR-den
Aela: AY-luh
Alyaa: AL-yah
Rythos: RYE-those
Silas: SYE-luss
Vitea: vit-AY-uh
Magus: MAH-goose

Locations:
Elysia: el-LIH-see-uh
Zarkuse: zar-KOOSE
Vernista: ver-NIH-stuh
Belharnt: BELL-harn-t
Shegora: sheh-GORE-uh
Mistwick: MIST-wick
Myrewell: MIRE-well
Ilgathor: IL-ga-thor
Metta: MET-uh

ELYSIA

ELYSIA
ENDLESS SEA
Shegora
Metta
Zenduro Wastes
Sarphan
Absult
Zarkuse
Royal Palace
BAYWOOD RIVER
BAYWOOD FOREST
Cottage
Belharnt
Vernista
ENDLESS SEA
ILGATHOR MOUNTAINS
Port of Pyrn
Mount Sunder
PYRN
MYREWELL
Mistwick
END OF ELYSIA
N
W
E
S

PROLOGUE

As time passed,
the Lone Dragon's malice toward his brother grew,
forcing the shape-shifter into hiding.
He started an uprising in an attempt to find him,
Slaughtering anyone in his way.
Humans and shape-shifters alike,
Murdered simply because of their blood.
But there were two humans
Who trained up a rebellion,
Determined to end the bloodshed.
Through sword and shield,
They planned to end the tyranny in Elysia.
On the eve of the Winter Solstice,
At the base of Mount Sunder,
The rebellion attacked The Lone Dragon's army.
The battle was bloody,
With little hope from the start.
The sides of the mountain were painted crimson as a rose
Until nearly all who bore skin were dead.
But amidst the chaos,
The two humans found their way to Xalerion.
They fought valiantly,
From dawn until dusk,
Until one by one,
The Lone Dragon struck them down,
Ending the Battle of Mount Sunder.
And thus, the reign of cruelty and terror over Elysia began.

—Legend of the Battle of Mount Sunder

CHAPTER ONE

KAIDA

SMEARS OF BLACK dotted the edges of my vision.

Rasping breaths sliced up my throat like hot knives. The streets were crowded with endless people scrambling about, street vendors selling supplies and food, and carriages clattering past as I weaved through the chaos. My eyes darted about as the slap and clunk of my boots on the cobblestone road was drowned out by the shouting of the humans surrounding me.

An assortment of smells assaulted my nose, some sweet and sugary while others were downright nauseating. A cluster of people shoved their way past me, forcing me to scurry back, landing my feet in a puddle of mud. A groan slipped through my lips as brown liquid seeped into the bottom of my pants. I paused on the edge of the street, wiping my clammy hands against my shirt before gulping down a breath.

Fighting through the thick crowd, I tried not to flinch at every elbow that jammed into my sides, or vomit at the stink of unwashed bodies that rolled through the air. A whip, a knife, even a hand coiled into a fist could burst from the crowd at any moment, finding me. The sound of my heartbeat thrashed in my ears, my arms curling around my stomach, and I pushed down the urge to curl into a ball on the ground.

Just as the end of the crowd appeared, a boot landed on my toes, eliciting a yelp as I tripped forward. Something cold and unforgiving met my face and scratched against my palms as I tried to regain my balance. It took a moment for the texture to register before my heart rammed its way into my throat. Gray scales bristled under my hands, and I jerked them back, falling to the ground in my haste to get away.

Blue eyes attached to a head with enormous curling horns narrowed at me. The dragon towered above me, and a flashback of Eklos snapped through my mind, sending a cold fever through my veins.

"S-sorry," I stuttered, my body automatically curling into a defensive position. I fully expected the dragon to backhand me, shove me, or pull out a whip to punish me for colliding with him. But instead, he simply stared at me for a moment longer before weaving his enormous body past the humans I had just jostled my way through.

I glanced around, waiting for another dragon to appear to mete out my punishment, but no one paid me any mind. I shook my head, trying to calm myself as I thanked the old forgotten gods that Mistwick was different from Vernista. I would have already been chained to a whipping post had I collided with a dragon in my home village.

It was a strange experience for me, seeing so many humans in one place, moving about and selling as they wished. They moved with purpose rather than fear. The dragons nearby were not whipping or punishing their slaves, nor were they screaming orders or reprimanding them. The first day I had set foot in this town, glimpsing this new form of freedom, I had fallen to my knees, tears streaming down my cheeks at the sight of it. Eldrin had warned me that Mistwick was different, but I don't think I ever fully believed him. Weeks had passed and I still struggled to walk through the town without peeking around every corner or searching for red eyes amongst the throng.

With a shake of my head, I shoved the thought from my mind, and continued down the path through the market.

"Care for a pie, miss?" a lady with silver hair asked, stopping me in my tracks. It was a harmless question, but it still made my muscles clench tight. I managed to make my feet move in her direction, stopping in front of her stand. Pies, pastries, and tarts of every color were arranged on a platter of wood. Some had spiced fruit fillings bursting from their sides while others were strange shades of orange, blue, and pink.

I pointed to a muted orange-colored one. "I'll take that one, please."

With a nod, she pulled out some cheese cloth and wrapped the pie, before tucking it safely into a burlap sack.

"How much?" I asked as she handed me the pie.

The silver-haired lady shook her head. "No charge." Without another word, she turned to help another boy wandering by her stand.

I stared at the burlap sack in my hands. I didn't feel right not paying for it. Back home, every coin counted. Even if humans had been allowed to sell goods in Vernista, none of them would have been able to survive if they gave them away for free. But this one had given me a homemade pie without requiring anything in return. She continued to talk with a younger boy, and I dropped two copper coins onto her stand. It wasn't what the pie was worth, but it was all I had with me. Our pockets were quickly emptying after weeks on the run.

Before the pie lady could respond, I turned on my heel and made my way back through the town, careful not to jostle the pie too much.

Three streets and two corners later, I breathed a sigh. There was less congestion here and my pace quickened as I thought of the cozy bed waiting for me. The weather had blessedly taken a turn for autumn, leaving the summer heat behind, with each new night bringing a brisk chill and leaving the days much more bearable. Colored leaves crunched beneath my feet as I turned the last corner and found the door I had been looking for.

The Briar Inn.

Three months had passed since Tarrin, my father, and I had escaped from Belharnt, leaving Eklos in its depths as it collapsed on top of him. Our flight south took four long, exhausting days as my wings were only strong enough to handle a few hours at a time. Truthfully, it was a miracle I had been able to learn to fly in the first place.

The memory of begging Tarrin to carry me at the end of the second day swept through my mind, sending heat rising in my cheeks. Though his physical body was stronger than mine was, the three of us had foregone food as we raced south, trying to save as much time as possible, not knowing if Eklos had escaped or if the Remnant of The Lone Dragon was hunting us. By the time we made it to the town of Mistwick, deep on the southern coast of Myrewell, we were all so drained, physically and magically, that we rented rooms in the first inn we came across and collapsed into our beds.

The last few months had been especially difficult on Tarrin. Word had spread that King Martik had been captured, the Council keeping him in the dungeons beneath the palace. He fought my father at every turn, trying to persuade him that we should return to rescue him. Tarrin knew the conditions of those dungeons, knew the dragon jailor that stood guard. There had only been bright, unfiltered fear in his eyes as he told me about it, the skin of his hands turning to damp ice in my own.

In the weeks we'd been traveling, there had been no sign of Eklos; no word if he had survived the mountain collapse, or if his body had been found. The Council had taken control of the palace and the surrounding villages in the Prince's absence. The Remnant was wreaking havoc in all the northern towns, slaughtering humans and burning down everything that belonged to them.

Fire blazed in Tarrin's eyes whenever we discussed it. And I agreed that something needed to be done. But my father was right, too. What could three shifters do against an army of dragons, magic or no?

The heat of a roaring fire smothered my skin as I opened the door to our suite of rooms that the three of us shared, my eyebrows rising as I noticed Eldrin's absence in his usual chair. My father had left a few days ago on a scouting mission, and I was surprised he hadn't returned yet. Swallowing down my unease, I shut the door behind me.

Tarrin was sprawled across the couch, in human form, and looked up at me blearily over the back of it. I smiled, hoping for that smirk I loved to light up his face. It didn't.

"Hi," I said, walking the pie over to the table in the corner then dropped onto the couch next to him. He scrubbed at his face with a hand, his fingers lingering over the burn scars on his cheek before he sat up and pulled me against him. I closed my eyes as his scent of night air and blue cypress filled my nostrils, releasing the tension that had been coiled in my body after walking through Mistwick.

"Any news?" he asked, planting a kiss on the top of my head, before using his World Weaver magic to settle a blanket around us. Though I understood what his special magic was, it never ceased to amaze me. Having the ability to weave the world as you desire; creating or moving existing objects almost anywhere… It had been a gift on our flight south.

Butterflies fluttered in my stomach as my face grew warm from his touch. After fighting our betrothal, not to mention our feelings for each other for such a long time, it still felt strange when he was so open with signs of affection. Since arriving here, we had not discussed our relationship or what exactly it was that we had. Was our betrothal even existent anymore? I wasn't sure since he was now a prince in exile. If the requirement of our marriage were removed, would he still feel the same way toward me? Self-consciousness reared its ugly head in my mind each time I thought about it, sending pangs of doubt into my stomach.

"No," I replied. "There hasn't been any sign of Eklos anywhere. If he somehow survived, he is remaining hidden."

Tarrin's body tensed. "And my father?"

I grabbed his hand and held it firmly between both of mine. "No one had anything new to report."

He closed his eyes, a shuddering breath working its way out of his throat.

"It'll be all right, Tarrin. Your father will be fine. He's strong, like you."

He gave my hand a grateful squeeze. "I know. I just can't help but feel like he needs our help. You know that the Council will never let him go. There are only two ways this can end if we don't rescue him. Either they will kill him, or my father will spend the rest of his life in a dank, dark cell, and die alone in those dungeons."

I avoided his gaze, offering a solemn nod. "I know. I want to help him too, but we have no idea if we're currently being hunted." I narrowed my eyes at the fire in the hearth. "If the Remnant is trying to find us, they've kept it surprisingly silent. I fear it would be foolish for us to travel north now."

Tarrin opened his mouth to argue before stopping himself. Resignation filtered down our mental shape-shifter bond, though it was reluctant, and I had a feeling that if I agreed, he would be ready to fly north in a matter of minutes.

I cleared my throat, wanting to lighten the subject. "I brought you something." I pushed to my feet and retrieved the pie from the table. Holding it carefully, I handed the wrapped package to Tarrin and offered him a smile. "I thought it might cheer you up."

He unwrapped it and I smiled in triumph as his eyes lit up.

"Mango pie," he said, the corners of his eyes crinkling. "It was my favorite as a youngling. How did you know?"

"I had a hunch," I replied ruefully, tapping at my temple. One day, he had let his mental walls fall as we walked the streets of Mistwick and I saw memory after memory float through his mind as he beheld the vendor selling an assortment of pies. The mango ones were his favorite—his mother used to make them for him.

"Thank you." His gaze seared into me, and my ears grew warm. Setting the pie down, he cupped my cheek with his hand and pulled me toward him. His lips met mine and my insides went molten.

I didn't think I would ever get used to being wanted and not being alone… being *happy.*

It was like a drug in my veins. The more I experienced, the more I wanted of it. I found myself longing for Tarrin each time we were away from each other, counting the moments until I was back by his side. The way his eyes flickered when he looked into mine always sent prickles of pleasure across my skin.

Needing more, I wrapped my arms around his neck and pulled him toward me. Tarrin was the first to break away with a wry chuckle.

"Eldrin could be back any minute."

I blew out a breath and sank back into the couch, my face hot. The reminder brought reality crashing in, and a new weed of worry sprang up in my mind. Why wasn't he back yet?

Embers popped in the fire, and the wood shifted, sending a plume of smoke up the chimney. One look at Tarrin and I debated kissing him again when a knock sounded at the door, smothering any lingering desire with a layer of ice. I glanced at Tarrin who eyed the door.

That couldn't be Eldrin. Why would he knock when he has a key? I said to Tarrin through our bond.

His eyes narrowed as he studied the door. *He wouldn't.*

Another knock sounded, louder this time.

Tarrin was the first to respond, moving on silent feet over to the door. He pressed his ear against it but quickly shook his head. The door was much too thick to be able to hear who might be on the other side. I watched from my seat on the couch as Tarrin grabbed a small dagger, hid it behind his back, and rotated the bronze doorknob, the metal creaking as the swung the door open.

The tension in my body eased when I saw that it was not a dragon, but a human. A middle-aged man with graying hair stood in the hallway, eyes wide as he took in Tarrin's tall frame.

"Can I help you?" Tarrin asked, the dominance of his royal upbringing lacing his tone.

The stranger hesitated for a moment as he glanced over at me before returning his gaze to Tarrin. "I am looking for Eldrin the Great," he announced, bringing a fist to his heart.

My heart sped up. That was the gesture used by the humans who had tried to fight back against the dragons a thousand years ago—when half the human population had been slaughtered. It was a gesture that could get us all killed if the dragons were to see it.

"I was told he may be staying at this inn," he tacked on.

"Who are you?" Tarrin demanded.

The man's eyes crinkled, clearly not viewing us as a threat.

"I am Noam, an old friend."

CHAPTER TWO

EKLOS

FRIGID DUNGEON AIR seeped beneath my scales as I crept my way down the lightless hallway. A throbbing ache echoed through my leg as I limped along, the memory of Belharnt collapsing around me and crushing my leg into small fragments replaying in my mind. I leaned my arm against the slimy wall as the flashback consumed my vision. My heart thumped erratically in my chest as I recalled trying to drag myself out of the mountain, only making it partially outside before it came crashing down on top of me.

A low growl reverberated in my throat, feeling immensely loud as it bounced against the stone walls surrounding me. Fate had been kind to me in Belharnt, my life not yet surrendered to the afterlife. I took it as a second chance to rid Elysia of those abominations—humans and shifters that did not belong in this world.

Another growl rippled through my chest. That infernal girl and her prince. I had been so certain that everything would go according to plan. The bluestone iron shackles would drain the life straight out of the girl, and I would kill the Prince and my blasted cousin when they arrived to rescue her.

And yet, even with my superior strength, they still managed to best me, bringing the mountain down to crush me.

And then they got away.

I shook my head as I pushed off the wall, my vison slowly returning to the dark hall in front of me. It didn't matter. A smile split my snout. Plans were in motion; I was on the verge of finding the shifters. And once they were dead, there was nothing that would stop me from enacting my plans for Elysia.

I just needed to find those infernal beasts.

Which brought me to my current location.

The dungeons beneath the palace were a pitiful, horrid place. They were rarely cleaned, remains of human feces and vomit piled into the corners of the cells. The cold, damp, mustiness of the earth penetrated through the stone, keeping the bars of each cell covered in a moldy slime. Dragons had never been kept down here.

Until now.

The silhouette of a dragon emerged from the shadows, and I narrowed my eyes to see through the dark. My snout spread into a grin when I recognized the dark-red form of the jailor.

Regam. This was the dragon the King and Queen had employed to stand guard over their dungeons. The hatred that filled his cold, calloused heart rivaled that of even my father. Every time I encountered him his bright silver eyes shone with the promise of violence. The stench emanating off him, even now, would make the weak lose the contents of their stomachs.

What I appreciated about the jailor was that he didn't care whether his prisoners were human or dragon, a king or a slave. He despised them all. He was ruthless, without an ounce of mercy in his ancient bones. Regam once told me how he had cut out a human's teeth as a punishment for chattering them too much in the cold of the dungeon.

I smiled. "How is my favorite prisoner?"

"Suffering," his hoarse voice ground out. "Just as you wished."

"Excellent." With a wave of my hand, I dismissed the jailor and he dissolved back into the shadows. I continued down the hall, allowing my footsteps to echo.

A wheezing cough rang through the cells of the dungeon as I came upon the one I was looking for. The pitiful sight that was King Martik, or rather just Martik, appeared as I lit a torch and hung it on the wall. I bit down on my tongue to hold in a laugh. There was no king of Elysia, not anymore. After laying the perfect trap for the Prince and that wretched girl, I had coerced Martik into signing away his right to rule and handing it over to me, effectively assigning me as Regent.

"Well, well. What do we have here?" I crooned. The metal bars plinked as I wrapped my claws around them.

Martik laid in a heap of scales in the corner, his wings wrapped around himself to stave off the penetrating chill that had his enormous body trembling.

"Get out," he snapped, but the words were weak.

I clucked my tongue. "Where are your manners, Martik? Is this really how you treat your visitors?"

A wet cough was his only answer. Martik drew his limbs in even closer, making his body impossibly smaller. "Where is my son, Eklos? What have you done to him?"

"I am sure you will be torn apart to know that your pathetic son escaped the clutches of Belharnt." I paused, studying the former king. "But no matter, I will find him, *Your Majesty*," I spat out the words. Satisfaction churned in my gut when he flinched.

"Leave him be!" Martik shouted, mustering all his remaining strength.

I sent a whip of noxious smoke circling around his neck. "You are in no position to be giving orders," I retorted, squeezing it tighter until I heard the breath rattle in his throat.

Martik's eyes blazed bright, murder flashing like a lightning strike within.

"Anyway," I tutted, ignoring the tense exchange of words, and releasing the smoke collar from his neck. "I come with a bargain for you. I offer you a chance at freedom."

The King's gaze was sharp as a knife trying to slice beneath my scales as he tried to catch his breath. "At what cost?"

I bared my teeth. "Cost? You think so little of me that I wouldn't offer you freedom out of the goodness of my heart?"

Martik remained silent, his eyes spearing daggers at me. I waved a hand through the air, dismissing his accusation.

"I have no qualms with you as you are not the beast that your devil of a son is," I said, fighting to hold back the flames that licked at the backs of my teeth at the thought of those abominations. Shape-shifters. Unnatural monsters that never should have been allowed to exist in Elysia. Humans were bad enough, let alone a dragon tainted by human blood, and shifting between the two forms.

My father's brother, Bakari, was one of the first of their kind. I still remember the potency of my father's hatred for his brother— the violent need to end his life. I held back a sigh. If only Xalerion had succeeded in killing Eldrin as a baby all those years ago when Bakari's wife tried to smuggle him away. Then I wouldn't have to deal with these vile beasts. Though we've weeded out much of their race over the past millennium, there remain a few that must be dealt with. My cousin and the Prince amongst them.

"Join my cause, help me find Prince Tarrin, and you will be free of this forsaken dungeon. I will put you at my right hand, Martik." I waited, half expecting the pitiful dragon in front of me to grovel at my claws. When almost a minute had passed, bitter outrage stoked the fire in my belly. "You would be a fool to refuse such an offer," I growled, the sound echoing and dancing with the faint sound of water dripping farther down the hall.

For a moment, it truly seemed that Martik was contemplating my offer, perhaps choosing self-preservation over pride. Ever so slowly, he dragged himself off the floor, wincing as his limbs lengthened. A grin spread wide across my snout, a weightlessness filling my bones as victory perched on my shoulders. Martik approached the cell bars, pulling himself up as much as he could in the cramped space.

"I will never join you, Eklos. You are the fool." Before the words even had a chance to register in my mind, flames barreled at my face as Martik unleashed volley after volley.

Summoning a shield of dense smoke, I wrapped it around myself as the fire fought to singe beneath my scales. A bottomless anger shone in his eyes and any chance of bringing Martik onto my side, was gone.

With a frustrated growl, I snapped a whip of smoke at the former king, a deafening roar reverberating off the stones as they cut beneath his scales.

"Wrong decision, Martik," I snarled, shoving toxic smoke into his nostrils. I watched as all emotion died in his eyes, and I couldn't hold back my smile as King Martik collapsed to the filthy floor in a heap of wings and scales.

CHAPTER THREE

KAIDA

AN AWKWARD TENSION hung in the air as we watched Noam pop grape after grape into his mouth. He sat slumped in a chair at the table, one leg perched on his knee, completely comfortable and not at all what a human should have looked like in a room of dragon shape-shifters. Normally, I would never have allowed a stranger into our room, but something about this man was calming my inner alarms rather than setting them off. I didn't fully know whether he was friend or foe, but my gut told me that we should let him in.

If I had known he'd be eating the assortment of grapes laid out on the table, I may have rethought that decision.

Tarrin and I sat on the couch, studying the strange man's every movement.

Who do you think he is? Tarrin asked through our bond.

My father has never mentioned having a human friend. I don't know.

Tarrin tensed beside me, and I noticed his jaw clenched tight, the throbs of a headache leaking through into my mind. While we needed to know if we were being hunted—whether the Remnant or the Council had sent dragon mercenaries after us—we also desperately needed Eldrin to come back to the inn. Neither of us trusted the man, but I knew that neither of us truly wanted to harm a human either.

I exhaled through my nose, glancing at the small clock on the fireplace mantle, then outside at the moon that was quickly rising in the sky. Why wasn't Eldrin back yet? My imagination went crazy as all the possible scenarios ran through my head, most resulting in my father being injured and alone or killed. I swallowed hard, taking Tarrin's hand in mine for comfort. I had to believe Eldrin was fine and would return soon. He had a thousand years of hiding and evading under his belt. He knew how to stay safe.

I studied the stranger eating all my grapes through narrowed eyes. Those were *my* grapes.

"How do you know Eldrin?" I asked, trying to keep the annoyance from penetrating my tone.

A small smile bent his lips around bulging cheeks. "We have been friends for the better part of the last two decades. He is my closest friend."

"He's never mentioned you before," Tarrin replied, arching a brow.

"Not surprising. Eldrin is the greatest secret keeper I have ever met. Fiercely protective too." Noam stuffed a piece of bread in his mouth, his lips smacking together as he chewed.

"How did you two meet?"

The man opened his mouth to answer just as a familiar feeling flickered down the bond. Eldrin was close by. No sooner had I thought it when the knob on the door began to rattle and the grind of a key pushing into the lock halted all conversation. The door clicked loudly before it swung open, revealing Eldrin in human form, a sack hanging over his shoulder and a deep cut across his left cheek that was caked with dried blood. His face was pale, and he staggered forward, knocking his shoulder into the door frame.

"Eldrin! What happened?" I ran to his side, wrapping his arm around my shoulders.

Tarrin used his World Weaver abilities to make a chair appear behind Eldrin and I eased him into it. With a flick of his hand, a small bag of medical supplies landed next to my feet. I had lost count of how many times Tarrin's World Weaver magic had come in handy since leaving Belharnt. Rummaging through the bag, I found a clean cloth and a bottle of alcohol. I pulled a leather tie from my wrist and handed it to Eldrin. His fingers felt like ice as he took it from me and gathered his hair into it.

"Had a run-in with a patrol on the road heading east. It would seem that the Council has put some new laws into place regarding traveling on the road at night."

"Did they attack you?" I asked, pouring the alcohol onto the cloth before bringing it to the cut on his face, gently wiping away the dried blood.

Eldrin groaned and clenched his teeth, eyes squeezing shut at the stinging cut.

"It was nothing I couldn't handle," he panted.

"Did you kill them?" I was unable to stop the question from coming out. I finished cleaning his cheek, thankful that it was not deep enough to warrant stitches and applied a salve to keep it safe from infection.

Eldrin kept his eyes closed and winced. That was the only response I needed. He wasn't like other dragons who relished taking the lives of others. He hated having to end a life, no matter how heinous.

"You killed an entire patrol of dragons and walked away with only a cut on your face and a limp?" Tarrin asked, his green eyes wide.

"I have seen him walk away from worse with less injury," Noam said from the corner. I flinched, somehow entirely forgetting about the stranger munching on my grapes.

My father's eyes snapped open. "Noam."

"Eldrin the Great," the man responded, bringing his fist over his heart again.

"What are you doing here?" Eldrin made to stand but I pushed him back down, forcing him to stay put. He gave me a sour look but obeyed.

"I heard rumor that you were spotted in Mistwick. Word has spread about what happened at Belharnt—that you escaped. I figured you might need some help if you had made it here in one piece and now have the forces of Elysia on your tail." Noam blushed as he realized what he said. "In a manner of speaking, of course."

Eldrin let out a short laugh, shaking his head, but my stomach dropped to the floor. Someone had recognized Eldrin in town? It would only take the right person to see him, or the right dragon, and the Remnant would know exactly where we were. It wouldn't be long until they showed up at our door.

"How did you know where to find me?" Eldrin asked, interrupting my anxious thoughts.

"You are a creature of habit, old friend. There were only a few inns in Mistwick that you would have gone to. I took my chances and started here."

"Does anyone else know we're here, Noam?"

"Just me and my lonely boat." He cracked a smile and Eldrin's face softened.

"Let's keep it that way," Tarrin interrupted, and I scowled at his rudeness.

His eyes met mine. "We can't afford for anyone else to find out we're here."

Eldrin nodded. "Prince Tarrin is right, Kaida. We don't have long before our presence here is noticed. If the Council has truly sent mercenaries after us, we are not difficult to find here."

"The Prince…" Noam whispered, eyes widening. Was he just realizing who Tarrin was?

"Relax, old friend," Eldrin said. "He's not what you think. He will not turn you in."

Tarrin's brow furrowed, and he looked questioningly between them.

"Noam escaped his former slave master," my father explained. "He has lived as a free human for the last seventeen years."

"Free?" It was my turn to gape. "How is that possible? How have the dragons not found you? Punished you?"

Noam's lips curled into a slight smile, though his forehead bunched between his eyebrows. "I live on a small boat by myself. I am often out at sea, where the dragons do not bother to search. I created an imitation slave crest that I wear whenever I come into town for supplies. The dragons are too stupid to check to see if it is real or whom I belong to."

His cheeks heated and he smiled sheepishly. "But *you* dragons aren't stupid," Noam pointed at the three of us. "You are smart dragons."

Eldrin laughed, his entire body shaking from the force of it. "Ah, I've missed you, old friend."

Noam slumped back into his chair, probably realizing there was no threat of being punished for calling us stupid. "Anyway, I figured I would offer my help, however little it may be."

Tarrin's face clouded over at the same moment that Eldrin's lit up.

What is it, Tarrin? I bumped my hand against his.

We shouldn't involve anyone else. If he was able to find us, it's only a matter of time before others do. We should trust no one.

I could hear the skepticism in his voice, could feel his desire for this man to leave and not return. I knew there was wisdom in his words, but the sound of Eldrin clearing his throat stayed my tongue.

"On the contrary, Prince Tarrin," Eldrin said aloud, interrupting our silent conversation. "I do believe Noam would be of great help to us. He has a wealth of knowledge that he can extend to us, and we would be foolish to refuse it. He poses no threat to us."

Silence fell like a pulsing drum in my ears. Noam squirmed in his chair causing the wood to groan beneath his weight.

"What help would that be?" I dared to ask.

Eldrin cleared his throat. "There might come a time, Kaida, where magic will fail and all that is left is the strength and skill that humans possess. You will need to be able to defend yourself with or without magic if you hope to stand a chance of defeating the Remnant." Eldrin paused, pushing himself out of the chair and walked to Noam's side, placing a hand on his shoulder. Noam's green eyes flickered in the candlelight around the room.

I exchanged a glance with Tarrin and asked, "What exactly do you mean, Eldrin?"

My father inhaled, steeling himself before he spoke. "Noam is a direct descendent of the man who stood face-to-face with the Lone Dragon a thousand years ago, taking a stand against the tyranny of the dragons in hopes of creating a better world." The floor dropped out from under my feet.

"He will teach you to fight," Eldrin declared.

"I'm sorry, what?" Tarrin and I exclaimed at the same time. A smirk lit up Noam's face.

"What are you talking about?"

"Why have I never heard this?"

Our voices ran over each other, getting lost in a cacophony of unanswered questions.

My father held up a hand, and both of us fell silent. His mouth was turned down into a scowl, but amusement shown in his eyes.

Noam chuckled. "Perhaps you should start at the beginning, old friend."

"Very well." Eldrin settled back into his chair, running a hand over his tired face. I packed up the medical supplies, and Tarrin wiggled his fingers and the entire bag disappeared from my hands. I rose an eyebrow at him, and he gave me his signature half smile that I loved. Pushing to my feet, I went to make some tea while my father began speaking.

"Back in the days when The Lone Dragon had first begun his campaign to end the human race, he didn't face much resistance. He had managed to gain quite the following, each member sharing his disdain for the humans. Whether the other dragons of Elysia agreed with him or not, none would dare go up against his might. Xalerion was one of the strongest dragons to ever walk the lands of Elysia."

Noam nodded in agreement. "I've heard stories passed down through every generation of my family about how terrifying he truly was. He was ruthless and cunning, without an ounce of mercy in his soul."

"Sounds like someone else I know," I muttered beneath my breath as I brought the tea over to the three males.

Noam met my gaze. "Believe it or not, Eklos is not his father. He has chips in his scales, so to speak, where Xalerion did not."

"That's difficult to believe," Tarrin said.

Noam simply shrugged. "It is the truth whether you choose to believe it or not. Eklos may be a cruel and wicked dragon, but there is a spark of life left in his soul. Xalerion's was utterly gone by the time he began slaughtering the humans, driven by nothing but pure hatred. Eklos actually did Elysia a favor when he ended his father's life." Noam's eyes flickered to mine. "But I imagine Eklos has quite a bit different motive than his father did."

The blood drained from my face as I recalled the confession Eklos had told me when he held me captive in Belharnt. His mother, the one and only good thing in his life, had been killed in a human rebellion when he was a youngling. He blamed the humans, wanting any alive in Elysia to pay the price for what had happened to her. I shook my head. Revenge was just as strong of a motive as hatred. Noam didn't know what he was talking about.

I glared at the man who ate all my grapes. "Are you actually defending Eklos? The dragon who enslaved me, imprisoned me in Belharnt for seven years while he tortured and abused me, then tried to kill the three of us simply because of the blood we carry?"

Noam shook his head. "I am not defending his actions, only his soul."

"You're a fool," I bit out.

"Kaida," Eldrin reprimanded.

"No, I'm not listening to this." I stood and made to leave the room. "I'm not going to sit here and listen to a man who's been *hiding* on a boat for almost twenty years defend the dragon who nearly killed me every day of my life and took my mother away from me."

I turned my back on the males in the room when a warm, callused palm encircled my wrist. I glanced over my shoulder to find Tarrin's pleading eyes on me.

Kaida—

No, Tarrin. I won't sit here and listen to some human defend that monster. I won't.

Tarrin shook his head. *I don't think he's defending him. I think he's right. The motives are different, and perhaps that's the key to defeating the Remnant.*

I narrowed my eyes, aware that Noam and Eldrin were watching us as we talked silently through our bond. *I thought you didn't want to involve anyone else.*

I didn't, but I've been thinking while they've been talking. Eldrin may be right. It would be good for us to train more without magic. It can only help us, even if they end up being wrong. His thumb stroked my palm, instantly calming the rage coursing through my veins.

"Let's find out what he has to teach us," Tarrin said aloud.

I glanced at Eldrin first, who was watching our internal exchange closely, then to Noam whose face was twisted in confusion. He likely didn't know about our shape-shifter bond; the whole staring intensely at each other probably came across as odd to him. I crossed my arms before lowering back onto the couch. "Fine."

Tarrin wrapped an arm around me, pulling me into his side and squeezing, before turning his attention back to my father.

"I thought that Xalerion started the killing in order to find you, Bakari's son."

Eldrin nodded. "That's how it started. That was his purpose. After about a month of widespread slaughter, some of the humans began to band together."

"Wait," Tarrin interrupted. "I thought that the dragons attacked the humans without warning, and half the population was killed in one bloody battle?"

My father shook his head. "That's the story the dragons want you to believe. Tell a lie enough times, it becomes true, no?"

Noam leaned forward, resting his elbows on his knees. "It wasn't over in one single battle like they claim. It took a few months of Xalerion and his dragons slaughtering villages for the humans to finally band together and try to stop it. *That's* when the actual battle happened."

Tarrin arched an eyebrow. "And you fit into this story where?"

Noam stared at the floor while he spoke. "Two of my ancestors, Silas and Vitea, were the ones that started the rebellion against what the dragons were doing. They began training the humans in secret, teaching them hand-to-hand combat… how to wield a sword—how to defend themselves against the might of a dragon."

Eldrin chimed in. "When Silas deemed the rebellion was ready, he and Vitea led them to Mount Sunder, where a majority of Xalerion's dragons were stationed. They moved in the dead of night, hoping to catch the dragons unaware."

A heavy sigh escaped through Noam's lips. "But The Lone Dragon was far too cunning. Somehow, he knew of the humans' plans. They fought valiantly, but the dragons murdered anyone who dared to stand against them. There was no mercy." He wiped at the corner of his eye as if he were struggling to keep tears at bay.

"But Silas and Vitea found their way to Xalerion. While their band of rebels fell in pools of their own blood, my ancestors stood against The Lone Dragon. They fought, trying in vain to end the vilest creature in Elysia. But in the end, they were both struck down, as was the final rebellion to end the slaughter of the humans."

Silence fell as the heaviness of their words sank upon each of us like a water-soaked blanket. We each took a turn sipping at our tea before Noam spoke again.

"Somehow, the training the humans received got passed down through the generations until my father did the same with me. Though I've never stood up to a dragon like Silas and Vitea did, I know how to wield a sword—how to fight."

"And yet you decided to spend your life on a boat, alone, rather than helping the humans fight back," I snapped.

Noam shook his head. "I am not my ancestors. I don't pretend to be brave or valiant like they were."

"He's trying to do the right thing now," Eldrin picked up where his friend left off. "You and Prince Tarrin are the hope of Elysia. Train in magic and train with a sword. Be ready for every possible outcome."

Sweat beaded on my temple as the fire in the hearth took the chill from the air but left the pressure I suddenly felt at being labeled Elysia's savior. Tarrin's fingers squeezed into my shoulder as my mind spun over the torrent of information.

It wouldn't hurt to have another weapon in our arsenal, Kaida, Tarrin said down our shifter bond. *If Eklos is somehow still alive, we can never be too prepared. Besides, the Remnant will never be expecting it.*

I considered his words for a few moments as Eldrin and Noam seemed to have some sort of silent conversation of their own.

With a sigh, I set my teacup on the table in front of the couch and looked at Noam.

"When do we begin?"

CHAPTER FOUR

TARRIN

I SAT AT A table riddled with chips and dings in the tavern of The Briar Inn, in human form to avoid drawing any unnecessary eyes. My dragon form was too recognizable, and fortunately not many knew what I looked like as a human, if they knew I was a shifter at all. At least that was the case here in Myrewell anyway. This was the first time any of us had risked dining in the tavern, rather than opting to eat in our room. But I had a gut feeling that our time remaining unnoticed was coming to an end, and we needed answers as to whether we were being hunted.

I clenched my fists beneath the table. I missed my dragon body. The steady warmth that it offered, the constant feeling of protection, of feeling invincible. Though emotions were heightened, which could be a burden at times, there was truly nothing as magnificent as being in dragon form. Plus, being stuck in human form set me on edge, knowing the Remnant might be searching for us. While I had studied hand-to-hand combat years ago, I hadn't spent as much time learning to defend my human body as I could have.

But more than my fears or my dragon form, I missed my father. A steady ache in my stomach had become my constant companion, my heart wrenching every time I thought about what the Council might be doing to him.

Tipping back my head, I chugged the remainder of my spiced cider, clanging the mug onto the table as I set it down.

"Another cider, sir?" A brown-haired girl with a distinct mole on her right cheek was standing in front of me, arms full of dirty plates and bowls. I nodded and she walked back into the kitchen. She returned moments later, plopping a mug and a bowl of fresh stew in front of me. "It's on the house."

I attempted to smile in thanks but based on the confused look that twisted her face, it ended up being more of a grimace.

"I haven't seen you here before. Are you visiting from somewhere?" the slave girl dared to ask, and I bit my tongue to keep from reprimanding her for asking such a question to the Prince of Elysia. I was not the prince here. I was just another human, renting a room, killing time before I moved on to the next place. That's what I needed these humans to believe. I could not risk revealing myself, not in a crowded room.

"Yes," I answered stiffly. "Just traveling south."

"Smart of you," she said, nodding her head.

Suspicion crept over me like a snake slithering through the grass. "What makes you say that?" I asked.

She swallowed, eyes darting to the tables around her. "Only rumors and stories I have heard from other travelers like yourself."

I narrowed my eyes. "And what have you heard?"

Her throat bobbed as she swallowed. She seemed reluctant to say anything, but she took a tiny step closer, lowering her voice. "The King is in the palace dungeons, and the Remnant are murdering and burning everything in their path."

There it was. The tiny bit of information I was fishing for that would hopefully get her to reveal what I was wanting to know. "What do you know of the Remnant, girl?" I asked, lowering my voice so only she would hear.

"Only what I've told you, sir." Her hands fidgeted at her sides, eyes darting around, avoiding my stare. I could tell there was something she wasn't telling me. Something that made her deeply afraid.

"Who is leading them?" I dared.

The girl's eyes widened, and I watched as she took a step back, hands clenching into fists at her sides. "I know nothing, sir." She took another step backward, intending to flee.

I leaned forward in my chair to grab her wrist before she could get away. I needed to know what she was withholding from me. "Who is leading the Remnant?" I repeated.

Silver lined her eyes and her chin visibly trembled. She yanked at my grip a couple times before giving up. Her body loosened before twisting tight. "Eklos." It came out in a fearful whisper.

The room spun around me, and I immediately let go of the girl, who then scurried back into the kitchen without a backward glance.

Alive? How could Eklos have survived the collapse of Belharnt? The memory of his roar as the mountain came down echoed in my mind, replaying over and over.

I jumped to my feet, sending my chair screeching against the stone floor. A few curious eyes looked my way as I threw some coins onto the table and hurried to the stairs in the back corner that led to the rented rooms.

My shaking hands struggled to fit the key into the doorknob. When I finally got the door open, I staggered into the room and saw Kaida rise to her feet from her perch at the table in alarm.

"Tarrin, what's wrong?" she asked, arriving at my side. She guided me over to the couch. "You look like you've seen a ghost."

The irony of that statement hit me like a slap, and I let out a nervous giggle. There was nothing funny about it, but the terror flooding through my body at the thought of Eklos coming after us was too much to contain.

I fought to piece together coherent words as Kaida looked at me, concern shining in her eyes.

"Tarrin, what happened?" Her voice trembled, taking on the fear that was sliding off me in waves.

"There is a slave down in the tavern," I began. "She told me…" the words refused to form in my mouth. I could not get my lips to say the name. The name that had all three of us holding our breath for the last few months. The name that had each of us waking, drenched in sweat, from nightmares of Belharnt.

The name that held so much power over us.

"Told you what?" Kaida said, fingers digging into my arm.

I inhaled a shuddering breath, before it exploded from my mouth in a loud whoosh.

"Eklos is alive."

☙

Eldrin returned a short time later to find Kaida and I sulking at the table.

"What's wrong?" he asked, a flicker of amusement in his eyes at our sullen faces, but with our emotions sifting down our shared shifter bond, all humor died a swift death on his face.

"What happened?"

I rubbed a hand over my face. "Eklos is alive."

His eyebrows climbed his forehead, but other than that, Eldrin didn't seem surprised.

Kaida caught his expression. "Did you already know that?"

For a moment, Eldrin looked like a child caught in a white lie, about to be reprimanded by his parents. But then his shoulders relaxed, and he slumped onto the couch, reaching his hands toward the fire in the hearth.

"Yes," he admitted. "I heard the patrol talking about it on the road before they attacked me."

"And you're just now telling us this?" Kaida said, struggling to keep her voice down.

Eldrin shook his head. "I didn't want to worry you needlessly. We're safe here."

"Are we though?" I retorted. "Noam heard a rumor that you were in Mistwick and knew exactly where to find you. How long until another person who knew you years ago is tortured by the Remnant for your location?"

Eldrin rubbed at his face. "Noam is the only person who would know my possible location." He blew out a breath. "I thought we would have more time."

Kaida walked over to him and stood between him and the fire. His mouth turned down at the corners.

"You don't understand. It's not just the Remnant hunting us anymore," she snapped. "We're not just part of their large target of ridding the humans and shifters from Elysia anymore. No… with him alive, that means we're *the* target. If I know anything about Eklos, he'll want his revenge, and that means that the target on our backs just tripled. The Remnant might be destroying everything in their path, but they're searching for *us*."

Eldrin's mouth opened but Kaida continued. "And what's worse… Eklos knows you, Eldrin. He knows your past. Don't you think with him alive and leading the Remnant that he could simply point to a place with a high likelihood of you being there? Their search isn't like looking for a ring at the bottom of the ocean anymore if Eklos knows where to find you."

"It does beg the question though…" I chimed in, unable to keep the ever-growing pile of questions in my mind at bay. "If he *could* find us, why hasn't he? It's been three months since Belharnt. Why haven't they captured or killed us yet?"

Kaida's mouth opened and closed like a fish.

Her father shook his head. "I hid from him for centuries. I don't think Eklos has a clue where any of my hideaways are. I think it's more likely that he has been biding his time. We know he was injured in the collapse of the mountain. Maybe he's been having the Remnant terrorize Elysia, building up our own fear, while he took the time to heal."

Kaida looked thoughtful for a moment, considering Eldrin's words. "Even so, we can't stay here much longer. If they don't currently know where we are, it's only a matter of time until they show up at our door."

"Where can we even go?" I asked. If the Remnant were searching for us, it would be a challenge to travel without being caught.

"The slaves in the northern villages won't hesitate to turn us in if they think it'll bring them favor and safety with their Masters." Kaida's bitter words were soft.

"We can't leave Mistwick just yet," Eldrin replied, ignoring her words. "You need at least some training with Noam before we leave, and he won't travel with us. It needs to be here. We'll be all right for a few more days."

My brows lowered over my eyes. "You really think that what Noam has to teach us is worth risking our lives by staying here?"

Eldrin glanced at Kaida, studying the hesitance and fear written on her face, before meeting my eyes. "Noam's knowledge goes well beyond simply that of wielding a sword. There are secrets passed down through the generations of his family… things that could change the tide for us in this war with Eklos."

Kaida sat forward in her chair, resting her elbows on her knees. "Like what?"

Eldrin met her unwavering gaze. "Secrets that may explain how you escaped your chains in Belharnt."

CHAPTER FIVE

KAIDA

THE NEXT DAY I stood on the roof of The Briar Inn, a wood sword in my hand, facing Noam. The autumn wind was brisk, biting its way beneath my layers of clothes and sending a shiver through my body. My fingers were numb as they wrapped around the hilt, my grip growing weaker with each minute that passed in the chilly air. Thoughts swirled through my mind like the wind twisting the fall leaves into tiny cyclones on the ground. I barely managed to duck as Noam swung his weapon at my head, forcing my thoughts to a halt.

"Focus, Kaida," he snapped.

I winced as I took another step back, swinging my sword up to block his attack just before it made contact with my face. I followed the motions with my body that Noam had drilled into me, muscle memory kicking in even as my mind drifted back to Tarrin's words, sending a shock through me for the thousandth time.

Eklos is alive.

I had always felt in my gut that he had survived the mountain collapse, but hearing the words made it real. The uncertain fear that I had lived in for months had transformed into a monster that bit, scratched, and clawed at my insides, trying to consume me. Panic was my constant companion, eating away at my stomach.

"Keep your guard up!" Noam barked, snapping me out of another internal bout of anxiety. He lunged for me, stabbing at my ribs with his wooden sword.

I scowled at him as the weapon met my flesh. Bruises littered my body, and I knew that they'd be screaming at me in a few hours.

"You have to keep your eyes on your opponent, your sword raised to defend yourself at all times. You never know when your enemy will move on you," Noam scolded, repeating the same words for the tenth time.

Back when I first arrived at the palace, Tarrin had been the one to train me. While we spent some time with non-magic defense in human form, most of my training had been centered on controlling my shifting and harnessing my magic in a way that would not kill me.

Who needed swords when you had magic?

"I see that look in your eye, Kaida. You think this is pointless," Noam said, letting his sword fall to his side.

I brought the tip of my sword down to rest on the ground and leaned on it for support. The autumn sun was just warm enough to cause sweat to bead on my forehead.

"Can you blame me? A sword will not bring down Eklos, with scales hard as stone and smoke capable of killing me with hardly a thought," I said, wiping at the moisture on my brow. "Learning to fight with a sword will not save me. Or Elysia."

Noam's eyes narrowed.

"And what if Eklos commands all the slaves to fight against you? Will you kill them, those unable to wield magic, with your own, when they are not able to defend themselves against it? What honor is there in that?" His words cut like a knife. "Would you kill *me* with your magic, Kaida? If I were a human forced to do Eklos's bidding, would you kill me without a second thought?"

I swallowed hard, attempting to block the picture that Noam

had forced into my head. Would Eklos send an army of humans? Surely not, when he has his horde of dragons. What would be the point?

To break you.

The words filled my head through our shape-shifter bond just as Eldrin climbed onto the rooftop, his face grim.

"Furthermore, what Eldrin said yesterday was right," Noam continued, glancing at my father before continuing. "Magic is not infinite. There is a limit, no matter who the dragon is or how deep their reserves go. If you are to face off with Eklos in the end, he will not be invincible. There *will* be an end to his magic. And yours. What will you do then?"

A shudder racked through my body, my muscles locking as his words sank in.

"He's right, Kaida," Eldrin said as he approached us. "You must be ready for whatever Eklos has planned."

A triumphant smile lit Noam's face as he nodded at my sword. "Again."

With a sigh, I lifted it in front of me, bending my knees slightly.

"Widen your stance. You won't do much good if you lose your balance."

Muttering a curse under my breath, I moved my feet wider, assuming a defensive position. Eldrin stepped back to the edge of the roof, watching, the barest hint of a smirk on his face.

Noam feinted left before twisting and coming at me from the right, but this time I was ready for him. My arms shook as our swords met and I groaned between my teeth as I pushed back with all my strength. My knees threatened to buckle beneath me as I pushed harder against him.

"Kaida!" Eldrin called.

My concentration broke, my focus going to my father for the briefest of moments, taking it away from Noam who took advantage of the distraction and skipped backward before swinging the wooden sword at my arm. It hit with a *thwack* and my arm burst into a fiery pain. I dropped my sword, clutching my arm with my other hand, and glared at Noam.

"Do not let yourself be distracted. Had I been a real enemy, I could have beheaded you just now."

His words sent a chill through me that had nothing to do with the brisk autumn weather.

Eldrin brought two mugs of water over to us and I gulped it down, not realizing how thirsty I had become. Noam chugged his too and wiped his mouth when he had emptied the cup.

I watched him, a sudden thought occurring to me. "Noam, how do you know so much about magic if you're a human?"

Eldrin's eyes widened, but Noam didn't seem fazed.

"I suppose it's time for that conversation," he muttered.

I arched an eyebrow but stayed silent, grabbing my cloak off the ground, and wrapping it around me. Eldrin took a seat on the edge of the roof, staying uncharacteristically silent.

"My family has passed down many secrets through the generations."

I glanced at Eldrin, remembering his words from the night before. Could Noam somehow know the answers to all the questions I had regarding my own magic? How would a human know such things?

"With each generation, the elders in the family would pass down their knowledge of fighting, as I have been teaching you, but also much about magic…" Noam hesitated, glancing at Eldrin before meeting my gaze. "Particularly about the Ancient Magic."

"Ancient Magic?" I asked. I had never heard of such a thing.

He nodded. "It's not something that's taught in Elysia anymore. It faded from history even before The Lone Dragon."

"Then how do you know of it?"

A sly smile spread over his lips. "My family was quite special."

I couldn't hold back a snort. "Isn't everyone's?"

Noam huffed out a chuckle, fixing his eyes on the ground. "Not quite like mine." He blew out a breath, the air in front of him clouding in the cold. "Kaida, dragons haven't always been the only race to carry magic in Elysia's history."

My jaw popped open. "What?"

"Have you ever heard of the Order of the Magus?"

I shook my head.

"Thousands of years ago, long before Eklos and Xalerion, there existed a group of humans who called themselves the Order of the Magus. Their line had been birthed right alongside Elysia. The five members of the Order were gifted with a particular magic to help the land grow, prosper, and protect itself."

"Humans with magic?" I asked, dumbfounded.

Noam gave a sharp nod. "Yes, they were the first beings with magic, in fact. It was the Order who gifted the dragons with magic in the first place."

Anger swelled hot and strong in my core. "Why would they give the dragons such a gift?"

Noam's eyes crinkled in the corners as if he were sad. "Remember Kaida, the dragons were once a peaceful race, living alongside the humans without any problems. The Order had given them magic as a gift for helping them protect Elysia." His brows lowered over his eyes. "They had no way of knowing that their magic would slowly corrupt the hearts of the dragons who desired power over all else. But once the magic was given, it could never be taken back. It could grow weak and fade over time, but it could never be taken away."

I felt faint, my head spinning at the torrent of information Noam had just spewed at me. "And what does that have to do with me?" I asked, unable to make the connection as to why he was telling me all of this.

"The Order of the Magus had one primary objective: protect

the Ancient Magic. It was the strongest magic in Elysia, without weakness, entirely unstoppable." Noam ran a hand through his hair, his eyes far away as if remembering memories that were difficult to recall. "What the Order didn't know was that by giving away parts of their magic to the dragons, they weakened their own. It was incompatible with the dragons' greedy hearts, and it corrupted them. They thought if they killed the humans in the Order that they would be given all their magic and grow stronger. So, the dragons began attacking the Magus, and one by one, the members of the Order were killed, the fullness of the Ancient Magic dying alongside them.

"The magic that exists in Elysia now is only small pieces of the Ancient Magic. It faded out of the line of humans, but somehow remained within the dragons, though it's fragmented, tiny portions of what it used to be."

I rubbed at my temple, struggling to keep up with Noam's history lesson. "Why are you telling me all of this?"

Noam's eyes grew bright. "You, Kaida, are the first human in millenniums to manifest the Ancient Magic."

I was shaking my head before he even finished his sentence. "No. You must be mistaken."

Noam offered a small smile. "But I'm not. The knowledge of the Magus and the Ancient Magic has been shared through each generation of my family. The original five members of the Order were my ancestors. I know what the Ancient Magic looks like. The fact that you've melted through iron shackles when the iron would have nullified any normal magic is only one small bit of proof. Never mind the fact that you have multiple magical abilities, where the average dragon only has one."

I chewed on my bottom lip, considering his words. "If the Ancient Magic didn't have a weakness, and I supposedly have it, then why do I need to train without it? I thought you said it was unstoppable."

Noam gave me a patient smile, like a parent gives a child who isn't understanding. "Because, though the magic you carry is incredibly strong, it is not the entirety of what it used to be. The magic inside you is no longer pure. It's been tainted through the centuries and is not the same magic that existed long ago. Don't misunderstand me, it is still the strongest magic currently in existence, but unfortunately it has a limit."

"Can it defeat Eklos?" I asked, hope flaring inside me for a brief moment before I tamped it down.

Noam looked at Eldrin, the two of them having some sort of silent conversation before he turned back to me. "It may be the only thing that can."

I plopped down on the ground, putting my face in my hands. This was all too much. I couldn't quite wrap my mind around all that he had shared. How could I have a magic that faded from our blood thousands of years ago? How was that possible? And better yet, why was *I* the one to carry it? Why not someone else? It made no sense.

"I know it's a lot to take in," Eldrin's said, his voice gentle.

I raised an eyebrow at him. "Is this why you all keep saying I'm the hope of Elysia? Because I have fancy magic?"

My father's lips scrunched as he thought out his words. "Partially. There are a lot of reasons, Kaida, but your magic alone is the best chance we have of defeating Eklos. When you combine it with Tarrin's abilities, you both are nearly unstoppable."

I shook my head. "Why me? Why wouldn't the magic go to someone stronger?"

Noam took a step closer. "I don't fully understand how, after all this time, you've managed to manifest the Ancient Magic. It's even more surprising that the magic appeared in a shape-shifter."

I blew out a sharp breath. A hot, knife-like feeling stabbed through my stomach. I didn't ask for this magic. I didn't want to be Elysia's savior or be the one that had to go face-to-face with Eklos in battle.

I wanted to *live*. I wanted to create a happy life, find out where exactly this relationship with Tarrin could go, and live in a prosperous world that no longer enslaved the humans. But none of that could happen unless Eklos and his army were destroyed.

But why did that have to fall to me? The cold air billowed in front of me as I stood and turned for the ladder on the side of the roof.

"I need some air," I muttered, leaving Noam and Eldrin behind as I climbed down the ladder. The metal rungs bit into my hands as my tired limbs struggled to hold my body weight. My feet had just hit the cobblestone road of the alleyway when a noise sounded behind me.

Swinging around, I saw a girl carrying a sack of garbage out of the tavern toward a pile at the end of the alley. The hairs on my arms rose. Intuition pricked at my mind, and I couldn't escape the feeling that I knew her. The girl's dull brown hair hung loose around her face, her back bent over with the weight from the sack. It hit the ground with a loud crash like metal striking metal, and when she turned around, the ground beneath me fell away.

There was a distinct mole on her right cheek. A face that I had seen every day for years.

That is, until she tried to take her younger brother and escape from Eklos's ownership.

I had assumed she was caught and killed since no one had ever successfully run away before.

The breath whooshed from my lungs as I struggled to right the world that was spinning around me. She looked questioningly at me at first before recognition lit her face up in wonder.

"Kaida?" she asked, her voice incredulous. I swallowed, trying to come up with words to speak but only one would come out.

"Jinna."

CHAPTER SIX

KAIDA

"KAIDA!" JINNA SQUEALED before rushing over to me and smothering me in a hug.

She's alive. She's alive. She's alive.

The words raced back and forth in my mind, stumbling over each other and sliding around. How could she be alive? No slave had ever escaped, especially not from Eklos. Why hadn't word of her escaping gotten out?

"What are you doing here, Kaida?" Jinna asked, her eyes bright, grabbing hold of my hands.

An absurd giggle bubbled out of my throat at her question. *What am I doing here?*

"Y-you're alive," I stuttered, ignoring her question.

"Last I checked," she smirked, tucking her hair behind an ear. "H-how?"

The smile faded from her face as memories clouded her eyes. Like the flip of a switch, she went from elated to see me to distant and cold as she stepped back, fixing her eyes on the brick wall next to us. "I can't talk about this now." Jinna cleared her throat. "I need to get back to work. I finish with the sunset. Meet me in the tavern then."

Before I could utter a word, she disappeared through the door that led inside. The chill of the air combined with the scent of garbage sent a nauseated pang through my stomach. I needed to know how she escaped, especially if it meant she was being hunted too. I rubbed at my face. Mistwick was suddenly feeling crowded.

∞

By the time the sun set over the sea, the chill of the autumn air dropped into a cold that seeped beneath my layers, sending shivers up and down my body despite the fire in the hearth of our room that attempted to infuse warmth into the air. The wind picked up outside, moaning against the glass panes of the windows, shuddering against the walls.

Tarrin and Noam had been training on the roof of the inn, but my sore and bruised body remained planted on the couch instead of joining them, my mind spinning over the news of Jinna surviving. What did this mean for the slaves? Were there more that had escaped over the years that we didn't know about?

I stared at the flames for what felt like hours, trying to figure out how Jinna could have escaped, and why none of the slaves had anything to say about it. I remembered the morning I went to The Den after she told me she was planning to escape. There had been a new boy in the kitchens, but neither him nor any of the dragons breathed a word of her disappearance. Everyone acted as if she had never existed.

Perhaps that was a worse fate than death—being wiped away from Elysia's history with no one to ever remember you.

When it was finally time, I pushed myself off the couch and made my way back down to the tavern, ready to hear Jinna's story.

The room was fairly crowded, though nothing like the night we'd arrived in Mistwick when we could hardly get to the counter to rent a room or make it up the stairs. I spotted a small empty table over in the corner and took a seat, trying to ignore the scent of unwashed human bodies and the dragons' carrion breath as they indulged themselves. I hadn't seen any sign of Jinna yet.

Another girl appeared at my side, her short blonde hair streaked with dirt. "What can I get you miss?"

"Oh," I stammered. "Nothing. I'm just waiting for someone."

Her eyes narrowed. "You must order something if you wish to have a table."

"I—"

"Hush, Emeryn," a voice said. "She's with me."

Over the girl's shoulder, Jinna's face appeared, a scowl twisting her lips. Emeryn looked surprised before lowering her head and sauntering back the way she came.

"Sorry about that," Jinna said, watching the girl's retreat. "The Master of the tavern has rules about strangers loitering, and Emeryn was only following them."

I gave a single nod in understanding as Jinna took a seat across from me. I knew from working in The Den my entire life exactly what that was like. Emeryn appeared once more, carrying two mugs of spiced cider, and set them in front of us.

"It's on the house."

I opened my mouth to protest, but Jinna only nodded.

"Thank you, Emeryn."

When the girl was gone, a moment passed as we both sipped at our ciders. I was ready to burst with questions when she finally spoke.

"I suppose you want to know how I escaped." Her words were bitter, not at all happy as I would have expected from a slave who managed to do the impossible—escape their cruel master.

"Amongst other things," I admitted.

Jinna took another drink, as if bracing herself, before she blew out a breath and began her tale in hushed tones. "I took Tal in the night and left Vernista, like I said I would." Her voice grew distant, as if she were reliving the memory of that night in front of her.

"Did you know there's a tunnel that runs under The Den? It runs between Vernista and several villages on the way south.

The tunnel was supposed to be deserted—any human who knew about it was long dead, and the dragons were unable to fit in the tight, narrow spaces." Jinna inhaled slowly before letting it out in a whoosh.

"Miles into the tunnel, Tal and I came across an area that had been dug deeper than any other part. There was an entrance in the ceiling. A big one. At first, we thought it was just an old cavern meant for storage. From what we could see in the dim light of our torches, it looked abandoned. But then we heard voices around the corner. We extinguished our torches and crept closer, quiet as a couple of mice. There was no way around the cavern. We would have to cut through the room in order to continue through the tunnel." She paused, her lips pressed into a thin line, chin trembling.

"Tal was always so clumsy. He was never good at sneaking." Jinna swallowed hard, fighting back the emotions that were trying to rip free of their bonds. "There was a large circular table in the center, with eight dragons around it."

A weight dropped in my stomach. "Who were they?"

She shook her head, smoothing down her dirty apron. "I don't know for sure… I was so focused on getting Tal out of there that I didn't pay much attention to them. I wish I would have." Her forehead creased, her mouth turning down into a grimace.

"One of the dragons either spotted or smelled Tal. I still don't understand how they discovered him but not me." Her hands clenched into fists. "I had just made it to the other side of the cavern, about to race into the tunnel when I realized Tal wasn't behind me. I glanced back and one of the dragons was holding him in the air by the throat." Fresh tears poured onto her cheeks.

"There was no fear on Tal's face. Only resignation. The look in his eyes told me to go. I knew he was telling me to run and never look back." Jinna's cold eyes burned into mine. "I left him there, Kaida. I left him to die. I never would have tried to escape if I had known he would die, and I would live."

I hesitated for only a moment before reaching my hand across the table to grab hers. The chance of a slave successfully escaping was less than zero. Dragons were stellar trackers, able to pick up on scents from miles away. When you add the scent of fear to a human, which no doubt clung to them like a second skin if they attempted to escape, it only made the slave's scent more potent. Dragons craved a human's fear like a human needed water. According to everything I'd ever been told they always found any who tried to escape. It wasn't a surprise that Tal had been caught. It was a mystery, however, how Jinna had managed to escape.

Jinna sniffled, wiping at her face with the back of her hand. "I made it all the way to Mistwick and Eklos never found me. I still work in a tavern, but I have a room in the inn that is better than a dirt cave. Slavery is not as severe in Myrewell as it is in Vernista. While there are still slaves down here, it is much closer to a cohabitation than one species dominating the other. This is a much better world to live in. More than I could have hoped for." Her voice dropped another level and her eyes blazed. "But none of it makes a difference because Tal didn't make it."

Lost for words, I remained silent, rubbing her hand in a soothing motion. My heart wrenched at the thought of Jinna risking so much, and losing so much, only to make it this far with nothing left. Jinna and I had never been close—we couldn't be. Eklos would have used any friendship against us. We hardly ever talked, except when we were truly alone, but the few occasions when we did, there was a kinship there. We knew we weren't facing that darkness by ourselves.

But now Jinna *was* alone.

Memories of my mother being murdered flooded into my mind unbidden, and I sat back in my seat, trying to hold back the tears. I was alone just as much as Jinna was.

Yes, I had Tarrin. And I had met my father.

But neither of them would ever know what growing up in

Vernista, under Eklos, in my dirt cave was truly like. They would never understand. Not like my mother. Not like Jinna.

With a loud sniffle, she sat back in her chair. "Anyway, I'm here now. Mistwick is much kinder to slaves than Vernista ever was. I don't have to fear for my life every moment of every day. Tal would have been happy. I won't let his sacrifice go to waste."

Jinna chugged the rest of her cider and stood. "I must go." She put a hand on my shoulder. "I'm glad you were able to escape him too."

Lost for words, I could only nod as Jinna turned and walked out of the tavern. As if my feet had a mind of their own, I followed after her, but by the time I made it outside, any sign of her was gone.

Sorrow was like a sharp knife through my stomach, and I turned around and ran. I didn't know where I was running to, only that my feet were moving over the stones beneath them, the sweet scent of salt and sea air beckoning me forward. I raced past dragons and humans, scampering between carts and carriages.

Gasping for breath, I came to a stop. It was as though I merely blinked, and I was instantly at the edge of the sea, the water lapping at my clunky boots. I looked around, the wind flipping my hair behind me.

"I come down here to think too," a voice said next to me, and I flinched.

"Sorry, I didn't mean to startle you," Noam apologized, offering a sheepish smile before he looked at the sea with a wistful gleam in his eyes.

I let out a breath, gazing back out at the waves frothing in the distance. The moon was bright overhead and sweat beaded on my forehead from the run despite the chilly autumn wind biting through my clothes.

"Is something the matter, Kaida?" Noam asked.

"I just saw someone I knew back in Vernista," I said. "She and

I were Eklos's slaves, worked at the The Den together. She took her brother and tried to escape several months ago, before Tarrin found me. Her brother didn't make it."

Noam was quiet for a moment, the skin between his eyebrows bunching as he narrowed his eyes. "I'm sorry to hear that." His words were simple, but I felt the walls I had built to contain my emotions as I ran down to the water beginning to crumble.

"Sometimes there are no right words to say," he continued. "There are never enough words, or the right combination of them to ease the ache of death. Fate often deals a terrible hand." I turned my head to look at him and was surprised to see his own eyes lined with silver tears.

"But we cannot let fate win. If we give up, fate wins. If we are swallowed in sadness and wish for death, fate wins. We must keep going, keep fighting. For those we have lost, and for ourselves."

Noam's words clanged through me like the strike of a gong.

His face was sad, but his voice remained strong, confident. It sounded as though he spoke from experience. Had he lost someone?

I opened my mouth, intending to say something when a bright smile spread across his face.

"Would you like to join me for a late dinner, Kaida? My boat is small and the food meager, but you are welcome nonetheless." His smile was so genuine, I couldn't help wondering if I had imagined the sorrow that had been on his face moments before.

Speechless, I nodded my head, wondering what secrets this man was hiding as I followed him toward the small wooden boat with a lonely mast flapping in the wind.

We climbed the rope ladder on the side, the rough threads biting into my skin, and I breathed a sigh of relief as I finally pulled myself over the edge, my boots hitting the wood floor with a thud. Noam disappeared through the only door, before popping his head back out to wave me inside.

The main deck sat empty, only a bucket with a mop propped up in the corner and a pile of rope. Turning around, I placed my hands on the rough wood railing, staring out at the sea beyond. The sandy shore stretched for miles, the dark blue of the water gently kissing it as the tide moved in and out. There were five ships anchored along the docks, varying in sizes but all bigger than Noam's boat.

Night had fallen over Mistwick; any heat from the sun had already faded and a chill settled into my bones. I could faintly make out the sounds of voices in the streets up the hill, but there wasn't a soul in sight down on the docks or on the shore. The waves gently hit the boat, a soft slopping sound echoing off the wood, setting the vessel bobbing up and down.

A sudden breeze blew across my hair, causing it to fly into my face just as a dull thud echoed behind me. I turned, shoving the hair from my face.

Eldrin and Tarrin stood in dragon form in the middle of the deck, their scales flickering dimly in the moonlight.

"I wasn't expecting to see you here," my father said.

"Noam found me down by the water," I explained. "He invited me to join him for dinner."

Eldrin's eyes widened and he shifted back into human form in a cloud of black, before Tarrin shifted in a flash of blue. He came to my side, wrapping an arm around my waist.

"I'm glad you agreed." Eldrin's face was full of delight.

He led us to a door near the rear of the boat which held a small cabin behind it. There was hardly enough room for all of us, the room stifling from the woodstove burning away in the corner. There was a set of bunks on the far wall, and a tiny wooden table built into the wall next to it. A meager assortment of plates was stacked on top, one holding a roasted chicken, another some fruit, and the last plate held a variety of cheeses.

My heart panged at the sight of the cheese, bringing back

memories of when I had first arrived at the Royal Palace, and I had stupidly asked Tarrin if he liked cheese. A blush heated my cheeks and I heard Tarrin chuckle.

Do you like cheese? he said playfully down the bond. I nudged him in the ribs with my elbow and he laughed out loud. Noam and Eldrin stared at us before glancing at each other with a shrug. I bit my lip to hold back a laugh. We took turns gathering food onto our plates before settling onto the dusty wood floor.

Noam's ears reddened. "It's no Royal Palace, but it's home."

Despite the sweat gathering on my lower back from the sweltering heat of the cabin, I nodded and offered a smile. "It's cozy."

Eldrin snickered before crossing his legs and sitting across from us. "I offered many times to buy him a bigger boat over the years, but he always turned it down."

Noam shook his head. "This is my home. I don't need anything more."

Tarrin cleared his throat before snapping us back into the present. "Have you thought any further about a rescue plan to help my father?" His eyes were fixed on Eldrin and his shoulders remained like ice as if he were holding his breath.

My father stared at his plate. "We cannot risk going north, and I cannot carry one, let alone both of you, that great of a distance," he answered. "Martik is smart. He will do what he needs to do to survive. He knew what he was doing when he signed that decree."

I could feel Tarrin's anger flare through our bond. Months ago, when Eklos's slave kidnapped me and took me to Belharnt, Tarrin and Eldrin had come after me. It had all been a trap designed for two purposes. The first for Eklos to get his hands on three shapeshifters whom he planned to kill. The second to get King Martik to sign over his right to rule Elysia. Martik thought he was signing it to save his son's life.

"He signed that decree out of desperation to keep me safe. Clearly, Eklos can't be held to his word, and that decree was for naught. We have to help him." Tarrin set his plate on the floor. His hands balled into fists, and I could see the invisible leash he kept on his restraint about to snap. I took his hand in mine and squeezed.

"The best thing we can do for Martik now is to stay alive and figure out a way to stop the Remnant from widescale slaughter," Eldrin said, keeping his voice gentle.

"Are we to abandon him then?" Tarrin asked at last, his mouth a firm line.

"Young Prince, we are not abandoning your father. He knows we would rescue him if we could. Right now, we must not allow his sacrifice to be in vain. We must take advantage of the time he has bought us."

Through our bond, Tarrin deflated like a popped balloon, all his hope and drive to save his father swept away like a broom to a pile of ashes. My heart ached as I felt his breaking in two. I knew there was little I could do. I was unable to change the situation, and I knew my father was right. The risk was too great to try to rescue the King. I shuddered to think what would happen if we attempted to get him out of those dungeons and Eklos caught us.

Tarrin… perhaps he's right. I spoke the words into his mind, keeping them gentle as a caress.

My father did what he thought was right in order to save my life. I only wish to do the same.

The fire in the wood stove crackled and snapped, embers popping as I processed his words.

But I don't believe your father would have wanted you to throw away the freedom he has given you by running back into danger, into the hands of the Council.

You have no idea what my father wants. His words bit into my mind, and I flinched.

"Your father loves you, Tarrin," Eldrin cut into our silent conversation. "He would want you safe, as any father would."

I met Eldrin's gaze, feeling the double meaning in his words.

"My father has worked closely with the Council. He could have information that would help us stop them—stop the Remnant," Tarrin argued. "There is nothing stopping them from killing him to keep their secrets safe. Especially if he has exposed that he was consciously playing their puppet."

"They will not kill him yet," Eldrin retorted. "Far more important than any information he carries is the control they have over you and Kaida by keeping him captive. They'll be expecting you to attempt a rescue. Don't fall into their trap."

The truth hit like a hammer to the back of the head.

"We should still try," Tarrin said, his words soft. He squeezed his eyes shut and pinched the bridge of his nose with his fingers. "I know the palace better than anyone."

"Tarrin, no—" I cut in, but Eldrin held up a hand to silence me.

My father's gaze was harsh, piercing as he looked first at Tarrin and then at me, a muscle in his jaw working.

Finally, Eldrin heaved a sigh. "Noam, do you have some parchment and ink?"

With a nod, the man stood and rummaged in a small box beneath his bunk. He brought it over to Eldrin who gestured to give it to Tarrin, whose eyebrows furrowed as he took them.

"Sketch the layout of the palace dungeons. Include where any guards will be stationed and any tunnels or escape routes that you know of. I need as much detail as you can provide."

Tarrin sat there, eyes wide, mouth gaping like a fish for several moments before he started sketching with renewed fervor. My muscles would not move as my eyes flicked back and forth between the two males. My mind refused to understand what was happening. Was Eldrin planning to rescue Martik? Even after all his reasons of why it would be foolish to do so? Even when his cousin, Eklos, would do anything to get his hands on Eldrin? Air squeezed in my lungs like fingers clenching into a fist. I couldn't catch my breath, couldn't stand the thought of losing him. Noam's lips moved in response to my father, but a deafening roar filled my ears, silencing everything. The room spun around me.

I lost track of how many minutes had passed when my focus suddenly zeroed in on Tarrin as he handed the parchment to my father. He studied the drawings for a moment before pushing to his feet.

"Eldrin?" I asked, unable to form a full question. My mind refused to accept what my heart already knew. I took a deep breath, bracing for his answer.

"I will go," he answered. "I'm going to rescue the King."

☙

The next morning, I stood once more on the roof of the inn, wooden sword in hand facing Noam. Tarrin was off to the side, moving through the sparring motions that Noam had drilled into our heads, attempting to infuse his fire magic within the movements. It was easy to become entranced by him, a person his size and build moving so gracefully. It made my clunky, off-balance movements seem like an injured animal swinging its limbs around.

I caught Noam biting his lip as if he were holding back a laugh.

I sighed. "I will never be good at this, Noam." Lowering the sword to the ground, I leaned my body weight against it.

"Well, not with that attitude," he scoffed, and I rolled my eyes. He wagged his sword in the air in his way of telling me to pick it back up.

"I'm serious," I groaned out as I clashed the wood against his. "If this wasn't good enough for your ancestors to defeat Xalerion, then what chance do I have against Eklos?"

Noam stilled, his wooden sword inches from smacking into my neck. His eyebrows scrunched over his eyes. "They could fight, yes, but they didn't have your abilities. They were limited by their human bodies, and they were alone. You are a shape-shifter, Kaida. You are strong and can utilize the best of both forms. You have magic to enhance your physical fighting, and even when that runs out, you *still* have something they didn't have."

A shuddering breath billowed from my mouth into the chill air. I shifted my cold fingers on the hilt of the sword. "And what's that?"

Tarrin suddenly appeared at my side, wrapping his arm around my shoulder. "You aren't alone." His lips were hot as they pressed against my sweat-covered forehead.

"He's right," Noam said, nodding his head.

"But we are alone. It's only us. There's no one to stand with us—no one to help us defeat Eklos's army."

"Not yet," Eldrin's voice came over the ladder to the roof. "But rescuing the King is the first step."

We all turned to face my father.

"Once we have Martik back, we'll find out what he knows and keep gathering supporters. Eklos's reign of terror must come to an end."

I swallowed, my mind spinning as Eldrin arrived at our side. "When will you leave to go after Martik?" I asked.

His amethyst eyes met mine. "I leave tomorrow."

"So soon?" Tarrin asked, his body stiffening.

Eldrin nodded, staring at the floor. "The sooner I leave, the quicker I can return, and then we can focus on ridding Elysia of Eklos and the Remnant." His face was contorted in a frown, his voice a low growl.

I wrung my hands together. "Are you afraid you won't return?" The words slipped between my lips before I could stop them.

His eyes snapped to mine, and a shiver prickled over my skin. "I will return," he replied, his tone leaving no room for argument or further conversation on the matter.

Noam took advantage of the lull in conversation and gestured for me to begin again. I ran through the motions that had become muscle memory, though my mind wouldn't concentrate. My stomach churned as I thought of what awaited Eldrin when he returned to Vernista. Would Eklos pick up on his scent immediately? Would he kill him or use him to draw Tarrin and me out of hiding? Was there even a point in fighting against the Remnant? Against Eklos? Hatred was a powerful tool. It fueled anger and bitterness, igniting its host to do its bidding. Eklos, and his father Xalerion, the Lone Dragon, before him, had infected dragon kind with such loathing.

I was so consumed by my thoughts that I barely registered surprising Noam with an attack, sending his sword flying across the roof. But I couldn't bask in the victory of finally besting him or enjoy the look of utter shock on his face, nor could I hear the words he spoke above the tumultuous current of my thoughts. Instead, I simply stared at his sword lying on the ground as I struggled against the hopelessness that settled into the pit of magic inside me as I wondered if all our efforts were futile. For what could such small numbers do against such evil?

"Kaida," Noam said, pulling me out of my incessant thoughts, and I flinched. His eyes softened as if he knew just how dark and twisted my thoughts had become. "That was good. Let's try again."

With a groan, I lifted the sword into the air, my arms trembling with fatigue.

A smirk lit up Noam's face as his eyes glanced over my body struggling to lift the tiny weight of the wood.

"Perhaps we should move on to magic for a while. Give your arms a break."

"We're training with magic?" I asked, relieved, letting the sword clatter to the ground.

Noam arched a brow. "That Ancient Magic won't master itself."

"And *you're* going to teach me about my magic?"

He shrugged. "Who else?"

I opened my mouth to answer but realized I didn't know. Neither Eldrin nor Tarrin would be able to train me in something they knew nothing about.

"All right… so what do I do, oh wise Magus?"

Noam went still. "Don't call me that." He fixed his eyes on the ground. "I do not deserve the honor of being called one of them. I am not my ancestors."

I glanced at Tarrin, who looked as confused as I did, but Noam cleared his throat and changed the subject before I could ask what he meant.

"Hold your palms out." He stepped directly in front of me and tapped my left hand. "Summon flames in this one."

I blinked. "You realize I'm in human form, right?" While I could use magic outside of my dragon form, it was harder, and often much weaker.

He waved a hand in dismissal. "Magic originated in the humans. If they can do it, so can you. Concentrate."

I blew out an exasperated breath with a scowl on my face but did as he said, drawing on the constant ball of fire in my core. I pictured a tendril of flame snaking off, flowing through my veins before it erupted above the skin of my hand.

"Good," Noam murmured, and tapped the other palm. "Now, hold the flame and summon water in this one."

I balked and the fire went out. "You want me to *what?*"

He gave me a patient smile. "You wielded two abilities in past encounters with Eklos," he offered as if that would help.

"But I was in dragon form then, and the beast had taken over at the point." I held back a shudder at the thought. I hated when my dragon side took control. Tarrin said it was entirely up to me when I let that happen, but sometimes my anger was so great that there wasn't really a choice in the matter. I wasn't sure which was more frightening—the fact that my dragon side took control at all or the fact that part of me enjoyed the pain I could inflict on my enemies when I was in such a state.

I shook my head, shutting down those thoughts. "How do I separate them at the same time? It takes all my concentration to summon simple flames. How do I split my focus to call on both?"

Noam waved his hand at me. "Call the flames back."

With a series of inhales and exhales I managed to bring the fire forth in my palm.

"Good. Now, picture a scale. Without your magic, the scale is equal, each side at the same height. When you summon your fire, imagine it to be a gold coin that you're setting on one side of the scale. Now, its unbalanced. Pretend your water magic is a second coin. Place it on the other side to balance it, letting the water pool in your palm."

As if the mental image were the key to unlocking my magic, the cool sensation of water spread through my veins, somehow intertwining with the fire before it erupted into my hand. It poured from my skin like a waterfall.

"Excellent. Hold the fire but control the water. Instead of letting it fall, work it into a sphere."

My first instinct was to laugh at him and tell him I couldn't do that, but with a single thought toward the magic, it began to react. The water that had spilled onto the ground ran backward, up into my palm. Like a wriggling ball, it floated in the air, both solid and liquid. The flames flickered in my other palm, in danger of going out, but I sent a wave of magic back into it and it flared.

In one hand I held a strong fire and the other a ball of water.

If only my mother could have seen it. She wouldn't have believed it.

I squeezed my eyes shut at the thought, and my core of magic went cold, the elements disappearing from my palms. I dropped my hands to my sides, expecting for Noam to perhaps scold me or demand that I try again, but when I looked up, he was grinning.

"If you ever doubt yourself again, Kaida, remember this moment. You held two different magic abilities within your hands and fully controlled them. You are stronger than you believe." He stepped up and poked my forehead with a finger. "Don't let those thoughts tell you otherwise."

He stepped back, gathering our swords. Eldrin was watching me carefully, and Tarrin appeared at my side.

"That was incredible." He planted a kiss on my temple.

When Noam had put the wooden swords in a case by the edge of the roof, he said, "That was a great start—a good place to stop and rest for the day. We can work on more of your abilities later."

My shoulders slumped. "More?" I couldn't fathom trying to control more than two types of magic.

Noam chuckled. "The Magus' magic was endless. Every ability in Elysia, all the different types amongst the dragons, both common and rare, once dwelt inside of them. The difficult thing about your magic is we don't know just how much of the Ancient Magic you inherited, and it may be something we don't discover for years yet. Some abilities may take longer to manifest than others, and some may be stronger, some weaker."

"So, how are we supposed to know what to train?" I asked.

He slung the case over a shoulder and followed Eldrin over to the to the roof ladder. With a wave, my father climbed down, Noam close behind him. Right before his face disappeared from view, he stopped and gave me a wink. "Take it one day and one magic at a time."

CHAPTER SEVEN

KAIDA

"TARRIN?" I CALLED as I stepped into the dark room, the only light being the fire blazing away in the hearth. It was the coldest night thus far and hours of wandering the streets of Mistwick contemplating Noam's words about my magic, and Eldrin leaving to rescue the King had the chilly night air seeping deep under my skin. In hindsight, it probably wasn't the wisest decision to walk the streets alone, but I had told Tarrin through our bond that I needed time to think. Besides, the shadows offered plenty of hiding places, not that I encountered even one suspicious-looking dragon.

Wishing I had warmer clothes, I grabbed one of the scratchy blankets off the back of the couch and wrapped it around me. "Tarrin?" I called again when there was no response.

"Out here." A faint voice responded from the other room.

I tip-toed on wobbly legs into Tarrin's room and found him standing on the tiny balcony attached to his room. I let out a breath, and scurried to his side, burying my face in his chest as his arms wrapped around me. The comforting scent of blue cypress and night sky enveloped my senses and all the apprehension and worry I had felt before began to fade into the background of my mind.

"What's wrong?" he asked, tilting my chin to look in my eyes. Creases appeared at the corner of his own.

I gave him a small smile and shrugged. "Why would you think something is wrong?"

Tarrin gave me a skeptical look and tapped my nose with his finger.

"I could feel your emotions the moment you entered the inn, Kaida." His mouth twitched as if he were fighting a smile. "What's wrong?"

I let out a sigh. "Eldrin is leaving tomorrow on a rescue mission that has more chances of going wrong than right. We haven't been able to find anyone to help us defeat Eklos outside of a human with a lot of knowledge, an old shape-shifter who has run from danger his entire life, and two young shape-shifters who are rather inexperienced." The words spewed from my lips like vomit, and I met his gaze. "All I can see is failure and death."

The corners of his lips twitched, and he cupped my face with his palm. "Is that all?"

I couldn't help it. A snort burst from my nose, and I dissolved into a fit of laughter. Tarrin laughed with me, though his eyes watched me carefully.

"Kaida," he whispered, before pressing a soft kiss to my lips. "Yes, the future is uncertain, and it's terrifying. There will always be more reasons to quit than to keep going. But if you let yourself live in that terror, of course everything we're fighting for will seem pointless. You must choose to see hope in each sunrise, come to love each sunset. Every day brings new chances for life, for hope. Though it's difficult to see when we're in the midst of it, if we stop now, all of Elysia will be lost. If we won't fight for this world, who will?"

I struggled to breathe as his words settled into me, soothing the ache, and calming the anxious thoughts swirling like bile in my stomach. He smoothed down my hair, a shiver crawling over my skin as he ran his fingers through it. The blanket that I had wrapped around me fell to the floor as I wound my arms around his neck. He offered a half smirk that made my heart stutter and begin to race as he leaned down and brought his lips to mine. One step at a time, he led us back into the room, never breaking contact.

Wrapping one arm around my waist, Tarrin pulled me closer, his other hand knotting in my hair as he deepened the kiss. Every clash of our lips sent stars flashing behind my eyelids, vibrant and extravagant colors swirling and igniting as each kiss, each caress, set my skin on fire.

The back of his knees hit the large bed that occupied most of the room and he fell backward onto it, pulling me with him. A small giggle escaped my lips and a grin lit up his face. His eyes flickered with an emotion that I couldn't quite place as he ran his thumbs across my cheeks.

"I love you, Kaida."

Time stopped.

For a moment, my entire body was doused in ice water, my muscles freezing. No one had ever said those words to me before. My mind clunked to a stop and refused to start moving again as I stared at Tarrin, his face going from happy, to confused, to a hurt expression that wrenched my heart in two.

Why wouldn't my mouth work? Why wouldn't my mind form a response?

Tarrin gently pushed me to the side and stood up from the bed, smoothing out his shirt.

"I'm sorry," he said, voice painfully quiet. "I shouldn't have said anything."

He began to walk away, and I grabbed his wrist, begging my lips to say something.

"T-Tarrin, w-wait!" I stuttered. "Please, just give me a moment!"

In the gentlest way possible, he pried my fingers from his wrist, and tears filled my eyes. He refused to look at me.

"I need some air," he said, walking out of the room, and I felt him shut me out as he threw his mental wall up, cutting me off from his emotions and thoughts, and stormed out of the inn.

CHAPTER EIGHT

TARRIN

*K*AIDA DOES NOT *love me.*

The words clanged through my mind, over and over, punching into me like a battering ram.

The memory of her face when I said those words was like a knife to my stomach. Her eyes had gone wide, mouth parting, and I felt every part of her body lock up.

What was I thinking?

I knew she had feelings for me. I felt it every time we were together, every time we touched or kissed. I thought we were on the same page. Why wouldn't she say it back?

The brisk night air slapped against my body as I left the inn.

"Should've grabbed a coat," I muttered to myself, my breath clouding in the air. The streets were deserted, all dragons in Mistwick likely in some tavern, and all humans were probably finishing up their daily duties or were at home with their families. Being in Myrewell was like taking a deep, unhindered breath for the first time in ages. Fear wasn't a slime over every surface, nor did hatred cling to every spoken word or action.

I didn't know when culture had changed in the south, but I found myself wishing that all of Elysia was like Myrewell.

When I'm King...

I stopped dead in my tracks at the thought. Only a few months ago I hadn't blinked an eye at the abuse that the slaves endured at the hand of the dragons. I remained blissfully ignorant, not bothering to care about any of the humans.

Until Kaida. She had helped me shed that insensitive skin and embrace a new way of thinking. She brought a passion, a light in my life that I had never experienced. How a girl who had been so horribly mistreated her entire life could still have such a good heart, I would never understand. But perhaps she was affected more than I thought if she wasn't able to love me the way I loved her.

Swallowing, I continued to meander through the empty streets, hands in my pockets, mind spinning in circles.

"Give it to me!" a voice growled, and I froze, instinct taking over as I backed into the shadows of an alleyway. Across the road a brown dragon stood on the other side of an open window, back hunched as he conversed with a yellow dragon. Something about their darting eyes and body language had my nerves instantly on edge. Holding my breath, I crept closer, sliding against the wall until I was hidden behind a bush just to the side of the window. I peeked over the window ledge, just enough to see who was speaking. My human ears strained to hear what they were saying.

"I want a census of any new visitors to Mistwick in the last three months," the brown dragon growled. Alarms started ringing in my mind.

The other dragon fingered through a stack of papers, his claws shaking as his gaze flickered between the other dragon and the paper in front of him.

"A-are you looking for someone in particular, my lord?" the yellow dragon asked, his slithering tongue stuttering over the words.

"*Someones,*" he retorted. "Not just one. I'm looking for three dragons or humans. They are both, you see."

The yellow dragon blanched and went back to his search.

My heart pounded so hard in my chest that I wondered if the dragons could hear it.

They're looking for us! My legs begged me to flee, but I fought the urge to run, needing to know for sure if the Remnant had discovered our location. I debated shifting into dragon form, but I knew that it was much more recognizable than my human body.

"Ah, here we go." The yellow dragon handed the paper to the other, his features calming infinitesimally.

The brown dragon scanned the list once, twice, and then a smile full of dagger teeth bent his snout. "Thank you, Ort. You've been most helpful." He crumpled the list in his claws and slammed the door as he left the house, turned down the street, and disappeared around a corner.

What was on that list? Our names? We were careful not to use our real names at the inn. Perhaps our descriptions? Did it list our location?

Deep in my gut, I knew I needed to get back to the inn—to Kaida.

My head throbbed, my stomach a writhing pit of fire. Desperate to make it back before he found her, I shifted into dragon form, and took off into the sky. For the briefest moment I relished the feeling of flying once again. Having to keep my dragon abilities silenced had begun to take its toll.

I flew headfirst into the wind, my neglected wings thudding in the air as they tried to keep me aloft. Time passed both too fast and painstakingly slow as I struggled to make it back to the inn to warn Kaida. When the familiar brick building came into view, I nosedived for the door, sending crimson leaves flying in my wake as I touched the ground and shifted back into human form. My feet felt sluggish as I rushed up the stairs, hands trembling as I struggled to fit the key into the door before bursting in with a shout. "Kaida!"

I came to an abrupt halt, my blood freezing in my veins, and my feet turning to puddles beneath me. For in front of me stood Kaida in human form, the brown dragon from the street standing behind her, holding a dagger to her throat.

CHAPTER NINE

ELDRIN

I STOOD ON THE bow of Noam's boat, staring at the stars. The vessel bobbed up and down in a gentle motion as the tide slapped against it. Though it was still tied to the dock on my left, I allowed myself to wish, if only for a moment, that we were out at sea, away from all the troubles that plagued my mind. Mistwick loomed behind me, and with it, a reminder that we needed to leave soon. If I knew my cousin, it would be only a matter of days until the Remnant started tearing through the town in search of us. I was surprised we'd made it so long already. Kaida and Tarrin needed to relocate while I went after the King.

My mind spun in a thousand directions, trying to throw together some semblance of a rescue plan to get Martik out of the palace dungeons. Even with the sketches from the Prince, I had to admit, there was a far better chance of things going wrong than going right. Fear tightened my stomach into a needle riddled ball.

Rescuing the King had never been a part of my plans. That was the point of his sacrifice. He thought what he was doing would keep his son safe, without an expectation of being saved. Knowing Martik, he fully expected to die in those dungeons. I let out a sigh, rubbing at my face.

The only thing that appeared to be in our favor was the fact that Eklos's cronies hadn't found us yet. I blew out a breath as a star raced across the sky, bleeding into the horizon.

"Sapphire for your thoughts?" a voice asked, before a small blue stone bounced on the railing in front of me. I huffed a laugh, finding Noam at my side before returning my gaze to the sky. The night air was brisk, the sea air whipping my silver hair behind me.

"I can't help but feel that all our efforts are futile," I said at last, voice like a whispering wind as I echoed Kaida's thoughts from earlier. "Eklos's numbers grow stronger each day, and the chance of finding supporters to help us defeat him grows smaller with it."

"You speak as though you have lost hope, old friend," Noam replied, narrowing his eyes at me.

I bit the inside of my cheek, refusing to say aloud what I was truly thinking.

At my silence, Noam's nails dug into the wood in front of him. "What happened to Eldrin the Great? The mighty shape-shifter who fought for justice, never ceasing, always striving to do good?" Noam's chest was heaving with the force of his words. "What happened to the Eldrin who always believed that there was some good in this wretched world? What happened to the dragon who befriended a human, saving his life countless times, never abandoning him or enslaving him as a dragon should?" A heated silence snapped into place between us.

"That Eldrin has grown weary, I'm afraid. A thousand years is a long time to fight against such evil."

"But you haven't been fighting it," Noam scolded. "You've been running from it."

A cold, empty feeling sunk into my well of magic, dousing the fire that had already faded to a small flame. The truth of the words sunk like nails into my skin, and I fought to keep my expression neutral.

"I wouldn't expect you to understand, Noam," I snapped, crossing my arms across my chest, immediately regretting my words.

Noam was silent for a moment, his brows furrowed over blazing eyes.

"No," he answered. "I suppose you wouldn't expect *me* to understand. Me, a lowly human born into slavery. Me, whose mother and father were brutally beheaded in front of my sister and me when we were children. Me, who fought for revenge against the dragon who murdered them, only to be caught and my sister killed in my stead." Steaming tears cascaded onto his cheeks as he spoke, a dam of long-held emotion finally breaking. "Me," he said, voice cracking, "who wanted to give up, to forget Elysia and the evil that resided in it. Me, who was ready to die. And then who happened to land on my boat?" Noam's silver lined eyes turned on me, and I flinched.

"Noam…" I began but he held up a hand.

"You are going to the palace, Eldrin. You will rescue the King, and we *will* fight." His tone left no room for argument and for a moment I marveled at my friend. At the courage it would take to face all he had gone through, and still want to fight back. To live in Elysia, with century upon century of slavery binding him and the other humans, but still retaining some semblance of hope.

I exhaled, looking up at the stars again, watching as another one shot across the sky and fell out of sight. I could see no way that we could win this fight. Three shifters and a human were hardly a formidable force—not against the Remnant nor Eklos's dragon army. I had traveled to all the surrounding villages in the three months we'd been in Mistwick, and none were willing to stand against the might of the new Regent of Elysia.

What could we do? There was no winning this battle.

Unless…

A bright flame suddenly flared in my stomach, deep in the depth of my magic. A small tendril of hope wriggled its way into my head, and, against my better judgement, I allowed myself to embrace it, letting it fill me to the brim. I considered it for another moment, trying to justify sending my friend on an uncertain journey that may or may not end in his death. I met his fierce gaze and saw nothing but fire. He wanted Eklos's reign to end just as badly as we did.

"All right, Noam," I said, drawing out the words. "We will fight." I put a hand on my friend's shoulder and squeezed. "This is what I need you to do."

CHAPTER TEN

TARRIN

"L ET HER GO," I said, taking a step forward.

"Not another step, or I'll make the girl bleed," the dragon growled, his sharp teeth flashing in the torchlight.

"You don't want to do this." My voice was hard, containing every ounce of that royal dominance I had acquired growing up. The brown dragon chortled.

"Oh, yes. I believe I do," he sneered. I had never seen this dragon before, and I took some small comfort that he was not one of the Council—or Eklos himself. I dared another step forward and watched in dismay as Kaida let out a tiny yelp, blood trickling down her neck.

"My reward will be great," the brown dragon snarled. "Delivering two of the most wanted fugitives in Elysia directly to the hand of Eklos and the Remnant." His sneer spread even farther, the dragon's scaly lips disappearing altogether.

"I can double your reward. Just let her go."

The dragon barked out a laugh, the sound like crunching gravel. I took advantage of his momentary distraction and took another step forward and to the right. If I could just get close enough…

"You have no power to offer me anything, *Prince.*"

Fire ignited in my gut, burning through my blood.

Tarrin, shift.

I wasn't sure why Kaida's voice in my mind caught me off guard, but I blinked before smoothing a blank expression across my face once more.

The moment I shift, the dragon will kill you.

You have to! Please, trust me!

A war battled in my mind as I fought out the choice before me. I could try to lunge at the dragon, defenseless in my human form, and still Kaida would likely die. Or I could shift, and the dragon would likely slit her throat before I had even made a move toward him. Though she had all but mastered the art of shifting over the past months, part of me worried that the days of her struggling to shift into dragon form would shove to the surface once more. The thought of what might happen if she failed to shift had bile rising in my throat.

I met Kaida's fierce gaze and the hair on my arms stood on end. Her eyes were *glowing*.

I swallowed hard and gave an imperceptible nod.

All right.

Inhaling slowly, I let the fire in my core swell and build until it flowed through every vein, and in a mighty exhale a blue light flared around me, scales flickering over my skin, my body racing toward the ceiling, wings erupting from my back. I opened my eyes again and lightning exploded in the room.

It spiderwebbed along the floor and ceiling, followed by a mighty clap of thunder, and I collapsed onto my knees, the sound rendering me momentarily deaf. Silence pulsed in my ears as I looked frantically around for Kaida and the dragon.

In the split-second distraction of my shifting, Kaida, too, had shifted. Her amethyst body towered over the brown dragon. He clearly had not expected it, nor had he expected the spear of white-hot flames now resting in her hands to be poised over his heart.

"How did you know where we were?" Kaida's eyes glowed bright like the sun; her voice almost otherworldly as she ground out the words.

The brown dragon trembled, falling backward on the floor, clawed hands outstretched in front of him. As if that would ward her away. When he did not answer, she touched the tip of the fire spear to the tender area just beneath his arm. The roar he emitted was almost as bad as the thunderclap from moments ago.

I fought the urge to cover my sensitive ears.

"How did you find us?" Kaida roared.

The dragon's snout twisted with a hatred that could stop a man's heart. He met her gaze only to flinch away, his eyes shutting tight.

"Last chance, dragon. Either tell us how you found us, or I will kill you."

My blood chilled at her words. Her dragon side was fueling this violent version of her, but I knew Kaida did not relish hurting—let alone killing—any living thing. Even back in Belharnt, she had hesitated to kill Eklos—the one dragon who truly deserved to die.

The tension in the air was tangible, ether coating every ounce of oxygen, only a breath away from shattering.

"Long… live… Eklos," the brown dragon snarled, enunciating each word and spit at Kaida, his steaming saliva landing in a wad on the ground.

Surprisingly, Kaida turned to look at it and then rotated toward the dragon, her head cocked at an angle. He cringed beneath the weight of her gaze.

"No," she said, voice strong and unwavering. "Long live the King." The dragon's eyes widened, and she thrust the spear of flames through his thick scaled armor, and plunged it deep into his heart, a thud echoing as it went all the way through and hit the floor beneath him. He groaned as blood seeped between his teeth before a mighty exhale escaped his lips, marking his passage from Elysia into the afterlife.

Kaida released her hold on the fire magic and spun to face me. My body responded before my mind could catch up and I took a step backward. The soul-crushing hatred still shone in her eyes, the beast within her not yet releasing its control over her body.

My pulse quickened as she took a step forward, then another.

"Kaida, it's me," I said gently, putting my arms out in a gesture of surrender.

Her eyes continued to glow, and a dark, poisonous hatred slithered down our shifter bond. It was like burning ice spreading through my blood, a relentless need to kill that consumed every other thought.

Ever since discovering she was a shape-shifter, Kaida had been afraid to give into her dragon side—afraid the beast would claim complete control and the human girl would no longer exist. I had assured her frequently that she was the master of her own body, not the beast inside. Though as she stalked toward me, I wondered if perhaps I had been wrong.

But no sooner had the thought crossed my mind when Kaida's eyes widened, losing their glow. She stumbled forward, shifting back into human form, and I caught her in my arms, shifting with her.

"Must… leave," she muttered, her eyes instantly falling closed. Though her magic was strong, the well much deeper than any dragon I had witnessed, these few months of not using any of it had taken its toll. Kaida had not required much to kill the dragon, but it was enough to exhaust her.

I managed to walk her over to the couch before she collapsed, asleep in a heap on the cushions.

CHAPTER ELEVEN

KAIDA

"HURRY," A MALE voice said, though it was far away in the back of my mind, the sound of it echoing behind my eyelids. I tried to pry them open, but the darkness had its claws buried deep. My stomach both ached and throbbed like the feeling of covering yourself in snow for too long. A shiver worked itself into my limbs but still I couldn't open my eyes.

"Hurry," the voice said again. "There's more where he came from." A loud sniff sounded. "Based on the smell, we only have minutes before they descend on the inn."

The more he talked, the more the black receded from my mind, consciousness creeping back in ever so slowly.

"Why hasn't she woken up yet?" It was a different voice this time, one that I would know even in the deepest pit.

"Tarrin?" I whispered, through cracked lips and a mouth dry as cotton.

I heard a sudden intake of breath before warm fingers were touching my cheeks. Still, I couldn't make my eyes open.

"Kaida." Strong hands tilted my face. "Can you hear me?"

My mouth wouldn't move. Rustling fabric sounded behind me before I felt the heat of another body close to me.

"Using such magic after months of suppressing it took its toll.

It's going to take some time for her to be fully conscious. We need to go. Now."

"Eldrin, I can't just throw her over my shoulder and run. Surely, we can wait a few more minutes for her to wake."

He emitted a low growl. "I just returned to the inn to find a dead dragon on our floor—only feet away from you that is leaking its scented blood all over the floor. Any enemy dragon in Mistwick will smell it and come running. We can't wait."

My face scrunched into a wince as Eldrin's stern voice grew louder, reverberating in the darkness. Through the chill encompassing my body, thin tendrils of warmth from the hearth seeped through the pores of my skin, warming me inch by inch, but it was still too slow.

"Kaida, can you hear me?" Tarrin's voice was right next to my ear. "I'm going to carry you. We need leave the inn. Sleep, my love. I'll keep you safe."

Scorching hot hands gripped my arms, and I tried to call out against the sudden heat, but my lips were glued shut. I was vaguely aware of a weightless feeling before the heat of Tarrin's body returned in full force and the darkness consumed me once more.

❧

The moon was high overhead, the cold of the autumn night slamming into my face like a punch as I finally pried my eyes open. I was perched on Tarrin's back, secured with an unreasonable number of ropes, as we flew through the starry sky. I could barely make out Eldrin's midnight-blue body soaring next to us. Clouds split and reformed, swallowing us whole; drops of water condensing on my skin before the wind swept it away.

Where are we? I asked Tarrin through our bond.

I felt his smile in my mind as if he had run a finger over my lips. *She awakens. We're perhaps a hundred miles from Mistwick, headed toward Pyrn.*

How long was I asleep? I rubbed at my temple, willing the pounding in my head to stop.

Several hours. The Remnant were scouring the streets when we snuck out of Mistwick. We didn't have time to wait for you to wake.

I glanced over at my father, expecting him to chime in, but he kept his snout facing forward, occasionally dropping through the clouds to see the landscape below before rising again.

I wriggled against the ropes, trying to free my limbs. *What is this infernal contraption?*

Tarrin's sultry chuckle had any lingering drowsiness evaporate into the wind.

Well, I couldn't have you snore so hard that you slid right off my back.

My eyes narrowed and I smacked my hand against the scales on his neck. *I do not snore.*

Another laugh whispered down the bond, and I glanced over at Eldrin whose gaze was fixed on me.

You snore like a male dragon. Amusement flickered in his eyes, and I huffed out a breath, managing to wiggle out of the ropes enough to cross my arms. Stupid dragons. I didn't snore.

In unison, both males burst out laughing, sounding a bit like barked growls and hissing in their dragon forms. But as quickly as the laugh surfaced, it disappeared beneath Eldrin's scales as he studied the ground.

We should land and walk for a bit. It's not long until dawn and we'll need to find shelter before then.

Without another word, he tucked his wings in and dove for the ground, Tarrin following suit. They aimed for a clearing of trees just large enough for the both of them to land. My stomach rose into my throat as we grew nearer, the thud of Tarrin's wings pulsing in my ears as we landed. As soon as their feet were planted on the dirt, my father swiped a claw at the ropes holding me down, and I slid off Tarrin's back. The ice-crusted grass crunched beneath my boots.

I swayed on my feet and before I could blink, Tarrin shifted into human form, and wrapped an arm around my waist, steadying me.

Eldrin shifted then headed for the woods. "We'll rest for a bit beneath the cover of the trees, then continue on foot until dawn."

I rubbed at my cheek, thankful that I wouldn't need to fly anytime soon. Every part of my body ached from the fight with the mercenary. Even if I were physically fine, I still wasn't particularly good at flying, nor had the weeks in Mistwick afforded much time for practicing. My wings weren't strong enough yet to handle the long distances that were second nature to my father and Tarrin. I hated the thought of being the reason we weren't already in Pyrn.

If I had been able to handle my magic better, use it without passing out for hours, or even fly longer distances, we could have been there by now. The urgency to get far from Mistwick, to find more support to help us defeat the Remnant, was like an enormous bell clanging in my mind, growing louder with each moment we were on the road.

We walked a ways into the forest before my father threw a pack onto the dirt and rummaged through it, pulling out a loaf of bread wrapped in cloth and a few apples. He tore off several hunks and handed it to each of us before settling down against a tree, the wet sound of his teeth sinking into the skin of the apple echoing. Holding in a groan, I lowered myself to the ground, sitting shoulder-to-shoulder with Tarrin as we each bit into our bread.

As if my brain knew I was out of danger, and in a place where my mind could wander, my thoughts immediately drifted back to the dragon that held a dagger to my throat. A sharp burst of remorse cut through my stomach, making the bread taste rancid. I killed another living being. Though it was a cruel dragon, intent on murdering me, I couldn't stop the tingle of regret, the numb feeling that was fighting to envelope my body. The dragon deserved it. He was going to kill Tarrin and me, without any hesitation. Why was I struggling?

Eldrin had determined that the dragon was a member of the Remnant—the amulet he wore around his neck indicating that he was a specially trained mercenary. There had been no choice in the matter but to take his life.

Yet, it still haunted me. Tarrin kept glancing at me out of the corner of his eye, likely sensing the direction of my thoughts through our bond, but I refused to look at him. He wouldn't understand. Dragons killed for sport—they were taught to do so from the time they were younglings. He wouldn't understand the soul-wrenching ache deep in my stomach. There was one less soul in Elysia, and it was my fault.

"How much farther?" I asked Eldrin, attempting to shut down those thoughts, shoving them deep inside.

Eldrin cast an annoyed look my way and returned his gaze to the treetops. Through the foliage, the sky began to lighten with the first signs of dawn. "We'll need to make camp and rest out of sight once the sun rises. We can't risk being seen and it's much harder to hide in daylight."

"Camp where?" I meant to say the words only to myself, but they popped out in a snippy tone that earned a scowl from my father.

"I know of a cave in these woods that will provide adequate shelter. We'll rest there until night falls and then we'll fly the rest of the way."

My stomach rioted against the bread I just ate. The first few times I had tried to fly, it had been an utter disaster. I had barely managed to catch an updraft before crashing back down to the ground in a pile of limbs and wings. I wouldn't describe my flying as graceful, but I had at least managed to improve enough to stay aloft.

"What will we do once we arrive in Pyrn?" Tarrin asked.

"You two will remain hidden in the first village we come across, and I will head north to the palace."

Tarrin studied my father, rubbing his chin. "You truly expect us to hide while you rescue my father?"

"Yes. I do," Eldrin responded, his tone shutting down any possible discussion on the matter.

We ate in tense silence for several moments. Tarrin's thoughts down the bond were loud, outraged, but he kept his lips pressed together. I wished we had another option—any option—but to send Eldrin off on his own to find Martik. I didn't know which I had more confidence in—Eldrin's intelligence to slip in and out of the dungeons or Eklos's ability to sniff him out and finally put an end to his cousin. If we had more dragons on our side that could help him rescue the King, or even if my father had a friend…

A sudden gasp escaped my throat. "Noam! We left him in Mistwick!" A sinking feeling settled into my gut. How had we forgotten him? Alarm flashed in Tarrin's eyes, but my gaze snapped to Eldrin.

"Noam is fine," Eldrin announced, his eyes on the apple in his hand. "He left Mistwick before we did."

"What? Why?" Tarrin said, suspicion creeping into his voice.

"I told him to leave." The words were cold, emotionless.

"But… why?" I tried to feel an explanation through our shifter bond, but Eldrin had strong stone walls erected around his mind. I couldn't find a way in. "He's your friend and he was supposed to continue training us. Why would you tell him to leave?"

"This is not his fight," Eldrin stated, though something strange flickered down our shifter bond for a split second. It almost felt like my father was… lying? I blinked against the breeze coming through the trees. Eldrin had never lied to me before. Why would he lie about why he sent Noam away? I glanced at Tarrin, but his gaze remained on the apple in his hand, as though he hadn't noticed the odd feeling down the bond us shape-shifters shared.

"He is better off out at sea, where no dragon can find him. Though the Remnant wasn't searching for him yet, it was only a matter of time before they learned of his involvement and began hunting him as well." He took another bite before tossing the core into the woods. A squirrel scrambled down a tree, grabbed it, and took off through the trees. "Noam was already gone before I arrived back at the inn to a dead dragon on the floor." His eyes met mine for the briefest second before looking away.

Though I hadn't spent much time with Noam outside of training with him, my stomach sank at the thought of never seeing him again. I had grown to appreciate his presence over the past few weeks, even if I despised it when he whacked me with a wooden sword.

"Come," Eldrin said, getting to his feet. "Let's get to the cave before the sun is fully risen." He turned his back on us, ending our conversation, and headed deeper into the woods.

Tarrin's eyes met mine. The memory of what happened in his bedroom hit me like a punch to the stomach. We hadn't had a moment alone since then to talk about it, to figure things out. Between the Remnant and leaving Mistwick, we'd barely had a moment to breathe. He had told me he loved me, and I froze like a fool, saying nothing. The hurt in his eyes when I couldn't say the words in return bit into my skin. I never wanted to see that pain on Tarrin's face again. Now, I feared that it had sat unresolved too long. That whatever we were, whatever we had, would simply cease to exist.

Is that how love worked? I didn't know. Did I love him? I didn't know that either. I had never known what love was. It had never existed in my world.

"Are you all right?" Tarrin asked, his deep voice rumbling in my ear as he walked beside me.

My cheeks burned. "Yes." That uncomfortable tension filled the space between us. I wanted to close the distance, to reassure him, do *something*. But my feet were glued to the dirt. Words warred in my mind, and confusion coated every thought. I didn't know how to do this. Whatever this was.

Figuring it out would have to wait. Eldrin's voice pierced the silence like glass shattering as he called through the trees.

"Come on. The cave is close."

CHAPTER TWELVE

EKLOS

A FIRE ROARED IN the hearth of the King's study—now my study—making it sweltering and stuffy, but I didn't mind. The torches remained unlit, leaving the flicker of the flames as the only light source. I stared into the fire, watching each lick of orange and blue dance around each other. It was mesmerizing as I envisioned the battle of finally capturing my cousin and killing the girl and her prince. It all played out perfectly in my mind, and I let out a triumphant growl that echoed between the bookcases as I finally struck down Eldrin. Slumping back into Martik's large chair—my chair—I smiled to myself as my eyes finally left the flames.

A light knock sounded from the other side of the door, and I straightened in anticipation, spreading my wings behind me to make myself appear more intimidating. "What is it?"

A dark-green dragon with one eye missing poked his long snout in through the door, glancing around the darkened room before his wide eye finally settled on me. When he didn't move, I waved my clawed hand impatiently, summoning the dragon into the room.

"My lord, I bring news from Myrewell." The dragon's voice made a hissing sound, like air escaping a small hole, and it set my nerves on edge.

I rapped my claws against the wooden desk, smoke leaking from my nostrils. "Well?" I snapped when the green dragon said nothing. He flinched, taking an involuntary step back.

"Our spies have discovered the shifters' presence in Mistwick, my lord, on the southern coast of Myrewell." Sweat glistened on his scales, dripping down the sides of his face. "Morsun engaged two of the three." He paused, his eyes darting to me then back to the floor. "The Prince and the girl. We were unable to locate the third."

Eldrin. How do you escape my grasp at every turn?

"Well, where are they?" I spat.

The dragon swallowed, his throat bobbing up and down, and he hung his head.

"They put up a fight when Morsun tried to capture them. By the time the other mercenaries in Mistwick arrived to assist, he was dead, and the Prince and the girl were gone." The dragon took another step back, his body coiling as if readying for a strike.

For a moment, all was still. Nothing moved or made a sound.

Then fire exploded in my stomach, burning through my veins, before erupting from my snout. It swirled like a vortex, twisting around the room, engulfing everything in its path. The green dragon collapsed to the floor, covering his head with his arms.

I stood from my chair, flames spilling from between my teeth. "You mean to tell me that they killed one of our own and escaped?" My voice was quiet as death, the promise of murder thick on my tongue. "Follow them!" I roared, and the dragon on the floor curled tighter, making himself impossibly smaller.

"They tried, my lord," he whined. "The trail has gone cold."

Like a candle being snuffed out, the room suddenly went dark, all fire ceasing. It took a moment for my dragon sight to adjust before I could see the charred ruin of the study left behind, and I felt a slight satisfaction that I had taken something else of Martik's.

I closed my eyes, inhaling the smoke around me, waiting for my furious trembling to subside.

My eyes snapped open, and I reached a hand forward, a whip of smoke lashing out and wrapping itself around the green dragon's neck, lifting him off the ground. He choked and gasped, clawing at the smoke collar, trying to get air into his lungs.

"There is always a trail," I growled, bringing our snouts together and baring my teeth. "I suggest you find it."

Releasing my hold on the smoke, the green dragon collapsed to the floor, wheezing heavily as the smoke from the charred room offered no relief to his starving lungs.

"Tell the Remnant if they do not find them, and soon, they will have proved their uselessness and will have to answer for it." I smiled, flames filling my mouth, shooting out embers as I spoke.

"As you will it, Master Eklos." The green dragon pushed himself up, staggering back toward the door, throwing one last look at me over his shoulder.

I allowed him to take a few more steps before I whipped a tendril of smoke at him. He roared as it sharpened, spearing under his scales. Wrapping it around his belly, I yanked him to me, bringing him snout to snout.

"Do not fail me," I whispered as smoke leaked from my mouth, shoving its way into his nostrils. His mouth fell open just before he blacked out, and I ripped the door open, throwing him into the hall.

CHAPTER THIRTEEN

TARRIN

THE OPENING TO the cave was hardly more than a crack in a wall of rocks, covered in moss and surrounded by foliage. It was almost impossible to see to begin with, and there was no possibility that a dragon would ever be able to fit inside it, making it the perfect hiding place. Eldrin shimmied through the crack, signaling with a hand to stay put until he inspected inside. A whistle sounded a moment later, and I glanced at Kaida.

An ache shot through my chest when she looked at me. When I had arrived at the inn to find that dragon holding a dagger to her throat, my heart froze in my chest. All previous thoughts of what had happened between us had fled, and my only focus was to get her out of there alive. But during the hours since then, flying in silence through the night, that hurt had begun to creep back into my heart.

I wanted to go to her, to kiss her, to tell her I loved her. But I didn't. I wouldn't. I laid my feelings out for her and received rejection. Now, I needed her to come to me. I wasn't going to force anything on her—not a betrothal or a relationship—if she didn't truly want it.

Swallowing down the lump in my throat, I gestured for her

to go first into the cave. Kaida hesitated, her mouth opening like she wanted to speak, but her eyes found the ground at the last moment, and she disappeared through the crack in the rock.

The coarse surface grabbed at my clothes as I squeezed my way through, the cold seeping into my skin. The crevice seemed to go on forever when the wall suddenly gave way and I stumbled forward. Kaida grabbed my arm to keep me from falling, and I blinked against the darkness. The sound of striking flint echoed between the rocks before a small torch flared to life in Eldrin's hands, and I squinted against the sudden light.

The cave was enormous. A cavernous ceiling loomed above us, every quiet breath of ours echoing. From outside, it would have seemed impossible for such a large room to sit behind it. It was easily large enough for all three of us to stand comfortably in dragon form. Though the rocks and dirt that made up the walls were cold to the touch, the cave was surprisingly warm, which was a good thing since there was no place for smoke to escape if there had been a need for a fire.

"I'll be back," Eldrin announced, placing the torch in a crevice in the rock, and then strode back toward the entrance. "I'm going to scout the area." He didn't bother to look back at us before he slipped through the crack and was gone.

A heavy weight fell on me. Hours of flying without sleep and running for our lives was beginning to catch up to my body. Invisible bricks sat on my eyelids, and I watched as Kaida swayed and dropped to her knees on the floor as if she could no longer remain standing. She scooted herself backward until her body met the wall and sighed, before fixing her eyes on me.

She patted the floor beside her, inviting me to sit with her. I hesitated for a moment before sitting next to her. I waited for that uncomfortable tension to settle into place between us, but Kaida shifted closer, wrapping her arms around my waist, and nestled her head beneath my chin.

The frigid ice of rejection that had surrounded my heart thawed ever so slightly. I put my arms around her and pulled her closer. Instead of dwelling on what happened yesterday with Kaida, I chose to relish this moment, holding her—the shifter I was in love with. She was alive and unharmed. That was all that mattered. I squeezed my eyes shut, forcing the image of the knife at her throat out of my head.

"I'm sorry." Kaida's voice was a whisper, but it echoed back and forth against the cave walls.

I tensed, swallowing down the lump in my throat. "What are you sorry for?"

"For… yesterday," she said, struggling to find the right words.

"It wasn't your fault they found us. You have nothing to be sorry for."

"No," she blurted. "Not for that." Kaida took a deep breath and it whistled between her lips as she let it out. "I'm sorry I wasn't able to say it back."

My stomach dropped like a ship anchor into the sea. I remained quiet, carefully choosing my words. "I would not want you to say it if it wasn't the truth."

Kaida pulled back to stare into my eyes. "Tarrin… I have never experienced this. I don't know what love truly is. I cannot distinguish between what is love and what is necessity."

"Necessity?" I repeated in disbelief. "You think I love you out of necessity?"

She took a shuddering breath. "If the betrothal were not in existence, do you believe you would have still come to love me, Tarrin?" Her words were sad, and clarity snapped into place in my mind.

"You think I love you only because of a betrothal? Because it's a requirement?" I took her face in my hands and searched her eyes. "I know that some way, someday our paths would have crossed if all of this had never happened. Whether the King and Queen arranged the betrothal out of necessity does not matter. It was always you and me. I knew from that first day I found you at The Den." Tears spilled onto her cheeks, and I smoothed my thumbs over them, wiping them away. "I love you, Kaida. Truly. Not out of necessity or because of a betrothal. I would have faced Eklos and the Remnant and fought through armies of dragons to find you." I paused, tucking a piece of hair behind her ear. "My heart is yours, if you will have it."

Fresh tears filled her eyes, pouring onto her cheeks and she collapsed against my chest.

You don't need to say anything right now. My words were a gentle caress from my mind to hers. *I'm not going anywhere.*

Kaida's tears fell harder, dampening my shirt, but it wasn't long before her sobs quieted, and her breathing became more even as she fell asleep. I smiled despite myself. Resting my head on top of hers, I pulled her tighter and closed my eyes, following her into the realm of dreams.

CHAPTER FOURTEEN

KAIDA

"WAKE UP!"

My heart threatened to burst from my skin at the startling sound of my father's voice. Tarrin and I had fallen asleep against the stone wall. Though the cave we were hiding in was huge and should have been musty and cold, it was stifling, and I found it difficult to take a full breath. It felt like the summer humidity in Vernista, but summer was months in the past. I glanced at the torch across from us on the wall and my eyes widened at the sight of it burning low, almost out of fuel. I blinked as I realized that hours must have passed.

Tarrin groaned, rubbing his scarred cheek with a hand before gently shifting me to the side, and getting to his feet. He held out a hand to me; I grabbed it and let him pull me up.

"Where have you been?" I asked, stifling a yawn.

Eldrin stood with his hands on his hips, a deep scowl turning his lips down.

"Making sure we were not followed," he snarled.

I stiffened at his tone and Tarrin stilled behind me. My father had not spoken to me in such a way before. Eldrin was always the calm and collected one. In the few months I had known him, I had never seen him lose his temper. Something was wrong.

"What happened?" I asked.

Eldrin ran a hand through his silver hair. "I was scouting the area, and I risked going into a nearby village for supplies. The Remnant were already there."

Ice prickled over my skin and my heart doubled in tempo.

"How?" Tarrin asked, his forehead creasing. "There's no way they could suspect we're nearby. We covered our trail."

Eldrin snorted. "Yes, but that does nothing when Eklos has mobilized his dragon army, and distributed members of the Remnant to every village across Elysia." His words were much too loud within the confines of the cave, and I winced, fighting the urge to cover my ears.

"Do you know this for certain?" Tarrin asked, some of that royal dominance creeping into his voice.

"Don't patronize me, boy," my father growled. "The news is everywhere, spreading faster than disease. They are looking for us—for *you*," he finished, his eyes finding mine.

My heart stuttered before racing to a gallop, sweat pooling on my neck and dripping down my spine. Would they be able to find us here? If we left this cave, where could we go? If what Eldrin said was true, the only place we could go was away from Elysia, out to sea like Noam.

For a moment I let myself welcome the thought. What if we *did* leave Elysia? We could leave Eklos and the Remnant, and his stupid hoard of dragons behind us. They would never find us. We would be safe, and Tarrin and I could live as we wished. We could be both dragon and human without fearing for our lives or being hunted. I ached for it like the desperation for water after too many days without it.

I dared a glance at Tarrin and that trail of thoughts immediately ended. He was the Prince of Elysia. Leaving wasn't an option. This new version of him that he had grown into since we had met was too invested in his country. He cared more for Elysia's inhabitants, both humans and dragons, than any other dragon I had ever met.

Tarrin would make a great King.

I couldn't ask him to leave. Not even for me.

I let out a breath, willing my heart to slow. "What do we do?"

"Stay here. There is no place safe for you." Eldrin grabbed his sack of belongings from the corner, thrusting it over his shoulder, and strode toward the cave entrance.

"W-where are you going?" I stuttered. "You can't expect us to just stay here indefinitely."

My father stopped but didn't turn to meet my gaze. His chest heaved, and although it was muted in human form, the boiling fire within his stomach roiled down our shape-shifter bond. Eldrin wanted this to end just as much as I did.

"I'm going to rescue a king." He paused for a moment, glancing back at us. "Don't leave the cave," he repeated. "Both of you. If I have not returned by week's end, find a boat, and leave Elysia. If I fail, there will be nothing left for you here."

A sharp pang shot through my stomach like an arrow. If he failed? Eldrin had seemed so confident that he would rescue Martik when we had discussed it on Noam's boat. I studied his face before he turned away from me trying to hide what was written plainly on his face.

My father, Eldrin the Great, nephew of the Lone Dragon… he was truly afraid. It shone in his eyes like a wild storm, waiting to be unleashed. I opened my mouth to speak but he moved to the cave entrance. Without another word, Eldrin squeezed through the crack in the stone, and disappeared into the dark forest beyond.

CHAPTER FIFTEEN

ELDRIN

WHITE PUFFS OF clouds blurred past beneath me as I flew through the sky, trying to remain as invisible as possible with the sun fully overhead. Fire singed through my veins, my breaths coming in short pants even though staying aloft required no physical effort. I could not recall a time in my thousand years of existence ever feeling this emotion. It was overwhelming and all consuming. It wrapped around each of my senses, smothering them until everything I heard, saw, smelled, and felt was coated in it. I had felt the weight of wariness and uncertainty, but never fear. Not like this.

I had been entirely confident that I would be able to sneak into the palace dungeons, find Martik, and escape. But after scouting around the nearby village and seeing the Remnant crawling around with the promise of death in their eyes and whips in their hands... I knew it would be a fool's mission.

The only hope I had now was that perhaps Eklos had sent most of his forces away from the palace and I would be able to slip in and out unnoticed. But Eklos wasn't stupid, and I couldn't bring myself to let that flicker of hope burn.

The air was frightfully cold as an updraft took me higher into the sky. Through the occasional breaks in the clouds beneath me, trees zoomed past, interspersed with huts made of mud.

My stomach sank as I crossed the border from Pyrn into northern Elysia. Only a couple hundred miles until I reached Vernista and then the palace. I could have made the jump right then, appearing at the palace in a second, but the simmering in my veins kept my wings spread wide, and my magic at bay. It was too far of a distance and would use up too much of my magic. I needed to reserve as much of it as possible in case I came face to face with Eklos. I blew out a smoke-filled breath.

Questions ran rampant in my mind, forcing out all other thoughts as I rose and fell on the currents of the air. Was all of this for naught? Were we fighting a battle already lost from the start? Each of us had so much to lose.

An image of Kaida flashed through my mind, quickly followed by Noam's face, then the Prince's, and then Aela's.

This is why you are fighting. Though he was hundreds of miles away on a boat in the middle of the sea heading away from Elysia, Noam's voice of reason filled my head. *You are fighting to give them hope, a better future, a better world. The numbers may be against you now, but the battle is not lost.*

The words strengthened me, like ice and steel reinforcing my veins, smoothing away the jagged fear that had been tearing through my stomach. I knew Noam was right. Though it seemed futile now, perhaps fate would show mercy. A better Elysia was worth fighting for.

I had run for years—centuries. I left Aela when she had needed me to protect her the most. Like the coward I am, I had fled every fight that came my way. But no longer. If my daughter, after facing Eklos's abuse and unfathomable pain, was willing to fight, then I would stand by her side. I was done running—done hiding.

I glanced at the earth below, taking note of where I was. There was a safe place close by that I would be able to utilize my magic to get to without diminishing it too much. Inhaling a deep breath, I closed my eyes, sealing out the sunlight and drenching my mind in darkness. I stoked the fire within my core, sending the flames roaring through my body as I called on my magic.

A picture of a small cottage in a wooded area west of Vernista appeared behind my eyelids. I knew that cottage well. I had built it… for Aela.

It seemed a lifetime ago.

I gripped that image in my mind and with hardly a thought, my magic burst forth, covering my body in black shadow before I disappeared from the sky entirely. Black and white swirled around my body, licking at my limbs as I traveled through that world between time and space. Before I could inhale again, the world stilled, sunlight streaming above me as my scaled feet settled into the grass.

I stood amidst a clearing, surrounded by forest, and a familiar structure standing in front of me.

The cottage.

It had been almost twenty years since I had stepped over that threshold and my heart pounded beneath my scales. I could remember every piece of wood, every tree I had cut down, and every nail I hammered. I had wanted to give Aela the world, starting with a safe home, one that was clean and warm, away from the dragons that sought to harm her.

Aela was the first human that truly made me think about the world in a different way. Much like Prince Tarrin, though I had grown up as half human, I had never spared much thought for the humans in slavery. She had just escaped her previous Master when I met her, and all I desired to do was to keep her safe.

So, I built her that cottage.

It was quite small, with only one room making up the entirety of it. There was a shallow porch attached to the front that I could remember building at her request. We spent many nights out there, staring at the stars through the trees—many mornings watching the sun rise. The roof was in surprisingly good condition, with minimal wood rot throughout the whole house. There were planter boxes under the two front windows that held the withered remains of old flowers. The memory of helping Aela build them, holding her hands as she hammered nails into the wood, my arms wrapped around her as we watched the shooting stars in the sky...

I closed my eyes against the memory, shifting into human form in a cloud of shadow, and willed my feet to move forward.

The wood groaned as I stepped onto the porch, my heart thrashing in my ears as my hand turned the doorknob. It creaked open far too loudly in the quiet of the woods and my jaw fell open.

I had half expected for the room to be just as I left it, our bed with the blue floral quilt over in the corner, the wood stove in the center of the back wall burning logs, a pot of soup simmering away on top. I longed to see that shelf filled with books on the wall to the right, where Aela had spent countless hours poring over book after book.

But there was nothing here.

The cottage was empty.

I fell to my knees in the middle of the room.

Every book was cleaned from the shelves, even the pots and pans that had littered the corner by the wash basin were gone. It was almost as if that life with Aela had never existed.

I swallowed hard, begging the memories to recede. Though she had been dead for years, I had only learned of her death months ago, and if I were being honest, I still struggled to believe it. I could feel her soul in the world, inside me. But seeing our home, empty and bare... the reality hit me square in the chest, my heart squeezing until it grew difficult to breathe.

A snap sounded from outside the cottage, and I froze. Summoning my magic, I jumped from the doorway to the space beneath the window where I was hidden yet was able to see if anyone approached the cottage.

My heart pulsed painfully against my chest as I strained to hear movement outside. No one should have known there was a house here, it was well tucked away in the woods. But then again much can change in twenty years.

Forcing the ice in my veins to thaw, I slowly peeked up over the window out into the clearing. Another snap sounded just as a doe pranced through the trees, and settled over a patch of grass, oblivious to the fact that I was there.

I blew out a breath as I attempted to calm the roaring in my ears. I watched the doe for another moment, debating whether I should leave or stay here to plan the King's rescue, but my thoughts were instantly cut off as an arrow shot through the doe's heart, and it fell to the ground, a thump and rustle echoing as it fell.

I ducked beneath the window again, closing my eyes as my limbs grew heavy like lead.

Surely Eklos had not found me already. I was not close enough to Vernista for the scent to have reached him. I studied every inch of the room. There was no way out of the cottage, not without being seen. I would have to leave through the front door, putting myself in the sight of whoever was hiding amongst the trees.

I let out a silent breath, my mind racing and stumbling as I fought for some solution. Crawling on my hands and knees, I knelt in the space behind the open door. If the intruder were to come inside, I could at least have the advantage of surprise.

Dusk was beginning to set, casting an eerie glow inside the house and the yard beyond. If it reached full dark, without a torch or light to see by, I would be in real trouble. Wiping my sweaty palms on my pants, I managed to peek around the door.

The doe was lying in the grass, the arrow still protruding from its heart, but there was no sign of anyone.

A dragon likely wouldn't have used an arrow to kill an animal, so I assumed it was a human hiding beneath the cover of the trees, though the thought brought little comfort. They were armed and

I was not, and I didn't relish the thought of attacking a human with my magic either.

Wait—my magic. I gasped as I realized fear had kept my mind from the obvious way out of the cottage. Smacking myself on the forehead, I scolded myself for my stupidity for a moment before I summoned that fire within my stomach. It scorched through my veins, thawing the ice that fear had deposited.

I inhaled, grabbing hold of that magic, readying to leave the cottage and those woods for good, when the front door creaked, followed by the sound of a boot thudding.

I didn't even have time to move before the door was thrown back, revealing the human intruder.

My stomach sank, my heart slowing to a trickle, and my mind fought to comprehend what I was seeing as I beheld the hunter, or rather the huntress.

"Well, well. If it isn't Eldrin the Great, returned to his humble abode," a female voice crooned, dropping her bow by her side.

It was Queen Lita.

CHAPTER SIXTEEN

EKLOS

I SAT AT THE head of a long table, the members of the Council, their wings, tails, and limbs spilling out of their too-small chairs. I had done it on purpose—given them youngling-sized chairs. I wanted them to remember their place, that I was better than them—their future High King. My claws were clenched so tightly into fists that they pierced beneath my scales. Sulfurous smoke trickled out of my nostrils as I glared down each dragon around me, their muted scales of browns and greens growing even paler with each second that passed.

"I gave you all one job," I growled. "Find the shifters and bring them to me." I met the gaze of each dragon, feeling satisfaction as one by one they all averted their eyes. "You were tasked with finding the most ruthless and cunning dragon mercenaries in the Remnant—those who *would not fail*. And yet here we sit. The shifters have disappeared, without a trace, and one of our own is *dead!*" Every beast jumped as I snapped the last word.

"Tell me," I continued, "why was the mercenary alone when he confronted the shifters? Why were there not more of the Remnant present?"

Roldan cleared his throat. "Morsun acted alone, my lord. The other dragons claim he didn't tell them about his discovery, or his plan to attack.

"How convenient," I drawled, and I saw the scowl cross Roldan's snout before he replaced it with a neutral expression. "And why would he have acted alone, Councilman?"

"Perhaps for glory... or the reward." The other Council members exchanged glances. Dragons were notorious for their greed over gold, silver, and jewels. If that were the true reason, it wasn't a surprise that the mercenary acted alone.

Silence smothered the room.

Another dragon, with scales a muted greenish-blue color, shifted uncomfortably in his seat, his tail thumping on the floor. I couldn't remember his name and my irritation rose as the chair creaked beneath his movements.

"Something to say?" I snarled at him. The dragon's eyes widened before swallowing.

"N-no, my lord."

The scent of fear covered his scales like a cloak, and I smiled. Good, they *should* be afraid. I would be High King of Elysia once all the shifter nonsense was dealt with, and I would only achieve that title by being unrelenting, unyielding, and vicious.

That was what my father taught me.

Before I murdered him.

I slammed the door on that memory before it fully came into my consciousness and brought my attention back to the males surrounding the table. Horns glinted in the torchlight as they exchanged uneasy glances with each other.

Another thought slithered into my mind. "Update Regam on the fugitive shifters. It has been months since we threw Martik in the dungeons. I'm surprised they've gone this long without attempting to rescue him." I peered at each dragon, narrowing my eyes as I looked for any sign of weakness I needed to weed out. Each male kept their gaze planted on the table. "I imagine it won't be long now until they try. Make sure Regam is armed and ready. When they come, they cannot escape."

I paused, pointing at the muted blue dragon from earlier. "You. See to it," I snapped. The dragon's face faded almost to white as the blood drained from behind his scales; he remained frozen in his chair, his wings drooping behind him. "Now!" I roared. He all but fell out of his chair and fled the room.

I let the tension settle, relished the fear and uncertainty swelling like the ocean tide before I turned to the rest of the dragons.

"You have one last chance. Pick your mercenaries, make sure they are in pairs. Do not let those shifters catch them alone. They have proven that they do not care for the lives of dragons." I stood from my chair, flaring my wings, and leaned forward onto the table, digging my claws into the wood until it creaked and groaned. "You will not fail me this time."

"But Master Eklos, their trail has disappeared," Roldan boldly declared, and I clenched my claws to keep from grabbing him by the throat.

"That's your problem, not mine." I started to walk toward the door, feeling the weight of their eyes with every step I took.

"There is always a trail," I replied, stopping just before the threshold. "I suggest you find it. Before they find *you*."

CHAPTER SEVENTEEN

ELDRIN

"LITA?" I BREATHED, mouth hanging open.

"It's good to see you, too," she chuckled, though there was no amusement in her eyes.

"W-what… h-how… but you were *dead,*" I stuttered, unable to put together a string of coherent thoughts.

Queen Lita huffed out a laugh, though it was laced with a bitter undertone.

"Yes, that devil of a dragon did kill me," she drawled.

Lita walked over to the woodburning stove and threw a log inside along with a lit match. Her dark-brown hair was tied in a loose bun at the nape of her neck, and dirt was smudged across her cheeks and forehead. The Queen was *dirty.*

"Are you quite finished inspecting me?" she asked, irritation darkening her face as she turned to face me, noticing the way my eyes assessed her. "I assure you it's me."

"You seem… different," I managed after a moment. I had never seen Lita in such a sour mood before. Sure, she had moments of general sass, but the darkness in her eyes told me this was something else.

"Yes, I suppose I do." She nodded her head before setting

down her bow and quiver in the corner and settling down against the wall as the room slowly heated from the fire.

"What happened? How are you here?"

Lita scoffed, turning her gaze away. Her brow was furrowed in concentration, her hands fisted as her arms rested over her knees.

"I was dead, yes. But the moment my heart ceased beating, the human half of me was ripped away. I watched my dragon body on the ground, motionless, as Tarrin cried over me. I was helpless to do anything as I was tugged away, and the world went black. The next thing I knew I woke up here, in this cottage. Human."

Lita snapped her eyes to me.

"If a shape-shifter is killed whilst in dragon form, they do not truly die. Their human and dragon forms are eternally separated, the dragon half ceasing to exist, while the human half remains. We lose all ability to shift, our magic is gone, and we remain as mortal humans, with their shortened life span for the rest of our days." She paused, closing her eyes. "Though it should be a mercy to still be alive, living in a world where you can no longer access magic and summon both scales and skin is an ugly thing indeed."

My mind raced as I struggled to understand what she was saying. I had never heard of a shifter surviving death, losing all connection to their dragon side. It was difficult to believe that such a thing could be true, but I had heard the story of how she saved Kaida during Eklos's ambush—I had seen her dead dragon body in that casket. It was impossible to deny with her sitting right in front of me.

"Did you know that would happen when you saved Kaida?"

She gave a violent shake of her head. "No. This appears to be a closely guarded secret, for I had never heard of such a thing before in my long life. Nor have I been able to find any sort of texts confirming this is truly what happens if you kill a shape-shifter."

My brows crawled up my forehead. "You've been searching for answers."

Lita scoffed. "Of course, I have. Do you think I want to be stuck like this?" She gestured to her body. "If there were a way to get my dragon form back, I would do it in a heartbeat. But there's nothing. This is it. This is all I'm left with, and if I perish in this form, I will cease to exist."

I lowered myself to the dusty floor, mimicking her posture as I pondered her words. Lita was right. It must have been a secret rarely shared, for I was older than her and had been around many more shape-shifters in my lifetime, and yet had never heard of such a phenomenon. More unanswered questions popped up like daisies in my mind.

Did that mean that all shape-shifters who were killed in dragon form are still alive, only in their human bodies? Would that happen if *I* were killed? Or was this a fluke occurrence where fate wasn't finished with Lita yet? Perhaps she still had a role to play before her soul left Elysia.

I blew out a breath. "If you have been alive all this time, why have you not returned? You are still the Queen. You could have stopped Eklos from taking over, from capturing Martik—"

Lita put up a hand to stop me. "I am human, Eldrin. I am no longer a shifter. If I had returned to the Royal Palace, Eklos would have easily killed me *again* without any effort because I cannot defend myself. There is a reason why the humans have remained enslaved for a thousand years. We are powerless against the dragons."

I didn't miss her use of the word *we*. I had to bite my cheek to keep my jaw from hanging open. Queen Lita, a fierce and strong shape-shifter, no longer thought of herself as such, but as a lowly human, incapable of standing against the dragons.

This was not the Lita I remembered. Perhaps the Queen I knew really had died.

As if sensing my thoughts, her eyes narrowed. "I wouldn't expect you to understand, Eldrin. You're still a dragon."

"Did you not wish to ease the heartache and suffering of your husband and son?" The question popped out of my mouth before I fully thought it through. I couldn't understand why she would remain hidden, allowing her family to believe she was dead.

A muscle worked in Lita's jaw. "I would only have been a distraction. Martik and Tarrin had more important matters to deal with."

"They would have kept you safe."

"I would have been a distraction," Lita repeated, shaking her head.

"But you are the Queen of Elysia."

"I am the Queen of *nothing*," she spat, her eyes blazing with ice.

My mouth fell open. "What has happened to you? The Lita I knew, that I grew up with and fought with, would never have given up so easily."

Lita was thoughtful for a moment, while the cottage grew warm and stifling.

"The world looks different when you are no longer a superior beast, Eldrin." She paused, searching for the right words. "There is less light and color, less confidence, less certainty. I am learning what it means to be Lita the human rather than Queen Lita the shape-shifter. I am doing what is needed to survive."

I chewed on my lower lip as I processed her words. "You would leave Elysia in Eklos's claws, forsaking your birth right as well as your husband and sole heir?"

"It's not as simple as you make it to be," Lita retorted as she pushed to her feet. She walked over to the corner near the bare shelves and stomped on one of the floorboards. One end of the wood sprung up and she bent down to lift it up. I watched her curiously, wondering if she had done that, or if Aela had when I built the house. I certainly had not made such a hiding space.

The muscles in Lita's arms strained as she pulled out a strange configuration of rope and wood that appeared to be folded in half.

Setting it behind her, she dug beneath the floor and pulled out a couple of quilts and a few pillows. My eyebrows rose as I watched her unfold the contraption of rope and wood and she set it against the wall. It was a cot. The ropes were tied around a wood frame, and ran horizontally down the length of it, easily fitting her petite body. She threw a quilt down on top, followed by a pillow before chucking the others at me.

"I only have one cot," she said, shrugging. "You are much too big to fit without breaking it into pieces."

I eyed Lita for a moment, before my gaze roved from the hole in the floorboards to the remaining empty room.

"You've been living here." It was meant to be a question, but surprise choked my voice.

"Only to sleep. There are too many memories here to stay longer than that." The wood and ropes groaned as Lita settled into the cot, the room growing steadily darker as the fire in the wood stove faded to embers.

"I understand," I said, voice quiet.

"Do you?" Lita's voice was a whisper, and I could see the unshed tears in her eyes flickering in the dying light of the fire.

After I had built the cottage for Aela, Lita had come to visit a couple times, checking in to make sure her friend was safe and well-cared for. Though the specifics of the memories had faded with time, I distinctly remembered the two of them playing a game of cards on the floor next to the wood stove, laughing at some foul joke Aela had learned. A small smile turned the corner of my lips before I shoved the thoughts away. It was no use to remember now. My love was gone, every memory I had tainted by the ache of missing her.

Ignoring the dust caking the floor, I threw the quilt down and settled on my side, propping my head up with my hand.

"This is the first time I have returned here since…" Emotion choked my voice, forcing me to stop.

"Why did you leave her, Eldrin?"

I bit the inside of my cheek. "I thought I was keeping her safe."

"You didn't consider your scent all over her? That Eklos would sniff her out?"

"I panicked. When I saw my cousin in Vernista, every rational thought disappeared. I should have taken Aela and run—left Elysia where we could be free and safe together. But in that moment, fear controlled my mind so thoroughly that it seemed like the best option was to leave her."

Lita made a noise of disgust. "After a thousand years of life, you sure have moments of sheer stupidity. You should have known—"

"I know, Lita!" I yelled, unable to take her scolding any longer. "I have had nearly twenty years to dwell on every mistake I ever made with Aela, to regret every choice I made. And when I found out that she was dead—at the hand of Eklos—it only renewed that shame and regret. Don't tell me I was stupid. I already know."

Silence filled the cottage, thick and oppressive. There were no sounds outside, the brisk autumn air quieting even the hardiest of bugs. She either had no response for my outburst or she chose to keep it to herself.

"I was going to marry her," I whispered, more to myself than her.

Lita's eyes widened. "There is no record of a dragon ever marrying a slave. Believe me. I've combed through the history books."

I glanced at her, knowing she had been searching through Elysia's history to find a way to bring her dragon form back.

I rubbed at hand over my forehead. "I loved her Lita. I think she was my one heart."

Her jaw popped open. "Your *cor unum*? A dragon and a human?"

"I know how it sounds," I said, shaking my head. "I can't explain it."

Cor unum was the dragons' term for soulmates. Dragons could live over a thousand years and yet there was still only one destined mate for them to find—their one heart.

"If that were true, Eldrin, you wouldn't have been able to leave her like you did."

I was already shaking my head before she finished speaking. "Sometimes love is so great that you're willing to do whatever it takes to keep them safe—even if that means leaving them."

Lita hesitated, dropping her eyes to the floor. "Then you understand why I've stayed away from Martik and Tarrin."

I gaped at her, comprehension falling over me like a wave. "Lita…"

"Are they safe?" The motherly concern sent a jolt of relief through me. Perhaps the real Lita was still inside her, just buried beneath her anger. I felt my hands that had unconsciously balled into fists relax.

"Tarrin and Kaida are in Pyrn. I left them in a cave where they will be safe." I hesitated before continuing. "The Remnant is hunting us."

"I've seen them crawling through the villages. Portraits of their faces have been hung all over Elysia. If they go into any town, they'll be recognized. Even the humans won't hesitate to turn them over to the Remnant—not if they think it will keep themselves safe."

I nodded. "I told them to stay in the cave until I return."

She arched an eyebrow. "And you think they will?"

"I'm foolishly optimistic."

Lita chuckled, the sound like a breath of fresh air after breathing smoke, before she gripped the side of the cot, the wood creaking beneath the pressure.

"And Martik?" Her lips barely moved as she spoke, her fear of the answer shining in her eyes.

"Eklos has him in the palace dungeons. He's alive. For now."

Lita swallowed hard, releasing her grip on the cot.

"That's where I'm headed. Your son was desperate to rescue Martik, but I couldn't let him face Eklos alone."

"So instead, *you* will face Eklos alone?" Lita retorted.

"If all goes to plan, he won't even know I'm there until I'm gone."

She looked like she wanted to say more but she bit her lip, keeping the words held tight.

Several minutes lapsed in tense silence as neither of us spoke. Exhaustion fell heavily on my eyes which kept slipping closed regardless of how hard I fought.

"What will you do now?" I asked, trying to wake myself up.

For a moment she said nothing, rolling onto her back to stare at the ceiling.

"I don't know."

The answer took me by surprise. Growing up with Lita in Shegora, I had never once seen her grasping for answers or unsure of what direction to take. She always knew what to do, even when we were younglings. I wanted to console my friend, to help her, but I knew that the path Lita was on was one she had to navigate herself. I could say all the right words or try to tell her what to do, but it would do little good when her heart wasn't listening. It was a road she had to reach the end of by herself.

I couldn't give her answers, but I could try to give her hope.

"You think you're weak as a human," I began, and Lita's eyes hesitantly met mine, tears spilling onto her cheeks at last.

"If there is one thing that I have learned in all my long years, it's that there is a strength in humans that the dragons do not understand. It's what keeps them fighting, despite the odds."

"What is there to fight for, Eldrin?" Lita whispered into the darkness. Noam's words came back to me, and I inhaled before slowly blowing it out.

"A better world."

CHAPTER EIGHTEEN

KAIDA

FOUR DAYS PASSED, marked by the faint hint of daylight shining through the crack in the wall at what felt like odd intervals. The nights seemed to last much longer than the days, and the bleakness of the dark danced on my growing nerves. Tarrin and I stayed in the cave, obeying Eldrin's orders. There were a few times in the middle of the night where we could hear branches cracking and footsteps, but whether they were dragons or some other beast, we didn't know—nor did we want to. Talking was sparse, our whispers far too loud in the echoing cavern, and we fell into an awkward rhythm of sitting, pacing, munching on jerky and bread, and sleeping.

Despair tried to slither over my bones. This was too similar to the dirt cave I grew up in. The walls were beginning to close in, the ceiling growing closer, ready to crush me. Not for the first time, Tarrin felt the terror that clung to me through our bond and grabbed my hand, tugging me to him. He would never truly understand, but he showed me repeatedly that he cared, and for the moment that was enough.

We sat on the dirt floor with our backs against the wall, his arm slung around my shoulders, and my face pressed into his chest.

"It's been four days, Kaida." Tarrin's whisper broke the silence like a clap of thunder, and I winced. Eldrin's week was almost up. Not wanting to add to the noise, I merely nodded.

"We can't stay in here forever."

"Eldrin told us to stay here," I said pulling back and meeting his eyes.

"He also said that he would be in and out of the palace and back here quickly." He hesitated. "We need to start thinking about finding somewhere else to go if… if Eldrin is captured or…" His words faded and I could tell he didn't want to say the words aloud.

"Eldrin will return," I replied, my voice firm though my confidence had evaporated.

"And if he doesn't?"

I closed my eyes, shutting out the question. It was something I couldn't bear to think of. Eldrin was the key to our survival. He knew Eklos better than any of us. He knew Elysia better than any of us. I couldn't fight the feeling that if we lost him, we would be doomed.

Tarrin squeezed my arm. "He said he would return by week's end. That's only a couple of days away. We need to start thinking of leaving, trying to find somewhere else that is safe."

"No—"

"Kaida, we are almost out of food. We're cold, tired, and hungry, and we desperately need baths." Amusement flickered in his eyes, cutting through the tension for a moment.

"What if Eldrin comes back and we aren't here?"

"Then he'll find us." His tone was strong and confident. He truly believed Eldrin would be able to find us if we left. "But Kaida… your father would not stay away this long. Not unless something happened."

My stomach sunk and my hands trembled in my lap.

"There is nowhere safe we can go."

I could see Tarrin's mind racing, trying to put together some semblance of a plan.

"We could leave at nightfall," he said finally. "We can fly north, steering clear of Vernista. Perhaps we can find shelter within the forest bordering the Ilgathor Mountains."

"Those woods are no better. You don't know what creatures inhabit them." The Ilgathor Mountains was where Belharnt was once located before I started an earthquake that brought it crashing to the ground. But there was a reason why Belharnt was never discovered. There were beasts and creatures that lived in the woods surrounding the mountains. Horrid, devious things that prowled in the darkness devouring any who were unfortunate enough to get caught within the trees.

"You're a dragon. You should fear no other creature."

I scowled at Tarrin, my human side automatically rebelling against the beast within me. Though I had done my best to make peace with the fact that I was a dragon, there were moments where I wanted to revolt against that fact, refusing to believe that I could be something I once hated desperately.

Part of me always wondered how Tarrin and Eldrin had wandered through that forest during the night to find me. I supposed he was right—nothing would try to attack a dragon.

"Still," I said, exhaustion smothering me like a blanket. "We are safe here, we shouldn't leave."

"What if Eldrin is in trouble?"

"He said he'd be fine." I forced myself to brush the question off, though I knew something likely had gone wrong. Eldrin should have been back by now, but I couldn't bring myself to face it. That brave, bold thing inside me had gone dormant ever since the Remnant mercenary attacked me in Mistwick. Killing that dragon had severed something in me.

I didn't want to run. I didn't want to fight.

I knew Tarrin could feel my thoughts, could feel the downward spiral I was falling into. His eyes flickered in the torch light as he watched me.

Kaida, what's wrong? Why don't you want to leave the cave?

I exhaled in a whoosh as his gentle voice caressed my mind.

I don't... know.

I could feel his lips spread in a smile as he brought his lips to the top of my head. *Tell me what's wrong.*

"I don't like it," I blurted.

"Like what?"

I wished I could sew my lips shut so that the words that were ready to burst from my lips could never be spoken.

"This feeling. I'm afraid."

"For Eldrin? If anyone can—"

"No, that's not it." Of course, I was worried for my father, but that wasn't what frightened me about leaving the safety of the cave. "I'm scared of the beast... the beast inside me."

A flood of understanding crashed down our shifter bond. His arm squeezed tighter around me.

"I just..." I choked out, trying to find the right words. "When I'm in dragon form, and the anger becomes so much that I let the beast take control... the bloodlust is maddening. When I'm in that state, I'm ready to kill, to take a life with no remorse. It's hard to escape it." I blew out a shuddering breath. "I don't want to be like him. Like Eklos."

Tarrin let out a sigh of his own. "Kaida, you could never be like him. Your heart is too good."

"I killed that dragon, Tarrin, and I wanted to. I enjoyed seeing the light leave his eyes. I loved causing him pain. What kind of a monster does that make me?"

"Perhaps there's a bit of monster in all of us," Tarrin admitted. "But that doesn't mean that's all you are. That mercenary would have killed us if you hadn't done what you did. Besides, that's not truly what matters. Want to know how I know you're not like Eklos? Because of this." He gestured to me with my head on his chest. "The fact that you're here, remorseful over taking the life of a dragon who would have taken yours, and that you're worried about becoming a monster as a result. That's proof enough that your heart is *good*. You are not Eklos, and you will never be, my love."

His words settled into me like a warm summer breeze, easing the ache that had made a home in my chest. Was he right? Could we all have pieces of monster in us without becoming one?

He cleared his throat. "When my father would do the Current each summer, infused with all that power from the sun, he would lose himself too. My mother was his tether. She would bring him back, remind him of who he was. I'll be your tether, Kaida. I'll help you remember who you are." Cupping my cheeks with his hands, he touched his lips to mine.

Tarrin smoothed down my greasy hair and I cringed and pulled back. He was right. We did need baths. He tucked my hair behind my ear and gave me a lopsided smile that made my stomach flutter.

"Can't you just magic more food and a bath into the cave?" I said, pulling away. It was my last attempt, the last excuse I could come up with to stay here.

Tarrin narrowed his eyes at me before poking my nose. "My magic will do nothing to tell us what is happening out there."

I sighed. "I know."

A heavy fabric was suddenly flung around my shoulders, and I looked up surprised. Tarrin had made two black cloaks appear, one now enveloping me, and the other was being tied around his neck.

"You couldn't have made these appear two days ago when we were freezing?" I asked, my eyebrows raising.

He gave me a mischievous grin. "Then you wouldn't have needed me to keep you warm." My cheeks warmed, and I looked away from his eyes, now burning with desire. He leaned in to kiss me once more but before his lips touched mine, he snapped my hood over my head, and it fell over my face.

Tarrin snickered and I scowled from beneath the fabric.

"These will help us remain anonymous. For a little while anyway." He tied the cloak shut around my neck and stepped back, evaluating.

"What's your plan?" I asked. He took my hand and kissed my palm.

"We will fly north once the sun has set. We can stop when we find a village, perhaps one large enough to hide our presence, and get supplies. Then we will continue toward the Ilgathor Mountains."

I swallowed hard, my insides twisting and coiling like a snake.

"Relax," he said, running his thumb along my cheekbone and jaw. "I won't let anyone hurt you." Bumps prickled along my skin, my cheeks heating at his touch. His gaze pierced into me, despite the darkness of the cave. "And I'll never let you forget who you are. You are strong and brave. You are *kind.*" Tarrin planted another kiss on my lips. "And you are mine."

CHAPTER NINETEEN

KAIDA

WE FLEW ALL night. I don't know how, but my wings managed to hold out for hours, far longer than they ever had before. We skipped over the first and second villages that we passed, wanting to get as far as possible before stopping. Dawn was only an hour away from breaking over the horizon, and I could feel Tarrin's anxiety rise at the thought of being in the sky when the sun would reveal our shapes soaring through the clouds.

Ice coated our scales and eyelashes, our teeth chattering against the frigid high altitude despite the fire burning away in our cores. My wings were beginning to tire, the muscles within them aching and pulsing.

"We need to land soon!" Tarrin roared against the wind. Our eyes scoured over the ground beneath us between the clouds, looking for an inconspicuous place to land, one perhaps that was close to a village where we could find supplies.

I still didn't like this plan. I couldn't escape the feeling of danger resting on my shoulders. Eldrin could have returned to that cave at any point. The thought of him finding it empty, our trail gone, made me shudder. And the idea that we were willingly stepping out into harm's way, not knowing who lurked in the shadows of these villages, or in the forest of the Ilgathor Mountains... It made the hair on my arms rise beneath my scales.

"There!" Tarrin yelled, pointing with a claw beneath us. There was a small clearing amongst some trees, and perhaps a mile or two farther sat a large village, a vast number of torches flickering in the minutes before dawn.

Snapping his wings into his sides, he dove headfirst for the ground. The first several times I had seen both him and my father do the maneuver, my stomach had sunk, every ounce of my body trembling in fear. All I could picture in my mind was my body splatting into the earth. Thankfully, Tarrin walked me through step-by-step how to dive with endless patience, and I had done it enough times now that it no longer frightened me, though the feeling of my stomach rising into my throat was still unpleasant.

I squeezed my wings in tight against my back and began to spin as I aimed toward the ground. Tarrin taught me to fix my eyes on one point as I spun so it wouldn't disorient me. My eyes snatched onto the clearing I was falling toward, and I fought the urge to close my eyes.

I counted in my head as the grass grew closer and closer.

One.

Not yet, Tarrin had told me when I was first learning this maneuver, though I had begged to open my wings.

Two.

I could see the frost-covered grass now, the air significantly warmer, though it still had a bite. Tarrin landed with a graceful extension and flap of his wings, only a soft rustle as the burst of air caused the grass to sway beneath him. I returned my attention to the ground.

Three.

Now, Kaida! Tarrin's voice yelled down the bond.

I clenched my teeth as I ripped my wings open a hundred feet from the ground, far too late and far too close to the earth. I couldn't help the roar that escaped my mouth as I barreled toward the dirt. With a sharp inhale, I braced for impact, but a sudden breeze caressed my face and I halted mid-air. Strong, scaled arms wound around me and I peeked an eye open. Tarrin was holding my enormous body suspended several feet off the ground. He met my eyes, amusement flickering in his, before slowly sinking to the ground.

"Are you all right?" Tarrin crooned in my ear, lighting my insides on fire, as he set my feet on the ground.

"I'm fine," I muttered, my pride the only injury.

He eyed me skeptically before taking a step back, crossing his dragon arms in a human gesture.

"I thought you had the hang of the fall." It was part question, part statement. We had practiced many times, but obviously I hadn't quite nailed the landing part of it yet. He shifted into human form, the smirk I loved twisting his mouth, and offered me his hand. I shifted in a dull burst of purple light before taking hold of it, my cheeks burning. I shrugged in response.

"You made it all night long." He pulled me into his embrace, barely touching his lips to mine. The pride in his voice was enough to wipe away the embarrassment of my fall. His lips were hot against the cold night. Hands sliding up my spine, Tarrin brought one hand to cup my cheek, tilting my head to deepen the kiss. Our breaths came faster, the heat of them pooling in the air around us, and we didn't pull away until the first tendrils of dawn began to tangle amidst the stars.

"Come on," he said with a light chuckle. "We need to get to that village before the sun crosses the horizon."

Our progress was slow and took the better part of an hour. By the time we reached the outskirts of the town, the sky had lightened to a dull tangerine rimmed with purple, the sun just beginning to break over the horizon.

Tarrin tugged my cloak tighter around my shoulders, pulling

my hood over my face before doing the same to himself. "We'll find an inn to rest at and figure out what's been happening. The taverns have the worst gossips." He smiled ruefully at me before tugging me forward, sticking to the shadows as much as possible.

The village was comprised of small huts made of wood and straw that were dotted here and there, rather than in a line or a circle like Vernista or Zarkuse. With the early hour, there were hardly any people or dragons on the streets. Dodging in and out of alleys, and dashing between houses, we reached the center of the village, which had carts and roughly built buildings in a sort of diamond shape. I assumed it was the market, where dragons could sell goods and services. I wasn't sure if this village allowed slaves to sell, like the ones in Myrewell. The market in Mistwick had been busy but beautiful. This was a foul sight in comparison. Everything was covered in mud, and some carts were so riddled with rot that it was a wonder they were even still standing.

Tarrin abruptly tugged me around a corner and hurried down an alleyway, stopping in the shadows.

"Wha—"

Tarrin put a hand over my mouth and pressed himself against me. I glanced up at Tarrin's face but instead of the desire I expected at his touch, his eyes were wide, fear flickering in them. My breath caught, brows furrowing as I tried to ask what was wrong. Before I could speak, he pushed tighter against me.

Then I heard it.

Thundering footsteps at the end of the alley. The crunch of pebbles beneath heavy feet.

My stomach filled with lead, sinking down to my feet as the unmistakable sound of a dragon stopped in the alleyway, the sounds of sniffing bouncing off the brick walls.

Don't make a sound. Tarrin whispered down the bond.

My heartbeat pounded beneath my skin, and I prayed to the old forgotten gods that the dragon couldn't hear it.

With the sun not fully risen yet, the shadows were darker, and I silently begged that it would be enough to keep us hidden. I risked a peek from beneath my hood. A dark-green dragon blocked the end of the alley, his large snout twitching as he smelled the air.

He can smell us!

I instinctively held my breath, willing my heart to stop pounding, and pretending I could control the shifter scent that I knew was potent on us. That was how Tarrin said he found me back at The Den so many months ago. All shape-shifters had a certain scent from the magic that allowed them to shift, which distinguishes them from all other dragons. Some dragons were ignorant to it, while others recognized it immediately.

Based on how this dragon turned down the alley, eyes narrowed, and roving over the shadows, it was clear he knew what it was.

Fools. We were fools. We hadn't been in the village for more than a few minutes and we had already been discovered.

Eldrin was right. There was no safe place for us. We should have stayed in the cave.

My thoughts spiraled out of control, and I fought to keep my shaking limbs still. Tarrin pressed tighter against me, his eyes never leaving the dragon. Through the bond, each beat of his heart was like a mini explosion.

The dragon took another step toward us, and I felt, more than saw, his eyes rove over the shadows we were hiding in. Stones crunched beneath his enormous feet as he shifted toward us. I noticed an amulet on a long chain around his neck, and it reminded me of the royal crest, only this one had the silhouette of a dragon surrounded by the sun.

It was the symbol of the Remnant of the Lone Dragon. Though the sun was the source of strength for the dragons, the members of the Remnant believed they were more powerful than even the sun, placing themselves at the center.

"Oi!" A deep voice bellowed behind the green dragon. He

spun around so quickly I was surprised he didn't lose his balance. With his body blocking my view I couldn't see who, or what, had drawn his attention.

"Dragon!" The voice spoke again. "I don't care what your purpose is in Feltar." I felt Tarrin stiffen. "You will not intrude on my property or be a nuisance." The green dragon shifted to the side, revealing a smaller brown dragon with silver spikes down his spine at the end of the alley, smoke curling from his nostrils. His blue eyes blazed with barely concealed fury.

"I have orders from the Regent of Elysia to search every village," the green dragon retorted, balling his claws into fists.

"I don't care who sent you here. You have already been here for days. This is a peaceful village, and I will not have you destroying everything we have fought to build." My mouth fell open at the bravery and boldness that this dragon had. He was standing against one of the Remnant. Though he wasn't defending *us,* I felt my heart swell. Perhaps there *were* some decent dragons in Elysia, who only desired peace and goodness.

The member of the Remnant took a menacing step toward him. "You will remember your place," he growled, flames coming to life in his palms.

I watched the smaller dragon from beneath my hood, prepared to see him back down in fear, but he lifted his snout higher in defiance and widened his stance.

"No, you will remember *yours.*" Both Tarrin's mouth and mine fell open at his audacity. "We haven't fought against Eklos's tyranny, or his command for his dragons to search every house, tree, and stone. We have allowed you to disturb our peace without retaliation. What you seek is not here, so you will leave Feltar, and you will not disrupt this village further."

For a shocking moment, the dark-green dragon looked cowed. It was not quite fear that flashed in his eyes, but perhaps intimidation.

"You—"

"Zeghar!" A third dragon's voice called, and Tarrin groaned down our shifter bond. It was getting crowded in this alley.

A light-blue dragon came around the corner, shoving the brown dragon aside. "Zeghar, the village is clear, we have orders to move out and keep traveling south."

"You have searched everywhere?"

The blue dragon nodded once.

Zeghar half turned, eyes scanning the alleys once more. His snout twitched as he sniffed, and I tensed my muscles, readying to be discovered, but after an endless number of seconds, he turned back to the other dragon and nodded.

"Let's go."

The dragons vanished around the corner, and relief swept through me so fast that the minute they disappeared, I collapsed to the stones beneath us. Tarrin, too, fell to his knees, unwilling to remove his arms from my shoulders. My breaths came in ragged gasps, my entire body trembling.

That was too close. Tarrin's voice shook, even in my mind. I grimaced, wrapping my arms around his waist, welcoming his comforting presence.

"You can come out now."

We froze, and the blood drained from my face.

"Come on out," the voice repeated. Pebbles skittered as footsteps shuffled toward us.

Tarrin stiffened and swallowed hard. I risked a glance up and found the smaller brown dragon who had stood up to Zeghar several feet inside the alley, looking directly at us. His emerald eyes met mine despite the shadows keeping us hidden.

"I won't hurt you."

"No, you'll simply turn us over to the Remnant," Tarrin snapped, standing in a brisk shove to his feet, and I winced.

"I am loyal to Elysia, and its Royal Family. I will not bring harm upon Elysia's Prince or his betrothed, regardless of whether his parents are currently in power. While you remain in Feltar, you will be safe."

"Who are you?" Tarrin asked, eyes narrowed.

"I'm the Town Keeper."

"Town Keepers were disbanded years ago." Tarrin's eyes narrowed as he studied the dragon.

"Not in Feltar. The Queen granted us the right to continue our tradition as a gift for our loyalty to the Crown."

"What is a Town Keeper?" I dared to ask, keeping my voice low. The smaller dragon's eyes snapped to mine.

"Before the Prince's parents took control of Elysia, the Queen's father rid the country of us. Town Keepers were once a highly respected position. There was one in each village, and they were charged with keeping the peace. They were a sort of king for their village. They handled disputes and disagreements, collected money when necessary, and swiftly dealt with any threat."

"My grandfather disbanded them long before I was born," Tarrin chimed in. "My mother never told me why."

"The old King was greedy for power and influence. He didn't like the idea of the dragons looking to someone else for protection," the brown dragon answered.

Tarrin winced. "He died before I was born. I didn't know him."

"Your mother was a far better Queen." Pride flashed in the dragon's eyes, and I wondered if he knew her personally. I saw Tarrin relax infinitesimally out of the corner of my eye.

"Come, I have a place for you to stay. You will be safe from the Remnant." He turned to walk away.

Tarrin and I hesitated, unsure whether we could trust him.

"My name is Kalev," the brown dragon said, half turning back to us. "No harm shall come to you while you are under my protection."

Tarrin's eyes widened when he said his name but said nothing.

Do you know him? I asked silently.

Kalev was the name of the captain of the King's Guard before my grandfather dissolved it. He was well known in Elysia, written in many of the history books. Female dragons sung lullabies and stories about him to their younglings. I don't know if this is the same dragon, but if he is, perhaps we can trust him.

I processed this information for only a second before deciding that I would trust Tarrin's judgement. If he trusted this Kalev, I would too. Even if he was a dragon. He already proved his loyalty by not revealing us to the Remnant. Perhaps he was telling the truth.

I nodded at Tarrin and he grabbed my hand, leading me toward the dragon. Kalev smiled, and for once it did not look like one that promised death.

It was one of hope.

CHAPTER TWENTY

ELDRIN

"ARE YOU SURE you won't come with me?" I asked Lita as I threw a sack of supplies over my shoulder. We stood on the small porch of the cottage, the first signs of dawn just peeking over the horizon. I should have already been to the palace and back, but instead, I had spent several days in the cottage with Lita as she helped me to plot out a more detailed plan to rescue Martik, knowing of hidden passages and tunnels that even the Prince had not known about.

"Yes, I'm sure. I think I'll head west. Something tells me that's where I need to be." Her brows furrowed as she looked in the direction of the Ilgathor Mountains.

"Foresight?" I couldn't help but ask.

She shook her head, avoiding my gaze. "My magic is gone, Eldrin, my foresight with it. This is only a gut instinct. Nothing more."

I gave her a skeptical look, but kept my lips closed. I had found it was useless to argue with this version of my old friend.

"Remember the instructions?" she asked, finally looking at me.

I gave a single nod. "Your drawing is ingrained in my brain." I tapped my temple with a finger.

"Be careful," she repeated for the hundredth time, glancing at the rising sun.

"Always am." Without another word, a cloud of black shadow smothered my skin as I shifted into dragon form and took off into the sky. I needed to get as far as possible before the sun was fully risen. I glanced back at Lita only once, prepared to wave goodbye to my friend. I didn't even know if I'd ever see the Queen of Elysia again.

I raised my hand to wave.

But Lita was gone.

☙

I snuck through the tunnels beneath the palace. It was bone cold, like the deepest parts of the sea, with dust and cobwebs lining the floor and unlit torches. I crept along, keeping my footsteps as silent as possible, wishing my human eyes were able to see in the dark as well as my dragon ones. I had shown Lita the map that Tarrin had drawn for me of the dungeons, but she had simply scoffed and told me about the secret passageways that would prove more useful. She drew in the dust that covered the floor with her finger, outlining the route I should take.

The tunnels were a maze that dragged on and on and my legs grew wearier with every step forward. I continued straight, ignoring each fork in the passages that I came to until there was a dead end, and the only option was to go right or left. The cold settled into my skin so thoroughly that my fingers and toes were numb, and my teeth chattered together, sending a throbbing ache through my jaw.

Looking to the right and left, I knew why Lita had specified to take the left one. Any fool would have gone down the right. The air smelled cleaner and there was a glimmer of light coming from the end.

It leads to the edge of a cliff, and you will fall to your death before you can stop your feet from going over the edge, Lita had said as she drew a giant X in the dust to indicate death.

To the left, it was dark, musty, and somehow even colder than the passages thus far. It reeked of moldy earth, and I fought the urge to gag. It was not the route I would have chosen.

Take the left tunnel, Lita's voice echoed in my mind again.

Swallowing hard, I turned down the passageway, every limb protesting as I moved forward. There was no sound outside of each shuddering breath I took and the pounding of my heart.

This was foolish. I knew it was. There was a good chance Eklos had already caught my scent from when I had entered the tunnels beneath Vernista that led to the palace. I imagined Eklos waiting in the dungeons to ambush me, and my stomach opened into a dark pit.

Not for the first time, I wished that I could use my magic to "jump" into the dungeons, retrieve Martik, and jump back out. Lita had mentioned the doors and cells were all made of iron, rendering my magic useless. Besides that, dragon magic leaves a strong scent when it is used. Eklos would have been alerted to my presence far too quickly. Plus, the distance was far too great to make in only one trip, especially once I had Martik in tow.

My breath puffed out in the cold air in front of me as I sighed.

Get in, dispose of the jailor and get the keys, find Martik's cell, and escape back through the tunnels.

That was my plan in a nutshell.

Unfortunately, I had a feeling it was going to be easier plotted out in the dust of the cottage floor than it would be to carry out. I released a soft breath as the ladder that led into the dungeons came into view. A shiver worked through my body, though it had nothing to do with the cold.

Regam is the dungeon jailor. He is ruthless and if he catches you, he will show no mercy. You will need to dispose of him quickly and silently. Regam has the key, so once you kill him, take them, and disappear into the dark cells and find Martik. Do not linger, no matter what else you find down there. I shivered again as Lita's words repeated in my mind.

The frozen metal bit into my skin as I grabbed the rungs on the ladder, trying in vain to keep my boots from scuffing with each step up. I didn't know how close to Regam the ladder would take me, and I didn't want to alert him to my presence before I even reached the top.

Taking a deep breath, I put the slightest amount of pressure on the stone ceiling, begging it to stay quiet as it moved. I risked a peek through the crack and found it dark, musty air hitting my face in waves. Pushing on the stone a little more, I took another breath and poked my head through the hole. My human eyes fought me, rebelling against my command to adjust to the complete darkness.

The stone was like a giant boulder as I lifted it and moved it to the side. My arms felt like icicles, but I managed to pull myself up and rolled onto my side before standing. My eyes roved the darkness but could see nothing— like the blackness that accompanied death. Perhaps Lita's memory had not been entirely accurate after all. It appeared as if I were *inside* the dungeons, rather than coming out before them where she said I would.

Hands shaking, I held them out, trying to feel for anything but all I found was the damp air kissed with mold and death. Dread set in as I realized I would need to shift into dragon form if I wanted to be able to see anything. It was much harder to keep a large body with wings and a tail silent, never mind my scent which would strengthen with the magic of shifting.

I held my breath as I stoked the fire in my core and shifted into dragon form, a blue light coating my vision enabling me to finally see. Glancing around, I saw crates of fruits and vegetables and barrels of ale, along with other various jars on shelves lining the walls.

I let out a sigh as I realized I had ended up in the root cellar beneath the palace, instead of the entrance to the dungeons. My relief was short lived as a low growl sounded from behind me and I spun. Only shadows greeted me.

Willing my large feet to stay quiet, I crept on my claws over to the outline of a door, pressing my ear against it, listening.

Another growl sounded and I skittered back, my heart jumping into my throat. Seconds passed but nothing happened. Inching forward, I listened again, only to hear the sound once more.

What is that?

Knowing I couldn't stay in the root cellar, I reached for the doorknob and turned it, painstakingly slow, and peeked into the room beyond.

There was a single torch lit on the far wall, a large iron door looming tall next to it.

Of course, it's iron. The iron would keep me from being able to use my magic to jump through to the other side.

Three more cave-like openings stood across from me, dark as a starless night, leading to various parts of the palace.

But that wasn't what caught my attention.

Guarding the door was an enormous blood-red dragon, wings spread behind him, spanning the width of the entire room, scales nearly bursting off his limbs from the bulging muscle beneath them.

Regam.

My stomach dropped. I had never seen a dragon with musculature like that.

My saving grace dawned on me a moment later when I noticed that Regam had not been growling because he knew I was there. No, he had been growling because he was asleep.

I suppressed a snort. Eklos would have flayed him alive if he knew his prize jailor was sleeping on duty. But perhaps this would play out well for me after all. My mind paced back and forth over my options. The obvious solution was to slip silently into the room and kill the dragon before he ever knew I was there. Though Regam had a terrible reputation, and he had undoubtedly murdered hundreds of humans, and perhaps dragons as well, I struggled with the idea of killing him. Though I had killed before, it wasn't something I enjoyed. Even after centuries of it, it never got easier.

But I also didn't want to deal with the terrifying dragon Regam would become if he were awake. In only a split second he would be able to raise an alarm, alerting the entire palace to my presence, effectively putting an end to this rescue attempt.

A silent breath escaped my lips. I had no choice—I had to kill him. Now.

Glancing around the room for anything that would be useful, I took my eyes off the dragon. The room was empty, save for a rat scurrying across the floors, and the spider hanging in the web in the far corner.

I brought my eyes back to the jailor and my insides turned to jelly.

Regam's molten silver eyes were open, shining like the liquid metal of a sword before it is forged.

"Eklos told me you might be coming." His voice rasped like a hive full of wasps.

I stumbled backward, barely keeping myself from falling to the ground.

Regam stood up straight, pulling a mace and a sword from behind his back, closing his eyes as flames erupted from his hands and encased the length of each weapon. "I thought your thousand years of wisdom would have taught to you stay away." He smiled, his dagger teeth gleaming in the dim light.

I cursed myself, wishing I had unsheathed my dagger before shifting into dragon form. It remained strapped to my clothes deep beneath my layers of scales. There was no way to retrieve it without shifting, and that brief moment would be all Regam needed to finish me. It wouldn't even be a fight.

All I had was fire magic. It was *something*, but I didn't think it would be enough. My eyes narrowed as I studied Regam and the weapons in each of his hands, while glancing around the room out of the corner of my eye. The door was made of iron, but nothing else in the room was. That meant I could use my magic in this room, just not to get through the door to the dungeons.

"Nothing to say, old man?" Regam taunted, taking another step closer.

"Would anything I say keep you from killing me?" I asked, stalling for time.

Regam only smiled, a menacing thing that chilled me to the bone. The jailor took a step toward me, then another. He was mere feet away now.

Eyes darting around the room frantically, I begged my mind to come up with a way out of this. If I could just get into that door to the dungeons and find Martik—

Regam lunged at me, releasing a roar that echoed endlessly in the stone room. He swung his mace toward my head while arcing his sword toward my stomach. Instinct flooded through me, and I reached for my magic, disappearing just as the jailor's weapons would have made contact with my body, appearing five feet to the right only a heartbeat later. I immediately felt the weakening of my body as the magic used my energy.

Regam paused, his brow furrowed in confusion as he glanced between where his weapons should have sunk deep into a dragon's scales and where I now stood.

I took advantage of the jailor's hesitation and leaped toward the door, grabbing the long handle and yanking with all my might.

It didn't budge an inch. I cursed before ducking just as Regam swung his mace toward my head, the impact on the iron door making my teeth ache.

"You think simply anyone could open the door to the dungeons?" Regam crooned, taking a step back, readying to strike again. "That would make it much too simple to get inside. Especially for dragons with magic such as yours." He tipped his snout down, silver eyes blazing. "The door is bound to my blood. I am the lock."

And just like that, the fight drained out of me, my arms going slack.

"That's right, *Eldrin*," Regam continued, spitting my name like an insult. "To get through the door, my blood must be spilled." He bared his dagger teeth. "You will have to kill me to get inside." He straightened, fueling the fire that burned over his weapons, the flames growing larger and hotter.

I created a spear with my fire magic and held it defensively across my body as I pressed my back against the iron door. The freezing metal bit into my scales, penetrating deep beneath them until I was shivering.

Regam feigned left with his sword, then lunged to the right, aiming for my ribs, and I whipped up the spear, sparks flying as our weapons collided.

The jailor's weapons were solid metal, while mine were only made of fire. My energy and magic would fail long before Regam's weapons did. I knew I had to find a way to end this battle. Quickly.

We took turns advancing on one another, each trying in vain to find an opening to finish the job. I lost count of the number of times I had to duck beneath that mace, and how many scalding sparks had skittered across my scales as Regam's sword met my fire spear.

I parried another blow and caught sight of something flashing in the jailor's eyes. I couldn't tell if it was surprise, exhaustion, or fear. Perhaps it was all of them mixed in the twisted fury of his gaze. Momentarily distracted, I missed Regam's movement, and a cry of pain erupted from my mouth as the sword cut deep beneath the scales under my arm. I summoned my magic and jumped away from the jailor just as he went to push the sword farther, up into my heart.

My breaths came in frantic gasps as I pushed my hand against it. Blood seeped from my wound, much too fast, and black spots were already crowding my vision. Regam stalked closer, like a predator waiting for its prey to die, lowering his weapons to his sides.

"So, this is how Eldrin the Great meets his end." He smiled again. "Eklos will be pleased."

Fire erupted beneath my scales, as anger ripped through my veins.

No, this is not how I die.

This was not where I would meet my end.

My energy was draining by the second, but I took a deep breath and closed my eyes. Regam grew ever closer, already basking in the victory he believed he had won.

The moment the jailor stepped up to me, nearly nose to nose, I moved.

Summoning the last dregs of my magic, I jumped to the space just behind Regam. Before the jailor could even blink, I created my spear of fire once more, gripped the dragon's shoulder, and shoved the spear up beneath his arm, plunging it directly into his heart. Instead of releasing the fire, I stoked the flames, willing it to burn hotter. The smell of burning flesh filled the room and I finally looked up and met Regam's eyes.

There was confusion there, as if he couldn't believe that he was now burning alive from the inside out. But there was also something else shining in his eyes. It almost looked like relief.

When my fire magic had done enough damage, I released it, instantly falling to my knees, and watched through the spots dotting my vision as Regam toppled to the stone floor beneath them, a slight shudder shaking the ground.

The jailor opened his mouth to speak, but before he could utter a sound, the light left his eyes, his final breath blowing the dust beneath his face.

I didn't allow myself even a breath of relief as I launched

myself at the iron door guarding the dungeons. I knew I would die soon if I didn't stop the bleeding. Putting my hands on the handle, I braced myself, expecting Regam to have lied and for the door to still be locked.

But when I pulled on it, the enormous door that should have required great strength to open, swung open easily, a putrid musty smell slapping me in the face. I coughed down a gag and swallowed the lump of relief that had risen in my throat.

Before I could second guess myself, I shuffled through the doorway, darkness swallowing me as I stepped into the palace dungeons.

CHAPTER TWENTY-ONE

TARRIN

I SAT IN A lumpy oversized armchair, in human form, near the hearth in Kalev's home. The autumn morning was the coldest thus far in the season and I was thankful for the warmth from the fire sizzling across my skin. Kaida was perched on the edge of the couch across from me, her knees bouncing up and down. I could tell she was nervous from the way she wrung her hands and how her eyes kept darting to the dragon who was pacing back and forth across the room.

"The Remnant arrived three days ago," Kalev said, as he finally settled onto the opposite end of the couch from Kaida. A muscle jumped in her jaw at the movement, her throat bobbing. I knew this was uncomfortable for her. It took a long time just for her to get comfortable with *me* let alone a brand-new dragon whom she didn't know if she could fully trust.

Admittedly, I didn't even know how trustworthy the male was. Yes, Kalev had saved us from being discovered, but I couldn't help but ask what the dragon had to gain from protecting us. What was the purpose of keeping us safe? Just how far did his loyalty stretch?

"They tore through the village like a disease," Kalev continued. "They scoured every house, cave, stone, tavern, and market cart. I have never seen anything like it in all my years, and I am grateful that it wasn't worse. With their reputation, we all believed they would pillage and burn everything in their path during their quest for you. That's what they've done everywhere else." He poured a cup of tea, setting the kettle back over the hearth, his claws clinking against the iron, before he offered it to Kaida. She shook her head, avoiding his eyes.

A silent sigh escaped my lips. More than anything, I wanted her to feel safe—to know that not every dragon would hurt her. But I knew that seventeen years of being abused by the dragons would take time to undo.

"Why did you protect us?" I asked, breaking Kalev's focus on her.

"I already told you. I am loyal to the Royal Family and those associated with it," he said, glancing at Kaida again before meeting my eyes. "Your mother would have wanted me to keep you safe."

"How did you know my mother?"

Kalev chuckled, memories flashing in his eyes before he mastered his emotions. "Queen Lita and I... well," he hesitated, searching for words. "I courted her for several years."

My jaw went slack.

"Before Martik, of course," Kalev hurried to add, glancing anxiously at me. "Once she met Martik, anything we had was long gone." He offered a half smile that had part of his lip curling up over his teeth, a wistful look crossing his face. "But I do believe she still cared for me. That is why she allowed Feltar to resume its tradition of Town Keeper once she came into power."

Skepticism coated me like a second skin. My mother had never once mentioned any sort of relationship with him. "Are you *the* Kalev? Of the King's Guard?"

The dragon paused, staring into the flames of the hearth. "Yes." He grabbed an iron rod and poked at the fire, stoking the embers back into flames. "That's how your mother and I met.

When I was not leading the Guard into battle, I was a part of her personal guard. We became close."

Out of the corner of my eye, I saw Kaida scoot back on the couch cushions, settling into them.

"Once her father caught wind of our relationship… he kicked me out of the King's Guard, saying a dragon soldier was no match for his daughter who would one day be the Queen of Elysia. He disbanded the entire Guard, with the cover story of the King and Queen being too powerful to need them any longer, while the true reason was that he didn't want word to spread that his prized soldier was in love with his daughter." Hurt flickered over Kalev's face and I felt a pang of sadness in my gut.

"I stayed near the palace as long as I could, but Lita met Martik not long afterward, and I was forgotten. I returned to Feltar." He paused, taking a shuddering breath. "A few years later, the King died, and your mother took the throne. One of her first decrees was for Feltar to resume its Town Keeper tradition, beginning with me." Kalev shifted his position on the couch. "She knew it was something I had always dreamed about. Though she had found love with another, I knew then that she still cared."

Silence descended in the room, and I grew uncomfortable. I was used to dragons showing adoration for my mother, but not in this way. It felt like a betrayal to my father, who remained prisoner in the dungeons of the palace.

"So, Prince Tarrin, that is why I protected you. She would have wanted me to."

"You loved her," Kaida said quietly, and Kalev's eyes widened as he looked at her.

"Yes." His eyes flickered in the light of the flames. Kaida nodded, returning her gaze to the hearth.

"How did you know it was us?" I asked, wanting desperately to change the subject away from another dragon's love for my mother.

Kalev cleared his throat and stood, his wings held tight to his back as he tottered over to a table in the corner of the room. When he returned, he had two pieces of parchment between his claws. He handed them to me.

My teeth clenched tight, shooting pain up my jaw as I looked at them. On one was a drawing of me, in both my dragon and human form, and the other held a drawing of Kaida's human face. Underneath each picture was the word *wanted.* A very generous reward was listed below it and I suppressed a shudder.

With their notorious greed for riches, there was nothing stopping every dragon from here to the palace from turning us in.

Kaida appeared at my shoulder, and I heard her shaky inhale, felt the spike in her fear through our shifter bond.

"They have hung your portraits in every village across Elysia. If I hadn't found you, someone else would have, and I don't believe that would have had a happy ending."

I sighed, looking at Kaida, a million thoughts passing between our connected eyes in a single breath.

"What do we do now?" she whispered.

"Stay here," Kalev responded. "Perhaps in a few days or weeks, the hunt for you will have quieted."

"You don't know Eklos very well." The sudden menace in Kaida's tone made the hair on my arms rise.

"We can't stay here for weeks, Kalev. Kaida's right. They will never stop hunting us. The hatred that drives Eklos is unquenchable. He won't stop until he has our heads, and every last shifter and human is slaughtered."

I saw Kaida flinch, and Kalev's eyes narrowed as he processed my words.

"My father is a prisoner in the palace dungeons," I continued. "Kaida's father went to free him nearly a week ago, but he didn't return. I fear the worst." It was the first time I had spoken my suspicion aloud. "We were headed that direction when we landed here. We were hoping to hear news of whether Kaida's father, too, had been captured."

Kalev grunted. "I haven't heard any rumors, but there's been little news out of the palace. Eklos has kept the doors locked tight."

"We can't stay here," Kaida repeated my words, her voice soft and tinged with fear.

"If you leave, you will die." The warmth in Kalev's voice disappeared, his eyes hardening. "I managed to send the Remnant away from you once, but don't expect me to be able to do it again. If you choose to leave, your death is on yourself. I cannot leave Feltar, or its inhabitants unprotected. Not with the Remnant crawling around like cockroaches."

Kalev stood abruptly, circling around the couch before heading toward the door. "I must get back to the village to ensure the Remnant is leaving Feltar's residents be. You will find food in the cupboards and sparkling ale in the cellar." He pointed to a door in the far corner of the room. "I will be back after nightfall. If you wish to remain alive, I strongly suggest you do not leave."

The hardened mask of the old King's Guard slid over his face, and he turned on his heel and left the house, closing the door with a soft click behind him. A brief chill from the autumn breeze skittered through the room.

Kaida exhaled in a whoosh, but I spoke before she could demand that we leave.

"We don't need to leave right this moment. We need food and rest. Why don't you go bathe while I find us some food."

She opened her mouth to argue but stopped herself, her shoulders slumping. I could feel her weariness through our bond, the heavy weight of exhaustion. With a nod, she stood from the couch and wandered through another doorway in search of the bathing room. After a few moments I heard the distinct sound of water sloshing before Kaida sighed.

Getting up from the armchair, I shuffled my way over to the

kitchen, dragging a chair with me to stand on so I could reach the cupboards. Rummaging through them, I found a loaf of day-old bread which I cut into slices, along with some dried meats and cheeses. Throwing everything onto a wooden plank, I brought it over to the table to the left of the hearth.

The cellar door squealed on rusted hinges as I swung it open in search of the sparkling ale Kalev had mentioned. The bottle was cold as ice as I grabbed it from the depths of the cellar and brought it over to the table. I poured a glass for Kaida and then myself and settled in to wait for her to join me.

A handful of minutes later, Kaida emerged from the bathing room, hair hanging in damp strands around her face, her skin glowing.

"Kalev has scrubbing salts," she explained with a smile, voice breathless. "I've never used them before."

Salts were wildly expensive in Elysia, only the wealthiest dragons purchased them. They used it to buff their scales so they were as shiny as possible, much like humans would use it to scrape off the dirt from their skin. The Royal Palace had the scrubbing salts in abundance.

I tucked her wet hair behind her ears, smiling. "Feel better?"

With a nod Kaida sat next to me, eyeing the food with the predatory intent of an animal. Her stomach erupted with a fierce growl, and I chuckled as she filled her hands with bread and cheese, piling one on top of the other and stuffed it in her mouth. As if she had washed off the fear and weariness in the bath water, I felt my own energy renewed at the light, almost happy feeling coming down the bond.

"We can stay here for the night," I said around a mouth full of food. "After a full night's rest, perhaps we will have come up with a better solution." Her only response was to take another big bite of cheese.

When we were finished eating, Kaida curled up on the couch

while I went to clean myself up. When I returned, she was asleep, her soft snores bringing a smile to my face. I squeezed between her and the couch, pulling her in tight to my chest. I loved the feeling of her between my arms. I couldn't stand the thought of her being anywhere else—especially in danger. The idea of the Remnant finding her... it had some deep part of me awakening, like a monster so terrible that it could crush worlds and reap destruction just to keep her safe.

I had never experienced anything like it before. A shaky breath worked its way between my lips as I kissed her temple. Kaida stirred, leaning back into me.

After a moment, she asked, "What if Eldrin is dead?" Her voice was a whisper, full of the fear of a child who had been told a scary story.

Her fear snapped me out of my thoughts, forcing me back into the present. "If he were dead, I think we would've heard. Eklos wouldn't keep that news silent." A yawn overtook my last words and I settled further into the couch, pulling Kaida with me.

"But something must have happened."

"Your father is smart. No matter what may have happened, he will find a way to survive. He will find a way back to us."

"We should go to him."

"Kaida—"

"I'm serious!" she snapped, her voice trembling. "He's the only family I have left. We can't just abandon—" her voice cracked, and she cut off, swiping angrily at her eyes.

"Kaida," I said, my voice softening as I wiped her tears away with my thumbs. "Your father knows Eklos better than anyone. He knows how to keep himself safe. If we leave now in search of Eldrin, we could be captured... or killed."

"What about your father?"

I fell silent, that pang of sorrow echoing in my stomach. I desperately wanted to rescue my father. I had been fighting for it for weeks. But after encountering the Remnant in Feltar, and seeing the wanted posters, I knew Eldrin had been right. There was no safe place for us. I would only be quickening the King's death if we were caught.

"I trust Eldrin."

Kaida's brow furrowed as she looked at me, studying my face. After several moments, she nodded, and relief flooded through my veins. I offered her the lop-sided smile I knew she loved and brought my lips to hers. It was a sweet kiss, full of reassurance.

"Rest, love. We can figure it out in the morning."

With a reluctant nod, Kaida settled back into the couch and stared at the fire blazing away in the hearth. A faint scratching noise sounded, but neither of us thought anything of it. Perhaps it was a mouse looking for scraps of our food, or footsteps outside on the street.

But then the noise happened again, louder. Scratching, a thud, and a gurgling noise. It sounded as though it were just outside Kalev's door.

I glanced at Kaida and found fear flashing within her eyes. A warning bell started ringing in the back of my mind. I pushed off the cushions and walked on silent feet over to the door. Pressing my ear to the wood, I strained to hear a clue as to what had made the noise, but there was nothing. Needing to know what the cause of the noise was, I reminded myself that we were safe in Kalev's home and reached for the doorknob.

My brow furrowed as I opened it and found Kalev standing there.

"Kalev?"

At first, he said nothing, but then his eyes widened, a pained gurgle escaping his mouth as the head of a spear ripped through the hard scales of his back, straight through to the front. My mouth fell open, my heart faltering before racing like a war horse.

Kalev fell to the ground, blood pooling around my feet. I

should have dropped to my knees and tried to find some way to save him, but ice coated my limbs, freezing me in place. For standing behind Kalev's dead body, still holding the spear that killed him, was Zeghar, the Remnant dragon from the village who had searched for us in the shadows.

With a wicked dagger-toothed smile, he aimed the spear at my chest. "Prince Tarrin and Kaida of Vernista. You are under arrest by order of Regent Eklos of Elysia."

CHAPTER TWENTY-TWO

ELDRIN

I DECIDED I BOTH loved and hated the darkness.

I loved it because it kept both me, and the owners of the screams and groans in the cells I passed, hidden. I hated it because this was a darkness made of death and fear and it blinded me, even with my dragon sight, forcing me to slow down and utilize other senses to locate Martik. It was taking far too long, and every second that passed was one more second that Eklos could find me.

Regam's death wouldn't go unnoticed for much longer, even if the dragons rarely came down to the dungeons. The smell of death mingling with my scent would move quickly, reaching the main level of the palace soon, if it hadn't already, and every bloodthirsty dragon within these walls, including Eklos himself, would come crawling down those stairs, drooling and chanting for my blood to be spilled.

The rancid, musty smell of this place made my head spin, and I cursed myself for having to lean against a wall *again* to steady myself.

Where was Martik? It was impossible to tell how far into the dungeons I had wandered or to tell how much farther in Eklos would have put the King.

Wings aching from being held tightly to my back, I let out a shaky breath, forcing myself to slow down even more to keep my claws from clinking too loudly on the ground. Frigid cold leaked through every scale on my body, my teeth throbbing at the effort it took to keep them from clacking together.

A faint splash echoed as my foot slid into a questionable puddle and a wince contorted my face as I tried not to think too much about what now dripped from my scales.

Come on. Come on. The desperation to find Martik grew with every step I took, and the darkness played tricks on my mind, moving and contorting into shapes that weren't truly there, making my head feel like it was being pricked by a thousand needles. My breaths were like screams in my ears. Calling Martik's name would be a mistake but if I didn't find him soon—

"He's down the stairs at the end of this hallway," a voice rasped, brittle and full of pain, and I froze.

"What did you say?" I turned in the direction the voice had come from and cursed as my dragon vision tried to adjust to the darkness.

"The dragon you are looking for is down the stairs." The male's voice clearly had not been used in weeks, perhaps even years judging by the sound of it, and I recoiled as the shriveled scales and gnarled bones that made up the dragon slowly came into focus. The male mumbled to himself, his face twitching and claws clinking together.

My feet remained glued to the ground. I didn't recognize him, but he had clearly spent years isolated and captive. Decades.

"Hurry dragon killer. They are coming." The dragon in the cell hissed and a numbing cold caused bumps to rise over my scales. My blood turned to ice, freezing my limbs in place. *Dragon killer.* How did this prisoner know what I had done?

"Hurry," he barked, and I sucked in a ragged breath as my feet moved of their own accord farther down the rank hallway. I wasn't sure what evil deeds or madness had landed that dragon in the palace dungeons, but I found myself immensely relieved to be out of his presence, despite the darkness growing thicker around me like a suffocating cloud.

My right foot stepped forward and just as I expected it to meet the frigid stone, the floor disappeared, and I half bounced, half skidded down the lengthy stairway. Slamming to a stop at the bottom, I held in a groan as my entire body throbbed from the impact. There was a concerning stickiness coating my left knee, and the wound from the fight with Regam continued to seep blood, but thankfully that was the worst of my injuries. Adrenaline pumped through my veins, and I pushed to my feet, pinning my wings in tight to my back.

Thus far I had remained quiet, not daring to utter the King's name in case there were other guards hiding in the shadows. But after that prisoner had said Martik was down here, I couldn't hold it back now.

"Martik?" I hissed into the gloom shrouding my dragon sight. Silence.

"Martik," I repeated, daring to say it louder.

For another moment silence reigned but then a soft scuffling sound, like claws dragging over rock, followed by a quiet moan had me moving toward it.

"Martik." The name came out in a breath of relief before I fought the urge to cover my snout with my hands, holding in the gasp and cry of despair as my eyes finally fought through the dark and found the King.

Curled up in a heap in the corner of the tiny cell, scales ripped off half of his body and the bones in both wings snapped in multiple places, sat King Martik. His eyes remained on the ground, as if he hadn't heard me speak.

Though Regam's death had unlocked the door into the dungeon, I noticed that all the cell doors remained locked. I didn't have time to locate a key, so I shifted into human form for a moment to grab the slim dagger attached to my leg and shifted back. I moved quickly, jamming it into the rusty lock until it clicked. The hinges creaked and groaned, echoing off the stone walls as it swung open.

At the sound of the door opening, Martik's eyes snapped up, and I could have sworn that fire was smoldering in them.

"Martik, can you—"

The words were only halfway out of my mouth before Martik, despite his plethora of injuries, sprang at me, clawed hands circling my throat.

I coughed and clawed at my old friend's hands, trying to free myself and get air into my lungs. His blue eyes blazed.

"Martik… it's me." Stars flickered in my vision as the King squeezed tighter. "It's Eldrin… I'm here… to… get you… out."

Martik held on for several more seconds, squeezing harder, before he blinked, the fire in his eyes suddenly winking out, and released me. I dropped on all fours, gasping for air, my body shuddering as oxygen burned through my starved veins.

"Eldrin?" The King's voice was not as I remembered. The once deep, rumbling voice full of that royal dominance was gone. Now, his voice was broken and small, indicative of the torture Eklos had put him through.

"Need to… get out," I stammered, swallowing repeatedly, trying to get the dry lump out of my throat so I could speak. Martik muttered something unintelligible under his breath and took a step back, staring at the direction I had come from. The ache in my throat finally eased enough for air to flow smoothly into my lungs and I used the wall to push myself to my feet.

I dared a look at the King and found that flickering fire back in his eyes.

"There's an escape tunnel." Martik's voice was lethal and quiet. "It's back up the stairs and to the left. There is a hidden door that leads to the tunnels beneath Vernista." He prattled the details off as if they had been stored in his mind for quite some time.

King Martik barely spared a glance back at me before taking off for the stairs. Knee throbbing from my fall, I limped after him, confused at Martik's sudden clarity. From what I knew of Eklos, the King would have been tortured relentlessly. With months having passed already, Martik should've been a shell of a dragon. There should not have been enough conscious thought left in him to be able to think clearly. Especially not to remember that there were tunnels out of the dungeon.

But perhaps King Martik had been pretending—putting on a façade—in order to escape Eklos's wrath. He was smart, would do what was needed to survive, even if it wounded his enormous dragon ego.

I hurried up the dark stairwell, hands braced on either wall to support myself.

"Hurry," Martik's whisper danced through the dark.

A faint clinking sounded in the distance, so quiet I might have missed it had I not already been on alert. The sound was unmistakable.

Claws on the dungeon floor. Someone was coming.

I could barely make out the shape of the King's body waiting at the top of the stairs. I knew I wouldn't be able to climb the stairs very fast with how much blood I had lost, so I put all my remaining strength into a mighty flap of my wings and propelled myself the rest of the way, landing silently next to Martik. The footsteps grew louder, unhurried, as if whoever was coming knew there would be no escaping.

"Where is it?" Martik muttered, voice so quiet that even I, standing next to him, barely heard it. Blinking against the smothering darkness, the King was sliding his hands along the wall, searching for something.

"Martik," I whispered before sniffing. The scent of Eklos permeated the air, and bile rose in the back of my throat.

An eerie sensation washed over me, and it was as if time stood still. I watched as Martik's eyes lit up in slow motion, pushing on a slightly protruding stone in the wall, just as a barrel of white flames hit the space above his head.

I whipped my head back and every instinct in me roared to life, screaming for me to run.

Eklos stood there, face twisted into a nightmare, the vengeful wrath coating his hands in fire flaring bright, ready for another attack.

The scene continued at half speed as I watched Eklos's eyes flash and his arm rose, throwing a burst of white flames straight at my chest. I closed my eyes, readying for the impact, and the excruciating pain that would follow. The heat from the flames closed in on my body and then suddenly it disappeared.

Blinking in confusion, I registered that Eklos was gone, a stone wall now standing between us, before Martik was hauling me by the arm up the secret passageway.

A roar shook the walls, dust and pebbles raining down from the ceiling as we both half ran, half limped as fast as we could move. Smoke filled the air, as if Eklos was using his magic to find a way into the tunnel.

A door appeared at the end of the hall and before I could think it through, I grabbed Martik's arm and used my magic to jump the remaining distance to the door. When the shadows dissipated, I steadied myself against the wall as Martik used his remaining strength to rip the door halfway off its hinges.

He wanted out of here just as much as I did.

Martik waited for me to head into the tunnels that led to our freedom, but I simply said, "After you, Your Majesty."

CHAPTER TWENTY-THREE

KAIDA

I OPENED MY EYES to darkness, blinking multiple times before I screamed against the cloth that was shoved in my mouth and tied tightly around my head. Cold iron shackles bound my wrists in front of me, preventing me from shifting back into dragon form or using my magic. My body bumped and skid around the floor I was laying on, a constant sound of metal on stone clanking nearby. An animal snorted and my mind snapped into focus, my ears straining to recognize the sounds coming from outside. Was I in a carriage of some kind? Despite the chill of autumn outside, the interior was stifling, sweat beading on my forehead and dripping down my spine. I winced as a pain lanced across my face. Gingerly, I touched my cheek and found a warm liquid trickling down, and memory flooded through me like plunging into ice water.

Kalev was dead. The dragon from the Remnant, Zeghar, killed him.

I remembered furniture and glass shattering as Tarrin and I fought against the dragon, desperately trying to get away before he could capture us. But Zeghar had a special type of magic we hadn't counted on—one neither of us had heard of before. All it took was our blood and his touch and he could send us into unconsciousness.

That was the reason for the sticky substance on my face. He had cut my cheek open with his claws. The memory of his scaled palm touching my forehead immediately afterward sent a shudder through my body. That was all I could remember. It was only darkness after that.

How had the Remnant dragon found us?

"Kaida?" A voice whispered behind me.

"Tarrin?" His name was a muffled gasp through my gag. Thankfully, my hands were chained in front of me rather than behind, which allowed me to work the cloth free, spitting the disgusting acid-tasting fibers from my tongue as it slid free.

Shackles clinked as he tried to move before letting out a groan.

"Where are we?" he asked at the same time I said, "What happened?"

A beat of silence passed as we listened to the sounds around us trying to figure out the answers to our questions. Outside of the snorting animals, and the wheels of the carriage crunching the stone beneath them, there were no other noises. Not even voices whispering.

"Are you hurt?" Tarrin asked, his voice hoarse.

"Just a cut on my cheek. I'm all right." I paused. "What happened after…"

Tarrin blew out a long exhale, before I heard the sudden intake of breath, like he was in pain. "After you… fell," he struggled to find the words just as I had, "Zeghar turned on me. He moved so fast… his claws sliced through my thigh, and I didn't even have time to cry out from the pain before blackness filled my mind."

"How bad is it?" I asked after a moment. He hesitated, and that told me everything I needed to know.

"It needs stitching," he said, defeated.

I closed my eyes, my stomach sinking, the fight sliding out of my limbs in response. He was losing too much blood. I yanked at my shackles, wrists aching, a quiet groan slipping through my lips as the frigid metal pierced the fragile skin beneath them. The iron leaked into my bones, preventing even the smallest tendril of magic from sneaking through.

The clanking of the metal wheels hitting stone suddenly changed, and the jostle of the carriage smoothed out. The bruises covering my backside rejoiced for a short moment as the violent jerks and bumps stopped.

My relief was short lived as I realized what the smooth road must mean.

"We're on the road to the Royal Palace." Tarrin's voice spoke the words just as they crossed my mind. It was the only smooth road in Elysia, made with some thick liquid that hardens flat and smooth like the surface of a diamond.

A shiver racked through my body despite the heat of the carriage, and I fought against the sinking feeling settling into my stomach.

"We don't have much time. If we're on this road, it's less than an hour to the palace. We've already crossed through Vernista." There was no emotion in his voice. "Feel around you," he began, determination fueling his voice. "See if there is anything we can use to pry off the chains."

"I don't think—"

"Just try." His stern reply sent a jolt through me, momentarily stopping the panic from subduing my mind.

Roving my hands around the rough wood beneath me, earning endless splinters, I swallowed down the lump that threated to bring tears to my eyes. There was nothing—only frayed ends of rotting wood jamming their way into my flesh.

I opened my mouth to tell him there was nothing we could use when the carriage stopped.

We froze. Pulse pounding in my throat, I instinctively held

my breath, begging the roaring in my ears to quiet so I could hear what was happening outside. There were murmuring voices at first and then it went silent.

Another voice echoed before a sudden bang on the side of the carriage caused me to jump. The ringing of steel weapons sounded before a chorus of shouts began. The scent of smoke drifted beneath the wooden slats followed by the roar of fire.

Someone was out there, fighting whoever was guarding us.

The smoke grew thicker and the already stifling heat of the carriage grew unbearable. The scent of charred wood filled the air and despair licked over my skin.

The carriage was on fire.

As if my thoughts had summoned it, flames shot through the side, illuminating the interior in a dull orange light. Tarrin sat against the far-left wall, one leg bent supporting his arms, the other stretched in front of him, a large gash leaking blood. His hair was in disarray, his clothes torn and streaked with grime. His brows were low over his eyes, a mingling of resignation and determination twisting his face as he stared at the flames burning through the wood like paper.

The smoke grew denser by the second, and coughs racked through my lungs.

"Tarrin," I gasped, trying in vain to get clean air.

He was once again pulling against his shackles, desperate to get free of this smoke-filled coffin. The flames grew larger, the entire side of the carriage blazing.

My body screamed as the heat grew more intense, licking against my skin, leaving the first sign of burns behind. Out of the corner of my eye, I noticed Tarrin's movements suddenly stopped. Squinting against the smoke, I saw that he was sprawled on his back, head facing the wall.

"Tarrin!" I tried to shout, but the smoke choked my voice. Spots flashed in my vision, and I knew I was only moments from passing out. The fire would consume the carriage and we would die.

For a minute I was tempted to let that despair take control, to give up and let the flames take me into the afterlife. There was no way out of here, no way to break the chains that held Tarrin and me inside.

But as the thought of accepting death crossed my mind, the fire in my core awakened despite the iron that had kept it cold and barren. Flames, born not of normal fire but of the magic burning through my veins, rushed over my body, and I instantly remembered when I was captured at Belharnt. I had been shackled to that stone table, the iron and bluestone draining my life away, when my magic had awakened, and the metal chains *melted* away. It felt exactly like that moment.

I inhaled a lung full of smoke and coughed, my entire body trembling. A dark-blue glow filtered through the smoke before a tingle prickled over my wrists and I realized my hands were free. The shackles were gone. Noam's explanation of me carrying the Ancient Magic came to mind once more.

I leaped at Tarrin and a sob broke from my throat as I attempted to melt his chains. I clumsily tried to grasp the magic and filter it into the iron around his wrists, but the frantic need to escape was causing the magic to slip away. When I was in dragon form, my magic often just came to me as the beast took control, but in human form it was much harder to summon.

Putting my fingers on his neck, I could barely make out his pulse thudding dully beneath the skin. The smoke was so thick it was impossible to see him, and my vision grew hazy. I couldn't concentrate on the heated metal around his wrists long enough to draw on my magic. The inside of the carriage spun around me.

The fire licked at the floorboards, and I knew we only had seconds left. Spots flickered in my vision as I kicked with all my might at the door, sending bursts of my fire magic at the lock, but unlike the shackles, it somehow remained intact. Perhaps I had already drained my magic. Either way, my body grew weaker by the moment, the well of magic within me growing cold and silent.

I bent over Tarrin's body, tears streaming down my cheeks. I flung the last of my magic at the door in one last attempt to open it before my head came crashing down to the wood floor. Darkness fought over my vision, and I glanced one last desperate look at the door and took in another lungful of smoke as I gasped.

It was open.

And a human stood on the other side.

Right before the darkness took me, a flash of recognition slammed through my mind as I beheld her eyes, now a fiery silver, so different from the last time I had seen them. A cut dripped blood over her left eye and down her cheek.

I didn't even have time to be confused at the sight of Queen Lita standing there in human form, a sword gleaming in the fire-light, before blackness covered me and I was gone.

CHAPTER TWENTY-FOUR

EKLOS

THE DUNGEONS OF the palace were ablaze. I walked amidst the flames, a gentle heat swirling and licking at my scales but I paid it no mind. My only thought was of my cousin's escape with the King. The scene replayed over and over behind my eyes: Eldrin and Martik, within my grasp, disappearing behind a secret passageway that wouldn't open no matter how much fire and strength I threw at it.

Rage twisted my heart, causing it to pound like a hammer in my chest as my claws burrowed into scaled palms. How had Eldrin even made it past Regam? There was a reason I had left him in charge of the dungeons. No one should have been able to get past him, let alone kill him. I was the one to tie the lock to the jailor's life, so I knew immediately when he had died.

It was hard enough to imagine weak, pathetic Eldrin managing to kill such a beast, but then to fumble his way through the dark of the dungeon and find the King, whom I had made sure was well hidden, far away from the other prisoners, was too much to swallow.

Such a failure was intolerable.

There was only one way that my cousin had managed to find

Martik before I had found them. Someone must have told Eldrin where the King was. Someone inside.

Thus, the inferno now blazing across the stones and mold of the dungeon. I wanted every creature within those cells to feel pain, to feel my wrath in each flame that scorched across their skin or scales. Everyone had to die, whether guilty or not, whether skin or scales.

Smoke swirled through my nostrils, but it didn't bother me for the smoke was mine to command. I embraced it, letting it fight off the flames that fought to claim my life too. Fire was no observer of persons. Screams and fierce growls ripped into my ears as the prisoners within those walls were devoured and turned to ash.

I smiled as the iron door clanged shut behind me, trapping the fire within. I stalked up the endless stairwells and came to a stop as I entered the foyer. The room was empty—all the humans within the palace had either been killed or assigned to the dragons in my army. The autumn sun did little to warm the space, and a dark, eerie chill crept through every inch of the palace. I took a deep breath, relishing it. This was what Elysia should have been all along. Dragons like myself sitting on the throne, commanding the rest of the weaker dragons to do my bidding. Not a pitiful piece of human flesh in sight.

A dagger-filled smile peeled back my lips as I sat on Martik's throne—*my* throne—in the Great Hall. I released a breath of relief, a ring of smoke escaping my lips.

"Master Eklos," a voice rang out, echoing in the cavernous room. Councilman Roldan hobbled down the gold carpet that led from the door to the dais upon which the throne sat.

"What?" I snapped, annoyance replacing every pleasant thought in my mind.

"I bring word of the shifters, my lord."

I perked up. "Are they here?"

Roldan's eyes widened and the scales on his throat bobbed as he swallowed. "N-no, my lord," he stuttered. "Zeghar found them in Feltar and apprehended them. They were on their way here when the carriage was attacked." Roldan paused, his claws clinking nervously at his sides. "The three Remnant dragons were murdered and… the shifters escaped." The dragon winced and took a step backward, preparing for retaliation.

I was silent as I processed his words. How had two shifters escaped iron shackles? My mind was immediately assaulted by memories of Kaida, moments from dying on that stone table in Belharnt, suddenly freed from her shackles. It never made sense and I had never found out how she broke free before the mountain collapsed.

"And how," I started, my stomach churning hotter as I wreathed my hands in white flames, "did Zeghar, one of the Remnant's best mercenaries, and his two companions manage to get themselves killed, allowing the abominations to escape?"

Roldan gulped, taking a step backward. "M-my lord, it would s-seem that they had h-help. S-someone freed them f-from the carriage." The Councilman's stuttering was like a headache hammering away at my temples. It only appeared when Roldan addressed me, and it took every ounce of self-control to stop myself from ripping the dragon's tongue from his mouth.

"Someone?"

"Y-yes, Master Eklos. We are unsure who it was as there were no witnesses, but we found the charred remains of the wagon. The door was unopenable from the inside so there is no way they would have escaped without someone else opening the door."

"And did you search the area?" I growled, smoke tendrils leaking from my nostrils.

Roldan nodded. "There were brief footprints in the mud, but the rain that night washed away any trail."

A deafening growl split the air, fire bursting from my mouth, stopping just before consuming Roldan.

"Find them."

"But—"

"Find them!" I roared, causing the floor to tremble. My blood blazed beneath my scales like the inferno I left behind in the dungeons. "Find them or your life is forfeit."

Roldan's black eyes widened to the point of bursting before he stumbled backward. "Y-yes, Master Eklos." He scrambled toward the door, using his wings to propel him faster.

"One more thing," I called, forcing the Councilman to halt mid-step. Roldan halfway turned, struggling to meet my eyes.

"The Remnant has failed me. Mobilize the dragon army. Send them to every village from here to the border of Myrewell. I want every human killed, each of their hovels burned to the ground. I want there to be no indication of humans having ever been in Elysia." I paused, my fire fading to a simmer as I gripped the sides of the throne, my claws gouging into the stone. "Kill every last person until you find those abominations."

"As you wish, my lord," Roldan managed before scurrying out of the Great Hall.

"Too long, Eldrin," I muttered to myself once he was gone. "Too long have you evaded me. Too long has your blood ruined my days and haunted my nights." I inhaled deeply, exhaling a lungful of noxious smoke. "I am coming for you, cousin. I *will* find you."

I stalked down the steps, leaving the throne I had plotted and schemed for behind.

"This ends now."

CHAPTER TWENTY-FIVE

KAIDA

I WAS SICK AND tired of waking up in the dark.

A stinging tightness wrapped around my arms, and I bit the inside of my cheek against the pain as I blinked into the darkness of the night. Mercifully, it was not the all-encompassing dark that I had become accustomed to all the times I had been captured recently.

I decided I was also sick and tired of being captured.

The grass was soft beneath my aching body, the stars flickering overhead between a canopy of trees that my human eyes could barely make out. The autumn night was cold, a shiver working its way over my skin, causing a ripple of prickling pain over my arms. Burns. That's what the sensation was. My arms were covered in burns.

I bit back the tears that welled in my eyes as the true extent of the pain flared in my mind. My body felt like it was smothered in fire, despite the chill in the air, causing a cold sweat to bead on my forehead.

An orange light danced behind me, and I held my breath as I turned my head to get a better look. A small fire burned a few yards away, illuminating the small grove of trees we were in.

We.

Prince Tarrin was lying next to me, eyes closed, though his chest rose and fell in a steady rhythm. Strange shapes covered his arms, and I gingerly touched them, finding a paper-like substance. Movement caught my eye by the fire, and I noticed someone sitting there, a black cloak covering their body, a hood hiding their face.

As if drawn by my gaze, silver eyes peered out from beneath the hood, meeting mine. The person drew back the hood and I gasped as the firelight revealed her face, bringing back the memory of who had rescued us from the burning carriage.

Queen Lita, in human form, stood from the log she had been sitting on and sauntered over to where Tarrin and I were laying in the grass.

"How are you feeling?" she asked, but all I could do was stare. Queen Lita was dead. I saw her die. She died in my place, to save me when Eklos attacked me at the Beginnings Festival.

I opened my mouth to answer her, but nothing came out.

Lita's furrowed brow relaxed as she glanced at her son and bent down to adjust whatever was wrapped around his arms and legs.

"They're mithdere leaves," she whispered as if she didn't want to wake Tarrin. "They help to draw the heat out of the burns so that they heal faster."

When she had assured herself that the leaves were still in place, Lita stood and nodded her head toward the fire, beckoning me to follow.

I suppressed a groan as I pushed to my feet, careful not to step on Tarrin, and limped over to the fire. Ignoring the log that the Queen was now sitting on, I plopped onto the ground, preferring the velvety grass after so many years of being surrounded by dirt and mud.

Silence fell between us as the fire crackled and popped, embers floating up into the trees. I risked a glance at Lita and found her gaze planted on Tarrin's sleeping form.

"H-how..." I tried, breaking the silence, wincing at how

loud it sounded in the quiet of the woods. "W-what… I don't…" Words stuttered and tripped over each other as I tried to form a coherent question. My mind raced trying to figure out how the beloved Queen of Elysia could still be alive when I had watched her die—when her blood had covered my hands.

"You're alive," I managed at last.

"Yes."

I blanched. "B-but… I saw you. I saw you die."

A wince twisted her face, the fire casting shadows over it.

"Yes, I died, Kaida," Lita said after a moment. "I died as a dragon, and that part of me was ripped away, gone into the after-life forever. It would appear that when a shape-shifter perishes whilst in their dragon form, the two halves are severed. My human form remained, stripped of all magic and shifter abilities. Now, I am utterly human. Mortal." There was a deep sadness in her voice, but it was tinged with something else that I couldn't quite place. Regret, perhaps?

"Did you know that would happen when you saved me from Eklos?"

Her throat bobbed as she swallowed. "No, I didn't."

I wanted to ask if she regretted taking the spear that was meant to kill me. If she regretted the promise that she had made to my mother to protect me. All the questions that circled my mind since her death stalled on my tongue, my voice refusing to speak.

An awkward tension hung between us as neither one of us spoke. The heat from the fire slipped over my skin and I cringed, scooting farther away as the burns on my arms flared. The frost-covered grass crunched beneath me.

"We need to leave," Queen Lita said, glancing at Tarrin, still lying on the ground. "We've already been here for too long. It's not safe here, especially once word gets to Eklos that you were freed, and that three of his prized Remnant mercenaries were killed."

"Did you…"

Lita's liquid silver eyes unsettled me, so different from her turquoise dragon eyes. She remained silent, but the answer was evident in the hard set of her mouth, the creasing of her forehead. The Queen had killed the dragons… but how did a human kill three dragons by herself?

"This was as far as I could carry the two of you, injured as you were. Tarrin's leg is still badly wounded. I was able to stitch it up, but he won't be able to put much weight on it."

"Where are we?" I asked, glancing over my shoulder to the trees surrounding us. A shiver crawled over my body as I noticed several pairs of glowing eyes watching us from beneath bushes and roots. We were all in human form, and there was nothing to deter the beasts of the woods from making a meal of us. I swallowed hard.

Lita let out a sigh, pulling herself to her feet. "Too close to Eklos. Much too close." She tossed a pot of water onto the fire and went to Tarrin's side, stooping to feel his forehead, before removing the bloody bandage from around his leg. She tutted and pulled another strip of cloth from her pocket and tied it tightly around the wound.

"Come, help me lift him, Kaida," she called.

Tarrin's human body was much heavier than I could have guessed, and it took both of us to maneuver him to his feet, each of his arms wrapped around our shoulders. I ignored the pain rippling across my burned skin as his head lolled to the front, bouncing side to side as we half limped half dragged him farther into the forest.

"Where are we going?" I asked between pants, trying and failing to catch my breath.

"There is a cottage a few miles away that will offer some amount of safety. Eldrin will meet us there once he rescues Martik."

The world dropped out from beneath my feet, and I stumbled. "You saw my father?"

The Queen hesitated, her eyes darting from tree to tree as we moved.

"I stumbled upon him on his way to the palace. Assuming he wasn't caught trying to free the King, they should be on their way now."

My heart throbbed and a swell of hope crashed over me like a wave.

"He's alive?"

Her only response was a nod before she moved faster, silently telling me to keep moving. We pushed on through the forest, our labored breaths puffing in front of us as the temperature grew colder. My limbs ached and my lungs begged for more air, but Lita only pushed harder, wordlessly telling me to hurry. It felt like days had passed when the first signs of dawn appeared through the trees, tendrils of golden light rippling upward through the dark blue of night.

"Hurry," Lita rasped. "We must make it to the cottage before the sun is fully risen."

"I could fly—"

"No," she snapped. "Someone will see you. We stay on the ground." She paused to touch the bark of a tree, looked up at the canopy above us, and then tightened her grip on Tarrin's arm. "Come on, it's just ahead."

Leaves crunched as our bodies barreled through them, sticks cracking beneath our feet as we picked up the pace. A branch whipped against my cheek, and I blinked against the sting just as a root caught my foot and I stumbled forward, the forest falling away as my knee crashed into the moist dirt.

Ignoring my fall, Lita exhaled in relief, and set Tarrin on the ground next to me, before leaving us in the shadows of the trees. The shape of a small cottage appeared between the trunks. I watched as she circled it, then creeped up the steps of the front porched and peeked in the windows. Her shoulders loosened when she must've found it empty, and she waved an impatient hand at me to come inside.

"Sure, I'll carry him myself," I muttered. Groaning, I grabbed Tarrin beneath his arms and dragged him toward the cottage. The grass flattened beneath his boots, coating the silky strands with pebbles of dirt as I pulled him, and his shoulders tensed, the first sign that he was waking up.

I managed to get him onto the porch, wincing as his feet bounced loudly against the wood, and pulled him inside after his mother. The door closed behind us, and I propped Tarrin up against the wall as he groaned and rubbed his face, squinting at me as his eyes opened and adjusted to the dim light of the cottage.

"What happened?" he asked, voice hoarse from the smoke in the carriage. He studied the room before picking at the leaves covering the burns on his arms.

"Leave those on, Tarrin," Lita said, and his body stiffened, before his eyes slowly rose to meet hers across the room. His face drained of color, eyes widening.

"Mother?" he whispered.

A sharp twist of grief, like a knife slicing through skin, tore through him, echoing down our shifter bond. My mind flashed back to the moments after his mother had died so many months ago—when he had sat in his room and screamed in agony through the bond.

"Am I dead? Is this the afterlife?" He looked at me with wide eyes. "Did you die too?" He tried to push to his feet, and I pushed down on his shoulders to keep him seated.

"No, Tarrin." I grabbed his hand. "We're not dead. She rescued us from the carriage."

"B-but... you..." Tarrin stammered. "I saw you die. I held you as you died." Tears filled his eyes and he struggled to his feet before limping across the small room to smother her in a hug.

My own eyes burned as I watched them embrace, the unhealed

wounds of losing my own mother seven years ago piercing through my chest without warning. They broke apart, each swiping at their cheeks, and Lita gestured for him to sit. She went on to explain what she had told me about shifters dying in one form but surviving in the other. I watched as Tarrin's skeptical face transformed from disbelief to awe. A light shone in his eyes that I hadn't seen since before his mother died. I couldn't hold back the small smile that curled my lips.

"So, you're human now? You can't shift at all?" Tarrin asked after several seconds of silence as he absorbed the torrent of information.

Queen Lita shook her head. "It's gone, all of it."

"How have we never known about this?" He ran a hand through his hair. "What if there are other shifters that have died but are still alive after all, like you?" A hopeful light entered his eyes.

"Tarrin, even if there were shifters who survived their dragon form's death, they would be mortal. Their long dragon lifespan would immediately cease, shortening to the mere brief years of a human. I may be alive now, but there is no telling how long my human body will last."

I watched as the light of hope faded from Tarrin's face and my heart crumbled. I couldn't imagine knowing my mother was dead, only to find out she was actually alive, but would die again, possibly one day soon.

He rubbed a hand over his face. "How long have you been alive?"

She hesitated. "I never truly died."

Tarrin's hands clenched into trembling fists. "Why didn't you send word? Why didn't you come find me?" The anguish in his voice was palpable. "How could you let us think you were gone?"

Lita shook her head. "It was better for you to believe I was dead. I would have only been a distraction."

Tarrin gaped at her. "A *distraction*?" He huffed out an unamused laugh.

Lita's brow furrowed. "I don't expect you to understand, Tarrin."

"No," he bit out. "How could you expect me to when you've been *hiding* while Eklos destroys Elysia? How could I understand when you made the decision for me that I was better off without you?" His voice cracked. "How could I understand when you let me believe you were in the afterlife all this time?"

Her eyes softened. "Tarrin—"

He dismissed her with a wave of his hand and said, "I don't want to hear it." Anger and anguish warred as dark shadows in his mind, sending thick, jagged tendrils through the bond.

I leaned my shoulder against his, unsure of how to comfort him.

Lita held her arms out to her sides. "I was no use to you like this. My magic is gone—my strength is gone. You didn't need me, and I had nothing to offer you anymore."

His eyes snapped to hers. "I said I don't want to hear your excuses."

Lita flinched, blinking at his tone, his words.

"Do not speak to me like that. I am your moth—"

"My mother is dead."

The oxygen disappeared from the room, and I couldn't move beneath the weight of his words. Lita went still as death.

"My mother never would have hidden herself away, letting the vilest creatures in this world destroy the country she worked so hard to build. My mother never would have willingly left her husband and son." Tarrin's eyes lit with magic, fire pooling in his palms in anger. "My *mother* never would have allowed us to believe she was dead. She would have fought back—fought to find us and get Elysia back." He shook his head, the fire vanishing from his hands. "I don't know who you are, but you are not her."

Silence fell over the cottage, thick and smothering, and I struggled to draw a full breath into my lungs. A faint thudding sound echoed in my ears, but I wasn't sure if it was my own heart pounding or Lita's. We no longer had the shape-shifter bond between us, but I could tell by the stricken look on her face that Tarrin's words had cut deep.

"I'm sorry, Tarrin," Lita said after a moment. "I thought I was doing what was best for you. I… I let my shame of being a human cloud my judgement."

"There is no shame in being human," I retorted, unable to hold my tongue.

She gave me a sad smile. "Perhaps you're right."

"You've raised Tarrin to be strong," I replied, glancing at him out of the corner of my eye. "He's a grown male now. You don't need to protect him anymore. He can do that himself, just as he can make his own decisions." I felt a pulse of warmth down our bond. "I don't care if you are no longer *mutator formarum*. That was not all you were back then, nor is human all you are now."

Lita opened her mouth to speak but I shook my head. "The Queen of Elysia was one of the strongest, bravest people I knew, regardless of whether she was dragon or human. I know it's hard that you've lost half of yourself, but you need to let it go and find the Queen again. *That's* what Tarrin—and Elysia—needs. She's still inside of you, Your Majesty. You need to find her."

Tarrin's mental arms wrapped around me, squeezing tight, his relief and gratitude shining like a bright fire through the shifter bond. His mother's face was pale, her hands loose by her sides. Tears lined her eyes, but I wasn't sure if it was because my words had hurt her or helped her.

Minutes passed, as if I had rendered her speechless, and none of us said a word. The heat of our emotions began to fade, and the cottage grew cold from the chill of the autumn night. I rubbed my arms, trying to infuse warmth into them. Lita missed nothing, watching my every movement, and rose from the ground without a word. She crossed to the opposite corner of the cottage, kneeling on the dusty floor, popping up a piece of wood, and rummaged around in the secret compartment in the floor as we watched with open mouths. A couple of threadbare pillows and a moth-eaten blanket were tossed in our direction; a wooden piece of furniture with ropes tied across the length was unfolded against the wall.

"There is only one cot and one extra blanket," she said. "We should all get some rest before Eldrin and Martik return. There is no telling what condition they will be in or if we will need to flee." Lita settled into the cot without another word, tension still thick in the air as Tarrin and I settled on the floor together. He leaned against the wall, tucking me into his side. I pulled the blanket over the both of us, careful to keep it away from Tarrin's burns. The sound of his hoarse breathing filled my ears as silence settled over the cottage.

"How did you kill those dragons by yourself?" Tarrin whispered loud enough for his mother to hear.

Lita let out a sigh before turning on her side to face us. Her eyes roved over our bodies huddled together against the wall, and I thought I saw a flicker of something in her eyes. Approval?

"Kalev managed to send word to me that you had arrived in his village. I'm not sure how he knew how to find me, or how he even knew I was alive, but it was shortly after I received his message that I heard he had been murdered. I knew if the Remnant had killed him, that they likely had the two of you as well." A slight tremble shook her voice at the mention of Kalev dying.

"Knowing Eklos, Vernista was the obvious destination to take you, so I picked a place along the road and waited." She paused, rubbing at her face. "I had three poisoned arrows with me, specifically made to pierce dragon scales."

"How did you get those?" Tarrin interrupted.

"It doesn't matter. Some things are better not spoken of," his mother replied before letting out a shaky breath. "When I saw the carriage barreling down the road with those imbecilic dragons riding out front, it was obvious you were inside. I hid beneath the trees and shot them down one by one." Her eyes grew distant, the memories playing behind them as she spoke. "Of course, they were stubborn and only one died at first. I shot a flaming arrow into the side of the carriage to distract them and killed the other two with this." Lita pointed to a long dagger strapped to the side of her leg.

"*You* set it on fire?" I blurted. "You could have killed us." The words were loud in my head, but they came out as a lethal whisper.

Lita winced. "I didn't expect the fire to spread so quickly. It had been raining and the wood was still wet. I thought I would have more time." She glanced at Tarrin's arms where he had been burned, her forehead creasing.

"It doesn't matter," Tarrin said on an exhale, snuffing the tension rising in the room like blowing out a candle. "You freed us, and we're alive. That's what matters." His mother's eyes flickered, and she hesitated before nodding once.

She had saved us and kept us away from Eklos. A shiver worked over my body at the thought of what might have happened if she had not found us.

"We should all get some rest," Lita said after a moment. "With any luck Eldrin and Martik will arrive tomorrow, and we can plan what to do next."

"What we will do next is kill Eklos," I muttered beneath my breath.

I expected her to respond, but Lita rolled over, pulling the blanket over her head, effectively ending the conversation. I glanced at Tarrin and found his eyes full of sorrow, and maybe even confusion, but he said nothing and kissed my temple before pulling the blanket up around us and closing his eyes.

My mind churned over this new Queen. She was not the same as the shifter I had spoken with in the gardens at the palace. This

Queen was hardened, a shell of bitterness encasing her heart, shutting off any compassion or warmth that had previously been there. I knew the Lita I met at the Royal Palace had to be in there somewhere, and for both Tarrin and Elysia's sake, I hoped she could find herself again. An ache throbbed through my heart.

Lita had survived. Jinna's words from back at The Den, the day she made her escape so many months ago, rolled through my head.

Just surviving is not living.

I blew out a breath, closing my eyes against my roiling thoughts. As I drifted off to sleep, I couldn't help but wonder if Queen Lita, stuck in her human form and devoid of magic for the rest of her life, wished that she had never survived at all.

CHAPTER TWENTY-SIX

KAIDA

A LOUD THUD JOLTED me from sleep, and I glanced out the window through bleary eyes to find dusk waiting. Pushing back the blanket, I crawled onto my knees to listen for what might have caused the noise. Tarrin and Lita were slower to wake, blinking the daze from their eyes. Another thud echoed outside the cottage. It sounded like boots clunking heavily on the wooden porch. The faint clinking of scales met my ears and my heart picked up speed.

Lita rolled herself out of the cot without a sound and crouched as she tiptoed over to the window to peek outside. Her dark-brown hair was in disarray over her hunched shoulders as she eased her face over the windowsill. I watched as her body tensed, and I barely registered Tarrin easing into a defensive position in front of me. Lita's forehead smoothed out and her clenched fists went slack at her sides.

She met my eyes, and a small smile tilted her lips before she threw herself at the door and whipped it open. I heard three distinct intakes of breath before Tarrin and I bounded for the doorway, our mouths falling open as we peered outside.

My father stood on the wooden porch in human form, blood soaking through his shirt beneath his arm. His face was alarmingly pale, his forehead creased in pain as his silver hair, drenched in sweat and tinged red from blood, fluttered on the breeze behind him. I took a step toward him but came to an abrupt stop when I noticed what stood behind him.

A dragon's turquoise form stood in the grass at the base of the porch. The last time I had seen the turquoise male, his eyes had been bright though full of sorrow and fury from losing his wife. But now they were dull, a painful haze smothering them caused by months of torture and lack of food. His once muscular body was now thin, large areas of scales missing from his limbs and torso. I swallowed hard at the sight of the King of Elysia. The once mighty dragon that ruled all of dragon kind, reduced to gangly limbs, drooping wings, and dull, battered scales. King Martik swayed before falling to his knees in the grass.

I glanced at Lita wondering why she was not rushing to her husband's side and found her cowering behind the door. Her eyes were wide, and she had a hand pressed to her chest. Tarrin wasted no time and limped to his father, wrapping his human arms around the massive dragon's chest.

I hurried to Eldrin's side and put his arm around my shoulders, helping him inside.

"What happened?" I asked him. His breathing rasped in short gasps, and blood dripped onto the dust-ridden floor beneath us.

I was vaguely aware of Tarrin helping Martik squeeze through the front door, the dragon's head skimming the ceiling even in a crouch, the rest of his wings and tail filling much of the one-room house.

"I rescued the King," Eldrin deadpanned, wincing as I helped him sit on the floor against the wall.

"How were you hurt?" I glanced at Lita, hoping she would grab medical supplies from her hiding spot in the floor. Thankfully, she scurried over to the hidden compartment and pulled out a small box, though she kept her distance from Martik.

I lifted Eldrin's shirt and had to stifle a gasp. A deep puncture wound, the width of a large coin, was directly over his ribs. Based on his slow pulse and the cold sweat on his skin, I knew he had lost far too much blood. Wetting a cloth with alcohol, I gave Eldrin a stern glance in warning before touching it to his wound. He could not hold in the scream that erupted from his mouth before clamping his teeth down on fisted knuckles. Tears swarmed his eyes, and I muttered a quiet apology. I pulled the cloth away, searching for something with which to close the wound.

"Regam," he gasped, and I saw Lita freeze out of the corner of my eye. "The dungeons were locked. The door would only open if the jailor died." His voice was hoarse, strained with pain. "We fought and I killed him, but not before he wounded me."

My hands were covered in Eldrin's blood, and they shook violently as I tried to fit a piece of thread through the end of a needle. My vision swirled at the sight of my father's blood coating my skin and by the third failed attempt a frustrated whimper escaped my lips.

Steady hands wrapped around my fingers, taking the needle and thread away. I looked up, tears spilling from my eyes, and Tarrin wiped the wetness from my cheeks.

"I'll do it," he said, his voice low and soothing. I managed a nod and scooted out of the way.

"What happened once you made it inside the dungeons?" Tarrin asked.

Martik appeared to be in a daze where he was curled up in the corner, his head and wings skimming the ceiling. Lita was on the opposite side of the room, watching him carefully, though he hadn't seemed to notice her.

"I stumbled through the darkness," Eldrin panted as Tarrin stitched up his wound. "I thought I would never find Martik. Those dungeons are endless." He took a deep breath as Tarrin finished and stepped away to wipe the blood from his hands before searching for some gauze to wrap it with. "There was another prisoner in one of the cells. I don't know who he was, but he knew where Martik was, and he told me where to go. I found him within minutes."

Eldrin's face contorted as Tarrin began wrapping his torso. "By the time I got to Martik's cell, Eklos had almost found us." He glanced at the King before continuing. "Martik knew of a passageway that allowed us to escape. Eklos was right behind us, trying to break through."

Tarrin stepped back, inspecting the gauze to make sure it was tight before clearing his throat. "But you made it out. That's what matters," Tarrin declared, clearly relieved to have his father out of those dungeons, and safe.

"Lita?" Martik's usual booming voice was tight and frail as he blinked at her and we all stilled, turning our attention toward them. The King's eyes narrowed at her small human frame, and her eyes widened as she took a step back.

She almost looked… afraid.

Why would she be afraid of her husband? After the conversation we had with her last night, I could understand her hesitancy to see him again, but based on the tightness in her face, her round silver eyes… Did she think Martik would love her less for no longer being a dragon?

The King's movements were awkward as he tried to navigate his massive body in the tiny space. He grimaced as parts of his limbs without scales scraped the floor. Extending his snout nearly to Lita's face, he squinted, trying to break free from the daze his mind must have secluded to over the last few months.

"Lita?" he asked firmer, his eyes beginning to clear. "Is that you?"

Lita's throat bobbed as she swallowed, her body tensing before she offered a resigned nod. "Hello, Martik."

Martik's eyes widened. "So, it's true." Before anyone could

move, he stretched out his arm and gently wrapped his claws around Lita, drawing her to his chest. Lita froze for several heartbeats before her body softened and she stretched her arms across his chest, tears spilling onto her cheeks.

Tarrin and I gaped at him, at what he had just revealed.

"You knew?" Tarrin breathed. "You knew she was alive?"

The King exhaled. "I had read of such legends in books as a youngling, that shape-shifters do not truly die their first death. When I received word that you had been killed, it brought back the words written in those pages." He paused, his claws tangling in her dark-brown hair. "But then I saw your lifeless body in that casket, the pale red your scales had turned... I thought it must have been lies—just an old tale that hopeful shifters made up centuries ago to ease the grief of death." A heavy silence filled the cottage.

I flinched as Lita cleared her throat, the sound delicate like her human frame.

"I thought you wouldn't..."

Martik's scales bunched over his eyes. "You thought I wouldn't love you because you aren't a dragon anymore?" He wiped a tear from her cheek with the back of a claw.

I had never seen the King be so tender toward Lita, even before everything happened with Eklos. Maybe losing her reminded him of everything he had taken for granted.

Martik's snout peeled back into a smile. "Though it will present some... challenges, I could never love you less. Dragon or human—it doesn't matter. As long as you're alive."

A smile brightened Lita's face, her silver eyes glowing as she gazed at her husband.

Tarrin cleared his throat, clearly uncomfortable with his parent's affection toward each other. I couldn't help the giggle that slipped through my lips, and he gave me a sheepish grin.

It's great that they're reunited, Tarrin said into my mind. *But they're my parents and... it's gross.*

I laughed down the bond. *Poor baby.*

He gave a shrug before we turned back to the others, finding them watching us.

I gave an awkward cough. "So… what do we do now then?"

Eldrin ran a hand through his long silver hair. "If I know my cousin, losing the King as a prisoner will only enrage him further. It will renew his sense of purpose. I imagine, if he has not already done so, he is moments away from sending his army to hunt us down. Eklos wants nothing more than our deaths."

"Where do we go?" I asked.

"We need to find a place farther from Eklos's grip where we can hide while we regroup. The King needs to recover, and I am in no shape to fight. We should do as we originally planned," he continued, nodding at Tarrin and me. "Search villages for humans *and* dragons that may support our cause."

Ice licked over my skin as his words settled into me. My father didn't know about what happened in Feltar—how quickly we had been discovered. I still couldn't fight the feeling that this was all for naught. Though we had gained the King and his now human wife, what good could a dragon, two shape-shifters, and a human do against the might of Eklos's dragon army? What can such meager numbers do against such unfathomable hatred?

"We were nearly caught in Feltar," Tarrin said, studying my father's face. We didn't even make it an hour in the village before the Remnant sniffed us out. Do you really think there will be other supporters in Elysia? Not many will want to risk Eklos's wrath, and many will want the reward that comes with handing us over."

"I think you will be surprised," Martik said around a groan as he leaned against the wall, "how many supporters you will find. There are many who have tired of the old ways."

Skepticism contorted my face, and I knew I wasn't alone. I took a deep breath. "Where do we go then?"

No one said anything for several moments.

"Shegora," Lita whispered from the corner.

Eldrin didn't look surprised. "That's a long journey."

"But it's far from Eklos and his army. It would take them much longer to reach it than our small group. He doesn't know where we are or where we're headed so that may give us an extra advantage."

My father pondered her words. "There's nothing left of the village. Xalerion had it destroyed."

"It still stands," Martik interrupted. "Though, it was in rough shape the last report I received."

It was Lita's turn to gape at her husband. "Report?"

Martik nodded. "I have scouts travel there several times throughout the year. I always knew it was a special place to you. Much remains in ruin from the Lone Dragon, but much has stood the test of centuries." The King adjusted his wings behind him. "It's a good place to hide for now."

"So, Shegora?" I asked uncertainly, glancing at Tarrin for reassurance.

He looked as skeptical as I was, but sat down next to me, taking my hand in his. We were in this together. That was his promise to me.

Martik and Lita shared a weighted glance and then nodded in unison.

"To Shegora then," Eldrin said, his eyes hardening and piercing into mine. "If it is a war Eklos wants, then it is a war he shall get."

CHAPTER TWENTY-SEVEN

TARRIN

THE NIGHT WAS never-ending as we went round and round in discussion of what to do next, including how to leave the cottage with our plethora of injuries. My mind swam in exhaustion, and I fought the heaviness persistently sitting on my eyelids. The cut on my thigh had long ago faded to a dull ache, but every shift of my leg sent a shooting twang cutting through it. I was unsure how I would make the journey to northern Elysia if I were unable to walk.

Both Eldrin's and my father's injuries were great enough that many of our plans were thwarted before they could come to fruition. My mother was in good physical shape, but the fact that she was human put a larger target on her back. She would be the first one that the mercenaries went for.

"Where is Shegora?" Kaida asked no one in particular, breaking me out of my spinning thoughts.

"It's at the very northwestern tip of Elysia, in the mountains. It's quite the trek to reach the village," Eldrin answered, rubbing the bridge of his nose.

"And how are we supposed to travel hundreds of miles and climb a mountain in our current states?" Kaida sounded exhausted, her voice strained. "Not only that, but all while avoiding detection by Eklos's spies." Her eyes constantly darting between the occupants of the cottage as if they might disappear at any moment.

Eldrin studied her before clearing his throat. "The fastest way would be to fly, but Martik and I are in no condition to fly such a distance, especially carrying someone." He nodded toward Lita. "On foot, the journey would take at least six weeks, and that doesn't include the time that would be added trying to evade and hide from Eklos's army."

"Do we even have that long?" I asked, brow furrowing.

"No," my father whispered before a growling cough interrupted him. "If we travel on foot the entire journey, we will be caught. Eklos has too many dragons covering these lands." He winced as he shifted against the wall. "We should spend the first two weeks on foot to give Eldrin and I time to heal, and then we'll fly the rest of the way. Perhaps Eldrin will be strong enough to use his magic to jump us farther."

I glanced at Kaida's father, his human form leaning heavily against the wall. Thankfully, the color was returning to his face, though his breathing was still short and shallow as if every breath pained him. His brow furrowed and skepticism twisted his face, but he remained silent.

The first trickles of dawn were beginning to peek through the window, and I stifled a yawn.

"What supplies do you have here?" Kaida asked my mother. "Is there enough food and blankets that we can travel with?"

"Not enough," she answered with a shake of her head. Mother pulled herself to her feet and brushed the dust from her worn brown pants. "I will go to a nearby village and get some food and essentials for the journey. You all should get some rest. When I return we need to leave. This cottage will not stay safe for us much longer."

Before any of us could utter a word, Lita was out the door, silent as a wraith. Kaida was unable to suppress a yawn as she laid her head against my shoulder and closed her eyes. Eldrin and Martik looked worried at Lita's sudden departure, but exhaustion kept them both firmly on the floor.

Though I fought it, sleep pulled me down into its depths, my mind lulled by the steady sound of Kaida's breathing. When I awoke, the sun was high in the sky, illuminating the cottage, and I blinked against the bright light. My father, Eldrin, and Kaida remained asleep, and I carefully moved Kaida to the side and got to my feet. The floor groaned beneath my weight as I tiptoed to the window and I winced, my eyes darting to the others. When no one moved, I let out a silent breath and looked outside.

The clearing the cottage was nestled in was full of color, the vibrant reds and oranges of autumn decorating the trees, even the green of the grass was brighter than I had ever seen it. Birds chirped in the trees and the sky was blue as the sea, absent of clouds. The air was unseasonably warm for late autumn, but I didn't complain. Cold weather would only hinder our traveling, and since winter was approaching, I would take all the warm days I could get.

There was no sign of my mother outside and worry sprang up like weeds in my mind. Surely, she should have returned by now.

With a glance back at the others, I slipped out the door.

Grass crunched beneath my feet as I navigated my way across the clearing and into the woods surrounding the cottage. Birds chirped in the nearby trees, the sunlight streaming through the leaves and branches warming my skin. Worms wriggled in and out of the dirt in front of me.

Farther and farther I went, winding around trees and roots that threatened to send me flying onto my face. The forest grew denser, all sunlight fading away, the chill of autumn biting at my nose in the shadows. A branch snapped in the distance at the same moment the wind changed directions and my head snapped up. Scanning the foliage around me, the hairs on the back of my neck stood on end. The birds were silent.

Something was out there. Was it just an animal? Or was it something worse?

The faint scent of ash met my nostrils, and I carefully took a step backward so that I was hidden behind a tree. I peeked over a shoulder but saw nothing lurking in the woods. Heart thudding against my chest, my mind frantically churned through my options. I was far enough away from the cottage that whoever was out there hopefully hadn't caught the scent of the others, and I didn't want to risk leading anyone back there.

Stomach sinking, I knew I had only one choice: run. Draw the intruder away from the cottage and find a way back to Kaida.

Taking in huge gulps of air, I prepared to take off through the trees. Another twig snapped, closer this time. I put my hands on the tree, ready to propel myself forward, when a cold hand slapped over my mouth, pulling me back toward the cottage. A scream built in my throat, and I was about to release it when the scent on the hands holding me came into focus.

I'd know that lemon pine scent anywhere.

"Quiet, Tarrin," Lita's hoarse whisper filled my ear. "We have to get back to the cottage before the mercenaries get there."

My mother released me, and we took off as fast as my injured leg would allow. It was quickly healing thanks to my dragon heritage, but it still ached as I pushed my legs harder. The sounds of branches cracking echoed in the distance, and I allowed myself a small sigh of relief that the mercenaries didn't see us retreat and weren't right behind us. I wasn't sure how much time that would buy us, but I hoped it would be enough.

The woods thinned out and the clearing came into view, Kaida appearing in the doorway, her brow furrowed as my mother and I half sprinted, half hobbled through the grass toward her.

"We have to leave. Now," Lita barked. Eldrin and Martik were instantly on their feet as she gathered the meager supplies from beneath the floorboards and threw them into three separate sacks.

"There's no way we can get far enough away if we leave on foot," I said, watching my mother. Eldrin was helping my father maneuver his large body out the door.

"No, we can't. The only way to outrun Eklos's mercenaries is to split up."

My mouth fell open, brows furrowing. "We can't—"

"We can and we must, Tarrin. If we all leave on foot in the same direction, that will be like leaving a trail of fruit that leads right to us. Our only option is to split up and meet in Shegora."

My mind spun and Kaida's eyes were ablaze with terror as she looked at me, then at our fathers.

"You and Kaida must go—head straight west and then head north along the coast. But don't cross too close to the remnants of Belharnt. I will head south and circle back north, and Martik and Eldrin will head east and fly to Shegora once they have healed." Lita stopped abruptly, and walked to me, gripping one of my shoulders.

"If there was another way, we would take it. But the males cannot fly, and you and Kaida cannot carry the three of us. This is our only option."

Lita lifted one of the three sacks at her feet and handed it to me. "There is some dried meat and fruit in there along with two bedrolls. Stay away from the villages as much as possible for you've become too recognizable. Only light fires if you have no other option." My mother leaned forward and placed a kiss on my forehead, then Kaida's.

"Above all, you two must make it to Shegora. You are the hope of Elysia."

My eyes narrowed at her words but before I could ask what she meant, she shoved me and Kaida out of the cottage. "Now, go!"

Kaida gripped my hand with a death hold and together we hurried into the forest, leaving the family that we had fought so hard to find and rescue in fate's hands.

CHAPTER TWENTY-EIGHT

KAIDA

THREE DAYS PASSED without food or rest, Tarrin and I dining on terror for meals, only stopping long enough to drink from our quickly depleting canteen. We took to the air in short stints but never made it far in case Eklos's scouts were nearby, watching for turquoise and amethyst-colored dragons in the sky.

"We have to be nearing the Ilgathor Mountains by now," I said, voice hoarse from disuse. Apart from the silent tears we both shed upon leaving our families behind, we didn't dare speak for fear of attracting the mercenaries. We even laid a false trail for them when we realized they were still following us. Whether it was only one, or if it were a group that split up like we did, we weren't sure, but we used precious time and energy to lead them away as best we could.

"It would be easier to tell where we are if we could go into a village," I muttered under my breath.

"You heard what my mother said. Eklos's eyes are everywhere. We have to stay away from them as much as possible."

I nodded, ducking beneath a low-lying branch in the dense forest around us. "We can't go much farther like this, Tarrin. There has to be a safe place we can rest."

"I know," he replied, rubbing at his temple. "Let me see if I can see the mountains. If we are close, we can hopefully find shelter in a hidden cave."

In a dull flash of blue, Tarrin shifted into dragon form and jumped up through the trees, unfurling his wings as he broke through the tops. Silence descended, heavy and thick in his absence, making my ears throb. Sunlight beamed through the leaves in thick shafts, highlighting the dirt and weeds surrounding my feet. The birds were strangely quiet as I waited for Tarrin to return. A twig cracked in the distance and my heart jumped into my throat until a squirrel scurried across the ground and jumped on the bark of a tree to my left.

Letting out a shuddering breath, I scolded myself for being so jumpy and forced myself to calm down.

Minutes passed and Tarrin didn't return.

I walked forward, continuing the trek west, thinking he would be able to find me with his dragon sense of smell once he was done scouting. Enough time passed that the angle of the sun had changed, and worry began to claw its way up my throat.

Where was Tarrin?

All the possible scenarios, from him being shot out of the sky with an arrow, to getting lost, however unlikely that would be, to being captured by Eklos's mercenaries spun out of control in my head. My feet moved faster and faster through the woods, my breath coming in panicked gasps. Tears threatened to spill from my eyes, causing them to burn and blur. A large root appeared in the ground before me and my foot caught beneath it, sending me flying through the air, landing in a cluster of thorny bushes.

A groan slipped through my lips as blood trickled down the palms of my hands and thorns tangled in the sleeves of my shirt and both pant legs. I struggled to pull myself from the bushes before studying by surroundings. Tarrin had definitely been gone too long. Where *was* he?

He would never purposely leave me to fend for myself. Without my dragon senses, I wasn't able to know if danger approached. Knowing it was a great risk, I shifted into dragon form, prepared to get above the trees to search for Tarrin. Summoning the last dregs of my strength from my exhausted body, I followed Tarrin's movements and jumped into the air, releasing my wings as soon as I cleared the trees.

At first, I was relieved, as I took in my surroundings and saw the Ilgathor Mountains just mere miles away. A smile crept over my dragon lips but faded when I saw a large shape flapping its wings frantically in the distance. It was headed straight for me. A distant roaring met my ears, but if there were words in the noise, I couldn't make them out.

Then horror seized my body, and it took everything within me to stay airborne. For it was Tarrin flying back to me, blood streaming from every part of his body. And that was three mercenaries behind him, gaining on him fast.

Run, Kaida! Hide!

I am not leaving you! I screamed the words in my mind. *Where are you hurt?*

Everywhere. They have arrows that pierce scales.

His pace was slowing, his wings barely keeping him in the air as they struggled to open and close. The mercenaries were catching up.

I am coming to get you! A plan slowly formed in my mind as I raced as fast as my wings would take me. It was risky, but it might work.

When I reach you, I want you to shift into human form. I will catch you.

What? Are you insane?

Just do it, Tarrin. Trust me!

In three deep breaths I reached Tarrin. *Now!*

Blue flashed, smothering my senses for a brief second before my eyesight cleared and Tarrin's human body remained suspended just long enough for me to snatch him out of the air. I didn't even have time to make a witty comment before an arrow zinged past my ear, forcing me to dive.

In a burst of wind, I snapped my wings behind me and soared higher into the sky.

"Where do we go?" I shouted into the wind. I held him aloft with one arm under each armpit and squeezed him tighter as his sweat-and-blood-drenched skin began to slip against my scales. His body was littered with gashes and wounds.

Tarrin pulled at his hair. "I don't know! I have been trying to escape them and get back to you for nearly an hour."

I shook my snout. "I can't outrun them. They're too fast."

"Our best chance is to land and try to fight them off." His voice was carried off in the wind. "We won't be able to fight if they shoot us from the sky."

Spotting a clearing in the forest, I dove for it, snapping out my wings at the last moment and surged into a run to slow my momentum. As we came to a stop, I shoved Tarrin behind my back and turned to face the three dragons that had just landed in the clearing. The one on the left was dark brown with red eyes, the one on the right was a green so dark it was nearly black, his eyes also red, and my heart stuttered in my chest as I beheld the center dragon.

At first glance I thought it was Eklos because this dragon's scales were dark gray like ashes. But then I noticed his eyes. They were pitch black, like an endless pit, and there were no whites surrounding them. Dagger like horns twisted and curled above his head, and he held a crossbow in his claws with iron tipped arrows in a quiver attached to his arm.

In unison they stepped toward us, smoke leaking from their nostrils. The center dragon sneered, revealing a mouth full of rotten teeth, though still deadly sharp.

I barely registered the dull flash behind me as Tarrin shifted back into dragon form and limped forward. His normally bright scales were dull. He had lost too much blood.

A laugh met my ears as the dragons stalked closer.

"This is the *great* shifter that bested Master Eklos and escaped from Belharnt?" the dark dragon sniped, offering another laugh that rose bumps beneath my scales. "I expected more."

Time stopped as the mercenaries, all three of them, raised their crossbows in tandem. I didn't even have time to look at Tarrin or say goodbye before the click of the bows sounded and the arrows were released, aimed for each of us, one for Tarrin, and two meant for me.

I closed my eyes, trying to summon any last trace of magic to incinerate the arrows before they reached us, but my reserves were empty after days of no food and little sleep.

One blink and the arrows were inches from us, and the next blink the arrows were suddenly gone, and three separate clunking noises echoed amongst the trees.

The arrows that had been meant to kill us were now jammed into the bodies of the mercenaries. I blinked again, trying to make sense of it as the three dragons dropped to their knees, blood leaking from the scales where the arrows had sunk into flesh, right in the center of their hearts. Ice began forming around the arrows, spreading over every scale like the swell of a tide, until each of their bodies were encased in it. The dragons gasped for breath inside their cages of ice, though it was muted, like being underwater.

The blood dripping from their wounds froze, and each of them stiffened inch by inch as if they were being frozen from the inside out. It was then that the ice cages cracked, before exploding outward, sending frozen pieces of scales flying in every direction. I cringed away, trying to cover Tarrin's body with my own.

Silence descended in the clearing, my heartbeat hammering in my ears before a group of dragons stepped from beneath the canopy of trees, layered in weapons that were now aimed at us.

Black smeared the edges of my vision, and I fought off the darkness. I squinted at them, my vision growing hazier as they stalked closer.

Tarrin shifted back to human form and slumped forward onto the ground, his body too weak and injured to stay conscious. The world spun around me as the strange dragons surrounded us, raising their weapons to signal they were ready to strike.

My shaking legs were unable to hold me upright any longer and I collapsed to my knees, the ground thudding beneath me. A dragon the color of the deepest part of the ocean inched out of the circle. His liquid green eyes narrowed as he studied Tarrin, then me. Ice rimmed the claws on each finger.

"Help him," I managed to whisper as I pointed at Tarrin, and the dragon's eyes widened. He hesitated for a moment before nodding at the beasts on either side of them who lowered their weapons and gathered Tarrin in their arms.

The leader extended a hand toward me, and my eyes narrowed as my exhaustion riddled brain struggled to understand who these dragons were. Tentatively, I extended my bloody claws, our scales scraping against the other, before my vision went black.

CHAPTER TWENTY-NINE

KAIDA

MY EYELIDS STUCK together as I pried them open. Sunlight streamed through the window, warming the chilly autumn air that permeated through the holes in the mud that appeared to hold the walls together. The room was tiny, barely large enough for a broom closet, and bare, save for the cot I was perched in. I could see a small fire crackling in the hearth through the doorway, and the thick blankets that smothered me grew unbearable.

Wriggling my way from beneath them, I realized I was back in my human form. I rubbed my forehead, trying to recall what had happened, and how I would have gotten here, but my mind remained blank.

Where was Tarrin? Muscle by aching muscle, I forced my limbs to stretch and pulled myself to my feet.

"Ah, she awakens," a male voice said, and I spun on my heel, fighting the wave of dizziness that came from the movement. Memories flickered through my mind as I studied the deep ocean-colored dragon from the clearing. Flashes of Eklos's mercenaries and their gruesome death in ice flooded behind my eyelids.

"Who are you?" I asked, taking a step backward, unsure if this dragon was friend or foe. "Where is my... companion?" I didn't know if the male knew who Tarrin was, but if he didn't, I had a gut feeling I should keep it that way.

"He is resting," he replied, nodding his head to the room behind him.

I wrung my hands. "Who are you?"

A smirk twisted his snout, and he crossed his arms in an unusual human-like gesture for a dragon. "You can call me Z."

"Z?"

"I don't know your name, so it's hardly fair for you to know mine." The dragon's eyes flashed, a mischievous glint setting my temper on edge.

"And I would assume that even if I told you mine, you would still insist I call you, Z," I snapped, crossing my own arms.

"Ah, there are some smart humans after all. Or should I say shape-shifter?"

Ice poured through my veins, though it had nothing to do with this dragon's magic. "What do you want?"

"I want to know why three infamous, previously undefeated mercenaries, employed by the Regent of Elysia, was hunting you and your... *companion*." A knowing look flashed across his face.

"I... don't know."

"You're a terrible liar." Z straightened and stalked back into the other room. Swallowing hard, I followed after him, stopping dead when I saw Tarrin on a bedroll in the corner, strips of bandages covered much of his body.

"Why is he on the floor?" I demanded, appalled that they would leave him on the floor with his injuries.

"I figured the female would want some privacy," Z answered flippantly, waving a hand at the broom closet he had stuffed me into.

"Well, you thought wrong," I snapped. "The Prince of Elysia should be treated as the highest guest."

My eyes widened and I slapped a hand over my mouth, wishing

I could rake the words back in. I watched as Z's face remained stoic while his eyes jumped from Tarrin to me. Had he already known who we were? What game was he playing?

"Prince Tarrin of Elysia, you say. So, that would make you… his betrothed?" Z smirked at me, and a blush creeped over my cheeks. "What did they call you? Keena, was it?"

"It's Kaida," I spit, fire spreading through my bones at yet another vital piece of information I had given away simply because this infernal dragon had stoked my temper. Who did he think he was?

Z repeated my name several times, testing it out and drawing the two syllables out. I wanted to plug my ears and hum to block him out.

"What do you want from us?" I asked, dread curling in my stomach like a snake.

"You realize there is quite a large bounty on both of your heads." It was not a question.

I narrowed my eyes. "Yes."

"And I would be an extraordinarily rich dragon if I handed you over to Eklos's males. I know the location of every single spy and mercenary from here to the palace. It would be quite easy."

"Then you would be a fool."

"A very rich fool." Z smirked, and I wanted to slap it off his face.

"Why did you save us?" I asked, dropping my hands at my sides.

All humor fled his face as he studied me, then Tarrin.

"Eklos's dragons have become a nuisance in these parts, not only killing humans and burning their property, but the dragons who do not join their cause as well." Silence fell as he scratched at the scales on his face before his liquid green eyes bored into mine. "We hunt the hunters."

A chill skittered down my spine. "And why did you save us?"

Z let out a sigh. "When we first saw them attack the *Prince*," he emphasized, "we didn't know who he was and simply thought the mercenaries were attacking another dragon. Then you zoomed through the air and caught a human mid-air where a dragon once was, and we all thought we had lost our minds."

I winced at the memory of how close we had come to being killed.

"We knew something was different about the two of you, so we put them down."

Unease spread like nausea in my gut. Who was this dragon that he could kill three of Eklos's best mercenaries without any effort?

"That was your ice, then?" I asked, trying to shut out the memory of the dragons freezing to death.

A smirk twisted Z's snout, and he spread his claws in front of him, palms up, before ice coated them. In the time it took me to blink, it all vanished.

I'd never met a dragon with such magic before and I had to bite my tongue from asking the endless number questions clambering for attention in my mind. Besides, I had a feeling that he was the type of dragon where fawning over his magic would only cause his ego to grow bigger.

Instead, I said, "Why did you take us? Why didn't you just leave us in that clearing?"

Z gestured to me with his claws. "Once the threat was eliminated, you begged for us to help him." He pointed at Tarrin and shrugged. "We were curious."

"Where are we?" I asked.

"Just north of the mountain that collapsed several months ago."

Belharnt. The name made me shudder.

Z scented my fear and lowered his voice. "You're safe for now, Kaida."

I didn't miss his use of the words *for now.*

"Then what do you plan to do with us?"

Z was thoughtful for a moment, studying the ceiling, then the floor in silence.

"I suppose you're free to leave as soon as the Prince is healed and able to travel."

"You would let us leave? Just like that?"

Z smirked. "Unless you give us a reason to keep you." Firelight glinted off his teeth as he grinned.

I huffed out a breath and headed to Tarrin's side, not wanting Z to see how flustered he had made me. Tucking my feet beneath me, I sat on the floor next to him, brushing back the brown strands of hair from his forehead.

"Where are you traveling to?" Z asked, lowering his voice even further.

My hand stilled, then dropped to my side as I looked up at the dark-blue dragon.

"Why do you ask?"

Z sighed, rolling his eyes. "You ask quite a lot of questions."

I huffed out an irritated breath. "We just danced with death. Can you blame me?"

Z snorted, embers flying from his nostrils.

When he didn't relent, I sighed. "Shegora. We're traveling to Shegora."

Genuine surprise widened his eyes before he could regain his composure. "For what purpose? Shegora was destroyed centuries ago."

"Eklos's reign of terror has gone on for far too long. We intend to raise an army to stop him. It's the only place left to go."

Z remained quiet, whether out of shock or thoughtfulness, I wasn't sure.

I turned back to Tarrin, gently lifting the bandages coating his arms to inspect the wounds. A breath of relief slipped from my mouth as the sight. They were healed much further along than I had anticipated. I had feared that we would be stuck with Z for a week or more, but by the looks of it, we would be able to leave in a day or two.

A knock sounded at the door before it swung open on groaning hinges. One of the other dragons from the clearing stood there, a long sword in a scabbard around his fat belly. Z's attention went to him, and I watched them out of the corner of my eye.

"Orders, sir?"

Z rambled out a long list of commands, none of which I paid any heed as I ran my fingers through Tarrin's hair. He didn't stir. Then I felt eyes boring in my back and I glanced over my shoulder. Z studied the Prince for a long moment, and then met my eyes, holding them as he said, "Call in everyone. Prepare to move out by the end of the week. We travel to Shegora."

CHAPTER THIRTY

TARRIN

A FIRE ROARED IN the hearth, though it did little to heat the room with walls made of dried mud. The whole house smelled like manure and mold, and I was forced to breathe through my mouth to endure it. This morning I had woken up tucked in a corner, buried in blankets, with Kaida sleeping leaned against the dirty wall next to me. With a nudge to her foot, she had awoken and launched into the tale of how a band of rebel dragons, led by a dark-blue dragon named Z, had saved us, killing the mercenaries that had been hunting us.

Memories of the attack flooded my mind unbidden, and I squeezed my eyes shut. Terrifying frozen moments in time replayed behind my eyelids as I recalled flying above the trees, seeing the three dragons coming toward me, followed by the arrows blasting through my wings. I winced as I squirmed in my chair. All the wounds I had sustained in my wings translated to a broken arm in human form, and though it was mending quickly, it still caused me quite a bit of pain.

I glanced over at Kaida who was conversing with a couple of dragons on the other side of the room. While I was obviously thankful that we weren't dead, I didn't trust these dragons. There was something to be said for a group of dragons showing up just in the nick of time to save us from certain death. It seemed too convenient. Besides, simply the fact that they called themselves rebels left a rancid taste in my mouth. Though Z had been brutally honest in the few words I had spoken to him, I couldn't escape the feeling that he was hiding something. There was something off about him, something that set my inner fire boiling.

I wished I could convince Kaida to leave, but she believed that these dragons would help us defeat Eklos. Z must have somehow earned her trust in the hours I had been unconscious. I had never known Kaida to trust a dragon so completely, especially not so quickly.

I narrowed my eyes as I studied the other dragons. Why would they risk themselves to save us? And why hadn't they turned us over to the Remnant?

A hand squeezed my shoulder. "How are you feeling?" Kaida said, coming to kneel in front of me. Her warm palm settled on my knee.

"Fine," I bit out, immediately regretting my tone. It wasn't her fault we were attacked and saved by a band of untrustworthy dragons.

Her features softened but a dark-blue dragon appeared over her shoulder, and I scowled at the sight of Z. I wished I could swat him away like an annoying bug. His snout twisted into some combination of a grimace and a smirk, as if he were able to hear my thoughts. Z held out a mug of tea. I tried to refuse it, but Kaida grabbed it and placed it in my hands.

"Thank you, Z," she said, and I scowled. Z grinned, an expression that set my temper to simmering.

"Is the Prince finally out of bed?" he crooned.

"I wouldn't call a pile of fabric on the floor a bed," I retorted.

Z huffed out an unamused laugh. "So ungrateful." He shook his head. "I'm the reason you're alive, Prince. You can thank me anytime."

Kaida let out an exasperated sigh and scowled at the dragon. "You're not helping."

Z simply shrugged and turned on his heel and left the room.

"Kaida," I said, keeping my voice down so the others wouldn't overhear. "You don't know these dragons. You can't trust them."

She tsked, busying her hands with checking the bandage wrapped around my arm. "You're the one who has repeatedly reminded me that not all dragons will hurt me. You've been trying to get me to become more trusting of dragons all along. Why are you so against them? They saved our lives, and they haven't turned us over to Eklos's spies."

"That doesn't mean they still won't."

Kaida stilled, fixing her eyes on me. "I am choosing to trust them. They plan to travel with us to Shegora. I need you to trust me, Tarrin."

"You don't know anything about them. We can do this without him." The words tasted sour as they left my mouth. We needed every dragon we could gather to help us defeat Eklos's army, but I didn't like Z. It was plain and simple.

"His rebels number almost fifty, Tarrin. We need them."

It seemed like a decent number of dragons, for a single dragon was a force to be reckoned with, let alone fifty. But the last reports we had heard numbered Eklos's dragon army in the hundreds. And that was months ago. There was no telling how many he had amassed since then.

Against anyone else, fifty would have been enough. More than enough.

But against an evil beast like Eklos?

I shook my head. Sensing my thoughts, Kaida knelt in front of me.

"It is better than none, Tarrin. Z's rebels are well trained. They took down those mercenaries like they were made of feathers. We are better for it if they join us. I fear we would fail without them."

That fear flickered in her eyes, sobering me. I blew out a breath. Though I didn't like it, nor did I trust this Z male, I would try to trust her judgement.

Without help, we would fail. Elysia would be doomed.

If these dragons were willing to put themselves at risk, and fight for that better world that Kaida had painted so clear in my mind, then I would work to trust them. Perhaps more dragons would still join our cause as we finished the last trek of our journey up to Shegora. Maybe when others saw that we had followers, they would be more inclined to join us.

I looked to Kaida, who had just finished fiddling with the bandages on my arm and leaned in to tighten the makeshift sling holding my broken arm in place. Her fingers were gentle, sending bumps up and down my body, despite the ache in my bone. Leaning forward, I brought my lips to hers, smiling to myself when Kaida's eyes widened before she melted against me, as if her body craved my touch as much as I did hers.

Wrapping my one good arm around her waist, I pulled her closer, silently cursing the shooting ache that throbbed in my arm as her chest pressed up against it. A scuff and a creak sounded behind us.

"Ahem," Z cleared his voice.

Kaida and I froze. I let out a shuddering sigh as she carefully extricated herself and sat back on her knees, a wicked blush coloring her face.

"If you two are finished, there is food." Z nodded his head toward the enormous table on the other side of the room, some mix of annoyance and amusement flashing in his eyes before he sauntered back the way he came. The floor rumbled at the weight of his steps.

Face still bright pink, Kaida pushed to her feet and extended a hand. "Come on. You need to eat something."

I exhaled a long breath before taking hold of her hand. The

room spun with a violent tilt as I stood, and Kaida wrapped her arm around my waist to steady me.

"See? Food," she said, nodding at my lack of balance.

She helped me limp to the other side of the room where I found one of the largest wooden tables I had ever seen, a bench on each side. A female dragon sat on the left side, smaller in size than most dragons I had seen, scales the color of dark lavender that were iridescent in the light. On the opposite side sat Z in all his grumpy glory, and a dark-brown dragon with spikes down the center of his head, on his right.

All three dragons ignored us as we eased onto the benches. I eyed the food warily though Kaida grabbed a large piece of tree bark from the center of the table and began adding spoonfuls of food to it. There was a large roasted bird, from which she pulled off a steaming piece of meat, but the rest of the food seemed to be picked straight from the forest. Different purple and red berries, varying sizes of mushrooms, and bunches of carrots that still had specks of dirt as if they were plucked from the ground and thrown on the table.

"We will plan to leave the day after tomorrow," Z said in a soft voice to the two dragons around him. My human ears strained to hear his words as I grabbed a few berries and popped them in my mouth.

"Are you sure about this?" The female dragon asked, her tangerine eyes, like a sunrise, flicked to me, before landing back on her partly devoured tree bark plate.

I saw Z nod out of the corner of my eye.

"This is the best course of action right now. Once Eklos is out of the way, everything will be made easier."

What will be made easier? Did Z have some hidden plans that he had not shared with Kaida? What was he up to?

"We will give the Prince one more day to recover and then we shall trek north toward Shegora."

The female dragon glanced at me again, studying me. "The shifter Prince looks fine to me," she sniped.

"The shifter Prince *is* fine," I retorted, unable to help myself, rotating my body on the bench to face them. "If you wish to leave, Z, then be my guest. We don't need you. Kaida and I can make it to Shegora without you."

"Can you?" the lavender dragon snapped, her voice ringing like steel. "Do *you* know where each one of Eklos's spies are located? Do you know about the secret paths through the Ilgathor Mountain woods? Do you know how to travel undetected, where even your smell is concealed?"

"Alyaa, enough," Z said, rubbing his clawed fingers above his eyes as if he had a headache.

"If the *Prince* thinks he doesn't need us, then let them go. See how far they can make it without being captured. We all saw how well that went a few days ago."

Z silenced Alyaa with a severe look before she huffed out a breath, dark smoke curling in the air between us, and stood, her footsteps rumbling through the dirt as she stalked away.

When she was gone, Z blew out a breath. "You will have to forgive Alyaa. She has lost much at Eklos's hands and the Royal Family's inaction."

"Inaction?" I said, eyes narrowed.

Z covered a red berry in ice between his claws before popping it in his mouth. The violent crunch of the ice breaking was unreasonably loud before juice burst between his sharp teeth.

"Yes. Eklos's reign of terror has spanned centuries, only worsening with each that has passed. The King and Queen have remained idle, unresponsive, letting Eklos get away with too much. Alyaa and her family were sympathetic to the humans. Eklos found out and had them all slaughtered, including her mate."

My stomach fell to the floor. "And she blames me?"

"Not truly, I don't think. She knows Eklos is at fault. You are just convenient to blame as you're right here."

"If it's truly a burden to take us north," Kaida chimed in,

changing the subject, "we will manage. I don't wish to make things more difficult for you and your rebels. You have helped us more than I could have asked for."

Z studied her for a moment before snapping his eyes back to me. "Your concern is appreciated, little shifter, but the decision is made. Eklos needs to be stopped, and you two will be the ones to do it. But I don't believe you can succeed without us. So, to Shegora we will go."

Kaida nodded, as if it was the simplest decision in the world and went back to her meal.

I wished I could trust wholly like she did, to believe that the rebels truly wanted to help for no other reason than it was the right thing to do.

But I couldn't help the curdling in my stomach.

The distinct feeling that something was not right. Dragons rarely did things out of the goodness of their hearts, or without a hidden agenda.

Kaida's eyes were bright, full of hope, for the first time in months. I couldn't bear to be the one who caused it fade. I would trust her judgement—I would try to trust Z. I just hoped my gut instinct was wrong.

CHAPTER THIRTY-ONE

EKLOS

THE SUNRISE WAS like the juice of squished oranges bleeding into the sky, staining the midnight surrounding it a dark blush.

It was a long night. For the first time, I traveled with my army as they destroyed village after village. It reminded me of when my father had started his crusade to kill the humans all those centuries ago. The screams of terror and pain, the pleas for mercy that went unheard, and the smell of flesh on fire permeating the air.

I wanted to enjoy it, wanted to bask in the glory of ridding Elysia of another village of those pitiful humans. But instead, I was consumed with thoughts of those shape-shifters.

My army had crossed hundreds of miles, scorching, pillaging, and laying waste to countless towns. And yet, there was still no sign of them. There weren't that many places in Elysia to hide—at least not many my spies couldn't find. So how was my cousin, that infernal girl, and the Prince still evading me? Why couldn't I find even a trace of them?

Breathing in the dawn, the scent of burnt wood and flesh coated my tongue. I usually enjoyed such a taste, but today it only angered me. The constant simmering fire in my core was now boiling day and night.

The charred grass crunched beneath my feet as I walked past piles of smoking rubble and the dragons of my army that were picking through the remains for gold and jewels.

"Master Eklos," a voice called, but I continued forward as if I hadn't heard it. "Master Eklos!" Wind whipped against my scales as a dragon frantically flapped his wings, landing in front of me. It was Councilman Roldan.

"What do you want?" I snapped, smoke already leaking from my nostrils. The dragons of the Council had failed me at every turn, and I was just about ready to rid this world of their pitiful, useless souls.

"I have news, my lord, of the shifters." He was panting, a slight sheen of sweat gathered on the tops of his scales, despite the autumn chill that was quickly deteriorating into winter. I turned my gaze fully on him and he flinched backward.

"Well, get on with it."

Roldan nodded and his snakelike tongue wet his lips. "One of your spies has caught the trail of the girl and the Prince. They are with a large group of dragons. Our spy has infiltrated their ranks, pretending to join their cause."

Well, well. What a pleasant turn of events. "And my cousin?"

The scales on Roldan's forehead bunched as he narrowed his eyes. His claws clinked together nervously, and I fought the sudden urge to cut them off. "Still no sign of him, my lord."

Flames gathered in my mouth, smoke leaking from my nostrils. "Then why are you here?" I snapped, the words grinding between my teeth. Wrapping my claws around his neck, I lifted Roldan off the ground.

He coughed and spluttered. "We... know where... they're going."

All at once, the anger fueling the fire inside vanished, leaving behind a pleasant cool breeze in the pit of my stomach. My snout spread into a dagger-toothed smile.

"Well then," I crooned, lowering Roldan to the ground, ignoring his irritating gasping as he dropped on all fours. "That is good news, indeed. And how did our spy manage to weasel their way in?"

Roldan coughed once more before easing himself back onto his feet. "They travel with a group that declares themselves to be rebels. They take in anyone who professes to be against you. It wasn't hard for our spy to sneak in and pretend to be one of them."

I fiddled with the amulet hanging around my neck—the dragon in the center of the sun. "And how many of these rebels are there?"

"Fifty."

This time I did choke. "They have fifty dragons gathered, standing against us, and you're just now mentioning it?" I growled, enjoying the way Roldan shrunk back and curled in on himself.

Flakes of snow drifted down from the sky, littering the ground like ashes; the shadows of night chased away by the sun which had made its appearance over the horizon. After surviving a winter in Baywood Forest, the coldest, most brutal climate in all of Elysia, the ice and snow no longer bothered me. Unfortunately, my army had not had the same experience and would be slowed by the elements. They were a sad lot, constantly complaining as the nights grew colder, the sun giving off less and less strength to us as the days faded into winter.

"We only just received the report this morning. But never fear, Master Eklos. Our army numbers in the hundreds. They are no match for the might you've created."

Knowing he had a valid point, I conceded with a growl and began pacing across the dirt which was growing colder as more snow fell. Dragons moved about us, arms heavy, laden with treasures of every size, shape, and color. I wished I could say that these dragons were motivated to fight in my army simply because it was the right thing to do for Elysia. I rubbed at my snout. I had a feeling it had more to do with their lust for gold and jewels, their need for glory, than wanting to rid the world of the filth of humans and shape-shifters.

I blew out a ring of smoke. "And where are they headed Roldan?"

"Our spy reported they're traveling north to Shegora."

Shegora? The old shape-shifter village that my father destroyed centuries ago? Why would they be headed there? With winter descending, it would be foolish to try to climb a mountain, especially with fifty dragons.

I narrowed my eyes at Roldan. "You're sure?"

Roldan gave a fierce nod. "Rythos said so himself."

"Rythos?"

"Yes, my lord. The spy who infiltrated the rebels."

I tapped my claws together. Rythos. Why did that name sound familiar?

"Well, relay the message to the army to make course for Shegora. And you tell this Rythos that if an opportunity presents itself, he is to strike. Dead or alive, I want those shifters brought to me."

Roldan's eyes grew wide as he nodded repeatedly, stepping backward, preparing to take flight.

"Why don't you tell me yourself?" a voice drawled. The wind picked up as heavier snow fell to the ground, making it difficult to see in the distance. But I could feel the unhurried, thudding footsteps through the ground. Slowly, as if emerging through the white shadows of snow, a dragon appeared. His scales were a pale gray that perfectly blended in with the whipping snow, his eyes a dark orange as if embers in a fire burned behind them.

And though I was Eklos, Regent of Elysia and soon to be High King, the blood drained from my face.

Now I knew why the name was familiar. I knew this dragon. I had grown up with him. Memories of him and Eldrin flying through drills in the air, tackling each other into the forest below, leaving me out of secret conversations… All before my cousin had manifested shape-shifter abilities, of course.

The dragon's snout split into a wicked grin that would send any human running in terror.

I swallowed hard and cleared my throat, but words escaped me. I could say nothing as memories flooded into my mind, effectively holding my tongue.

"Ah, I see you remember me then," his deep voice crooned, like velvet.

I couldn't contain my scoff. Swallowing the anxiety that coated my nerves for the first time in years, I forced my lips to move, my voice to utter the words.

"Of course, I remember you. You were Eldrin's best friend."

CHAPTER THIRTY-TWO

KAIDA

Z HADN'T BEEN LYING. Somehow, he knew where every Remnant mercenary was located and was able to navigate our large group around them, while avoiding detection as we traveled through the night. It had been an impossible feat just for Tarrin and me to avoid being seen. I had no idea how Z was managing to keep fifty dragons hidden.

Unfortunately, the past two days did nothing to help Tarrin's relationship with Z, Alyaa, or the rest of the rebels. He questioned Z's authority and decisions at every turn. I caught him watching Z any time he was around, as if he expected him to slit our throats as we slept.

If I were being honest, I wasn't entirely sure Z wouldn't. This had all seemed too easy. Too simple. I couldn't quite get over the haunting question of whether Z was working with Eklos. How else would he know every single location of the Remnant dragons? The main thing keeping me from running with Tarrin was the fact that we were desperate for support. We needed more numbers, and whether the rebels had hidden intentions or not, we had to work together.

I told Tarrin as much and he begrudgingly agreed.

Tarrin walked on my left, in human form, as we made our

way through the northern part of the forest bordering the Ilgathor Mountains. His arm was in a makeshift sling, and a large scabbed-over cut ran from his temple to his ear. When the mercenaries attacked, they pelted him with iron arrows which pierced beneath his scales, and the bones in his wings were snapped in several places, preventing him from being able to fly.

Unfortunately, the shift into his dragon form was still too painful while his bones continued to mend, so I remained in human form next to him, trying to lift his spirits.

I could tell through the bond that it made him nervous to be surrounded by dragons we didn't know while being stuck in skin rather than scales. There was a desperate need to protect me, a strange feeling that I hadn't felt from him in such a strong, unrelenting way before, and it irked him that he was forced to stay in a body that didn't allow him to do that as easily as it would in dragon form. We were placing an enormous amount of trust in Z, and every time I caught him whispering and conferring with his dragons, I had a sinking feeling that perhaps I was wrong to trust him in the first place.

But he hadn't betrayed us yet, and we had made really good time on our journey north to Shegora. I never imagined we'd make it so far so fast. I supposed that had more to do with being able to avoid Eklos's mercenaries than anything.

When Z deemed it safe, the rebels stopped at three small villages, though we remained in camp, trying to gain both humans and dragons alike who might sympathize with our cause and want Eklos out of power. We hoped to find more dragons like Kalev who were loyal to the Royal Family and not to Eklos. Unfortunately, fear of Eklos ran deep, and whether they agreed with us or not, not many joined us.

"Hey," Tarrin's voice said softly next to me. I glanced up at him, the light from the torch he was carrying casting half of his face in shadow. His eyes were full of concern as they studied my face.

"Hmm?"

"I can see those thoughts in your head. Don't go down that road."

I sighed. "What road?"

"Don't give up hope." Tarrin handed his torch to the dragon on his other side and interlaced his fingers with mine. "These villages may not join us immediately, but we are planting seeds. Perhaps we will be surprised to find them in Shegora when we arrive." He shrugged. "Eklos has governed with fear and destruction. He has taken away Elysia's peace and squashed any hope of a better future they may have had." He paused, lips pursed as he contemplated his next words.

"Hope can be paralyzed. Hope can be dragged into the mud and buried. It can be hidden and quelled. But it cannot be killed." Tarrin offered me my favorite half smile. "And it only takes a small seed to rekindle it into a bright flame. Do not underestimate what you have given Elysia."

Tears welled in my eyes, and I squeezed his hand. "I hope you're right."

Tarrin's half smile turned into a grin. "I'm always right." He winked at me.

I let out a small chuckle and returned my attention to the soft crunching of leaves and rustling of whispered conversations.

I swallowed the lump in my throat. "What if no one comes to Shegora? What if all of this was for nothing, Tarrin?" I couldn't help the question from slipping through my lips, nor the desperate tone that accompanied the words.

"Then we will figure out another plan."

He said it so nonchalant, like it was the simplest answer in the world. But it wasn't. If no one came to our aid, if we were unable to gather any humans or dragons to fight with us, there would be no other plan. Because Eklos would wipe us from the face of Elysia.

I wish I could be as optimistic as Tarrin, but I had grown up under Eklos's thumb. I knew what he was like, and I knew he would not relent. I was sure word had reached him by now of the mercenaries that Z and his rebels had killed. How many more would he send before he tired of their failure and came after us himself?

How long until his army found us and obliterated all of us?

I glanced around at our group. The season was growing closer and closer to winter, the chill clinging to my skin, and I fervently wished Tarrin was healed so we could shift and enjoy the warmth of our dragon bodies. The others trotted through fallen leaves, heads held high, eyes bright. Unlike me, with my eyes pinned to the ground, shoulders slumped in defeat.

I glanced up for a split second and caught Z staring at me.

It wasn't for the first time. It should have been disconcerting that a rebel dragon kept watching me, but it didn't seem to be in a malicious or malevolent way. It almost seemed as though he were watching me for direction. As if I had any say in our plans or what would happen.

I was just Kaida, a human from Vernista who happened to be a shape-shifter. I wasn't a leader, or a figure of hope.

So why did they all keep watching me as if I were?

Ever since Eldrin and Noam brought up my Ancient Magic, they had acted as if I was the leader to end Eklos's reign of terror. I didn't see myself as a leader then, and I certainly didn't now. I simply wanted Eklos's evil that corrupted Elysia like a fatal disease out of this world. I wanted to fight, not lead.

A sinking feeling settled in my stomach as we pressed on through the woods, the first tendrils of dawn spearing through the starry night sky.

Out of the corner of my eye I was vaguely aware of Z breaking from the line and coming to stand next to Tarrin and me. "Dawn is coming. We will need to stop and rest for a few hours before continuing. It should only be a few more days until we reach Shegora."

Tarrin nodded at him but said nothing. I saw his jaw clench as he bit back whatever remark he wanted to say.

"There is one more village that we will be crossing paths with—another opportunity for you to recruit more dragons," Z remarked, his eyes piercing into mine. A scowl was my only response, and with a smirk he moved back to his place in line.

A frustrated grunt escaped my lips.

Tarrin glanced at me, eyebrows furrowed. "What?"

"Why does everyone look to me and act as if I'm the one leading us? If anyone should be their leader, it should be you," I snapped at him. "You're the Prince of Elysia."

He sighed through his nose, not meeting my gaze. "That may be, Kaida, but I believe they have chosen you regardless."

Sweat pooled on my low back despite the cool air smothering my skin.

As if sensing my inner dread and tension, Tarrin said, "Don't worry, love. You were born for this."

My gaze snapped to his. "No, I was born a slave. That's what I was meant for. Not this."

He shook his head. "That's only part of your story, Kaida. It's what happened to you, but not who you are." Tarrin kissed the top of my head. "You are strength. Look at all you've done thus far. Look at all you've come through, and how much stronger it has made you." I moved my gaze to the ground before he cupped my cheek with his palm, bringing my eyes back to his. "Kaida, you are hope. You've given the humans and dragons of Elysia a better world to dream of. It doesn't matter what you were born into. All that matters now is that you take the lessons you learned and take the next step forward. Fight for that better world that you've painted so clearly for all of us."

"Why me, Tarrin? Any of you are more fit to lead than I am."

The corners of his lips turned up. "I imagine it has a lot to do with your magic. It draws all of us in, even me. There's a power in you that we all can sense." Tarrin searched my eyes for a moment. "But more than that, Kaida, word about you has spread. These dragons know who you are, how you grew up, the abuse you endured. Despite it all, you still stand for Elysia. You still fight. And that gives them a reason to follow you."

Hot tears leaked onto my cheeks. "I'm scared."

Tarrin gave me his signature half smirk before wiping the wetness from my face. "I am too." He kissed me once, twice. "But you're not alone."

Tarrin pulled me into his chest, wrapping his good arm around me.

"You're never alone."

CHAPTER THIRTY-THREE

TARRIN

EVERYTHING HURT. DESPITE being in my human form, I could feel each injury that I had sustained as a dragon aching beneath my skin. Though it only translated to a broken arm and a nearly healed cut on my temple, I could still feel each snapped bone in my wings, each place where those iron arrows pierced into my scales.

My whole body ached, even with my body healing at a fast pace.

But I didn't complain, didn't mention it once. Making sure Kaida was safe and that we made it to Shegora was the main priority. Everything else could wait. Healing could wait. It had to.

Another day of traveling had passed. It felt like an innumerable number of miles were covered, though it should have been impossible. Anxiety pricked at the back of my mind. This had all been too easy...

It was no secret that I didn't trust Z. What should have taken three weeks of travel, including time to evade the Remnant, had only taken a week and a half. We were nearly to the base of the mountain that Shegora was nestled atop.

What was Z's hidden agenda? He had to be working something behind the scenes. No one was *that* good. It didn't make sense, and it ate away at me that I couldn't seem to fit the pieces together.

The moon was bright as we all rested at the edge of the Ilgathor Mountain's woods. It pierced through the treetops, illuminating our makeshift campsite. Dragons lay scattered here and there, rumbles and grumbles echoing quietly through the trees. Kaida was wrapped in a bedroll next to me, her soft snores giving me a small sense of peace. She hadn't been sleeping much.

I swallowed a lump in my throat. She carried the weight of Elysia on her shoulders, though it was not hers to bear.

It was mine.

But Z's rebels, and those in the villages we risked entering, had looked to her.

Like I had told her, there was a draw to her, something that was impossible to stay away from. I knew the other rebels could feel it too in the way they watched her, followed her. I didn't entirely understand it, but if she was the leader they needed, I would accept with that. Someday, hopefully, we would marry anyway. They already saw her as their queen. Perhaps that was a good thing.

I was trying to be strong for her, to keep her hope alive. But I too was beginning to be discouraged by the lack of support we had been able to find in the villages the rebels stopped at.

Either loyalty to my family was not as common as I thought, or fear of Eklos was overriding it.

"Still awake?" Kaida whispered, breaking the suffocating silence of the night.

"Mmm," I answered, turning my head to the side to meet her eyes. They glistened in the light of the moon and my stomach tightened at the sight.

She rolled onto her side and reached out to grab my free hand. "Something on your mind?"

If only she knew. But I couldn't share the fears that plagued me. I couldn't share my deep distrust of Z, or the anxiety that we were missing something important that would allow us to be crushed by Eklos's army.

I wanted more than anything to tell her all of that, but I needed to be strong for her. So, instead, I said, "Just enjoying the peace of the night."

Kaida offered a small smile as if she knew I was lying but wriggled closer anyway.

"It's a little chilly."

I wrapped my arm around her and pulled her tight into my side. "I could warm you up." I winked at her and felt satisfaction when a pink tint rose in her cheeks.

Tilting her chin up, I brought my lips to hers.

Sparks erupted behind my eyelids. It didn't matter how many times I kissed Kaida, there were always fireworks. Shockwaves erupted through my nerves, heating my core.

It wasn't enough.

Stolen moments and brief kisses were never enough.

A dragon wheeze echoed through the forest, followed by a loud cough.

I peeked an eye open and glanced over Kaida's shoulder and saw several pairs of dragon eyes watching us with a mix of disdain and amusement.

I let out a rattling breath, reluctantly pulling away. "We have company."

Kaida rested her forehead against mine and let out a breath, the heat of it clouding in the air between our mouths.

And then the last thing I wanted to hear cut through the trees. Z's voice.

"You could at least have the decency to sneak away from the group." His eyes shone in the dark, the moonlight casting eerie shadows over his face. His voice gave away amusement, but his face remained blank. "Dawn is approaching," Z continued with a sigh. "Might as well pack up and head out now that we're all awake." He smothered a nearby fire in ice before he cast one last look at us and moved to the front of the rebels.

The camp became a muted flurry of activity. Where there should have been the rustle of fabric as tents and blankets were packed away, the distinct sound of steam as the fires were doused, or even the grumbles and complaints of tired dragons… there was nothing. It was all muffled, as if balls of cotton were stuffed inside my ears.

I helped Kaida roll up our blankets, stuffing them into a sack when my gaze caught on something in the distance. I could faintly make out a dragon standing on the other side of camp, with scales a light gray color, like soot-smeared snow. His dark-orange eyes were watching us, and I couldn't escape a gnawing sensation in my stomach. Something that told me to watch him—something that said he was not an ally.

"You all right?" Kaida's voice broke the odd trance that had fallen over me as I maintained eye contact with the dragon. I blinked several times, glancing at her before swinging my gaze back only to find the dragon was gone.

"Tarrin?" Concern filled Kaida's face as her brows lowered over her eyes.

Clearing my throat, I gave a half-hearted smile. "Yes, I'm fine." With a small smile, she moved to grab the last of our belongings.

Twenty minutes later the group was packed up and ready to move out. Kaida stood next to me, wringing her hands, her knuckles turning a bright red. Two shrill whistles echoed through the trees. That was the sign to begin moving. We stepped from beneath the canopy of the forest, the last of the stars beginning to wink out as tendrils of a tangerine dawn reached upward across the horizon.

Z appeared in front of us, causing my feet to dig into the mud to keep from colliding with him.

He smirked. "There is a village at the base of the mountain. We can try our luck once more before ascending to Shegora."

Without even waiting for a response, Z stalked off. I glanced at Kaida who was chewing on her bottom lip.

I squeezed her hand in reassurance. "Stop worrying. We—"

A commotion up ahead dried up the words in my mouth.

"Z!" a male voice shouted. "Z!"

"Quiet!" Z snapped up ahead, and I stretched onto my toes to try to see over the other dragons. I couldn't see who had been shouting, and all the rebels seemed to press in around us, getting closer and closer.

"What's going on?" Kaida whispered, her eyes darting from dragon to dragon.

"I don't—"

And then Z was in front of us, as if he walked through the shadows of the night. Ice perched on the tips of his claws.

"We must hurry." For the first time since I had met Z, his calm, cool demeanor cracked. Anxiety coated his voice like bitter ale.

"What's going on?" Kaida asked.

"My scout just returned. Eklos's army is on the move."

I heard Kaida release a sharp breath. "Is that all? We already knew that, Z."

The dragon shook his head. "No, you misunderstand me. They're on the move. Right behind us. My scout said they're only a couple days away and gaining. Fast."

"H-how did they know where to find us?" Kaida stuttered out.

My stomach dropped to the floor. "How far to the village?" My only concern was getting Kaida to safety. I didn't know if the village would offer us any advantage if it came to a battle, but anything was better than being caught in the open unaware.

Z opened his snout to respond, but a short whistle followed by a long shrill one pierced the air and every dragon around us froze.

"What does that mean?" Kaida whispered, her eyes frantically scanning the group around us. Z's eyes narrowed as he swung his head toward the front of the rebels, then shoved his way through the dragons.

A cold sweat broke out on my back, my heart hammering in my chest. I tugged Kaida toward me, tucking her into my chest as if that would save her from any sort of attack. The murmuring of the dragons settled, a strange silence descending on the forest like a blanket.

And then it all happened at once.

Every single rebel dragon in Z's party fell to their knees, eyes closed, and heads bowed. A larger group of dragons surrounded us in a circle, holding spears and swords directed at our heads. Z stood at the front, the only rebel not on its knees, dragon arms crossed, staring at the new arrivals, without a hint of emotion on his face.

A dark-green dragon with horns like a ram stepped forward and walked toward Kaida and me. He stopped before us, eyes narrowed as he studied and sniffed us.

"Prince Tarrin and Kaida of Elysia," his deep voice boomed, causing both of us to flinch as the tense silence shattered.

I couldn't help the pit that opened up in my stomach. Was this a friend or foe?

"Word has spread far over Elysia that you seek an army to rival that of Eklos, who hunts you not two days from here. You seek those who remain loyal to the Royal Family, those who would openly rebel against Eklos, despite the promise of death that that would bring. You seek those who are tired of the old ways of dragon versus human, those who will stand with you and fight. You seek those who desire a better future. A better world." The dragon's eyes narrowed, his deep voice echoing endlessly after each sentence.

"Thus far your search has been in vain. You have traveled many miles, visited countless villages, and yet not a soul has promised you aid." He paused, and my heart threatened to beat out of my chest. Kaida's hand was a mess of sweat.

At last, he spoke, eliminating all the air from my chest. "But what you seek you will find here." The green dragon extended his clawed hand to Kaida. "I am Gendon. Welcome to the village of Metta."

CHAPTER THIRTY-FOUR

KAIDA

GENDON, AS THE leader of the town, led us through the winding streets of Metta. The village sprawled over two miles at the base of the mountain, packed with cottages and huts where both humans and dragons lived together. When I had raised my eyebrows at Gendon's explanation of their peaceful cohabitation, Z had smirked at me and said, "not all of Elysia is like Vernista, though Eklos has tried very hard to make it appear that way."

Tarrin and I both gaped at the sight of it. Could it really be true? We had seen evidence of less severe slavery in Myrewell, but Metta didn't even seem to *have* slaves. They lived together. In peace.

I couldn't help but wonder if Eklos even knew about this place. It was hard to imagine that he would let such rebellion stand if he did. What would happen when his army arrived here? The thought of this place being destroyed because of me cracked through my heart.

Mud squelched beneath my boots as we walked, the first snowflakes of the oncoming winter drifting down like feathers and settling in my hair. I pulled my cloak in tighter around my neck, trying to stave off the chill seeping through the fabric.

There was no sign of my father or the King and Queen, although we had made it much faster than expected so I assumed they were probably still days behind us. I muttered a prayer to the old forgotten gods that the mercenaries had not caught up with them.

Gendon led us to his home, which ended up being a large cave in the side of the mountain. Despite being made of rock and stone, the place was enormous, easily fitting Z, Gendon, as well as Tarrin and me if we were in dragon form, all with plenty of room. It was well lit, and luxurious furnishings were carefully placed through the rooms. I met Gendon's eyes and cocked my head in silent question.

"Working together rather than fighting against one another allows us to enjoy the finer things of life. War and strife only bring poverty. Metta is a haven."

"How long have you sustained this way of living?" Tarrin asked.

Gendon was thoughtful for a moment. "For the better part of the last six hundred years."

Tarrin's mouth fell open. "How?"

Gendon smiled, somehow coming across as warm despite his mouth full of dragon teeth. "We have protocols in place that allow us to know if adversaries, such as Eklos and his minions, are close by. We have managed to stay out of their sights." He paused, letting the information sink in before he drove it home. "But the main reason is because King Martik and I grew up together. He has known of Metta his entire life. He regularly sends supplies and aid when needed. Until recently anyway. That is why Metta remains loyal to the Royal Family."

I was sure both Tarrin and I looked like floundering fishes with all the gaping our mouths were doing.

"Z sent word several days ago that you would be arriving here. We took the liberty of sending supplies up to Shegora for all of you and preparing the houses that are still standing for you to stay in. You may rest here as long as you need before you journey up the mountain." His large green head nodded as he spoke, and he gestured toward a doorway behind him. "Through that door is a suite of rooms. You and the Prince are welcome there as long as you need." I glanced at Tarrin, and he winked at me.

"We have begun preparations within the village," Gendon continued, "having weapons forged and training those without experience in war. Metta is prepared to fight with you, young shape-shifters. We know the army is not far behind you. As soon as we receive word that Eklos is here, we will join you."

Relief, thick and strong swept through me like a gentle wave carrying me out to sea. "I was expecting to have to fight you, to beg and plead for your assistance," I said honestly.

Gendon just smiled. "Not everyone in Elysia is blind. Eklos and his ilk have reigned for far too long. All of Elysia deserves to prosper like Metta has. A better world is worth fighting for."

A shaky breath worked its way out of my throat. I never imagined a village of dragons would be willing to help a human. Let alone for there to be a village of dragons *and* humans that would be willing to help two shape-shifters try to create a better future for Elysia.

Perhaps Tarrin had been right. Perhaps hope was not lost after all.

CHAPTER THIRTY-FIVE

ELDRIN

IT HAD BEEN two weeks since Martik and I had left the cottage, separating from Kaida and the Prince. Lita had gone her own way and we hadn't seen or heard any word from her. Part of me wondered if we had all imagined her for how well she had become a ghost.

It had taken three days for us to lose the mercenaries that Eklos sent after us. If it weren't for my ability to jump to other locations, there would have been no way for us to escape without leaving a trail. I was eternally thankful that my magic had not wavered in those moments, taking us farther than I ever thought I could carry the two of us.

We were only two days from the base of the mountain that held Shegora at its tip. I was surprised at how fast we were able to travel despite our various injuries, but even more surprised that we had not encountered any more of Eklos's mercenaries.

I couldn't help the nagging feeling in the back of my mind. Something wasn't right. Either Martik and I were *incredibly* good at hiding our trail, which was not that likely, or Eklos knew something that we didn't, and he was biding his time. I was afraid it was the latter. It kept me awake at night, kept my appetite suppressed, had me jumping at every snap of a twig beneath our clawed feet.

Thankfully, our injuries had healed enough that we were able to fly off and on, but only in short bursts. We had a lot of training to do to build back up the muscle we had lost.

Martik had been strangely silent as we traveled, barely speaking to me. Was he thinking about Lita? She had been so different back at the cottage—not at all like the female I had grown up with. Or maybe he was dwelling on the army that we would soon be battling—the fact that he no longer reigned over the country he and Lita had spent so long ruling.

"Martik?" I tried, seeing if I could get him to let me in his head.

A grunt was his only answer.

I let out a soft sigh as we weaved through the trees that lined the road we were following. Traveling on the main road was out of the question, but I figured there wasn't much harm in *following* the road, since it was the quickest way to the mountains, as long as we remained hidden beneath the canopy of trees. It was difficult, however, trying to navigate our large dragon bodies through the narrow trees while trying to be silent. It forced us to go painfully slow.

I cleared my throat and tried again. "Lita sure was… different."

A spark of life flashed across his eyes, and he finally deigned to look at me. "She's angry."

I snorted. "That much was obvious. I've never seen her like that."

Martik narrowed his eyes at me. "You've never lost half of yourself. She has every right to be upset. I, too, know what it's like to lose—"

He abruptly cut himself off, his lips pressing into a tight line across his snout, and when he met my eyes, for a brief second, I thought I saw a flicker of panic.

"To lose what?" I asked.

"Nothing."

"Martik—"

"Leave it be, Eldrin. I have secrets too—ones that have been buried so long I can hardly find them anymore. They're not worth digging up again."

I blinked, both at his tone and what he revealed. It had been decades—centuries—since he had spoken to me in such a way. Back when he and Lita had first begun courting, there were times when we would argue over her. She had been my closest friend, and both Martik and I had been a bit territorial over her.

But in all the years of friendship with the King, I had never known him to keep secrets, at least not ones that needed to be buried. He wasn't a shape-shifter, so how could he act as though he understood what she was feeling? What was he hiding?

I opened my mouth to ask what he meant when he suddenly went still, his snout twitching as he sniffed the air. His eyes narrowed and whipped his head to the side. Martik swallowed hard, and his eyes snapped to mine.

"We're being followed."

Panic coiled around my heart like a snake. In any other scenario, I would have simply used my magic to jump us to a safer place. But it hadn't been that long since the last time, and my magic had not regenerated enough.

There weren't many options. The trees were much too close to each other for us to try to run and getting airborne would only make us easier targets. Seconds passed and the scent of the stranger began wafting into my own nose. It definitely wasn't a human.

Had the mercenaries finally found us?

"What do we do?" I whispered.

A few more tense seconds passed as Martik's eyes scanned the woods, not uttering a word.

"You really shouldn't be here, Your Majesty," a raspy voice carried through the trees.

"Yesss," a second, more nasally voice hissed coming from the other direction. There were two of them—they had herded us.

Martik straightened at the sound of their voice, his eyes narrowing. "Roldan. Barden," he growled as both dragons stepped out of the trees and slowly circled us. "What are you doing here?"

The brown dragon, Roldan, passed another step closer. "I think the better question is what are *you* doing here, Martik? You're supposed to be locked in the palace dungeon."

Martik's eyes narrowed. "And you're supposed to be kissing Eklos's feet. So, I suppose we're both disappointed."

Barden hissed out a chuckle. "Now, now, Martik. We've only come to bring you back. No need to be cruel." His snout spread in a devilish smile, his teeth glinting in the filtered light through the trees.

Roldan took another step, forcing us back a step toward Barden who had moved behind us. His gaze found mine. "And what a pleasant surprise. The shifter with a death sentence on his head."

In a perfectly choreographed movement, both dragons summoned orange flames that perched above their scaled hands. My body ached as I drew on my depleted magic, and I could see the strain in Martik's body as he did the same.

Though much of my injuries had healed, Martik wasn't in as good of shape, his body needing longer to recover after months of living in those dungeons. I reached for the magic that allowed me to transport us, but it was still too weak. Perhaps in another hour I'd be able to manage a short distance, but that did nothing to help us now. Our only option was to try to fight or try to fly, both of which felt impossible.

My stomach churned like a violent storm at sea at the thought of coming so far, only to be bested by Eklos's minions. If we had been at our full strength, Roldan and Barden wouldn't stand a chance since they were significantly smaller and weaker than us.

I glanced at Martik and he shook his snout at me. We couldn't escape, and we certainly weren't going to give up. Letting out a long breath, I spread my legs into a fighting stance, similar to what I would use in human form, and raised my tail into the air for better balance.

I always found it frustrating that the dragons refused to look to the humans for anything but slave labor. Humans were surprisingly resilient, and there was much to gain from them, like their techniques in hand-to-hand combat. I often adapted their strengths in physical fighting to how I fought in my dragon body. It added a lot to my own personal skills, plus the dragons never anticipated my movements because they were unfamiliar.

I ran through the facts in my head.

It was two against two, and we had limited magic available, while our opponents seemed filled to the brim. We were still two days from the mountain, and there was no guarantee of safety there.

Truthfully, it didn't look good for us.

"Come willingly with us and we won't have to hurt you," Barden said, his voice shrill.

I watched Martik's snout spread into a sneer as he laughed, and then time seemed to move in slow motion like it had in the dungeons. Orange flames flared from his mouth and hands in a wild burst, aimed straight for Barden's chest. I wasted no time and followed his lead, sending an attack of my own at Roldan.

Roldan ducked beneath my flames in an effortless maneuver before spinning to slam his tail into me. I scrambled back just before it made contact, the wind from the force of it whipping against my face. Martik continued his assault on Barden, slowly pushing him back toward the trees they first appeared through. I could hear the sounds of growling, roaring, and the unmistakable scent of smoke as their fire was unleashed.

"Imagine my reward," Roldan growled, drawing my attention back to him, "when I bring Master Eklos the head of the shapeshifter he has sought to kill for centuries." Red flames that matched his eyes flickered two feet high in his palms. His enormous footsteps rumbled, the sound of popping sticks and crunching roots echoing.

"Too bad you'll never find out," I snapped before lunging at him. If I couldn't use much magic, I'd have to resort to physical strength. I managed to block his flames with a burst of my own, before tackling him around his middle. With the force and weight of my own body, we crashed to the ground, the long black spikes along his back sinking into the dirt, momentarily stunning him.

I dug my claws into the tender area just beneath the arm, ripping into his scales as he let out a roar that shook the trees. I summoned a flicker of fire, forming it into a short dagger. Drawing back, aiming for that spot where I ripped away the scales under his arms, I made to drive it in before I heard Martik yell, "Watch out!"

I glanced up and saw a huge green shape flying through the air toward me, and I flung myself off Roldan the best I could before Barden's body crashed down on top of him. I pulled myself up, using a tree trunk to steady me, and glanced at the two dragons. Roldan was still on the ground, bloody scales dripping onto the dirt beneath him. His snout hung open as he stared at the smaller green dragon on top of him. Barden's neck hung at an awkward angle, his scales several shades paler than mere minutes ago.

Martik stepped through the trees, blood smeared on his scaled palms, his eyes blazing with the fiery wrath that so often consumed dragons. I looked at Barden again. There was no mistaking it.

"B-Barden?" Roldan stammered, his eyes wide, before he shoved the dragon off him in a panic.

"He's dead," Martik growled, the sound setting even my nerves on edge.

I had seen it many times throughout my lifetime. Because a dragon's emotions are felt so strongly, oftentimes the anger that they experience turns into something stronger and more powerful, causing them to lose themselves in the act of whatever it takes to resolve that emotion. Lita had always been there to pull Martik out of moments like that, but now she wasn't. The darkened eyes of the King told me he was buried deep into his fury.

And I didn't know if I'd be able to pull him back.

I jumped in front of him, putting my hands on either side of his neck, trying to force him to look at me. Martik ignored my presence entirely and kept stalking toward Roldan, forcing me backward.

I knew the cruel dragon on the ground behind us should die. For all his treachery, treason, and plotting with Eklos, but if it meant Martik losing what was left of his sanity, of his *goodness*, then it wasn't worth it. We could deal with the Councilman another time.

"Martik!" I snapped, trying to draw him from his haze of wrath. He utterly ignored me. I swung my tail around and smacked him in the side. No response. I tried once more, harder this time, and the King finally deigned to look at me. I fought the urge to cringe away from his stare.

"He has to die," he growled, his voice shaking.

"Not like this, Martik." I shook my head, hoping he heard the plea in my words. "He's injured. Leave him here for the beasts of the forest to find."

For a moment, the clouded look in his eyes faded, as if my words were getting through to him. But then he blinked, and the haze of hatred had returned.

"No," he ground out between his teeth. "He must die."

Before I could move, Martik lunged after Roldan. I barely managed to jump in front of him, taking the brunt of his attack as we both crashed to the ground. The King's claws encircled my throat.

"Martik," I gasped. He only squeezed tighter. I tried to bring my tail up to knock his body off me, but he anticipated it and blocked it with his own. Black stars danced in my vision and still his claws grew tighter around my neck. I was running out of time. Martik would kill me before the wrath released his mind.

Drawing on the very last dregs of my magic, I managed to cover my body in shadow, jumping out from beneath him. His eyes blinked at where I should have been, but only rumpled grass remained. Before he could move to attack me again, I bashed the side of his head with my tail. Hard.

The King froze, blinking rapidly as he lifted his hands to his head. Ever so slowly, like smoke dissipating after a doused fire, I watched as the fog over his mind receded. His eyes roved over my face as if seeing me for the first time.

"Eldrin?"

I nodded, a deep, wracking cough erupting from my throat as I fought to get air back into my lungs. Martik looked from me, to Roldan's unconscious body, trying to fit the pieces together as if he weren't fully conscious for the last few minutes.

"Leave him, Martik," I said, voice hoarse. I couldn't let that angry haze take control of him again. "Let's get away from here."

Endless seconds seemed to pass until he let out a ragged exhale and nodded, his shoulders slumping as if he were defeated, though he had just succeeded in killing one of the dragons who had committed treason against him.

Every part of me ached, but I pushed to my feet, grabbing hold of Martik's arm. I had seen the darkness that lived inside the King, and I wasn't about to tempt it to make an appearance again. I dragged him through the trees, away from any sign of battle, throwing one last look over my shoulder.

That was when I saw the empty, bloodied earth where Roldan should have been.

But he was gone.

CR

After a couple hours limping and crashing through the woods, we collapsed to our knees in a clearing of trees. Based on the distance of the mountains we were headed toward, I guessed we had traveled roughly five miles. We needed to keep moving—try to get to shelter or safety before Roldan found us, or worse, more of the Remnant.

"Come on, Martik, we need to move." I offered him a scaled arm and he hesitantly took it.

"I wanted him to die," the King whispered once he was on his feet. "I want them all to die. For what they did to Lita—to Tarrin." Tears swarmed his eyes.

"And they will," I responded with all the conviction I could muster. "Once we get to Tarrin and Kaida at Shegora, they will all die for their crimes."

He kept his eyes on the ground, his entire body slumped in defeat. A moment of silence passed before I saw Martik's body tense and his head snapped up, his snout twitching.

He smelled something. *Not again. There is no way Roldan found us already.*

And then the fight completely drained from the King's body. His shoulders drooped as he looked to his right. A small purple dragon stepped out from the foliage, just a youngling, and offered a tentative wave.

"Your Majesty?" he asked, his voice quiet and high pitched like a child.

And then King Martik grinned. *Grinned.*

I was confused.

"Phelix," Martik said, relief lacing his voice as he dropped to one knee and opened his arm. The purple dragon scurried forward and all but jumped into his waiting arms.

"Martik?" I asked, needing to know what was going on.

Several heartbeats passed before Phelix stepped back from the King and rose to his full height, which was still only half of ours.

"What are you doing here?" the King asked the youngling, placing a clawed hand on his shoulder.

"Father sent me. The Prince and his betrothed arrived a few days ago. They said you were headed our direction."

Phelix's eyes flickered to me, noting my tense body language and winced. "I didn't mean to frighten you."

"We were attacked a few miles ago," Martik explained. "Forgive us for being wary." He waved his claws in the air. "How is my son?"

The youngling's eyes grew bright. "Better now. He and the girl were attacked on their travels, and Tarrin was shot from the sky with iron arrows."

"Kaida? You mean Kaida?" I interjected, only understanding pieces of what the young dragon was saying.

"But Tarrin is all right?" The scales above Martik's eyes bunched in concern.

"Who attacked them?" I asked, raising my voice so they'd hear me. They didn't.

"Yes, he had a broken arm, but it's nearly healed. He hasn't been able to shift for a couple weeks, but I think he is close now." Phelix's eyes shone.

Martik nodded. "Good."

Martik and Phelix continued to speak, ignoring me completely.

"Martik," I snapped, scaring the birds in a nearby tree into flight.

Both dragons froze and turned toward me.

"Ah," Martik said at last, finally remembering that I was there. "Eldrin, this is Phelix. He lives in the village of Metta. He's the son of an old friend."

Phelix nodded in affirmation, his snout bobbing up and down.

"I've never heard of Metta."

Phelix's mouth split into a smile. "Oh, you'll love it Master Eldrin. Metta is a village of true peace."

I couldn't hold back the wince at being called *master*. "Never call me that, youngling." My voice was cold, but Phelix took it in stride.

"As you say." He returned his attention to the King.

"Father is eager for you to join him." He jumped in the air a couple of times, flapping his wings like an excited child. "Come on. If we hurry, we can reach the village by sunset tomorrow."

CHAPTER THIRTY-SIX

EKLOS

ROLDAN LIMPED INTO the dimly lit tent I set up in camp as my office, and smoke immediately started billowing from my nostrils. Blood was smeared over his scales, particularly across his chest, still seeping from an open wound beneath his arm. His red eyes were dull and unfocused, and he stumbled forward, as if he couldn't take another step, catching himself on the back of the wood chair next to him.

"Sit," I ordered, and the Councilman fell into the chair. His breathing was wheezy and rattling, as if there were blood in his lungs as well. "What happened?"

He opened his mouth to speak and started coughing. My teeth ground together, a harsh metallic ringing filling my ears.

"Barden and I found the King and Eldrin in the north." He let out another shuddering cough, spitting blood on the floor. If any other words had come out of his mouth, I would have killed him on the spot for staining the priceless rug beneath him. Fire filled my mouth as the magic in my core grew unbearable. "They were only days from the mountain that holds Shegora."

Embers danced on my tongue. They were getting too close. Though we had been on the move for days, we still were too far from the shifters to catch up. The army needed to hurry.

"Why isn't Barden with you?" I barked.

For the first time in all the long years I'd known the Councilman, I watched as tears lined his eyes.

"He's dead."

I felt my mouth drop open. "How?"

Roldan looked me square in the eye. "The King killed him."

Martik? That absurd excuse for a dragon? How in Elysia did he manage to best Barden?

"We had the element of surprise when we found them. We managed to herd them, cutting off any escape. I took on the shifter while Barden dealt with the King. We thought it would be quick and simple, especially given the fact that neither of them were in good shape."

I clicked my claws together, one by one. "So, you had the advantage, they were both hurt, and yet Barden was still murdered by that coward of a King and you're sitting here bleeding out on my rug?" My voice started soft, but I was growling by the end of my accusation.

Roldan cowered in the chair before wincing and pressed a hand against his wound. I let out an aggravated sigh. As much as I despised his presence, and his insane ability to fail me, I needed the Councilman alive. For now.

"We'll discuss this further after you've rested." I reached beneath my desk and grabbed a small bell, ringing it three times. Before a heartbeat had even passed, the small slave boy who had cleaned my own wounds appeared at the tent entrance. His entire body trembled as he kept his gaze firmly on the floor.

"Yes, Master?"

"See to Roldan's wounds. Make sure he doesn't die."

The boy nodded fervently before fetching clean towels and gesturing for Roldan to follow him. I didn't know where the boy planned to take him, nor did I care.

I grabbed a handful of maps from the desk and ruffled through them, looking for one that highlighted the northern region. Most of the land was forest, right up until the boundary of the mountains at the northern edge of Elysia. It had been a difficult journey north, especially for those who had no experience with the northern climate—how brutal the winter days and frigid nights were.

Our numbers were well in the hundreds by now. Flying straight there would have been the obvious choice, and I could hear the grumbling amongst the other dragons. They didn't understand why we continued to walk in the elements, when we simply could have flown. While they were technically correct, it wasn't the *best* choice. With winter on our doorstep, we would only be able to fly so far up the mountain until ice and the cold-encrusted air stopped us. Besides, I knew that if we marched instead, word would spread like a blazing wildfire through Elysia. And once word reached Kaida and my cousin, there would be no peace for them. They would live every second of their remaining lives in fear, looking over their shoulders to see if I was coming.

I took to the air, intending to land in the center of our camp. There were dragons huddled around campfires, fighting, and flying through the air, trying to warm their bodies. I landed with a crunch in the snow. They all froze as I rose to my full height.

"Dragons," I called, a growl reverberating in the back of my throat. They hurried over, bunching together as they stood to listen to me. "Victory is within our grasp." Though I half expected them to cheer and celebrate, it brought me immense satisfaction that they all remained deathly silent, and I could feel their determination doubling down like a livewire running between us all. Smoke leaked from their nostrils, filling the air with a haze. A wicked smile twisted my snout as I looked out over the army I had secretly built over the years. They were the shifters' and humans' undoing.

A laugh burbled up my throat, but I bit my tongue to keep it down as my smile spread wider. Based on Rythos's reports, the shifters were only a day ahead of us. That distance could be easily crossed if we hurried. For now, I would let fear do what it does best: sow anxiety, sow paranoia, and hasten poor decisions.

"The shape-shifters are close. We will remain here and let their fear build into a monster they see in every shadow."

At the confused looks of the dragons around me, I snarled. "Do not question me! If we pause our advance, they will wonder why. Their fear and paranoia will grow, and they will make hasty decisions that will only benefit us. Let their dreams be troubled as they think of this army on their doorstep." I paused, glancing at the dragons closest to me. They all curled in on themselves, desperate to escape my attention.

"Keep training, keep busy. Don't let the cold weaken you." I let out a barrage of flames at the bodies in front of me, and they scurried backward. "Now, get out of my sight!"

The army scattered. I stayed in place until every dragon had disappeared but one.

Roldan limped to my side. "What now, my lord?"

I bared my teeth and snarled. "Bring me Rythos. I have a job for him."

CHAPTER THIRTY-SEVEN

KAIDA

"HARDER!"

My dragon-sized fists slammed into Z's enormous, scaled palms over and over.

"You're not even trying. Harder," Z snapped, voice cold as his ice magic.

Sweat slid down from my temples, over my scales, dripping off my snout, as I fought to catch my breath.

"What do you mean… I'm not… trying?" I managed to get out between panting breaths.

Z's snout did that infuriating smirking thing that made me want to grind my teeth and punch him for real.

"There is a point to this training, little shifter."

"Last time I checked, I couldn't win in a fist fight against a dragon," I barked before gulping straight from a pitcher of water. I bit down on the magic surging through my veins from being in my dragon form.

"Perhaps not, but you can outlast one. This is building your endurance. If you rely on only your magic, you'll regret it."

Noam's words back in Myrewell about my magic being limited and the benefits of fighting with swords flitted through my mind.

"What about swords?"

Z's scaled eyebrows crawled up his forehead. "You can barely make an indent in my palms, and you want to pick up a piece of steel that probably weighs as much as your human form?"

My own eyes narrowed, scaled lips pursing at his haughty tone. "You know, I don't like you much."

Z barked out a laugh, his teeth flashing in the fading autumn sun.

"That matters not, little shifter, as long as you are able to out-maneuver Eklos.

"An entire mountain collapsing could not even best that snake. What makes you think I can fight him and win?" I asked, the thought of finally facing Eklos shooting ice shards through my blood.

"Because you must," Z said simply, raising his clawed hands once more, waving for me to begin again. "Through brawn or through brains, little shifter, you must."

❦

The sun had fully set by the time I finished training with Z and found Tarrin back at Gendon's home. He had just returned from a tour of Metta, led by none other than Gendon himself, who somehow had endless patience for all the incessant questions Tarrin pelted him with. His arm was almost fully healed which meant he should be able to shift in a matter of days.

Now, he sat in human form in an oversized armchair, book in hand, near a window in the upper level of the cave-home. It over-looked the entirety of Metta, which lined the base of the mountain as far as the eye could see. With the darkness of night, I could see the torches and lanterns in the distance, making it appear as though burning stars were carefully placed amongst the earth.

I plopped into the chair across from Tarrin with an *oomph*. After training so long in my dragon body, my human limbs felt both leaden and floppy.

"It went that well, huh?" Tarrin asked, eyes not leaving the pages of his book as he propped his scarred cheek on a hand.

"How could you tell?"

Tarrin's eyes finally met mine, a mischievous gleam flickering in them. "Just a hunch."

"Why aren't *you* training?" I asked, blowing the sweaty hair out of my eyes. I desperately needed to bathe.

"I spent most of my adolescent years training," he answered, flipping a page in the book on his lap.

"Magic, maybe, but not like this."

His eyebrow arched. "What makes you so sure? Besides, how do you know I'm not training when you're not looking? It wouldn't be fair if I constantly whooped your butt."

My cheeks grew warm. "I'm going to pretend you didn't say that," I spit out in a haughty voice. "I assumed if you knew how to fight without magic, you would be the one training me, not Z."

The corners of his lips twitched as though he were fighting a smile. "I don't think we would get much accomplished if I were the one training you." His eyelids lowered as he fixed me with a sultry gaze.

Heat swirled in my core. "Are you saying you are unable to touch me without pouncing on me like a wild animal?"

Tarrin grinned, the expression purely feline. "No, I am saying *you* would be doing the pouncing."

I grabbed the decorative pillow on the chair next to me and chucked it at his face. He caught it with ease and burst into a fit of laughter. The book he had been reading made a slapping noise as he closed it and stood in one fluid motion. Only a few feet separated our chairs, but it seemed to take endless seconds for him to arrive in front of me. Tarrin's one arm remained in a sling, but that did not stop him from kneeling before me and running a strong hand up my leg.

Desire clouded his eyes and my own breathing quickened.

"Shall we test that theory?" I breathed.

He arched an eyebrow. "I wholeheartedly support that idea."

I huffed out a laugh, and before I could lose my nerve, I grabbed hold of his hand, and led him down the meandering hallways until I found a familiar door.

Turning around, I leaned my back against it and Tarrin's body pressed up against mine. Inching up on my toes, my breath caressed his lips, but I held a sliver of distance between us. He ran his free hand up the bare skin of my arm, eliciting bumps and a heat that flared in my core.

I closed my eyes to make him think I was about to kiss him but lingered an inch away. "Touching me already, hmm?" I teased, my voice hitting a low octave. "You didn't make it very long. Seems I was right."

Tarrin froze as the words settled in him, then chuckled. "You play dirty."

My hand found the metal doorknob and twisted as I gave him a wicked grin. "You have no idea."

The door opened without a sound as I took hold of Tarrin's hand once more and led him into our suite of rooms. We shoved the red velvet couch and coffee table out of the way in the sitting area, before I removed my boots, and stood barefoot on the plush rug that filled most of the space with a red and blue intricate geometric design. I raised my fists in a ready position.

Tarrin's eyes widened. "You were serious?"

I simply smiled. "Time to back up that big mouth of yours."

Tarrin ran his free hand through his dark hair as he huffed out a laugh. He gestured to his arm. "If you haven't noticed, my arm isn't fully healed."

I bent my knees, inhaling a deep breath as both Noam and now Z taught had taught me. "Don't worry, I'll go easy on you."

My favorite half smile twisted his lips, and it set me off balance enough that when he lunged at me, I let out a yelp and tripped backward. Tarrin laughed and tried to catch me, but without both arms to center him, he fell right along with me.

We crashed to the ground in a tangle of limbs.

The air filled with the sound of our laughter. Tarrin ended up mostly on top of me, twisted slightly to prevent his arm from being injured further. The laughter faded as he skimmed his fingertips over my cheek, tucking my wild hair behind my ear.

I opened my mouth to speak, but Tarrin was faster.

"I don't care if you're not ready to say it back yet," he began. "I don't care if you never do. All I care about is right now. This." Tarrin gestured to us, the mere inches of space between us. "Being with you, always." He swallowed hard, pressing a soft kiss to my lips. "I love you, Kaida."

At that moment, a realization struck me that set my brain to spinning.

Perhaps love was less about it being a feeling and more about the choice to love, regardless of the vulnerable state it puts you in. Tarrin saw all of me: the fears, the insecurities, both the bravery and meekness, and yet he loved me in spite of it all. He *chose* to love me in spite of it all.

Maybe that was the secret I had been missing. I was so worried that I didn't truly love him because I had never experienced love before. I was scared that I was mistaking what I felt for something that wasn't love.

But did any of that matter if I *chose* to love him back?

Maybe the feeling of love, or the fears of not feeling it, mattered far less than choosing to love a person regardless of those feelings.

The epiphany swirled through my brain, lifting a burden I hadn't even realized I was carrying from my shoulders.

I placed my palm against his cheek, and he leaned into it, closing his eyes.

"I love you too, Tarrin."

And I did. The words had never felt truer than in that moment.

His eyelids snapped open, revealing wide eyes. As the words settled into him, his lips spread into a glowing smile. It was like seeing sunshine after months of dark clouds.

Tarrin's lips were soft like a cloud but hot as a forge as they pressed to mine, and I smiled against them. The brightest summer days, or the most beautiful flowers, or even the rare moments of happiness of the past months could not compare to this feeling.

This was where I was meant to be, who I was meant to be with.

Despite all odds, Tarrin had found me. He loved me. And I loved him.

Nothing that was to come would ever change that.

Nothing could take that feeling away from me.

CHAPTER THIRTY-EIGHT

KAIDA

THE SUN WAS high in the sky the next morning, though it did nothing to warm the chilly air at the base of the mountain. Clouds heavy with snow sat atop the mountains surrounding us, promising a storm soon in the future.

Tarrin studied the sky. "We'll probably want to head up to Shegora before that storm hits. We might not be able to get through if we wait until after."

I nodded as we made our way up to one of the rooftop balconies built into the side of the mountain above Gendon's house that served as our training space. "We can let Gendon know after training. I'm sure he'll send supplies with us that need to be prepared." Tarrin pulled me into his side, his lips brushing mine just as a voice called across the roof.

"Well, well. Look who finally decided to grace us with their presence," Z's voice rang out across the balcony as we arrived at the top of the stairs. My ears burned and I avoided his stare.

I felt something strange filter down our bond. It was deep and… protective? It flared bright as a flame as Tarrin shifted slightly in front of me.

Z laughed at the look on Tarrin's face. "Down, boy. She's not my type."

I blinked and Tarrin lunged for Z, shifting mid-air and crashing into him.

It had been two weeks since I had seen Tarrin in dragon form and I had nearly forgotten just how large he was, how strong. I think Z had forgotten too. For a moment, he allowed Tarrin to press him into the ground, pummeling at his snout and scratching at his scales. Z only continued to laugh.

I wasn't sure whether to be flattered by Tarrin's violent outburst or outraged. The old Kaida would have run as fast as she could to get away from the violent dragons, but after everything we had been through, cowering was no longer my first response.

With a sigh, I stepped forward. "Tarrin," I called. No answer. "Tarrin!" He continued his attack.

Then without warning, Z sliced at Tarrin's legs with a dagger made of ice, eliciting a pained growl before he flipped Tarrin onto his back.

"Z, stop!" I yelled.

"I'll stop as soon as this brat of a Prince apologizes." Z had Tarrin pinned down with all four of his limbs, reinforcing his hold with ice, both of their chests heaving.

A dangerous emotion flitted down our shifter bond. If I didn't get them calmed down, Tarrin would do something I knew he'd regret.

"Z, his wing. It's only just healed."

"Maybe he should have thought of that before he attacked me," Z snapped.

Without fully thinking it through, I grabbed a wooden training sword and stalked over to the dragon and gave his shoulder a mighty thwack. Z looked up at me, his snout dropping open.

"Did you really just smack me with a training sword?"

I let out a growl of my own. "I said enough. Get off him. We stand no chance against Eklos if we can't stop quarreling amongst ourselves." I smacked him once more with the sword for good measure.

He still didn't move.

A snarl ripped out of my throat, and I shifted into dragon form, relishing the warm heat of my scales against the frigid rooftop wind. I stooped down, grabbing Z's arm in one hand, and the top of his wing in the other.

"I said… get off him!" I yanked his body off Tarrin, spun on my heel, and released him, sending him sliding across the ground. When Z came to a stop, he gaped at me, his snout hanging open.

I crouched next to Tarrin. "You all right?"

He nodded, keeping his eyes on ground.

"Why did you do that?"

He winced, refusing to look at me.

"He did that because he's territorial now," Z teased as he rose to his feet. "It happens to young dragons." He winked at him.

Tarrin jumped to his feet, and I grabbed his arm to keep him from launching himself across the roof. "You're not helping, Z," I said over my shoulder.

"On the contrary, he needs to get it out his system or his emotions will become a liability in any fight with Eklos. You're going to be surrounded by a lot of males in the coming days. He can't fight every one of them. Might as well get it out now and get some good training in while we're at it." He switched his attention to Tarrin. "That was good work shifting in the air like that, but your attack itself could use some work."

Smoke billowed out of Tarrin's nostrils. "I don't need any help from you."

"Tarrin," I scolded.

Z laughed. "I think you do."

I rubbed at my temples and let out a sigh. "Z, can you give us a moment?"

With a chuckle and a roll of his eyes, he opened his wings and took off into the air, flying circles around Gendon's home.

"Insufferable prick," Tarrin muttered.

I blew out a breath. "Tarrin, what was that?"

With a pained inhale, he shrunk down, shifting back into human form. I followed him as we walked over to the bench on the right side of the balcony.

He took a seat, rubbing at his temple. "I don't know. I just… couldn't stand the way he looked at you."

"He wasn't looking at me any certain way."

Tarrin scoffed. "I beg to differ."

I grabbed his hand, lacing my fingers through his. "Was Z right?"

He ran a hand through his hair. "Yes… he was right. A declaration of love between dragons has the same level of bonding as, um…" His ears turned red as he cleared his throat and continued, "As sharing a bed." He gave me a sheepish smile. "Young male dragons can experience a heightened sense of… protectiveness because of it."

I rose my eyebrows, gaping at him. I had never heard such a thing about dragons. I supposed that I had never actually seen dragons in love. "I wasn't aware that was a thing."

Tarrin nodded. "Declarations of love between dragons are not exactly common since they desire power more than love—more than anything."

"Hmm," I hummed, at a loss for words. It made sense and though his attack on Z was stupid and foolish, the fact that he was suddenly overbearingly protective of me was somehow endearing. I leaned forward to kiss him.

Tarrin returned the kiss, pulling me tighter into his side before he leaned back, resting his forehead against mine.

"Z is right though, as much as I don't want to admit it. If we're raising an army of dragons, there are going to be a lot more males that we will have to deal with. I need to get a handle on this feeling before then."

I glanced at the clouds that hung thick and low over the mountains above us. "What about the storm?"

Tarrin looked up and studied them. "We would need to leave in the next couple of hours to beat it."

"Which I would advise against," Z interrupted as he landed in front of us with a crunch. "It would be better to wait out the storm, continue to prepare for the coming battle, than to chance getting caught in a snowstorm that you've no experience trying to survive in."

"No one asked you," Tarrin snapped.

Z's snout twisted into a smirk.

A surge of fire speared through our bond as Tarrin struggled to contain the fury boiling in his stomach at the sight of it.

"Still testy, I see."

Tarrin jumped to his feet, but I anticipated it this time and put myself between them, though Z towered above us. "That's enough." I blew out a frustrated breath. "Where is Eklos's army now? Are they still approaching?"

"My scout has informed me that their army has paused their movements for the time being. They remain roughly a day's walk away."

I turned my head to look toward the forest, wishing I could see past them to where the army waited. "Why would they stop?"

Z shrugged, not meeting my eyes. "There's a plethora of reasons why Eklos may have stopped them. I won't attempt to understand his mind. We've been granted at least another day to prepare in any case."

"I thought you knew everything about Eklos," Tarrin muttered, rolling his eyes.

Suppressing a groan, I glared at him. "You're not helping either. Go cool off, take a walk around Metta or something. I'll stay and train. I can fill you in later and we can practice."

Z winked. "Right, *practice.*"

I had to hold a hand against Tarrin's chest to keep him from charging. "Not. Helping," I bit out. I turned around and planted a light kiss on Tarrin's lips. "Go, it's all right." I tried to send as much reassurance through our bond as possible.

He studied my face, before glancing at Z. "Fine." Planting a peck on my forehead, he sauntered off, before disappearing down the staircase in the corner.

"Why do you put up with that brat?" Z asked. His eyes were narrowed as I turned to him, his snout scrunched like he smelled something rancid.

"He's only a brat around you," I snapped. "Why must you goad him like that?"

"I'm trying to get him to grow up before this war with Eklos begins. He's been spoiled and cooped up in that palace for his entire life, never having to deal with anything difficult. His attitude will get him killed, and I fear what that will mean for you."

Z's words ran true, at least partly, but I felt the need to defend Tarrin. "You don't know what you're talking about."

"Don't I? What do you think would have happened if you two had gone to Shegora today, found a company of male dragons ready to help you, and Tarrin lost it? Do you think they would have stayed to help after their prince attacked them? Or better yet, do you think they would have let Tarrin walk away alive? It's time to wake up, princess."

I took an automatic step back. "Don't call me that."

Z took a step toward me. "Why, princess? Isn't that what you are?"

As he took another step, my instincts kicked in and I shifted into dragon form. The fire in my core swirled and flared, my magic begging to be released. "No," I growled as he continued to back me into a corner.

"You're the Prince's betrothed. That makes you a princess, doesn't it? Spoiled, just like him, right?"

My vision went red as his words sank into me and I couldn't hold back the fury that had built in my bones. Adapting the human motion to my dragon body, I clenched my claws into a fist and swung my arm as hard as I could. It connected with Z's jaw with a satisfying crack. His head whipped backward, and he stumbled, barely catching himself on the side of the mountain. I swung my tail, crashing it into his stomach, sending him falling onto his back. I was on him in a moment, my claws circling his throat. I squeezed, harder and harder, lightning and flames circling my wrists, ready to join the fight.

Only, he wasn't fighting. Z was just lying there, letting me hurt him.

The thought was like cold water being dumped over my head and my magic sputtered out, my drive to hurt him shriveling like a flower in a drought. He coughed and gasped for air as I released him. I crawled to the side and tucked my wings in as I leaned against the cold rock of the mountain.

"Sorry," I muttered, though I knew he heard me.

"You're strong," Z gasped out between breaths.

I rolled my eyes. "You mean stubborn."

"No," he said with a firm voice. "You're strong. Very strong, especially for a young shifter. Don't let anyone tell you otherwise."

I wasn't sure what to do with his words, so I pushed to my feet, extending a hand to help him up. "Sorry about your face."

Z offered an apologetic smile as he grabbed my hand and pulled himself up. "Sorry about your Prince."

I scoffed. "No, you're not."

That smirk I hated made a reappearance. "You're right, I'm not."

I pushed on his shoulder, the reality of everything that just happened descending like the snowstorm about to hit. "Do you think we stand a chance?"

Z immediately sobered. "There's always a chance, Kaida."

I blew out a breath. "That's not what I mean." I slumped onto the bench, my enormous body taking up the full width of it. "I mean, do you think we can win against Eklos and his army? Is this all a waste of time?"

Z remained silent for several moments as I looked out at the village of Metta. Despite all odds, a city of peace had prospered with both humans and dragons. That had to prove that change was possible, right?

"I think," Z began as he crouched in front of me to look me in the eye, "you will drive yourself mad with those kinds of thoughts. No matter how dark things seem, there is always hope. Always a light. The reason I push you so hard, Kaida, isn't because I dislike you. It's because I see strength in you. I see a hope that Elysia can be made better. No one has fought for Elysia in a millennium. Perhaps it's time someone finally tried." The first hint of a true smile spread over his snout.

"But why me?" I asked at last.

Z searched my face before he stood and offered me a hand. "Because *you* are what Elysia needs." His eyes drifted to the ground. "I lost someone a long time ago, thanks to Xalerion's madness." He blew out a smoke-laced breath. "It all could have been prevented if I had stood up for what was right—if everyone had. I didn't do the right thing then, but I'm trying to now."

His eyes pierced into mine. "If you're willing to fight for this world full of hatred and destruction because you truly see something worth fighting for, then I will stand by your side, Kaida. Until my last breath."

CHAPTER THIRTY-NINE

TARRIN

THE SNOWSTORM LASTED for two whole days.

Needing to get away from Gendon's house—and Z—for a while, I wandered the streets of Metta in human form now that the snow had lifted.

As much as I hated to admit it, Z had been right. It would have been foolish for Kaida and me to leave before it hit. We likely would have only made it a quarter of the way before the icy snowflakes would have stopped us in our tracks. Even at the base of the mountain, in Metta, the winds were wicked, whipping the snow around like frozen daggers. It was hard enough to make our way through the village streets, let alone climb a mountain.

Thankfully, Eklos's army remained camped exactly where they were. They had made no attempt to advance or attack, and it had all of us on edge. None of us could figure out what his motive was for waiting.

After being stuck inside for the past two days, and having to put up with Z's irritating countenance, I was beginning to feel restless. There was still no sign of my father, mother, or Eldrin. I knew they would arrive well behind us, but they should have been here by now. I had hoped they would be able to make the journey up to Shegora with us.

The residents of Metta were in cleanup mode, using brooms and shovels to clear the deep snow from the streets and storefronts. The temperature was mild, though still cold enough to keep the snow from melting into puddles.

Everywhere I looked were signs of both human and dragon life, coexisting in peace as if that was the normal way of Elysia. Small little huts were packed together next to large, dragon-sized homes. Humans and dragons chatted on their front lawns while cleaning up the mess from the storms, others helped pile snow into big drifts for the children and younglings to slide down.

I had never seen anything like it. Who knew that there was a place in Elysia where such a thing was possible? That despite dragons like Eklos and his followers, a place like Metta could not only exist, but thrive?

If I wasn't convinced before, I certainly was now. Kaida was right. A better way existed—a better world was possible. I blew out a breath, watching as a small boy bent to pick up a handful of snow, rolled it into a ball in his hands, and chucked it at the snout of a small dragon next door. My first instinct was to run and protect the child, expecting the dragon to hurt him. But the youngling simply laughed and mimicked the boy, pelting him with a snowball of his own.

I scratched at my scarred cheek. As I passed by, both of them stopped to stare at me. The young dragon bowed his head, somehow recognizing me in human form. I watched for the boy's reaction, expecting for him to cower perhaps, or his eyes to alight with fear like the slaves in Vernista, but they remained bright, and he waved at me.

I offered a weak wave back and continued down the road, my mind spinning. Tugging at my cloak to block my neck from the frigid wind, I had just turned a corner when Z landed in front of me. I couldn't hold back my scoff.

"What do you want?" I kept walking as if he never arrived.

"Is that any way to talk to the dragon who saved your life?"

I fought the urge to roll my eyes. "Why are you here, Z?" I'm sure he wanted me to have more of a reaction, but I wasn't about to give him that satisfaction.

He gave a derisive snort. "Gendon's son, Phelix, just arrived in Metta. With your father and Master Eldrin."

Every muscle in my body relaxed, melting like ice falling into hot water. *Finally.*

"Kaida asked me to come find you. She is tending to them. They were attacked a couple days ago before Phelix found them."

"But they're all right?" I asked, my stomach clenching.

Z hesitated long enough to set my nerves on edge. "They're alive."

My eyes narrowed. "What kind of an answer is that?"

"An honest one. You'll see."

With a scowl, I turned on my heel to go back. My arm was finally healed, thanks to my accelerated dragon healing, but I didn't want to strain the unused muscles in my wings by trying to fly quite yet. I inhaled, preparing to run when Z cleared his throat.

"There's something else."

I glanced over my shoulder, barely holding back an impatient growl. "What is it?"

"Gendon received a written message early this morning. The messenger was nearly dead by the time he delivered it."

My brows furrowed. "Why do I need to know this?"

For the first time, something that resembled remorse flickered in his eyes and he glanced at the ground, rubbing at his neck. He blew out a breath before meeting my gaze.

"The message is from Lita."

My body turned to ice as if I had thrown it into the snowbanks around me. Without a second glance, I shifted into dragon form. My wings ached as they stretched from my back for the first time in weeks. They wouldn't sustain me in the air quite yet, but

I could use their momentum to get to Gendon's home quicker. In an awkward series of running and flapping, I landed with a crunch in the snow outside the cave-home before shifting and hurrying inside into the foyer. Z entered mere moments after me, situating himself against the far wall, his eyes studying my every movement.

There was a small table tucked into the corner. A vase of snow-flowers, tall stems with little white buds that looked like snowflakes and only bloomed in the winter, was perched on one end, and a hastily scrawled note, riddled with wrinkles and creases, rested on the other. My hands shook as I picked it up.

Dearest Tarrin,

I will not be coming to Shegora. My efforts are better spent in Vernista, trying to infiltrate Eklos's spy network, and taking them down from the inside. I hope you understand, Son. You and Kaida must win against him, and you don't need me there to do it. I know you will be victorious. You and Kaida are strong apart, but together you're unstoppable.

Remember, whether skin or scales, it matters not. Only the heart. A better world starts in each of us.

All my love,

Your mother

I bit down hard on my tongue to maintain a neutral expression as I read and reread her message, memorizing every word. My knees grew weak, my legs wobbling beneath me, but I wouldn't let Z see me fall apart. I would give him nothing to use against me, not even the heartbreak of my mother choosing to stay away.

I flipped the parchment over, examining it for any words I may have missed—anything that might make sense of her decision to stay away from Shegora. There was nothing. Tiny blood and ink smears, and plenty of crinkles creased through it as though it had changed hands many times, but there were no other words. A deep ache of betrayal sat low in my gut. How could she think that was more important than our efforts here? I couldn't imagine one person being able to take down Eklos from the inside, even if it was her.

Warm arms smelling of lavender and cedar wrapped around my waist. Heat pulsed from Kaida's body as she leaned against me, my arms moving around her of their own accord.

"Tarrin?"

I couldn't meet her eyes. The realization of what her note meant was like a bitter tonic sliding down my throat, burning in my stomach. I shook my head.

"What is it?"

Opening my fist, Kaida hesitated a moment before she took the crumpled paper from my palm and carefully smoothed it out. Her body stiffened as she read, winding tighter and tighter until at last she let the parchment flutter to the floor. She blew out a breath before wrapping her arms around me once more.

"I'm sorry."

I swallowed down the lump in my throat, vaguely aware of Z leaving the room. I needed to keep moving, to go see what state my father and Eldrin were in, to help prepare for our journey up to Shegora. I couldn't afford to break—I didn't have the time.

But I didn't do any of it. Instead, I let Kaida hold me while my mind swirled in thoughts that threatened to drown me. Discovering my mother was alive after all these months was like a lightning jolt to my heart, infusing life in all the places that had died alongside her. My eyes burned and I squeezed them tight, gripping the hot, writhing anger in my core as if it were my only lifeline.

Because deep down I knew that if my mother was trying to get inside of Eklos's circle, if she could manage it at all, she wouldn't be coming out.

And I would have to lose her all over again.

◌

"They're doing better now, thanks to Gendon's healers," Kaida said as we walked down a hallway toward the infirmary, the chill of winter nipping at the edges of the windowpanes as night fell over Metta.

"What happened?" I asked, voice hoarse.

Kaida shook her head. "They wanted to wait until you were around to explain." She led me around two more corners before stopping in front of a black wooden door. Turning the knob, she pushed it open and led me inside. The room was unusually humid, the damp air sticking to my human skin. The torches were heavy with the moisture, casting shadows over most of the room. I could faintly make out two enormous beds on opposite walls, Eldrin's dark form in one, and my father's bright blue in the other. His chest rose in a steady rhythm, and it wasn't until that moment that I realized how worried I had been that my father wouldn't make it here. Splitting up back at the cottage had been the last thing I wanted to do, and the decision had haunted me the entire journey north.

I settled into the chair next to my father's bed, not wanting to wake him up. Kaida did the same next to Eldrin. He was sprawled on his side, his wings draped behind him, hanging toward the ground. The bed was dragon sized, but definitely not sized for a dragon as large as the King. Though the lighting was dim, I could make out the deep gashes and missing scales on parts of his body, other areas showing signs of magic burns.

As if he sensed my presence, his eyes peeled open, narrowing as they tried to see through the darkness.

"Tarrin?" my father rasped.

"I'm here," I replied, reaching out to touch his scaled hand. Normally a dragon's scales were cool to the touch—that was how their bodies regulated the heat from their internal fire, but my father's scales were scalding, and I yanked my hand to my chest.

"He was sick with fever when he arrived," Kaida whispered into my ear. "His wounds were infected which caused the fever. The healers were able to rid his body of the infection, so now we wait for the fever to break." She rested a hand on my shoulder, and I couldn't help but remember only a few months ago when she was chained to a stone in Belharnt. Infection and fever had nearly devoured her body by the time I had found her. Between that and the bluestone Eklos has chained her in, if it weren't for that Ancient Magic awakening in her, she would have been dead.

I shook my head, sending the memories away. "What happened, Father?"

His eyes flickered open and closed as if sleep were trying to drag him under again.

A voice spoke up from the other side of the room. "We were attacked not two days from here. Members of your father's Council." I glanced at Eldrin and found him sitting up in his bed, his amethyst eyes glowing in the torch light.

"Roldan and… B-Barden," my father stuttered out before going still once more.

I glanced at Eldrin. "How did they find you?" I expected Eklos to send mercenaries after us all, but I didn't expect him to send members of the Council itself.

"I'm still not sure. We covered our tracks well, and I moved us place to place as I was able. There should have been no trail for them to follow."

Kaida settled on the arm of my chair. "What happened when they found you?"

"They appeared out of the trees like demons. Martik managed to kill Barden, but Roldan escaped. We lost any trace of him after a few yards. He just *vanished*."

Kaida's brow furrowed. "Does he have magic like yours?"

Eldrin shook his snout. "I've never met another with my abilities."

Kaida wrung her hands together and I could see her brain trying to make sense of it.

"Eklos must have some tricks hidden beneath his scales if he can move dragons in a second, without a trace. If he can do that with him, could he do that with an army?" Her voice rose in pitch as she spoke, showcasing her fear.

I pulled her into my lap, feeling the need to comfort her. I ran my fingers through her hair and down the length of her spine. I was vaguely aware of Eldrin's eyes watching my every movement, but I paid him no heed.

"There's really no telling what he's capable of anymore. He finds ways to surprise us at every turn," Eldrin answered, studying the two of us. "I sense we're missing something vital, but I cannot for the life of me figure out what it might be. Were you able to gather any supporters?"

Kaida's lips flattened into a thin line. "Some."

Her father was quiet for a moment before his voice broke the silence like a clap of thunder. "But not enough." It was part question and part statement.

My arms tightened around Kaida as her eyes dropped to the floor.

"We have Z's rebels, and Gendon has promised the support of Metta," I chimed in, wanting to ease the defeat and failure I could feel through our bond.

Eldrin only nodded.

"More may come," I offered, remembering the villages we passed through before arriving here. Perhaps some would change their mind and we'd find them in Shegora when we arrived. I inhaled the humid air of the healing room, still running my fingers down Kaida's back.

"For all our sakes, I hope you're right, Prince," Eldrin's voice trickled across the room as if he, too, were fighting a losing battle with sleep. He winced as he slid down into the bed, draping his wings over the edge in the perfect mirror to my father.

Kaida curled into me, nestling her head beneath my chin.

"It'll be enough," I tried to reassure everyone. We couldn't see ourselves as already defeated. We had to cling to hope, no matter what.

The dragons and humans of Metta, and whoever else showed up, would be enough.

They had to be.

CHAPTER FORTY

KAIDA

IT TOOK ANOTHER day for the King's fever to break and for both him and Eldrin to be able to get out of bed. Thankfully, their dragon genes helped them to heal quickly, but every minute, every hour that passed felt like a lit fuse traveling down a wire to an explosive. With Eklos's army sitting on our doorstep—not moving—it pricked on all of our nerves like tiny needles shoved into our skin. None of us could understand why he hadn't attacked yet.

I watched from the rooftop balcony that Z used to train me while Eldrin and Martik flew through the sky. It was the first time either of them had been able to use their wings in weeks. A shiver shuddered over my body as a particularly cold gust of wind sliced through the air. Each day that passed brought us closer and closer to the Winter Solstice when the coldest weather would descend over Elysia.

Tarrin and I had no experience with winter conditions since it never got cold enough for snow to stick back in Vernista. Though Gendon had supplied us with everything we could possibly need, from thick fur coats, gloves, and wool socks to extra rations of foods in case any spoiled, I couldn't help but feel as though we were about to make a mistake leaving Metta.

Part of me wanted to wait before traveling up the mountain.

I wanted more time to train, to meet the people in Metta, both dragon and human, that were going to risk their lives to help us defeat Eklos's army. But staying wasn't an option. Eklos would only halt his attack for so long. I blew out a breath, a burst of cloudy air pooling in front of me as I grabbed the wooden railing of the balcony.

"Flower for your thoughts?" a voice said next to me, and a beautiful purple flower that appeared to be a combination of a tulip and a lily hovered in front my face. A startled laugh bubbled out of me before a warm set of lips pressed into my cheek. I turned to find Tarrin and took the flower from him as he wrapped me in his arms.

"I could feel your emotions from across Metta," he said.

Tarrin had gone with Gendon into the village to talk with some of the other villagers about strategies and plans for defeating Eklos. I knew nothing about such things, so I stayed behind in the cave-house. In hindsight, that was probably a poor decision since I had nothing to do, and my mind decided to run rampant instead of resting as it should have been.

I huffed out a breath. "Sorry."

Tarrin's arms squeezed tighter. "You have nothing to be sorry for. Do you want to talk about it?"

I couldn't help the small smile that spread across my lips. That was one of the things I loved most about Tarrin. He never forced me to do anything or tell him anything. He always let it be my choice. After growing up as a slave, it was something I wasn't sure I would ever get used to.

"It's cold here," I said after a few more seconds of silence. The wind whipped my hair into my face and Tarrin gently smoothed it out of my eyes.

He chuckled softly. "It is."

"It doesn't get like this back home." I picked up a handful of snow that was piled on the railing, presenting it to him.

Tarrin pulled back to look at me. "What is it, Kaida?"

For some reason, I couldn't meet his eyes and instead stared at his chest, at the top button he left open that revealed the tanned and muscled skin beneath the shirt.

"What if trying to travel in winter is a mistake?" I asked, voice hardly more than a whisper.

Tarrin's brow bunched together. "Gendon has everything prepared for us."

"No, I know..." I trailed off, taking a breath. "I just... feel like something isn't right. Like we shouldn't try to travel now. Not only do neither of us have experience trying to navigate in frigid cold and snow, but I can't escape the feeling that we're missing something, or that we shouldn't leave Metta."

He was thoughtful for a moment, the wind snapping his hair around. "If we were to stay here, we would bring down Eklos's wrath and destruction upon Metta. The children and elderly who want no part in this war would be at risk."

"I know," I said, pulling out of his arms. "It's not fair of me to even suggest. I would never want to put these people in danger." A thought occurred to me then. "Do you really think Eklos will leave Metta alone when they pass by on the way up the mountain?"

"Gendon has protective measures in place to keep him from detecting the village. If we stay here, we put that in jeopardy."

I turned my back to Tarrin, unwilling to let him see the tears filling my eyes.

"Kaida," his voice was heartbreakingly soft. "Eklos will not wait for winter to pass. He won't care if he loses numbers to the elements. He's hellbent on destroying us, and no amount of cold or snow will stop that."

"I know." My lips moved but no sound came out.

He turned me around, wiping his thumbs across my cheeks. "What is it, my love? What's really bothering you?"

I choked down on a sob, swallowing the hard lump in my throat.

I wasn't sure how to put my fears, my hesitations, and my inner warnings into words, so instead of trying to explain, I settled for, "I'm terrified."

Tarrin tucked my head beneath his chin, squeezing my body tight as if he could force reassurance into my bones. He was quiet for several minutes while he held me, which surprised me. I expected him to present me with evidence of why I was being silly, how prepared we were, and that we would defeat Eklos in the end. But instead, he stayed silent, never releasing his grip.

At long last, he replied, "Me too."

My eyebrows shot up my forehead. He was always trying to be brave, trying to be strong for me. I appreciated his constant attempts to keep me calm, but I appreciated this honesty even more.

I inched my arms out from between our bodies and wrapped them around his waist. I had no words to say but I knew Tarrin could feel everything I wasn't saying out loud through our bond. His body fended off the cold wind as we stood there for countless minutes.

I noticed the thickening clouds, as if another bout of snow were on the way when suddenly the balcony trembled and made a cracking noise as something enormous landed behind us. Tarrin and I swung in the direction of the noise, automatically shifting into dragon form in defense.

Eldrin and the King stood panting in the middle of the balcony, leaning on each other as if they had no strength left to stand. I could feel some sort of alarm down the shifter bond with my father.

Tarrin took a step forward. "What's wrong?"

Eldrin wheezed as he fought to catch his breath, Martik doubled over as if he were about to vomit.

"Eklos," Martik ground out.

Eldrin panted next to him. "He's coming. The army is moving."

No. It can't be.

My stomach twisted and churned into a tight knot, my limbs trembling. After having his army camped in the distance for days, part of me had begun to hope that they would never attack. Dread spread through my veins like an icy poison. Needing to be out of my dragon body, unable to handle the intensity of the emotions surging through me, I shifted back into human form.

"How many?" Tarrin asked, breaking through my spinning thoughts.

It was Martik who answered this time. "Too many. As far as our dragon eyes could see."

Even though our bond was muted now, I could feel Tarrin's terror slice through him like a knife. He turned to look at me before shifting into human form himself.

Now what? he asked into my mind.

I shook my head. *Despite my reservations, we must get to Shegora. We cannot risk Metta.*

The temperature was plummeting by the minute, thick heavy snowflakes beginning to tumble down from the sky. I looked up just as one landed on my nose, melting instantly from the heat of my body.

I summoned a small flame in my palm, the most I could muster in my human body. I held it up and watched as it sent steam spiraling into the air as it melted each snowflake it came into contact with. Tarrin watched my every movement and I fought to tune out his emotions and tried to settle my own.

There was one question I was dreading asking. One question I needed the answer to but didn't want to hear; the answer would determine everything. It determined when we left Metta, how much more training I had to squeeze in, how much longer I had with Tarrin before there was a chance we could be separated forever. I swallowed hard and took a breath.

"How long until they get here?"

At first, no one answered. I looked at Martik, who was sitting on the ground, his scales a paler blue than normal. Then I looked at my father, noting the devastation flickering in his eyes.

"How long?" I repeated. The scales on his throat bobbed as he swallowed. I held my breath as he opened his mouth to answer.

"They'll be here by nightfall."

CHAPTER FORTY-ONE

ELDRIN

I HAVE KNOWN FEAR before.

Fear every time I had to escape from my cousin in the past.

Fear like when I discovered I had a daughter, whom my cousin was hellbent on killing.

Fear like when I found my daughter in Belharnt, moments from breathing her last breath.

But I have never known fear such as what I felt when I beheld Eklos's army on the march toward Shegora.

I never should have let Roldan escape. I should have hunted him down like the beast that he was and killed him. He never could have reported our whereabouts if I had. I knew Eklos would have figured out where we were eventually—he always did. He knew my past, knew of my connection to the small mountaintop village. It was only a matter of time.

The sheer number of dragons was impressive. It stretched like a black cloud over the ground as far as the eye could see. The most eerie part of seeing my cousin's army of dragons was the fact that they were *marching*. They could have flown and killed us all in a moment. It would have been much simpler and easier. But I knew why they marched instead. It was to unsettle us. Eklos wanted to toy with us, build up our sense of dread and fear. He wanted to draw out the slaughter as long as possible, and it started with building the anticipation of an army marching toward us.

I exhaled and a puff of white billowed in front of my face. I stood in front of the open window in my chambers that Gendon was gracious enough to grant to both Martik and me. I had hoped that the chill air would be enough to numb some of my fear, but to no avail. Martik was down in the healing room, still being tended to for his various wounds that were taking much longer than usual to heal.

Dragons usually healed fast, much quicker than any human. That is, unless they've been poisoned, or were hurt by iron weapons. Even so, Martik should have been healed by now. Outside of some general soreness from not being able to fly for weeks, all my wounds were healed. He should have been right along with me.

Though perhaps his wounds were more emotional than physical, and it was leaking over into his physical body. I couldn't imagine the agony of losing his wife and partner in life, being tortured in a dungeon afterward, only to find out she was actually alive, but was no longer a dragon. And now that Tarrin had received that letter from her, Martik seemed to share the same fear as his son: Lita would not be walking out of Eklos's circle alive.

With a sigh, I snapped the window shut and went back to gathering the meager belongings I had brought to Metta. After the news came about the army, we all decided we would head up the mountain within two hours. Kaida, Tarrin, Martik and I would travel together to Shegora, and Gendon and Z would join us on the mountaintop in time for battle.

Thick, dark clouds sat low over the mountain promising snow, and we all knew that it was going to be a difficult trek up the mountain. Winter this far north in Elysia was brutal, snowstorms popping up at random, sometimes lasting for days. The passes we needed to go through to make it up to Shegora would be full of snow, if not completely blocked. But we were out of time. Eklos was coming, army in tow, and we had to be ready and well away from Metta. It was unfortunate the icy air was so thin up there, otherwise we all could have just flown, but there was not enough air for our wings to hold to and stay aloft.

I rolled my bedroll into a tight bundle and stuffed it into a sack. My only other belongings were a small book that was the perfect size for traveling and a locket I kept hidden beneath my clothes that held the last written note Aela had ever given me.

I blew out a breath, darkness enveloping me for brief moment as I shifted into human form. It was always easier to deal with reading her note for the umpteenth time when I was in skin rather than scales. The slip of parchment was yellowed and crinkled from the number of times I had folded and unfolded it over the years. The words were barely discernible anymore, and I fought the fear of the day when it would no longer be legible.

Though it didn't matter much. I had every word, every letter memorized as if it were inscribed upon my heart.

My beloved Eldrin,

*You are my treasure and my greatest love. Your love is a gift
I've never deserved but I will always be eternally grateful that
I found. I am better for knowing you, stronger because of
your unconditional love. No one would have ever expected a
human and a dragon to fall in love, but even the storms of this
world could not have kept us apart. Though I won't be in this
world forever, I cherish every moment we have. I love you, my
midnight darling.*

Forever Yours,

Aela

A tear slipped from the corner of my eye, but I ignored it as it slid down my cheek and hit the stone floor with a soft *plunk*. Missing Aela was a deep ache in my gut that never healed—never went away. A ragged sigh slipped through my lips just as a tentative knock sounded at the door.

"Eldrin?"

I hurriedly folded the paper back into its tiny square and hid it within my palm, swiping at my cheek before turning around. Kaida stood in the doorway, dressed in warm traveling clothes. A thick fur coat nearly swallowed her small frame, covering all the way down to her knees. A pair of black sheepskin lined boots adorned her feet, lacing up just beneath her knees. Her brown hair, so similar to Aela's, was tied behind her head.

"We're ready," she declared.

"I'll be right there," I said, popping the parchment back into the locket and tucking it under my shirt. Swinging the sack onto my shoulder, I picked up the wool coat that Gendon had supplied to me. Though it would be warmer to travel dressed in scales, there were some areas of the mountain where we'd need our smaller bodies to get through.

Before I crossed the threshold, I glanced back at the room—at the normalcy of having beds, a wardrobe of clothes, and a solid roof over my head. It might be the last time I ever had such luxuries if things with Eklos went poorly. I didn't know what state Shegora would be in when we arrived, but I wasn't too hopeful for accommodations as nice as the ones that Gendon had supplied.

"You coming?" Kaida called from the end of the hallway, halting my thoughts.

My eyes swept over the room one last time before I said, "Yes, I'm coming," and shut the door with trembling fingers.

ᛟ

"Well, aren't you all a lively bunch," Z said as he walked through the front door, brushing snowflakes from his scales.

The four of us stood in the entry to Gendon's home, wrapped in fur coats and cloaks, save for Martik who towered over us all in scales. Kaida's face had the same dread that was seeping through my veins like poison written all over her face. Tarrin's eyes flickered, though I could tell he was trying to be brave for her. My own shoulders were set in determination, though it was a struggle to keep my face neutral and not show every emotion like my daughter was. Martik, on the other hand, stood there, bedroll hanging from his claws, with a look of concentration on his face.

"Where is it?" the King muttered under his breath. "It's been buried too long…"

"Did you say something?" I asked him. The words were so quiet that I wondered for a moment if I had imagined it.

Martik snorted, embers shooting from his nostrils, and his eyes widened in alarm as if he said something he shouldn't have, but just as quickly as it appeared, his face smoothed out and his shoulders relaxed. "No, I didn't," he replied, turning his attention back to the others.

Through narrowed eyes, I watched him closely. Ever since we left the cottage, he had been acting strange. What was he hiding? I opened my mouth to question him further, but Z's voice boomed through the room.

"You're about to take on the foulest dragon in all of Elysia. You could show a little more excitement," Z quipped, looking at Kaida.

I felt Tarrin's hackles rise through the shifter bond the three of us shared.

"Why don't you face him and then see if you're still just as excited," he snapped.

"I'm just saying," Z continued, throwing his claws into the air, "you're being given the opportunity to finally kill the dragon responsible for the mistreatment and slaughter of slaves, and you're acting as though it's an enormous burden."

While I could see Z's point, he had a habit of coming across callous and harsh. I knew it rubbed Tarrin the wrong way.

"It *is* a burden when the world is counting on us to succeed— when we all have so much to lose," Tarrin bit out.

"Consider it a gift. A noble sacrifice."

Tarrin rolled his eyes and gestured to the door. "Then by all means, Z, if you have nothing to live for, then sacrifice away."

Z's eyes narrowed. "You don't know a thing about me."

"Yes, and who's fault is that?" Tarrin snapped.

"All right, enough," Kaida declared. "For the hundredth time, we will never defeat Eklos if we can't stop fighting with each other. This is bigger than any of us." She put herself between both males and pushed on Tarrin to leave Gendon's house. "We'll see you soon, Z."

The dark-blue dragon gave a nod. "Gendon and I will arrive with the others in time to face Eklos."

"You better be," she said before turning her back on him and heading down the street, arm in arm with Tarrin.

Z smirked and gave a stiff nod to the King and me before heading into the village.

Tension sat heavy in the air as, one by one, we walked in a line down the narrow path out of the village. The snow had been cleared so we could walk without hindrance, though the air nipped at my skin. This would be a brutal climb to say the least.

When we had walked about two miles, we reached the pass that would officially take us out of Metta, likely for the last time, and we all paused to look back. The flickering torches and sounds of children playing in the snow filtered up to us. None of us said a word as we silently said goodbye. Within the span of a blink, it all vanished. Every sound, every light, every home. Gone.

I heard Kaida's sudden intake of breath. "How?"

I offered her a sad smile. "Gendon is a Shielder. He has the ability to shield people or specific areas. The magic doesn't last forever, which is why he has scouts throughout the forest to give him ample warning to extend his shield over Metta. That's how he has been able to keep the village beneath Eklos's nose for so many years. He should be able to hold it long enough for my cousin to pass by unaware."

Tarrin studied the area where the village sat moments before, as if trying to understand the magic.

I put one scaled hand on his shoulder, squeezing in reassurance. "Elysia is full of wild and incredible magic, young prince. There is much you haven't seen yet." With a deep breath I turned my back on Metta for the last time. "Come," I said to my daughter, her betrothed, and the King. "Let us defeat Eklos so that you all may have the chance to truly see the beauty of Elysia that has remained hidden all this time."

CHAPTER FORTY-TWO

KAIDA

I F I COULD have murdered the cold, I would have done it in a heartbeat.

It seeped into my bones like the bluestone that had drained my life in Belharnt. It was unforgiving, brutal, and unrelenting. No matter how many pairs of socks I layered on my feet, or the thick, fleece-lined gloves that adorned my hands, I couldn't get warm. My toes had gone numb hours ago, my fingers stiff and throbbing. If it weren't for the need to be in smaller bodies to fit through some of the passes on the mountain, we would all be in dragon form. I glanced at Martik, wondering how Eldrin planned to fit him through the tight spaces.

Tarrin trudged along beside me, and my father and the King were several paces ahead of us. We made it an hour into the journey before the snow started to fall. It was a light, gentle flurry at first, but it had quickly grown into a blustery storm. Though I had never wished for it before, I found myself yearning for Vernista. For the warmth and humidity that was a different type of torture than the cold.

"How l-long are w-we going to t-travel in this?" I stuttered out through chattering teeth. My voice was barely audible over the wind, but Eldrin halted in his steps and turned halfway back to us.

"We're almost to the first campsite," my father yelled through the blowing snow. "We'll stop there for the night and continue in the morning."

Relief flooded my bones, giving me a sudden burst of energy that I hastened my steps. *Find camp. Find camp.*

"How many campsites are there?" Tarrin shouted over the gale of the storm.

Eldrin stopped again to face us. "Three. Once we get past the first one, the road becomes much more difficult. There will be more climbing and less walking. It'll be even harder on the army. That is, if they can even make it up the mountain."

"They will," Martik whispered, though it drifted like the wind past our ears. He hadn't said much since we left Metta, and I could feel Tarrin's concern for his father growing stronger through our bond. According to him, it was unusual for the King to be so quiet and reserved, and I had caught Eldrin studying Martik more than once, as if he, too, knew something was wrong. Part of me wondered if killing Barden had severed something vital within him, or if the thought of losing Lita again had forced him to withdraw further into his mind.

"We don't know what tools Eklos has at his disposal. It would take weeks for an army of that size to scale the mountain up to Shegora, but if I know my cousin, it won't be much longer after we arrive that they show their ugly snouts." Eldrin rubbed at his neck before turning back toward the path and continuing on.

I know the first thing I want to do when we make camp, Tarrin's voice drifted down the bond into my mind.

I looked sidelong at him. *What's that?*

Well, considering I can hear your bones shaking from here, I think the first order of business is to warm you up. Tarrin turned his head to wink at me.

Despite the cold, my cheeks grew hot, and I concentrated

on where my footsteps were landing in the snow. *And how do you propose we do that?*

Tarrin grinned. *Well, first I'll—*

"Hide!" Eldrin's voice speared through the air, whipping our attention forward. His eyes were narrowed, focused on something in the sky. Glancing over my shoulder, there was a winged shape in the distance barely visible amongst the white whipped wind.

One of Eklos's spies? I asked Tarrin.

Let's not find out. He grabbed my hand, and we stiffly ran as fast as our frozen limbs would carry us toward a cluster of boulders near the cliff face. Mercifully, there was a small overhang that offered a reprieve from the wind as we burrowed as deep and low as we could. I wasn't sure where my father and Martik were hiding—we had lost track of them in our haste to find shelter.

A roar split the air directly above us and I instinctively curled into Tarrin's side. The deep groan of muscled wings thudding in the air hammered into my skull. The dragon could have been miles away or right above us; my body knew no difference. Every part of me was shaking, and not just from the cold.

Another roar, closer and louder than the last ricocheted against the cliff above us. I counted the seconds until the sound stopped echoing back to us. When I had finally counted to ten, everything was still. Silent.

Is he gone?

Tarrin let out a shuddering breath. *I think so.*

If he knew we were here, why would he leave us alone?

It was a warning. Eklos wants us to know he's coming. Eldrin's voice filtered down the bond connecting the three of us. *Wait a few minutes longer and then continue up the path. We'll wait here to make sure no one is following you.*

Tarrin nodded at the silent words. For several tense minutes we hunched together against the cliff side, trying to ignore the biting cold of the stone that seeped into the thick fabric of our coats. The overhang provided blessed relief from the whipping wind and snow, and exhaustion reared its ugly head throughout my body. We hadn't eaten since we left Metta, and even with my training with Z, the physical exertion was beyond anything I was prepared for.

After a few minutes, Tarrin grabbed my hand. He pulled me out of our hiding spot, studying the sky for any sign of the dragon before we all but ran up the narrow path, our steps clumsy as we crashed through the snow, squeezing through a tight pass. When we made it to the other side, and I saw what awaited us, my stomach sank to my feet.

The snowy path forked into three different directions. One went to the left, into a copse of trees that seemed to lead back down the mountain. The one on the right led into another grouping of trees but appeared to go nowhere beyond it. The third path, which I knew in my bones was the one we were supposed to follow, led to a cliff face so sheer and steep that my brain couldn't reason how anyone was supposed to climb it.

My arms weighed a hundred pounds, each of my legs easily double that as I stumbled forward after Tarrin. He walked to the wall of rock, rubbing at his chin.

"There are not many handholds or footfalls to grab onto. It'll be a rough climb."

I blew out a frustrated breath. "I can't make that climb, Tarrin."

"No one can," Eldrin said from behind us, making both Tarrin and I flinch. His midnight-blue scales steamed as snow landed on them and instantly melted from the heat of his body. Martik stood behind him, somehow managing to squeeze through the crevice, his eyes on the cliff.

"What do you mean? We have to go *up* to Shegora, don't we?"

"There's a reason why it was a village for shifters," he said as he arrived at my side. "We have to use our wings."

Tarrin's brows bunched together on his forehead. "I thought you said we can't fly there because the air is too thin."

Eldrin nodded. "It's not technically flying. There are many walls of rock like this one that are impassable unless you have wings. It's more like using their momentum to jump high enough to make it to the next level than flying."

"So, we're *jumping* up the wall?"

I craned my neck to try to see where the cliff was that we had to land on. It was difficult to see through the snow, but it looked impossibly far. I shook my head. "I have no energy left. My fingers and toes are in great danger of falling off at this point."

Out of the corner of my eye, Martik moved off to the right, heading into the trees.

"We won't be attempting it tonight," Eldrin said, gesturing after the King. "Our first campsite is in there." He pointed to the trees.

"It doesn't seem very far from where that dragon almost found us," Tarrin quipped.

"It's not," Eldrin said, before following after Martik.

With no choice but to follow, we stumbled after them, breathing a sigh of relief as the thick trees cut off most of the snow and wind. Though the temperature was frigid, the dirt beneath my feet was warm to the touch as I stopped to clear aside a pile of leaves. Eldrin grabbed the sack from Martik and began unpacking it. There were two tents wrapped into bundles, one of which he handed to Tarrin. The idea of two dragons fitting into a tent seemed absurd until I saw the one Eldrin put together. It was easily the size of the cottage we left near Vernista. How had he folded it so small and carried it all this time?

Tarrin got to work pushing the corners of our tent into the ground with sticks before propping up the middle. My cheeks warmed as I realized it was *our* tent. For we would be sharing it together. It made sense I suppose. We would need each other's body heat to stay warm. As if sensing my thoughts, Tarrin glanced up at me and winked.

Needing something to do with my hands, I rummaged through my sack and found an apple. The wet crunch as I bit into it had my mouth watering for more. Tarrin finished setting up the tent and I tossed him the other apple. Though the trees protected us from the worst of the weather, the wind howled above us like a moaning ghost, hell-bent on finding us. It made bumps rise on my arms beneath all my layers.

Light disappeared by the second as dusk descended, and I was immediately glad that we had stopped for the night. Trying to make it any farther in the snow *and* dark would have been impossible. Tarrin finished his apple and chucked the core into a cluster of bushes before he looked at me and nodded his head toward our tent. Not needing any more encouragement to get out of the elements and into a warm bedroll, I followed him.

I desperately wished for the smothering heat of a fire and a hot meal, but with one of Eklos's spies possibly close by, it was an unspoken agreement that we'd forgo the fire and meal tonight in favor of silence and darkness. I crawled under the flap and Tarrin snapped it shut behind me.

I unpacked my bedroll, flinging it back until it laid flat on the ground. Saying a silent thank you to no one in particular, I kicked off my sheepskin-lined boots, setting them in the corner before tucking my feet beneath the blankets. Instant relief swept through my bones, and I let out a sigh, causing Tarrin to chuckle.

"Better?"

I nodded. "Much."

He dug in the sack next to him and produced a small bundle of dried meats that Gendon had given us. Handing a piece to me, my teeth tore into it as if it had been days, not hours, since I had eaten. The salty and smoky flavor coated my tongue and made me reach for more. Tarrin chuckled.

"While I don't mind sharing, it might be best to save some for the remaining days until we reach the village," he said with a sly smile on his face.

I gulped around my third piece of jerky, my cheeks bulging from trying to fit the whole thing in my mouth at once. "Thowy," I apologized, the meat blurring the word.

Tarrin threw his head back and laughed. It was a sound that he so infrequently made, and I hoped that this wasn't the last time I'd ever hear it. It was a sound that reminded me of sunshine and chocolate mixed with lilies. It was a happy noise that seemed in stark contrast to everything going on around us. Racing up a mountain, trying to get to safety while Eklos's army was right on our tails. Death sat like a cloud on the horizon.

A shiver worked through my limbs as I swallowed the rest of the jerky, and Tarrin put an arm around my shoulder, misreading the shiver.

"It's quite cold, even in here. We'll probably have to sleep curled together if we want to stay warm, even with the blankets." His fingers fiddled with the blanket pooled at his waist. I nodded in agreement.

"We'd get warmer faster if we slept naked," he drawled with a wink.

I shoved at his shoulder, chuckling.

He shrugged and gave me that half smirk. His eyes twinkled with mischief, and he pecked a kiss onto my lips. Before he could pull away, I latched onto him and he wrapped his arms around my waist, eliciting a shiver as his warmth seeped into me. His hands moved to cup my cheeks as he deepened the kiss.

A distant cough sounded, making us both freeze. Both of our throats bobbed as we swallowed, and Tarrin offered an apologetic smile before he pulled away, settling next to me on his bedroll. I squashed the desire down that flared in my core and took a long, cold drink from the canteen. When I was done, I handed it to him and laid down, burrowing into my blankets. Within moments, Tarrin was curling against my back. The tent was dark, barely illuminated by the shafts of moonlight that filtered through the trees. I could just make out the edges of the tent and Tarrin's arm wrapped over my stomach.

"Sorry, love," he whispered into my ear. I grabbed his hand and squeezed in reassurance.

"What do you think is going to happen when we get to Shegora?" I asked, unable to quiet my mind.

His arm tightened around me. "I'm sure Eklos and his army will be close behind us. I imagine it will be a battle that will be written in Elysia's history books." His lips brushed the shell of my ear. "And we'll be the victors."

I hummed, trying to disguise both the flare of desire from his lips on my ear, and the relief I felt at his words.

That was the scary thing about the future. It was always uncertain. We could win or lose everything at a moment's notice. It could take only the prick of a dragon's claw to topple Eklos's regime, or it could take a single arrow to destroy everything I held dear. And that thought was truly terrifying. It twisted my stomach into a painful ball of fire.

I opened my mouth to say as much when soft snores sounded behind me, and I held back a laugh at how quickly Tarrin had fallen asleep. Every muscle in my body was still coiled tight from Eklos's spy flying over the mountain mere hours ago. What if that dragon had attacked?

I shoved my face into my pillow, trying to block out the thoughts. We were somewhat safe now, and I was curled in Tarrin's arms. I forced myself to breath, letting out a long shuddering exhale before inhaling. I repeated the sequence numerous times, as Z had tried to teach me to calm my mind. Ever so slowly, sleep stretched over my mind like a warm trickle of water pooling outward, and each part of my body, starting with my fingers, and ending with the muscles in my legs, relaxed and loosened.

A snap sounded not far in the distance and my eyes flew open. My ears strained as I tried to listen over the sound of the wind, trying to hear if there was anything out there to make that noise. There was nothing—only the flapping of the tent fabric as the wind brushed against it. Realizing I had probably imagined it as I dozed off, I shut my eyes again, fighting once more to get my body to relax. Tarrin's arm was a dead weight over my side.

Another snap followed by a crack and a thud sounded and I shot up, flinging Tarrin's arm off me.

He rolled backward, squinting at me through sleepy eyes. "What?"

I put a finger to his lips, staring at the tent fabric as if I could see through it. Another thud, lighter this time. I looked over at him. *Something is out there.*

He rubbed at his eyes. *It's probably just your father relieving himself. I'm sure it's nothing to worry about. Go back to sleep.*

I blew out a breath. He was probably right, and I was just on high alert from earlier in the day. I laid back down, my ears still straining to hear any other sounds. My eyelids struggled to stay open, and I finally relented in letting them close.

A low growl echoed just outside the tent, and I shot out of my bedroll, violently shaking Tarrin awake. *Something is out there. It's outside the tent.*

For a moment, he looked skeptical, like he still thought I was imagining it, but then the growl happened again. I watched as the color drained from Tarrin's face.

What do we do? I searched his eyes, praying he had a solution that my fear-addled brain couldn't think of. We were trapped in this tent with either a dragon or some other beast on the other side of the thin fabric. Our tent wasn't as big as Eldrin's and there wasn't enough room inside for us to shift without destroying it completely.

Silently, he slid from the blanket and pulled his boots on. I followed suit.

When I say go, we'll run out of the tent and shift. If it's some animal, they'll run away with their tail between their legs.

Nausea swirled in my gut, and I regretted the dried meat and apple I ate earlier. *And if it's not some animal?*

Tarrin's eyes flickered in the dark and I could feel the pulse of fear down our bond. *Then we fight.*

He grabbed my hand, as if he could squeeze reassurance and strength into my skin. I tightened the tie holding my hair back and stood, though we were both hunched over awkwardly from the angle of the ceiling.

Ready? Though Tarrin's voice sounded unafraid, I could feel the tension rolling off his body in waves.

No. I admitted.

He squeezed my hand again. *One.* We both took a deep breath. *Two.* We braced our feet apart, preparing to run. Tarrin put his free hand on the flap, preparing to rip it open as we fled. *Three!*

We burst from the tent, fabric ruffling and tearing in our haste, each of us shifting in a dull flash of purple and blue. We spun to face the cause of the noise, and I fell to my knees, at the sight. Nausea erupted in my stomach, and I doubled over.

A behemoth of a dragon, with scales the color of dirty snow, stood in the clearing a few feet from our tent. His eyes burned orange, glowing even brighter in the moonlight. But it wasn't the sight of the dragon, or the threat he posed that sent icy daggers piercing into my skin from inside my body. No, it was who laid on the ground next to him, and whom he held in front of him.

In a pile of faded turquoise scales, King Martik laid at the feet of the dragon, blood coating his scales and seeping from a gaping wound where his heart should have been. I heard Tarrin's intake of breath as his eyes fell on his father.

But what had tears flooding my eyes and cascading down my cheeks was Eldrin, my father, held off the ground by the neck, a long black sword shoved through his back, protruding from his chest. Blood dripped down between his teeth, seeping down his scales as his mouth opened and closed like a fish gasping for water.

I tried to crawl toward him, knowing that nothing I did would save him. Tarrin's father was dead, and my own was seconds behind him. How had we missed a dragon of that size sneaking around our campsite? How did we not hear him? Surely Eldrin and Martik would have fought back, tried to alert us, but we never heard a sound.

"R-run, d-daughter," Eldrin croaked out, blood flying from his mouth. His words were my undoing.

A sob broke from my chest as I summoned flames that circled and flared over my scales. "Let him go," I commanded.

The dragon just laughed, not deigning to respond. He shoved the blade deeper into Eldrin's back, eliciting a bloodcurdling roar from him that had me covering my sensitive ears.

"Let him go," I warned, taking a step forward, trying to keep control of the magic fueled by my anger. It was harder to control— easier to burn out.

The dragon's dagger teeth glinted in the moonlight as his lips spread in a sneer. "As you wish."

My heart stopped in my chest as two things happened simultaneously. He clenched his claws tighter, a snap echoing between the trees as my father's neck broke before the dragon released him. Eldrin's body fell to the earth with a deafening thud, the sword still in his back, now piercing through his heart. His midnight-blue scales instantly faded to the color of dust.

A scream worked its way up my throat, my magic flaring in

my core in response. I opened my mouth to release a roar that would shake the trees from the earth—

I shot up from my bedroll, gasping for air.

Darkness surrounded me, the frigid temperature of the mountain inching beneath my skin like a rabid worm.

Dream. It was all a dream. A nightmare. The realest nightmare I had ever had.

I scrubbed a hand over my face. It was a struggle to calm my breathing as I peered through the dark to find Tarrin sound asleep next to me.

Martik and Eldrin weren't dead. It was all in my head. I blew out a long, shaky breath. But still… the hairs on the back of my neck stood on end. Something wasn't right.

We needed to get to Shegora. We couldn't wait any longer.

I shook Tarrin's shoulder to wake him and he jerked forward, his bleary eyes searching for danger in the darkness of the tent. "What is it?" he rasped, his voice hoarse from sleep.

"We need to leave," I replied, throwing the blanket back and gathering my warm clothes and boots, putting them on as quickly as possible. "Now," I amended when Tarrin didn't move.

He grabbed my arm, forcing me to still. "It's the middle of the night. On a mountain. In a snowstorm. We can't just leave."

I shook my head. "You don't understand. We have to leave. Eklos knows where we are. His spy is coming for us."

His eyebrows bunched together. "What are you talking about?"

I rubbed at my temples, knowing how crazy my explanation would sound to him. I sighed through my nose. "I just had a dream. An enormous dragon with gray scales found us while we were sleeping." Tarrin's eyes widened for a fraction of a second before he replaced it with a blank expression. "He… murdered our fathers." My voice cracked as I struggled to get the words out. The sudden need to go check on them, to see with my own eyes that they were indeed alive, and not dead, was overwhelming.

"Kaida, it was a dream," Tarrin said, using the calming voice he utilized when I was freaking out.

"But it wasn't. It was the realest dream I've ever had. And I can feel it in my bones. We need to leave here. Something is coming."

I could tell that there was something Tarrin wasn't saying, but my terror held me by the throat, and I couldn't bring myself to ask. After another moment studying my face, he finally nodded and pushed himself up, rolling up the blankets and stuffing them into a sack.

When everything was packed, I flipped open the tent flap and stepped outside, automatically looking for two dead dragon bodies in the snow. There was nothing. I could hear the soft snores coming from their tent, and there weren't any tracks in the snow to indicate someone had been there. Snow pelted my face, seeming to switch back and forth between snow and little pellets of sleet. I studied the trees around us, looking for that gray dragon or orange eyes, but I saw nothing.

"Kaida?" Eldrin's voice was barely audible over the wind. His human form dropped from the nearest tree, a bow slung over one shoulder as he stepped into a shaft of moonlight, face grim. "What is it?"

The relief I felt from seeing him alive, without a sword sticking out of his chest, or blood dripping from his teeth was almost too much to bear. I flung myself into his arms, wrapping my arms around his torso. He was so tall my head barely reached his pectorals. Eldrin's body stiffened at the sudden contact before relaxing the tiniest bit to wrap his arms around my back.

"What's wrong?" he repeated.

With a deep breath, I stepped back, looking him in the eye. "We need to keep going."

"It's the middle of the night," he said, repeating Tarrin's sentiment from earlier.

"I know!" I growled out, struggling to keep my voice down.

"She had a dream," Tarrin said.

Eldrin grabbed my shoulders, holding me at arm's length. "A dream? About what?"

I shook my head, unable to meet his eyes. "He found us. Eklos's mercenary killed you and Martik."

His eyes widened, but thankfully, Eldrin didn't press me for more info, most likely reading my emotions through the shifter bond.

"We need to get far away from here," I pleaded.

His eyes flickered back and forth over my face for several tense seconds before his body relaxed. "All right, I'll wake Martik." He turned back toward their tent, his footsteps silent as a ghost.

Are you sure about this? Tarrin asked.

No, not really. I couldn't find a way to put into words how real my dream had felt, how sure I was that it was real life. And there was no way to reconcile the fact that I *knew* what I dreamed would come to pass if we didn't leave right away.

"Yes, I'm sure."

The wind was relentless, but thankfully the snow had stopped falling. I could deal with the wind as long as it wasn't throwing ice and snow into my eyeballs. Within minutes, Eldrin reappeared with Martik in tow. His eyes were narrowed, though I couldn't tell if it was because he was still half asleep or if he was annoyed that we woke him up in the first place.

"All right," Eldrin declared. "Let's move."

In a single file line, Eldrin in front and Tarrin in back, we made our way out of the woods and back to that cliff face we were supposed to climb. Thankfully the moon was bright enough to illuminate our surroundings, so we didn't need to risk a torch drawing unwanted attention.

A dense, wispy darkness covered Eldrin for a brief second as he shifted into dragon form. Tarrin and I followed suit, turquoise and amethyst lights dancing on the rock before everything went dark once more. Relief flooded my body, relaxing the tension that coiled my muscles as the warmth from my dragon body heated my frozen limbs.

"It's rather simple," Eldrin explained, keeping his voice soft. "There aren't enough hand and foot holds to be able to climb, but there's enough to land on. Use your wings to propel you up to each spot."

"Why don't we just fly up the cliff?" Tarrin asked.

Eldrin squinted at him. "Have you ever tried to fly up a sheer wall of rock, Prince? It's too steep, and we risk whatever is hunting us hearing the thudding of our wings as we try to fly straight up." He turned to face the rock again. "At least this way, we stay relatively silent." My father dug his claws into a crevice as far above him as he could reach. "Just mimic what I do."

With a burst of his wings toward the ground, he launched himself up the cliff at least twenty feet before grabbing the rock once more. His snout moved back and forth as he searched for the next hold. With another silent beat of his wings, he continued up in four more winged launches before he pulled himself over the top. His midnight scales were nearly invisible in the darkness, the slight iridescence catching the moonlight as he peered over the edge to wave us onward.

"You both go first," Martik said, nudging us forward. "I'll keep watch until you're safe."

I could tell Tarrin wanted to argue with him, but I silenced him with a look. "Go on, I'll be right behind you."

He followed Eldrin's motions exactly, though it took him several minutes longer to reach the top. Tarrin's snout popped over the edge as he waved, beckoning me up. I glanced back at Martik who gave me a tight nod.

Slipping my claws inside the highest crack I could find, I counted to three in my head. With a giant inhale, I unfurled my wings, snapping them down behind me while I pushed up from the rock crevice. My stomach dropped to my feet as my body went weightless for a moment, my eyes searching to find the next place to grab onto. I didn't jump nearly as far as Eldrin or Tarrin had, and after only a few feet, I felt my body begin to sink backward.

Grab the wall! Tarrin shouted into my mind. I was less than a second away from tumbling back to the ground.

On your left.

Just as he said, there was a deep crack on my left and I shoved my claws inside, bracing for the impact as my body swung into the cliff. It took all my strength to keep from slipping as I felt the collision with the rock down in my bones.

Come on, Kaida. Just a few more, Eldrin encouraged, sending a pulse of reassurance into my mind.

Holding in a groan, I repeated the motion, flinging myself up the cliffside, though this time I soared much farther before my claws sent a throb of pain up my arms as I jammed them in another crack. It took three more tries before Eldrin's and Tarrin's clawed hands wrapped around my arms and helped pull me over the edge. I laid on the ground, chest heaving as I fought to catch my breath.

"Please tell me that's the only time we have to do that," I begged, looking at Eldrin.

A small chuckle escaped through his lips. "I'm afraid we have to do that several more times."

I couldn't hold back the groan this time. By the time I finally caught my breath and peeled myself from the ground, Martik was crawling over the edge. I let out a sigh of relief. Somehow, we had all made it up the first cliff, safe and sound. Had my dream been wrong? Was my mind just imagining ridiculous scenarios?

"Come on, let's get as far as we can before dawn, then we'll rest for a few hours," Eldrin announced, once again taking the lead. All of us followed, exhaustion causing our wings and limbs to droop.

I turned to look over the cliff one more time and felt the blood drain from my face. Hidden amongst the trees we had just come from were a large pair of orange eyes, staring straight at me. I rubbed at my face, making sure I wasn't imagining it.

But when I looked again, the orange eyes were gone.

CHAPTER FORTY-THREE

ELDRIN

IT WAS SLIGHTLY disconcerting that Kaida had a dream about Eklos's spy murdering Martik and me. It kept running through my mind like a spinning wheel. As far as I knew, she didn't have the gift of Foresight like Lita had, but through the bond I could tell she was telling the truth. I could *feel* the truth in her words. She truly believed we were in danger and needed to leave our campsite. Though I would have rather stayed and rested as much as possible, I also didn't feel like dying just in case she was right. Could Foresight be another ability granted to her by the Ancient Magic?

The first tendrils of dawn were beginning to peak over the horizon, and I stifled a yawn. The night felt never-ending as we fought against the bitter cold wind, and the snow that kicked up again after we made it up the first cliff. Despite everything against us, we still managed to climb two more cliffs before we were all too exhausted to continue.

We half walked, half limped our way up a narrow path, even with our dragon limbs frozen in the elements, when it veered sharply to the right into a copse of trees. The farther we traveled, the thinner the air became, making it difficult to breathe. I knew it was long past time for us to stop and rest.

I pointed to the trees. "We'll make camp there for a few hours."

Kaida and Tarrin both groaned, slumping against each other as they tried to hold the other up. Martik's wings dragged on the ground behind him as he, too, stumbled forward. I handed him the sack that held our tent.

"I'll keep watch, go get some rest." I knew the King had no energy left because he didn't argue, and instead struggled to remain upright as he half-heartedly shoved sticks into the ground to raise the tent before throwing himself inside. A quiet rumble echoed as his body hit the ground.

I chuckled to myself as I watched my daughter and her betrothed shift back into human form. Kaida wrestled with the pack, trying to pull out the tent before the Prince's hands gently covered hers and she stilled. Her normally bright eyes were lackluster and dull, and I had a feeling that if it weren't for her desire to get out of the cold and wind, that she probably would have collapsed right onto the ground to sleep.

"Let me," Tarrin offered. He pulled the rough fabric out of the sack before waving his hand in a gentle motion. A handful of sticks appeared at his feet before he made a sharper motion with his hand and the sticks were shoved into the ground. Holding both hands in the air, he held one arm straight which brought the canvas tent into the air and moved his other arm toward the sticks in the ground. Like a blanket settling over a bed, the tent floated down into place before leather ties secured the corners to the sticks.

I felt my jaw hanging open. "Have you been able to do that this whole time?" I asked.

He shrugged. "I'm a World Weaver."

It was so easy to forget what the young prince was. I rarely ever saw him use his magic.

"Why haven't you used it to help before?" I gestured to the tent now perfectly secured to the ground. Kaida swayed on her feet and Tarrin put an arm around her shoulders.

"I don't like to rely on my magic," Tarrin replied. I could feel his defenses rising, though I had not intended to insult him. "I'm not incapable of pitching a tent with my hands. My mother made sure I could survive and live my life without the aid of magic. Just because I *can* use my magic, doesn't mean that's always the best option."

I arched an eyebrow. Such wise words for a young shifter. I nodded in response. "Sounds like something Lita would do."

"Are you sure we'll be safe here?" Kaida asked.

"Safe or not, we can go no farther until we've gotten some rest."

Tarrin squinted. "That's not entirely reassuring."

I shrugged. "That's the reality of the situation. Lying about the danger we're in won't make it disappear. Better to be prepared than to be caught unaware."

A shaky breath escaped Kaida's lips before she turned to go inside their tent.

"Have you ever had dreams like that before?" I blurted.

Kaida froze, keeping her back to me. She glanced over one shoulder. "Never ones as real as that."

"Are you sure?"

Tarrin took a step toward me. "What are you getting at, Eldrin?"

I cleared my throat. "Lita used to have dreams like that. Things that had not yet happened." Kaida turned to face me, meeting my gaze. "But they always came to pass."

The shifting of the trees in the wind filled the camp as my words settled between us.

"I don't have Foresight, Eldrin," Kaida said at last.

I took a step toward them. "There's so much we don't know about your Ancient Magic. Who's to say this isn't some manifestation of it?"

Kaida shook her head. "I'm tired, Eldrin. I don't want to

theorize about this fancy magic. I just want to make it to Shegora, with all of us alive, and defeat Eklos."

Without another word, she turned and went inside her tent. Tarrin looked torn as he watched the flap close and then glanced back at me.

"Do you think that's what her dream was?" he whispered.

Truthfully, I didn't know. But my gut told me that it was too similar to Lita's magic for it to be a coincidence. I gave him a single nod.

He blew out a breath. "We need to learn more about her magic. Just when I think we've reached the end, there's something new."

"The Ancient Magic was gone long before I was born. It will be difficult to learn much, especially with Noam no longer with us."

Tarrin's eyes narrowed. "Where did you send him?"

I stared at the ground. "I likely sent him to his death."

He scoffed. "How kind of you."

"The less you know, the better. That's less information Eklos can use against you."

"But what if understanding the magic is the key to defeating Eklos? You sent away our only source of learning more about it."

I rubbed at my snout, my mind spinning over his words.

"When she lets the beast take over, it's like she becomes someone else entirely. There's no struggling to use her magic. There's no questions. She just does it, using magic in a way that only a dragon of your age should be able to." He ran a hand through his hair. "She hates it, the beast inside her."

A sinking feeling settled in my gut. "I need you to trust me, Prince. I sent Noam away for a reason. Where I sent him might mean the difference between winning this war or being slaughtered." I gestured at his tent. "Get some rest." I glanced at the lightening sky through the trees. "You're going to need it."

CHAPTER FORTY-FOUR

KAIDA

IT TOOK THREE days to scale the mountain. Three miserable, long, frigidly cold days that held nothing but exhaustion, hunger, and as close to frostbitten limbs as I had ever had. According to Eldrin, the cliff we had scaled an hour ago was the last of them, and now it was a straight road to Shegora.

The problem was it wasn't an easy trek but more of a hike. Thick grasses and bushes had overgrown any sign of the path, and the ice-covered snow made walking through it almost impossible. Every crunching step felt unnaturally loud, using up enormous amounts of energy just to drag ourselves through the deep snow.

"We should be there soon." Eldrin's voice broke through my thoughts, shattering the silence. "I can see the shallow valley ahead. Shegora is just on the other side."

I peered over everyone's shoulders but couldn't see what he was talking about.

"Gendon said he sent someone up to prepare the village for our arrival," Tarrin said, glancing first at me then at my father.

Eldrin nodded. "I always thought it had been destroyed, but apparently it was preserved somehow. I'm anxious to see the state of it."

"When exactly is Gendon planning to join us?" I asked,

knowing Eklos wasn't far behind us. Being this far up the mountain, we had started to see a black stain near the bottom. It was too far for even our dragon eyes to see details, but we all knew. It was the army.

"All he said was that they'd arrive in time to help us defeat Eklos."

Martik cleared his throat. "Knowing Gendon, it will likely be at the very last moment."

The thought had a tight ball of anxiety forming in my stomach. Why hadn't they just traveled with us? Surely there was safety in having more numbers. Perhaps if they had been with us, the dragon with orange eyes that I dreamed about wouldn't have dared to follow so closely.

There had been no sign of him since that first campsite, though that feeling of being watched had never left. I knew that Tarrin saw every glance over my shoulder, or every time I stared a little too long into the woods. But something was out there—whether it was the dragon in my dreams, I didn't know.

We crested over a hill and came face-to-face with the shallow valley that my father had mentioned. The sun peeked out from behind the clouds for the first time in days, indicating that it was still early morning. Rays of sunlight flooded the valley, reflecting off the snow and frost, forcing me to squint against the brightness. The brief burst of light warmed me enough to send a shiver through my dragon body, a shot of energy zinging through my veins like lightning.

"Silverdew Valley," Eldrin announced, halting my thoughts. "We named it that when I was a youngling. When dawn comes in the summertime, every leaf and blade of grass has shining beads of silver-colored dew. Something about the climate up here, and perhaps a bit of magic, causes the change in color." My father looked thoughtful as he studied the landscape.

Up on the opposite side of the valley, built into the side of the mountain, were black shadows that looked a lot like little huts.

"Is that…?" I began to ask.

Eldrin nodded. "Shegora."

"It seems so… small," Tarrin said.

"That's because it is. It was a small village of shape-shifters. Not many were willing to put up with the harsh conditions this high on the mountain, and there weren't many who remained the last time I was there." Eldrin's voice grew somber as he spoke.

The snow melted beneath my feet, causing my clawed toes to feel damp and uncomfortable. "Well, what are we waiting for?" I asked, impatient to reach the village and be inside, out of the elements, for the first time in days.

Without another word, Eldrin led the way as we descended the hill and entered the valley. The snow was even deeper here, easily reaching to my knees in dragon form. I shuddered to imagine how deep it would be if I were in human form. At least to my neck. A renewed sense of energy permeated our small group. The end of the journey was in sight, and we were all anxious to get there. I was about to open my mouth to suggest we use our wings to propel us faster across the valley, when an enormous shadow barreled toward the earth, shooting snow and ice in every direction as it landed.

Every drop of warmth in my body drained away, a cold sweat breaking out over my scales. I felt a pulse of dread down the shifter bond from both Tarrin and Eldrin. I peered into the orange eyes of the light-gray dragon that now stood in front of us, his muscles so thick beneath his scales that he appeared to be twice the size of any of us. Smoke spewed from his nostrils in black tendrils.

It was the dragon from my nightmare.

An eerie prickle danced over my scales. He was exactly how I had dreamed him, down to the matte black horns protruding from his skull and the specific shade of gray his scales were—like dirty snow. Was it simply a huge coincidence or was it my magic, like Eldrin had suggested?

"You will go no farther," the dragon growled, his voice gritty like sliding on gravel pebbles.

Eldrin situated himself at the front of our group, Tarrin behind him, and Martik behind me. With their bodies and wings, both my father and Tarrin's father created a protective circle around us.

"Who are you?" Eldrin called, not taking another step forward.

The dragon laughed. "Don't recognize me, old man?"

My father stilled. "Should I?"

The dragon's laugh turned into a cruel-sounding thing. "Manifesting your shifter abilities for the first time all those years ago must have clouded your mind. I would know. I was there."

Eldrin stiffened before his eyes widened in recognition. "Rythos?"

His snout spread in wicked delight. "That's right, old friend."

"What are you doing here?" My father asked, and I could feel his confusion down the bond. "I haven't seen you since—"

"Since the first day you shifted. When you left me behind to come *here*." The dragon pointed behind him to Shegora.

My father still looked lost. "I hardly remember anything about that day. It was a thousand years ago."

"How convenient," Rythos crooned, taking a step forward. For the first time in the short number of months I had known my father, I watched as he took a step back.

Rythos turned the full brunt of his gaze on me. "Your father never mentioned me?" I refused to give him the satisfaction of responding. "Pity," he continued. "I was his best friend. We grew up together. That is until his shape-shifter abilities manifested. The moment he shifted for the first time, he forgot all about me. Left me behind like an unwanted animal."

Eldrin's face crumpled in outrage. "I did no such thing. I was taken away from home to a place that would help me develop my magic. I had no choice in the matter."

"And yet you hardly remember me," the dragon finished.

My father shook his snout as if he were trying to dispel the accusation from his mind. Rythos took another step toward our group and Eldrin retreated another step.

"Unlucky for you," he drawled. "I waited in the wings of Eklos's Remnant, readying myself for the day when I could help him erase you, and the humans, from Elysia."

"You're talking about mass genocide," I spit, unable to take the fact that he talked about slaughtering the human race without any hesitation or thought.

He shrugged. "See it how you wish. Eklos's plan will bring nothing but good to Elysia, especially when unnatural beasts like you are finally gone."

I couldn't hold back my scoff. Rythos's gaze snapped back to me.

"Eklos sent me to end you." His snout spread into a twisted smile, his dagger teeth flashing. "I think I'll start with you," he growled, lunging for me. Instead of jumping toward Rythos, Eldrin disappeared in a blink, reappearing at my side, and grabbed my arm. Black smothered my senses before I was blinded by the snow again. We were several yards away from where I had stood. I glanced over at Eldrin to find him panting, before Martik planted a firm kick into Rythos's chest. It barely moved the beast.

"You need to get to Shegora," my father gasped between breaths. "There's a… barrier around it. It won't keep an army out, but it will keep *him* out." He nodded at the enormous dragon who sent a barrage of flames toward the King who ducked and spun away from the attack. Tarrin's eyes were locked on me.

Go, Kaida! We're right behind you. His words were frantic down the bond.

"I can't leave you," I said to my father. "I can help."

He shook his head. "I have no doubt, daughter. But I can't risk you. Elysia needs you. Now, go. Once you reach the end of the valley, there's a path that leads into the village. You can't miss it."

I shook my head, tears filling my eyes. I couldn't turn my back on them. I wouldn't run like a coward. Surely, we were stronger together than we were apart. He gave me a little shove.

"Trust me, Kaida. Get to the village." Without a backward glance, Eldrin disappeared again and reappeared directly in between Martik and Rythos. I could see their mouths moving, but I was far enough away that I couldn't hear the words being spoken.

Run, Kaida. We're right behind you. Tarrin repeated, throwing his words down our bond.

Though the beast inside me was thrashing, begging to be let out to destroy Rythos, I forced myself to listen to the pleading of Tarrin and Eldrin. Though it made my stomach clench into unbearable knots, I turned my back on them and ran as fast as my feet would take me toward Shegora.

◌

I made it all of twenty feet, my heavy and tired limbs struggling to get through the deep snow, before Rythos landed in front of me, spraying snow everywhere. I heard Tarrin shout my name, but my only focus was to get away from the dragon. My magic flared to a roaring fire in my core.

"Where do you think you're going?" he growled before swinging his arm at me. I wasn't fast enough to duck, and his rough scales slammed into the side of my snout, sending me careening backward onto my tail. A shock wave of pain bloomed on my backside, but I bit it down and pushed to my feet again.

"Ah, the female shifter has more bite in her than her father. How precious." Before I could think through his words, or even blink, he sent the biggest wave of fire I had ever seen a dragon produce, spiraling toward my face.

I managed to expel a brief burst of fire that collided with his, flaring and crackling as they connected. Embers popped all over my scales. I exhaled, a cloud of air pooling in the cold. I needed to get on the offensive. I was too tired, cold, and hungry to continue with only defensive magic.

I stepped forward, summoning blue flames into my palms when Rythos used his tail to smack the earth with all the force of an earthquake. The ground rumbled beneath my feet, forcing me off balance. He took advantage and used his wing this time, with sharp spikes ridging the edges and slammed it into my side. The force was like all the times Eklos hammered the bones in my hand in Belharnt, only magnified a hundred-fold all over my body. I couldn't stop it as my body spun from the impact, and I landed in a heap in the snow. It instantly melted beneath the heat of my scales.

My gut churned with fire. He was much too strong for me, even with my exceptional strength. Z's words flickered through my mind. He said through brawn or brain, I must defeat Eklos. I wouldn't be able to withstand physical attacks from him for much longer, and based on the smile on the dragon's face, he knew it too. Rythos stalked closer, his eyes blazing bright, sulfurous black smoke billowing from his open snout.

I blew out a breath as I pushed to my feet, only to duck beneath another barrage of flames, his movements identical to his previous attacks. I studied his stance, the way he held his arms, the way his eyes sometimes snapped to a particular spot before he moved. I watched him do the exact same thing once more, his large nostrils flaring just before releasing magic. I sent up a weak wave of fire as a shield, but it wasn't enough. His fire slammed into my chest, and I let out a roar as my mind flashed back to when I was burned by Tarrin's fire during a training session, right before I was kidnapped and taken to Belharnt.

Rythos's magic burned into my scales, but I refused to let him win, summoning a tendril of water magic to smother the fire over my chest. The heat of it winked out in a plume of steam, and his eyes widened.

I let a smile creep over my snout. I would not allow another injury to reduce me to a slave in bondage.

Rythos's eyes snapped to my chest, then my wings before his nostrils flared. That's where he was going to attack next. Drawing on my water magic once more, I managed to snap a wall of water up in front of me just as another sequence of fire magic collided with it, a thick wall of steam erupting.

His attacks grew sloppier—easier to predict. I had seen the attack coming. Perhaps his magic was weakening. It was clear that I couldn't beat him with physical strength, especially when my body was already exhausted from the trip up the mountain, so I would have to outsmart him. An idea came to mind just as I ducked beneath Rythos's swinging tail.

That's it! I shouted in my mind to no one in particular. *Get the King to safety!* I shouted down the bond to my father.

No, Kaida. Rythos is too strong. You have to get to Shegora if we stand any chance!

I blew out another breath just as the sun broke through the clouds once more, infusing my body with strength.

Just trust me. I have a plan. You and Martik get to the village. We'll be right behind you.

I knew it took every ounce of self-control for my father not to barrel through the snow and throw himself between the dragon and me. I knew he didn't want to leave me to face him alone. But I wasn't alone. I glanced at Tarrin, remembering our stolen kisses and moments together. As long as I had him, I wasn't alone.

Together, we could defeat Rythos. Both Tarrin and I were strong separately, but not strong enough to win against Rythos. Lita had been right—if we fought together, we were unstoppable.

Eldrin finally nodded, though his eyes gave away how much

he hated that I asked him to leave. He grabbed Martik's arm, and they disappeared, appearing several yards away. Rythos paid no attention to them—his attention solely on me.

Good. Tarrin, can you move the snow? Bury him?

I felt his incredulous look even in my mind. *The snow is… quite heavy.*

Can you do it? I repeated. *We have to try to break his pattern.*

Hesitation flowed down the bond before he gave a single nod. *I'll try.*

"Ah, young love. Such heroics, stepping up to save your beloved," Rythos crooned. A deep vengeful protectiveness flared down the shifter bond. Even if it was immensely difficult, Tarrin would lift that snow with his World Weaver ability. If for no other reason than that primal need to protect me.

I'm going to try something new. I knew Tarrin could likely feel my uncertainty. What I was about to do was a feat in itself, taken from a move I had seen Z do. I wasn't sure I'd be able to do it, let alone with Tarrin trying to lift several feet of snow into the air.

Is now really the best time, my love?

I ducked beneath Rythos's wing as it soared over my head. His eyes widened. We were running out of time before he figured out that I could tell where he would attack next.

I'm going to summon a wave of water… and then I'm going to try to freeze him inside it.

His surprise flared in my mind.

That's when you drop the snow on top of him. Hopefully it will hold him long enough for us to make it to the village. My father said we'll be safe there.

You really think that will work?

I took a step forward, drawing Rythos's attention. *Only one way to find out.* The sun broke through the clouds again, filling my body with a burst of strength. I couldn't help but think that the long-forgotten gods of Elysia were perhaps watching over us, wanting to help us defeat the evil in our world.

I called on the small kernel of water magic within my core, pushing and pulling until it pooled inside my palms. We really should have spent more time with water. I groaned down the bond.

"How cute," Rythos drawled. "You really think a little water is going to defeat me?"

I let my snout split into a grin, let the dirty snow-colored dragon see the anger, the bits of insanity, and the inner beast full of wrath in my eyes. "Stronger than you have fallen from less."

With a roar that shook the snow from the evergreen trees, I unleashed my magic on Rythos. I squatted low to the ground, hovering my scaled hands an inch above the ground. I felt every drop of water within the snow—felt it calling to me. With a jolt, I stood to my feet, drawing the moisture from the snow surrounding me, arranging it into a thick box-like shape in the air. One breath and it hovered above the ground and the next it enveloped Rythos's body.

The dragon thrashed and roared, but it was muted and garbled beneath the water. He released scorching flames from his mouth, over and over, but to no avail. It just turned to steam inside the water box I kept him in. If I had been strong enough, I could have held him under the water until he drowned. But after days of travel on little rest and food, my strength would give out soon. The prickling feeling of using too much magic too quickly lingered on the edges of my vision, swarming like biting insects.

Tarrin moved behind me, and I felt him drawing on the entirety of his strength through our bond, readying to lift the dense, wet snow. Rythos let out a particularly strong barrage of flames and I almost lost my grip on the magic.

Now, Tarrin!

With a mighty inhale from both of us, I blew out every last ounce of air in my lungs, infusing it with my magic while Tarrin lifted his arms into the air, drawing the snow up with him. His entire body shook with the effort, and he roared against the weight of it. As I intertwined my breath with my water magic, ice began to form around the edges of the box Rythos was caged in, but it was moving too slow. He would be able to break out before I was able to fully freeze him. Drawing on every last bit of energy I could muster, I infused my breath with the water one more time and watched in amazement as the water froze.

Tarrin didn't miss a beat, dropping the snow on top of him with a fierce growl. The ice was so heavy it dropped deep into the snow, encasing it further. I called on the water within the snow to freeze as well, adding an extra layer that would hopefully give us enough time to run for Shegora.

I jerked my head toward the village, beckoning Tarrin to follow. We started to run, our enormous bodies heavy and clunky as we fell through the snow, trying to get traction.

It's too far to run. We need to try to fly! Tarrin shouted into my mind.

The air is so thin. We won't be able to stay in the air.

A loud cracking noise sounded from behind us, and I knew our time was running out. I glanced over my shoulder and saw that the huge lump of snow Rythos was frozen under was glowing orange as he used his magic to try to break out of the ice.

Fly! Now! Tarrin shouted as he gave his wings a mighty flap. He managed to get aloft for a few seconds before he crashed down again, but his feet kept moving. *Use the momentum!*

I mimicked his motions, struggling to keep up. We were only a few hundred feet away from the village border. I could see Eldrin and the King waiting at the edge where I assumed the barrier my father had mentioned started. A fresh wave of energy crested through me as I realized we were almost there, that safety was in sight. My wings flapped, desperately trying to grab onto air that wasn't there, my lungs aching from the lack of oxygen.

Almost there! Tarrin yelled. Somehow, I had overtaken him, keeping several strides ahead of him.

Three hundred feet. My vision blurred and I felt the edge of exhaustion about to slam down on me.

Two hundred feet. Tarrin's panting was loud behind me, but I fought the urge to stop and help him. I heard the final crack of the splitting ice before an ear shattering roar rent the valley.

One hundred feet. *So close!*

Eldrin's arms were held wide, ready to catch us.

Fifty feet.

With one last inhale, I jumped into the air, snapping my wings down, letting it propel me through the barrier around the village. I collided with my father, and we both collapsed to the ground. An absurd giggle burst from my lips as I realized we actually made it— that despite everything, we made it to Shegora. Rythos couldn't get to us now that we were inside the border. He'd have to wait until Eklos's army arrived.

I looked behind me, my mind slowing to a crawl as I realized Rythos had disappeared, and my blood turned to ice, every limb going numb when I found the snow behind me empty. In the spot where my beloved should have been, where his footsteps simply stopped… there was nothing.

My betrothed wasn't there…

Tarrin had vanished.

CHAPTER FORTY-FIVE

KAIDA

I BLINKED, STARING AT the spot where Tarrin should have been.

My mind couldn't make sense of it. He had been steps behind me. I had felt his panting breaths on my neck as we ran, his footsteps rumbling the ground next to my own as we beat our wings to propel us faster. Tarrin's smiling face should have been standing next to me, an arm around my waist as we celebrated finally reaching Shegora. But as I looked to where he should've been, where his large footprints ended in the snow five feet from where we were, everything within me stilled—went silent.

There was no trace of him. He was simply gone.

Tarrin? I called down the bond. There was nothing—not even a pulse of his heartbeat in answer.

"Tarrin?" I whispered aloud, needing this to be some cruel joke. Eldrin and Martik moved behind me, the snow crunching under their weight.

"Tarrin!" My eyes scanned the snow, the trees, everything I could see. I sniffed, trying to find that familiar night air and blue cypress scent—*anything* that would give me an explanation as to why he wasn't standing next to me on this side of the barrier. My heartbeat like a banging drum in my chest, the inner dragon thrashing to be let out—to go find him. I *needed* to find him.

"Where is he?" I asked. Nobody answered. I looked where Rythos had been encased in ice. Giant shards of ice laid on top of the snow, but there was no sign of the gray dragon that had been inside.

"Where is he?" I screamed. My breaths came in frantic gasps—I couldn't breathe—couldn't get air into my lungs. The world grew larger as I shrank back down into human form, unable to stand the strength of the emotions I was trying to hold back in my dragon body.

"Tarrin!" I shouted, taking off into a run, my footsteps clumsy as I tried to push through the deep snow. "Tarrin!"

Strong arms encircled me—the familiar scent of leather mixed with the metallic tang of a forge covering me. Eldrin's arms squeezed tighter, keeping me from crossing the magic barrier.

"Kaida…" he whispered, and I hated his tone. I could hear every word that went unspoken. I shook my head, my brain rattling in my skull.

"No," I whispered. "No!" I struggled to get free from his arms. Tarrin couldn't be gone. I needed him. We were supposed to stop Eklos together. How was I supposed to do this without him?

"Kaida," Eldrin repeated, his arms growing ever tighter, his silver hair whipping in the wintry winds.

"Where is he?" Tears filled my eyes before spilling onto my cheeks. The heat of them searing my frozen skin. Fire burned in my throat.

"He's gone," the King's voice rumbled in the softest voice I'd ever heard from him.

"Rythos took him," Eldrin explained, and everything in me went preternaturally still.

"What do you mean he *took* him?"

Eldrin loosened his grip on me before letting go, running a

hand through his silver hair. "I lied before when I told you I had never met another with my abilities. Rythos is the only dragon I have met in a thousand years that can jump from place to place like I can." My stomach dropped as realization took hold. "Only… he doesn't have the same limitations as I do. His magic will take him any distance without running out, whereas mine will only take me as far as the amount of magic I have left."

"No," I whispered, staring at the invisible barrier, then to the snow where his footprints ended. *Tarrin!* I tried to call again through our bond, but he was too far away.

"It happened too fast," Eldrin explained. "He was right behind you. Rythos broke out of the ice cage as you jumped through, and when Tarrin pulled in his wings to jump after you, Rythos managed to grab his arm. That's all it took."

"There was nothing we could do," Martik added.

My eyes snapped to him and the tight ball of anger in my gut begged to be released. Magic itched under my skin. "You didn't even try," I spat. "He's your son and you let one of Eklos's beasts take him." I shook my head as I studied the King's face. "Do you even care that they took Tarrin, your son? Do you realize what Eklos will do to him?"

"That's enough, Kaida," Eldrin interjected.

I scoffed. "Don't you understand that Eklos with torture him within an inch of his life and then kill him just because he can? Do you have any idea the evil and cruelty that dwells inside that beast?" I turned back toward the barrier, readying my magic to shift and go find Tarrin.

Eldrin grabbed my wrist. "Don't be a fool, Kaida. Rythos could have taken him anywhere, and wherever that is, it is where Eklos will be. You'll get yourself killed."

I looked over my shoulder at my father. "I won't just abandon him and leave him to die."

I could tell by the brief hurt that flickered over his face that he heard the double meaning in my words. He may have been fine leaving my mother all those years ago, but I would not abandon Tarrin to the hands of a beast like Eklos.

I turned back to the barrier and stepped a foot forward when a large shadow landed behind us, spraying us with snow. All three of us spun on our heels and found Z, his dark-ocean blue scales reflecting off the snow. Where had he come from? He studied the three of us, his gaze lingering in the space where Tarrin should have been. When his eyes found mine, a strange emotion flickered in them, one that I had never seen on his face.

"I was stuck on the other side of the valley when I saw what happened," he said in a soft voice.

He took a step closer, and I crossed my arms, inching backward.

"There's nothing you can do for Tarrin right now."

I opened my mouth to give a slimy retort when he held up a hand to stop me.

"Tarrin is strong, he can survive for now. There's another problem to be addressed now."

Eldrin rubbed at his temple. "Now what?"

Z blew out a breath, his hesitation dancing on my nerves like an acrobat with knives. "It's about Eklos's army."

"We already know they're behind us. We saw the black stain of their ilk at the base of the mountain," I retorted, but Z was shaking his head before I had even finished speaking.

"That's where you're wrong, little shifter."

"What are you talking about?" Eldrin asked, and I could feel his body tense through the shifter bond.

Z looked at me, and only at me. "Eklos's army has disappeared."

ʘ

We all sat around a rickety wooden table inside one of the homes in Shegora, and I was immensely grateful to be out of the biting winter wind that had whipped the snow into a frenzy on the mountaintop. The house was in surprisingly good shape for being abandoned as long as Eldrin and Gendon claimed it had been. The kitchen area was fully stocked with meats, cheeses, fruits, and rice thanks to the supplies Gendon sent up ahead of us.

I crunched on a slice of apple, the fruit tasting like ash in my mouth. "What do you mean his army is gone?"

Z bit into his own apple, eating half of it in one bite. I saw a piece of skin get stuck in his teeth and forced my eyes away. "I mean *gone*. Poof. They are no longer at the base of the mountain."

Eldrin cleared his throat. "How?"

Z shrugged. "Gendon and I aren't sure. We had scouts out keeping an eye on their movements. They said they had quite literally disappeared before their eyes."

"I don't suppose we can hope that they're all dead?" Martik deadpanned.

"No, Eklos is too smart for that," I said, popping the last slice of apple into my mouth. Everyone was quiet while I chewed. The sound was deafening in the silence.

Z finally nodded. "Kaida is right, Eklos has something else planned. Something we don't know about."

"And now he has Tarrin." I struggled to keep my voice from cracking and the tears from lining my eyes. I would have time to cry later. Tarrin needed me to be strong. That was the only way we'd be able to rescue him.

Z gave a single nod and changed the subject. "The people of Metta—those willing to fight—are on their way up the mountain."

"Even though the threat of the army is gone?" Eldrin asked.

Z swallowed a chunk of cheese whole. "Yes. Gendon believes that they will return and wants his people ready."

The food I ate sat heavy in my stomach. The thought of facing Eklos's dragons without Tarrin made me want to find the nearest hole and hide in it.

I swallowed the lump in my throat. "What now?"

"We wait," Martik said.

"We train," Eldrin declared.

"We hide like cowards and force Tarrin to endure the worst torture imaginable," I finished.

Martik's scales bunched on his forehead. "We did not endure everything we have to make it here, simply to turn around and leave. I love my son more than anything, but we have to be smart about this."

Eldrin nodded in agreement. "He's right. We must stay the course, train those who arrive here, and prepare for the battle ahead. I know without a doubt that when Eklos makes his final stand, if we're not ready, all that will be left is our ashes on the ground."

Tears filled my eyes, but I bit the inside of my cheek to keep them at bay, rising to my feet. How could they be such cowards? To leave Tarrin in the claws of Eklos… I bit harder on my cheek, forcing down the primal need to go after him. Every inch of my body begged to walk out that door and find Tarrin. It consumed every thought, ate away at my core, and set my inner fire to blazing. The beast pleaded to be let out of its cage.

I shook out my clenched fists, forcing a shuddering breath through my lips.

Eldrin's eyes softened as he watched my anxious movements. "You should get some rest, Kaida." He pointed to a doorway on the other side of the room. I wanted to snap at him, to lunge at Z and fight—anything to expend this restless energy—this need to *go*. But instead, I listened to my father and stalked into the bedroom.

It took everything in me to strip down and put clean clothes on, to wash my face in the corner basin, and to wrap myself under the blankets on the scratchy bed. Every time I closed my eyes, I saw Tarrin's face—the stark look of terror as we ran for our lives toward Shegora.

Though my body was exhausted, and my eyes weighed a thousand pounds, my brain continued to swirl with nerves and what-ifs. After countless minutes or hours—I wasn't sure—my eyes slipped closed, the first fingers of sleep began to pull me under.

And then I felt it. My eyes snapped open. It was sudden and faint, but it was there all the same. A small sliver of a pulse, straight down the shifter bond I shared with Tarrin. I was still too far to hear him or talk to him, but he was out there.

And he was alive.

I had to find Tarrin. I knew he was strong, but Eklos was relentless. I didn't know how long he would be able to last before Eklos broke him irreparably. I blew out a breath and rolled onto my side. For now, I would rest, let my body recover, but I would not stay here. I would scour the earth and soar over Elysia until I found a shred of our shifter bond again.

Because I would find my Prince.

Whether it took hours, days, or scales forbid, weeks, I would find him.

That was a promise.

Hold on, Tarrin! I shouted as loud and strong down the bond as I could.

I'm coming for you.

TARRIN

THEY LEFT ME in the dark.

Seconds turned into hours. Hours into minutes. Minutes into days, then weeks. I had nothing to count the passing time. I had no way to know just how much time had passed since I was ripped from Kaida's side. All I knew was that I was far away from her for the shifter bond between us was utterly silent. Not even the faint beat of her heart.

The absence of it was a deafening ache in my ears.

The moment I had felt Rythos's arm coil around me, I knew that was it. There was no escaping. His grip was like iron, and then darkness smothered me, and I never emerged again. The floor beneath me was hard and damp, like wet stone, and my limbs had gone numb long ago. I was shackled to a stake in the floor. The chain wasn't very long, but by the stumbling around I did trying to escape, the cell I was in was merely a small box.

Piercing aches ripped through my stomach followed by a loud growling sound, reminding me that it had been far too long since I had eaten. When would my next morsel of food be? Would I even get any? Would they let me starve to death?

I let out a shuddering breath, rubbing my hands up and down my arms, trying to regain any ounce of warmth. My core was barren, thanks to the iron shackles adorning my wrists and ankles, but thankfully there was no bluestone like Eklos had used with Kaida.

Kaida. Missing her was like a sharp throb that never left, much like the hunger slowly eating me alive. Without her, it was even darker, colder. She was always the ray of sunshine when everything around me was black clouds. She reminded me that I was strong; helped me be a better male. A single tear slipped from my eye, gliding down my cheek.

What was she doing now? Was she still in Shegora? Had the army attacked? Would she die alone while I wasted away in the darkness? I should be at her side, protecting and defending her.

A sudden bang ricocheted between the walls before what sounded like several locks sliding open. Light burst into the room as the door peeled open and I immediately covered my eyes which burned against the brightness. I squinted against the harsh light to see scales the color of ash and smoke filling the doorway. Those signature red eyes made the blood freeze in my veins.

His snout spread into a razor-sharp grin of wicked delight.

I blew out a shuddering breath, this time having nothing to do with the cold.

I was in the lion's den. Only I certainly wasn't the lion this time.

What did that make me?

Hold on Tarrin! I'm coming for you.

Kaida's voice was faint in my mind as I recalled the words somehow sent down the bond weeks ago, so faint I wasn't sure if it was real or if I had imagined it. But it was what I needed in the moment. I knew she would never leave me to the whims of Eklos, even if I wished she would stay far away from danger. I would gladly take the onslaught of his wrath if it meant keeping her safe.

Her words were peace. Her words were fuel to keep going—to not give up hope.

My beloved would come for me just like I came for her in Belharnt. I couldn't feel her on the other side of the bond, but I sent the strongest feeling of warmth and love that I could, hoping that wherever she was, she could feel it.

She believed I was strong. She knew I could get through whatever this beast unleashed on me until she could find me.

Kaida survived for seven years in that dungeon with him. If she could survive, so will I.

I love you, Kaida.

Eklos took a step into the room, slamming the door behind him, and darkness descended, heavier and more frightening than before. I heard footsteps scuffing against stone, but each one echoed in the small space and I couldn't tell where exactly he was. That was, until hot carrion breath whispered against my ear.

"Let us begin."

ACKNOWLEDGEMENTS

I never thought I'd see the day where not one, but two of my book babies were out in the world for people to read. And let me just say…writing a sequel is HARD. Not only do you have to keep writing and progressing the story, but there's also an unseen pressure that it needs to be perfect—as good or better than the first. There were a lot of times I wanted to give up on this one, and Imposter Syndrome hit incredibly hard. It's difficult to pull yourself out of it, to find motivation again, and to finish the dang thing even despite your fears of people hating it. But we made it! *Scales of Ice & Shadow* is in your hands, and there are a few people I could not have done this without:

To my husband, Cody—thank you for dreaming big with me, and for supporting this scary dream of mine. Though there is a wide margin for failure when publishing books, you've never once told me to quit. You've always encouraged me to push through and to keep going. You believing in my dreams, even when my mind told me I'd never achieve them, means more than you could ever know. I love you, honey bunches of oats.

To my Beta Readers—thank you for reading the scary draft of my book, for all your constructive criticism, as well as your encouragement. I don't know that I would've had the courage to put this in the world if not for your constant love of this story. Y'all are the best!

To Kevin and Heather Bergsten—thank you for being obedient to the prompting of God. If it weren't for you both, I'm not sure if this book would have ended up in people's hands. I'm so grateful for you and your belief in me.

To all my author/bookstagram friends—I'm so thankful for each of you! Your excitement, encouragement, and every like, comment, and share mean so much to me. I couldn't have finished this without you.

To Andrea Hurst and Lucia Ferrara—thank you for editing my book and encouraging me along the way. This never would have been possible without both of you.

Thanks be to God—for His never-ending faithfulness and provision throughout this entire process. He gave me the gift of writing, and a passion for it, and I am forever grateful. I couldn't have done any of this without Him.

And to my readers—I am beyond honored that you chose to pick up this book and give it a chance. All I've ever wanted was to write stories that provide an escape from reality for a while. Stories that have light and hope in what often feels like a dark world. Books are keepers of magic that can transport us out of anything we're facing and into something greater. I hope when you pick up this book, you feel uplifted, hopeful, and have a big old grin on your face. Thank you for reading the next part of Kaida and Tarrin's story. It means the absolute world.

ABOUT THE AUTHOR

Emily Schneider is an award-winning author who grew up in Minnesota where she spent most of her life studying music and singing, which ironically has nothing to do with writing fantasy novels. While music had always been a passion, Emily could never get away from her love of reading and writing books full of dragons, Fae, monsters, magic, and romance. When she is not writing about dragons and magic, you can find Emily chasing around her two dogs, Pixel and Frodo, playing Mario Kart with her husband, or watching The Lord of the Rings for the one-hundred-and-eleventh time.

Emily is the author of *Scales of Ash & Smoke,* fantasy winner of the 2021 Best Indie Book Award.

emilyschneiderwrites.com

IG: @emilyschneiderwrites

www.ingramcontent.com/pod-product-compliance
Lightning Source LLC
Chambersburg PA
CBHW051218190726
48288CB00006B/2010